MOLLIE'S PRINCE: A
BY
Rosa Nouchette Carey

MOLLIE'S PRINCE: A NOVEL

Published by Silver Scroll Publishing

New York City, NY

First published circa 1909

ABOUT SILVER SCROLL PUBLISHING

Silver Scroll Publishing is a digital publisher that brings the best historical fiction ever written to modern readers. Our comprehensive catalogue contains everything from historical novels about Rome to works about World War I.

CHAPTER I.: IN THE LIME AVENUE.

In this age of transition and progress, when the pleasure-seeker, like the Athenian of old, is for ever searching for things new and strange; when old landmarks are ruthlessly demolished, and respectable antiquities are shelved in outer darkness; then to some conservative minds it is refreshing to stumble upon some old-world corner, fragrant with memories of the past, and as yet untouched by the finger of the destroyer.

Cleveland Terrace, Chelsea, is one of these spots—the cobwebs of antiquity seem to cling with the vines to the tall, narrow old houses, with their flagged courtyards, and high, iron gates and small, useless balconies. There is something obsolete, old-fashioned, and behind the age in the whole aspect of the place.

One could imagine some slim, demure damsel in a short-waisted gown, not long enough to hide the dainty shoes and sandals, with a huge bonnet disguising a pyramid of curls, tripping down the few worn steps and across the road, on her way to join her friends at Ranelagh.

Just opposite is Chelsea Hospital, with its scarlet and blue-coated pensioners, basking in the sunshine; grand old veterans who have grown grey with service, their breasts decorated with the medals they have won—some in a hale, green old age, others in the sear and yellow leaf, toothless, senile, tottering slowly but surely towards their long home.

One reads a whole page of history as one gazes at the worn, wrinkled old faces; ah! they have been young once, but now the battle of life is nearly over for them; the roll-call will only sound once more in their ears. Let them sit in the sunshine and tell their old stories, and fight their battles over again in the ears of some admiring recruit. How their dim eyes sparkle with senile enthusiasm! "There were two of the black devils, but I bayoneted them one after another— spitted them like larks; and serve them right, too. That's where I got this medal;" and here a fit of asthmatic coughing impedes the bloodthirsty narrative.

One can imagine the thrilling tales told round the fire towards night as the grim old warriors nestle cosily in the high wooden settle, while envious comrades watch them from afar. How heavily the poor wooden legs stump through the long, echoing corridors! Grey hairs, old wounds, the chill stiffness of decrepit age—well, thank God for their peaceful harbourage, where the weary limbs can rest in comfort.

There is a sweet old spot just where the long Lime avenue leads to old Ranelagh, adjoining the little plots of garden ground cultivated by the pensioners. One golden afternoon in September, when a fresh, pleasant breeze was rippling the limes, a girl in brown came down the avenue, and, as she tripped past the gnarled and twisted tree-boles, the slanting sunbeams seemed to meet and envelop her, until her shabby frock became like Cinderella's robe, and the green and golden banners overhead were a canopy of glory above her.

Who does not know the beauty of a lime avenue in the early autumn, when the very air is musical with faint soughing, and every leaf adds its tiny, vibrating voice to the universal symphony—when children and birds and sunshine, and all young living things, seem to have their own way, and play in unison.

The girl was coming up from the river in the direction of old Ranelagh, and she was walking with so light and airy a step that one could have imagined it set to music—for her feet, which were very small and pretty, though, alas! shabbily shod, seemed scarcely to touch the ground.

She was small, almost childish in stature, with a thin, erect little figure, and a pale oval face, framed in short, curly hair, and at first sight people always called her plain: "an insignificant, puny little thing"—that was what they said until they saw her eyes—and they were the most wonderful and spirituelle eyes in the world. And after that they were not so sure of the plainness.

For comparisons are odious, and there is no hard and fast rule with respect to feminine beauty; at least, tastes differ, and here and there a Philistine might be found who would be ready to swear that dark spirituelle eyes, brimful of intelligence and animation, with a mirthful sparkle underneath, were worth a score of pink-and-white beauties, in spite of their fine complexions and golden hair.

Just at the end of the avenue two old pensioners were sitting; and at the sight of them, and at the sound of their raised voices, the girl began smiling to herself. Then she stepped quietly across the grass, picking her way daintily, until only a tree divided her from the old men; and there she stood shaking with silent laughter.

"I tell you it is a lee, Jack; there were three of them, as sure as my name is Fergus McGill. Look here"—and here the speaker rose stiffly to his feet. He was a tall old man, with a long grey beard, and the pinned-up sleeve and the filmy look of the sightless eyes told their own tale. His breast was covered with decorations and medals, and in spite of his high cheek-bones, his massive, almost gigantic, figure and grand face would have become an Ajax.

His companion was a short, sturdy man, with a droll physiognomy; his light, prominent blue eyes had the surprised look of a startled kitten, and he had a trick of wrinkling his forehead as he talked until his eyebrows disappeared; and when he took off his cocked hat his stubby grey hair looked as stiff as Medusa's crest of snakes.

Wide-awake Jack was the name by which his mates accosted him—in reality Corporal Marks. He, too, was decorated, and had a wooden leg, which he found useful in conversation, when emphasizing some knotty point. He was tapping the ground pretty smartly at this moment, as he cut himself another quid of tobacco.

"Lees!" he returned, in a huffy voice, "it is the truth and nothing but the truth, and I'll take my oath to that."

But here a little peal of girlish laughter interrupted him. These two old men loved each other like David and Jonathan, or Damon and Pythias, or like any other noble pair of friends, and would have died for each other, and yet would wrangle and argue and spar fifty times a day; and the chief bone of contention was a certain episode—on an Indian battle-field half a lifetime before.

Human nature is sadly faulty—and even in Chelsea Hospital there were mischievous spirits; and on cold, windy nights, when old bones ached, and there was general dullness, and the draughts made one shiver and huddle round the fire—then would one or another slyly egg on Sergeant McGill—or Corporal Marks—with some such question as this:

"Was it three of them Sepoys that McGill bayoneted before he got that sword-thrust—or only two?"

Or perhaps more cunningly and artfully,—

"I wish I had nabbed two of those dratted Sepoys like McGill. Marks can tell that story best——"

"Two, John Perks!" interrupted McGill, wrathfully, "it was three that I killed with my own hand, and the third was so close to me that I could see the whites of his eyes—and the devil's smile on his wicked lips—and I laughed as I ran him through, for I thought of those poor women and children—and it is the goot English I am speaking, for I have forgotten the Gaelic, I have lived so long in the land of the Sassenachs—not but what the Gaelic is milk and honey in the tongue that speaks it."

When that little mocking laugh reached their ears, both the old men reddened, like children discovered in a fault. Then they drew themselves up and saluted gravely; but the girl's eyes were full of mirth and mischief.

"Aren't you ashamed of yourselves, you two, quarrelling over a silly old battle, that every one else has now forgotten? One would think you were heathens, and not Christians at all, to hear you talk in that sanguinary style." The girl's voice was deep, but very clear and full, and there was a curious timbre in it that somehow lingered in one's memory—it was so suggestive of sweetness and pathos.

"Are you fery well, Miss Ward? Ah, it is always a good thing when one has the joke ready,"— and Sergeant McGill's tone was full of dignity,—"but it is not quarrelling that we are after, Miss Ward—only a little difference of opinion."

"Yes, I know. But what does it matter, McGill, how many of those poor wretches you killed?" But she might as well have spoken to the wind.

"It was three, Miss Ward," returned McGill, obstinately; "and if you had seen the sight that Jack and I saw you would not be calling them poor, for they were the devil's sons, every one of them, and their hearts was black as sin, and it was the third man that I got by the throat; and when Jack came up——" But here the girl shrugged her shoulders, and a little frown came to her face.

"Yes, I know, but please spare me those horrible details," and then she laughed again; but there were tears in her eyes. "I daresay there were more than three if the truth were known. Corporal, why do you vex him with contradiction? If you were in another part of the field how could you know what he did?"

"Ah, it is the goot English that Miss Ward speaks," murmured McGill; but Corporal Marks struck in.

"Hold your tongue, McGill—you are like a woman for argifying—argle-barking, as Sergeant Drummond calls it—from noon to night. This was how it was, Miss Ward. Our company was scattered, and I found myself suddenly in the corner of the rice-field where McGill was. There was a barricade of dead Sepoys round him, and he had his foot on one of them, and had got another by the throat; and then——" But a peremptory gesture stopped him. "Thank you, I have heard enough; but I am inclined to take McGill's part, for how could you see clearly in all that smoke and crowd? Come, let us change the subject. I owe you sixpence for those flowers that you brought yesterday, for my sister tells me that she never paid for them."

"No, Miss Ward, and there was no sixpence owing at all. I left the flowers with my duty."

"Ah, but that is nonsense, Corporal," returned the young lady quickly. "I will not rob you of all your lovely flowers."

"It's not robbing, Miss Ward," replied McGill, in his soft thick voice. "It is a pride and pleasure to Jack that you take the flowers, for it is the goot friend you have been to us, and the books you have read, and the grand things you have told us, and what are roses and dahlias compared to that?"

"Well, well, you are a couple of dear old obstinate mules, but I love you for it; but please do not argue any more. Good-bye, Sergeant. Good-bye, Corporal," and the girl waved her hand, and again the old men saluted.

"They are two of the most pugnacious, squabbling old dears in the whole hospital," she thought, as she walked quickly on. "I wonder which of them is right? Neither of them will yield the point." And then she smiled and nodded to a little group that she passed; and, indeed, from that point to Cleveland Terrace it was almost like a Royal progress, so many were the greetings she received, and it was good to see how the old faces brightened at the mere sight of the girl.

Presently she stopped before one of the tall old houses in Cleveland Terrace, and glanced up eagerly at the vine-draped, balconied windows, as though she were looking for some one; but no face was outlined against the dingy panes. Then she let herself into the dim little hall, with its worn linoleum, from which all pattern had faded long ago, and its dilapidated mahogany hat-stand with two pegs missing, and an odd assortment of male and female head-gear on the remaining ones, and then she called out, "Mollie! Mollie!" finishing off with a shrill, sweet whistle, that made an unseen canary tune up lustily.

And the next moment another whistle, quite as clear and sweet answered her, and a deliciously fresh voice said, "I am in the studio, darling." And the girl, with a wonderful brightness on her face, ran lightly up the stairs.

"Oh! what an age you have been, Waveney! You poor dear, how tired and hungry you must be?" and here another girl, painting at a small table by the back window, turned round and held out her arms.

When people first saw Mollie Ward they always said she was the most beautiful creature that they had ever seen; and then they would regard Waveney with a pitying look, and whisper to each other how strange it was that one twin should be so handsome and the other so pale and insignificant.

But they were right about Mollie's beauty: her complexion was lovely, and she had Irish grey eyes with dark curled lashes, and brown hair with just a dash of gold in it; and her mouth was perfect, and so was her chin and the curves of her neck; but perhaps her chief attraction was the air of bonhomie and unconsciousness and a general winsomeness that cannot be described.

"Where is father, Mollie?" asked Waveney; but her eyes looked round the room a little anxiously. "Ah, I see the picture has gone;" and then a look of sorrowful understanding passed between the sisters.

"Yes, he has taken it," almost whispered Mollie, "but he will not be back yet. Ann is out—she has gone to see her mother; so I must go and get your tea. Noel is downstairs;" and, indeed, at that moment a cracked, boyish voice could be heard singing the latest street melody, and murdering it in fine style.

Mollie rose from her chair rather slowly as she spoke, and then—ah, the pity of it!—one saw she was lame—not actually lame so as to require crutches; but as she walked she dragged one leg, and the awkward, ungraceful gait gave people a sort of shock.

Mollie never grew used to her painful infirmity, though she had had it from a child; it was the result of accident and bad treatment; a sinew had contracted and made one leg shorter than the other, so that she lurched ungracefully as she walked.

Once in the night Waveney had awakened with her sobbing, and had taken her in her warm young arms to comfort her.

"What is it, Mollie darling?" she had asked, trembling from head to foot with sympathy and pity.

"It means that I am a goose," Mollie had answered. "But I could not help it, Waveney. I was dreaming that I was at a ball, and some one, quite a grand-looking man, in uniform, had asked me to dance, and the band was playing that lovely new waltz that Noel is always whistling, and we were whirling round and round—ah, it was delicious! And then something woke me and I remembered that I should never, never dance as long as I live, or run, or play tennis, or do any of the dear, delightful things that other girls do;" and here poor Mollie wept afresh, and Waveney cried too, out of passionate love and pity.

Mollie did not often have these weak moments, for she was a bright creature, and disposed to make the best of things. Every one had something to bear, she would say with easy philosophy— it was her cross, the crook in her lot, the thorn in her side; one must not expect only roses and sunshine, she would add; but, indeed, very few roses had as yet strewn the twins' path.

When Mollie had lumbered out of the room, Waveney folded her arms behind her and paced slowly up and down, as though she were thinking out some problem that refused to be solved. It was really two rooms, divided at one time by folding-doors; but these had been taken away long ago.

It was a nondescript sort of apartment, half studio and half sitting-room, and bore traces of family occupation. An empty easel and several portfolios occupied one front window; in the other, near the fireplace, was a round table, strewn with study books and work-baskets. Mollie's painting table was in the inner room.

A big, comfortable-looking couch and two easy chairs gave an air of cosiness and comfort, but the furniture was woefully shabby, and the only attempt at decoration was a picturesque-looking red jar, in which Corporal Marks' flowers were arranged. Presently Waveney stopped opposite the empty easel, and regarded it ruefully.

"It will only be another disappointment," she said to herself, with a sigh. "Poor father, poor dear father! And he works so hard, too! Something must be done. We are getting poorer and poorer, and Noel has such an appetite. What is the use of living in our own house, and pretending that we are well off and respectable and all that, and we are in debt to the butcher and the coal-merchant; and it is not father's fault, for he does all he can, and it is only because he loves us so that he hates us to work." And then she sat down on the couch as though she were suddenly tired, and stared dumbly at the vine-leaves twinkling in the sunshine; and her lips were closed firmly on each other, as though she had arrived at some sudden resolution.

CHAPTER II.: "MONSIEUR BLACKIE."

A shrill, ear-piercing series of whistles, of a peculiarly excruciating description, broke in upon Waveney's meditation. She shook herself, frowned, ran her fingers through her short, curly hair, thereby causing it to wave more wildly than ever—then ran downstairs.

The ground floor room corresponded with the one above—only the folding doors had not been removed, and over them, in a schoolboy's round hand, roughly painted in red and gold, was "Noel Ward, His Study," with a pleasing and serpentine ornamentation embellishing the inscription. In vain had Mollie, with tears in her eyes, implored her father to obliterate the unsightly record. An amused shake of the head only answered her.

"Leave it alone," he would say. "It is only a nursery legend, and does no harm—when Noel evolves another original idea it will be time to erase it." And so "Noel Ward, His Study," still sprawled in ungainly characters over the lintel.

As Waveney entered the room with rather an offended air, she saw the youthful student standing in the doorway. He was a tall, thin stripling of fifteen—but looked older, perhaps because he wore spectacles and had classical, well-cut features, and an odd trick of projecting his chin and lifting his head as though he were always on the look-out for celestial objects. But notwithstanding this eccentricity and a cracked and somewhat high-pitched voice, the heir of the Wards was certainly a goodly youth.

"Well, old Storm and Stress," he observed, with a derisive grin, as he balanced himself skilfully on his heels between the folding-doors, "so the pibroch roused you?"

"Pibroch!" returned his sister, wrathfully. "How often have I told you, you bad boy, that you are not to make this horrible din. Caterwauling is music compared to it, or even a bagpipe out of tune."

"It was my best and latest work," returned Noel, regarding the ceiling disconsolately. "A farmyard symphony with roulades and variations of the most realistic and spirited description, and would bring the house down at a Penny Reading. At present we had only reached the braying solo—but the chorus of turkeycocks, with peacock movement, would have created a sensation."

"They have," returned Mollie, stealing softly behind him and treating him to a smart box on the ears; but Noel merely pinned her hands in a firm grasp and went on with his subject: little interruptions of this sort did not disturb him in the least; he rather liked them than otherwise. Nothing pleased him better than to get a rise out of his sisters, for, whatever virtues he possessed, he certainly lacked the bump of veneration.

Dear, sweet Mollie, with her angelic face, was often addressed as "old Stick-in-the-mud," "Pegtop," or "the wobbly one," while Waveney, his special chum, the creature whom he loved best in the world next to his father, was "Storm and Stress," a singular soubriquet, evolved from her name and her sudden and sprightly movements.

"For one is nearly blown away," he would say. "There is always a breeze through the house when that girl is in it; it is like playing a scale upside down and wrong side outwards to hear her coming downstairs;" and very often he would come to his meals with his collar up, and flourishing a red silk handkerchief ostentatiously, and speak in a croaking, nasal voice, until his father asked him mildly where he had caught such a cold; and then Waveney would nudge him furiously under the table.

On the present occasion poor Mollie was kept in durance vile until Noel had finished his disquisition on his novel symphony; then he released her, and contemplated the tea-table with a fixed and glassy stare, which conveyed mute reproach.

"Noel, dear, it is a fresh loaf," she said, hastily and apprehensively, "and it is beautifully crusty, and the butter is good—a penny a pound dearer, and at the best shop."

"Where are the shrimps?" asked Noel, and he so lengthened the word that it sounded almost as terribly in Mollie's ears as Mrs. Siddons' "Give me the dagger!" for so much depends on expression, and if one is only melodramatic, even the words "shrimps" can be as sibilant and aggressive as the hissing of snakes.

"Oh, dear, how tiresome you are, Noel!" returned Mollie, quite sharply for her, for she was housekeeper, and the strain and responsibility were overwhelming at times, especially when her poor little purse was empty. "I could not afford them, really, Noel," she continued, welling into tenderness at the thought of his disappointment. "There were some nice brown ones, but I dared not get them, for I had only twopence left, so I bought watercresses instead."

"Ask a blessing, my child, and I will forgive you;" and then, much to his sister's relief, Noel subsided, and began cutting the bread, while under cover of the table-cloth, Waveney slipped sixpence into Mollie's hand, and made a movement with her lips suggestive of "to-morrow;" and Mollie nodded as she poured out the tea.

Noel had a volume of "Eugene Aram" propped up before him as he ate, but it did not engross him so utterly that he could not interpolate the conversation whenever he pleased, and it pleased him to do so very often.

Mollie was giving a graphic and heart-breaking account of the way in which she and her father had packed the precious picture, "and how it had been bumped three times while they carried it down the narrow stairs." "I quite missed the dear old thing, Wave," she went on, "and the studio looked so dull without it. Noel was so absurd; he threw an old shoe after it for good luck, and it nearly knocked father's hat off—and then he bolted indoors, and there was father looking at me so astonished, and he was not quite pleased, I could see that, so I said, 'It is not me dad, it is the other boy.'"

"Yes, and it was real mean of you," grumbled Noel; "but there, what are you to expect from a woman? Poor old padre, he will be precious tired with hauling along 'King Canute,' and it will bump all the worse going upstairs."

"Oh, Noel!" exclaimed both the girls, in a shrill crescendo of dismay. "You don't really believe that the dealers will refuse 'King Canute'?" ejaculated Mollie. "Father has worked so hard at it, and it is really his best picture."

Noel shrugged his shoulders; then he pointed his chin in an argumentative way.

"The dealers buy awful rubbish sometimes, but they won't buy this. Every kid knows how the old buffer gave his courtiers a lesson, but no one wants to be always looking on while he does it;

the public hates that sort of thing, you know. I told father so, over and over again, but he would not listen. 'Why don't you try something lively and less historical?' I said to him. '"The Two Grave-diggers" in Hamlet, or "Touchstone and Audrey." We might get Corporal Marks to sit for "Touchstone"—the public would think that fetching.' But no, nothing but that solemn old Dane would suit him—the Wards are terribly obstinate. I am my father's son, and speak feelingly;" and then Noel shouldered his book and marched back to the study.

"Do you think Noel is right?" whispered Mollie. "He is very clever, for all his ridiculous nonsense, and I am not quite sure whether 'King Canute' will really interest people."

"Oh, don't ask me," returned Waveney, in an exasperated tone. "If only dear father would stick to his schools, and his drawing-classes, and not try to paint these pictures! They seem grand to us, but they are not really well done. Don't you remember Mr. Fullarton said so? We were in the back room, but we heard him plainly. 'You are too ambitious, Ward'—that was what he said; 'the public is tired of these old hackneyed subjects. Why don't you hit on something pathetic and suggestive—some fetching little incident that tells its own story?' '"Child and St. Bernard Dog," for example,' returned father, grimly, 'and write under it, "Nellie's Guardian." Would that do, Fullarton? But I suppose anything would do for pot-boilers.'"

"Oh, yes, I recollect," returned Mollie, with a long-drawn sigh. "Poor old dad! How low he seemed that day! And this evening, if——" But Waveney would not let her finish the sentence.

"Never mind that just now. It is no use crossing the bridge till you come to it; let us go upstairs and be cosy, for I have a lot I want to say to you;" and then they went up arm-in-arm—Mollie was almost a head taller than her sister—and sat down side by side on the big couch; and then Waveney began to laugh.

"Oh, Mollie, I have had such an adventure; I did not want Noel to hear it, because he would have teased me so unmercifully. Don't you recollect that horrid note-book that we found?" And then, at the recollection, Mollie began to giggle, and finally both she and Waveney became so hysterical with suppressed mirth that they had almost to stifle themselves in the cushions for fear Noel should hear them.

For it was only lately that they had become acquainted with the dark and Machiavellian policy of that artful youth. Evening after evening, as they had exchanged their girlish confidences, Noel had sat by them with a stolid and abstracted look, apparently drawing pen-and-ink devils—a favourite amusement of his; but it was Mollie who found him out.

"The Adventures of Waveney Edna Ward, alias Storm and Stress," was scrawled on the title-page, and thereupon followed a series of biographical sketches, profusely illustrated.

"Storm and Stress with the Bull of Bashan"—a singularly graphic description of Waveney's terror at meeting an angry cow in the lane.

"No. II.—Storm and Stress. Saving an Orphan's Life—the Orphan being a deserted, half-starved kitten, now an elderly cat rejoicing in the name of Mrs. Muggins;" and so on. Every little incident touched up or finely caricatured in a masterly manner.

Père Ward had been so charmed with this manifestation of his son's talent that he had carried off the note-book and locked it up amongst his treasures. "That boy will make his mark," he would say, proudly. "But we must give him plenty of scope." And, indeed, it could not be denied that Noel had a fairly long tether.

As soon as Waveney could recover herself, she sat up and rebuked Mollie severely for her levity; "for how is a person to talk while you are cackling in that ridiculous manner? And it is really quite an interesting adventure, and"—with an important air—"it is to be continued in our next." And this sounded so mysterious that Mollie wiped her eyes and consented to be serious.

"Well, you know," began Waveney, in a delightfully colloquial manner, "father had told me to take the omnibus that would put me down at King's Street. All the outside places were taken, but there was only the usual fat woman with bundle and baby inside; and presently a gentleman got in. You know I always make a point of noticing my fellow passengers, as dad says it helps to form a habit of observation; so I at once took stock of our solitary gentleman.

"He was a little dark man, very swarthy and foreign looking, and he wore an oddly-shaped peaked sort of hat—rather like Guy Fawkes' without the feather—and he had a black moustache that was very stiff and fierce, so of course I made up my mind that he was a Frenchman, and probably an artist; for, though his clothes were good, he had rather a Bohemian look." Here Waveney paused, but Mollie gave her a nudge.

"Go on, Wave. I am beginning to feel interested. Was he really French?"

"Not a bit of it, my dear, for he talked the most beautiful English; and directly he opened his mouth I found out he was a gentleman, for his voice was perfectly cultured and so pleasant. I rather took to him because he was so kind to the fat woman; he held her bundle while she and her baby got out, and he scolded the conductor for hurrying her. I thought that rather nice of him; so few young men trouble themselves about fat women and babies."

"Oh! he was young?" in an appreciative tone.

"Well, youngish; two or three and thirty, perhaps. But now I am coming to the critical point of my story. Directly we were left alone the conductor came to ask for our fares; he was a surly-looking man, with a red face, and his manner was not over civil; most likely he resented the scolding about the fat woman.

"Well, no sooner had Monsieur put his hand in his pocket than he drew it out again with a puzzled look.

"'Some one has picked my pocket,' he said, out loud, but he did not look so very much disturbed. 'My sovereign purse has gone, and some loose silver as well.' And then he searched his other pockets, and only produced a card-case and some papers; and then he began to laugh in rather an embarrassed way. 'My good fellow, you see how it is; the beggars have cleaned me out. Five or six pounds gone. Confound those light-fingered gentry! If I had not left my watch at the maker's it would have gone, too.'

"'That is all very well,' returned the conductor, in a disagreeable voice, 'but what I wants to know, sir, is how am I to get my fare?'

"'Oh, you will get it right enough," replied Monsieur (but he was not Monsieur at all, only the name suited him); 'but for the present I can only offer you my card;' and then he held it out with such a pleasant smile that it might have softened half-a-dozen conductors. But old Surly Face was not so easily mollified.

"'I don't want your bit of pasteboard,' he growled. 'Do you call yourself a gentleman to ride in a public conveyance without paying your fare?'

"Then the motto of the Wards flashed into my mind, 'Open hand, good luck,' and the next minute I produced a sixpence from my purse—there were just two sixpences in it.

"'Will you allow me to offer you this?' I said, in my grandest manner, but I felt a little taken aback when he lifted his hat and beamed at me. I say beamed, for it was really the most friendly, jovial smile; his whole face quite crinkled up with it.

"'I could not refuse such a good Samaritan. A thousand thanks for your kind loan. There, sir,' handing over the sixpence, sternly, 'give me the change and next time keep a civil tongue in your head.' And then, greatly to my surprise, he pocketed the threepence.

"'I am in your debt for a whole sixpence,' he continued, 'and I am as grateful to you as though you had returned my missing sovereigns. Is it not Kingsley who points out the beauty and grace of helping "lame dogs over stiles?" Now will you add to your kindness by informing me of your name and address?'

"I stared at him blankly, and I am afraid I blushed.

"'There is no occasion,' I said, feebly, at last. 'Sixpence is not a great sum, and I was very glad to be of service;' for I could not help feeling how absurd it was, making so much of a trifle. But Monsieur seemed indignant at this.

"'I could not be in debt to any young lady even for sixpence,' he said, severely. 'I was too well brought up for that.' And then of course I was obliged to tell him where I lived; and he actually made me repeat it twice, he was so anxious to remember it.

"'Miss Ward, 10 Cleveland Terrace, Chelsea,' he observed. 'Why, that is just opposite the Hospital. I know it well. Strange to say, I am staying in Chelsea myself.' Then he took out his card-case, hesitated, and grew rather red, and finally put it back in his pocket. 'My name is Ingram,' he said, rather abruptly; and then the omnibus stopped, and he handed me out.

"'I must be in your debt until to-morrow, I fear,' were his parting words—and oh, Mollie, do you really think that he will actually call and pay the sixpence?"

"Of course he will, and of course he ought," returned Mollie, excitedly. "Oh, Wave, what an adventure! It was just like a bit in a novel when the hero meets the heroine—only an omnibus is the last place for a romance." Then Waveney made a face.

"No, no, Mollie, little dark Frenchified men are not my taste, even if they have nice voices. My private hero must be very different from Monsieur Blackie." Then a crackling laugh from behind the sofa made both the girls jump up in affright, and the next moment Waveney looked not unlike her soubriquet, as, uttering dire threats of vengeance, she flew round and round the room after the treacherous eavesdropper, until Noel, exhausted by laughter, subsided into a corner and submitted to be shaken.

"'Monsieur Blackie, to be continued in our next,'" exclaimed the incorrigible lad, when Waveney grew weary with her punitive exertions. "My word, there must be a new note-book for this. 'Storm and Stress enacting the part of Good Samaritan';" and here Noel fairly crowed himself out of the room.

"He has heard every word," observed Waveney, in a dejected tone. "I am afraid we laughed too loud, and that roused his curiosity. Oh, dear, what a boy he is! And none of us keep him in order;" but Mollie was too exhausted to answer her.

CHAPTER III.: "KING CANUTE" COMES BACK.

"Care to our coffin adds a nail no doubt. And every grin, so merry, draws one out." John
Walcot.

"And Nature swears, the lovely dears Her noblest work she classes, O; Her 'prentice han' she
tried on man, And then she made the lasses, O." Burns.

As the soft September twilight stole over the room, the girls became more silent. Waveney
seemed buried in thought, and Mollie, tired out with laughing, nestled against her comfortably,
and very nearly went to sleep. But she was roused effectually by Waveney's next speech.

"Sweetheart"—her pet name for Mollie—"I am going to make you miserable, I am afraid, but I
have been telling myself all day long that we must face the situation. If father does not get a good
price for his picture, what are we to do?"

"But he must sell it," returned Mollie, in a distressed voice. "Barker is getting disagreeable
about his bill, and his man says nasty things to Ann when he leaves the meat. And we owe
Chandler for two tons of coal."

"Yes, I know;" and Waveney sighed heavily. "Those two tons have been on my mind all day."

"You poor dear, no wonder you looked tired. Ah, how hateful and mean it is to be poor! Ah,
you are not as wicked and rebellious as I am, Wave. I sometimes cry with the longing for the
pretty things other girls have. I cannot resign myself to the idea of being shabby and pinched and
careworn all my life long. If this goes on we shall be old women before our time; when I am
ordering dinner I feel nearly a hundred."

Waveney stroked the glossy brown head that rested against her shoulder, but made no other
answer: she was thinking how she could best break some unwelcome news to Mollie. Mollie was
emotional, and cried easily, and her father always hated to see one of his girls unhappy. "Father
would cut the moon up into little pieces and give them to us, if he could," she thought; "nothing
is too good for us. But when Mollie frets he takes it so to heart. Oh dear, if only doing one's duty
were made easier; but there is no 'learning or reading without tears' in the Handbook of Life;"
and then she set her little white teeth together firmly, as a child does when some nauseous
medicine is offered.

"Mollie, dear, I cannot keep it back any longer—it makes me miserable to have a secret from
you. I have been to Harley Street to-day, and talked to Miss Warburton, and she has something
on her books that is likely to suit me."

Then the sob she dreaded to hear rose to poor Mollie's lips.

"Ah, Wave, you can't really mean it! This is worst of all. It is positively dreadful. How am I to
live without you? And father, and Noel, what are they to do?" and here the tears rolled down her
face; but Waveney, who had been schooling herself all day, refused to be moved from her
stoicism.

"Mollie, please listen to me. It is childish to cry. Do you remember our last talk—the one we
had in the Lime Walk, and how we agreed that we must do all we could to help father!"

"But I do help him," returned Mollie, in a woe-begone voice. "I keep the house and mend things, and look after that stupid, clumsy Ann; and the fine-art publishers seem to like my little drawings, and I am never idle for a single instant."

"No, darling, you put us all to shame. Do you think I am finding fault with you? But you must not do it all, that is just it; and as Mrs. Addison no longer requires me, I must look out for another situation"—for during the past year Waveney had acted as secretary to a lady living near them in Cheyne Walk. It had only been a morning engagement, and the pay had not been much, but Waveney, and Mollie too, had found immense pleasure in spending the scanty earnings.

"Of course, I know you must do something," returned Mollie, rather irritably, for even her sweet nature resented the idea of losing Waveney as an insufferable injury; "but you might find something in Chelsea."

"No, dear," returned Waveney, gently. "I have tried, over and over again, and I can find nothing suitable. I cannot teach—I have never been educated for a governess; and no one near us seems to want a secretary or reader, or companion."

"Are you quite sure of that, Waveney?"

"Quite sure. I have been wasting two whole months waiting for something to turn up, so this morning I made up my mind that I would see Miss Warburton. She was so nice, Mollie. She is such a dear woman; a little quick and decided in her manner—what some people would call abrupt—but when she gets interested in a person she is really quite soft and kind. She heard all I had to say, asked me a few questions, and then turned to her book.

"'It is rather a lucky chance you came in this morning, Miss Ward,' she said, 'for a lady who called yesterday is in want of a young person who can read well.' And then she explained to me that this lady's sister was troubled at times with some weakness in her eyes that prevented her from reading to herself, especially of an evening, and that they required some pleasant, ladylike girl, who would make herself useful in little ways."

"And the name, Waveney?"

"The name is Harford, and they live at the 'Red House,' Erpingham. They are very nice people, but at the present moment she is staying with some friends in Berkeley Square, and she will interview me there."

"Oh, dear, you speak as though everything were settled."

"No, indeed, no such luck. Miss Warburton was very kind, very sympathetic, and anxious to help me; but she advised me not to set my heart on it for fear I should be disappointed. 'Miss Harford may think you too young,—yes, I know,' as I was about to protest indignantly at this,— 'you are really nineteen, but no one would think you were over seventeen.' Isn't it humiliating, Mollie, that strangers will always think I am a child? If only my hair would grow and not curl over my head in this absurd way. People always take you for the eldest." "And you are to see Miss Harford to-morrow?"

"Yes, dear; and you must get Noel to throw another old shoe after me for luck." Then her lip trembled and her eyes grew misty.

"Dear, do not make it harder for me than you can help. Don't you know how I hate to leave my old Sweetheart? I would rather stay at home and live on bread and water than fare sumptuously in other folks' houses; I feel as though I should die with home-sickness and ennui. Oh, it is no crying matter, I assure you; it is the rack and the thumb-screw and the burning faggots all in one, and if you want a new martyr for the calendar, and have any spare halos on hand, I am your woman." And then, of course, Mollie did as she was expected to do, left off crying and began to laugh in the manner that often made her father call her "his wild Irish girl." And, indeed, there was something very Irish in Mollie's mercurial and impressionable temperament.

The next minute their attention was attracted by strange noises from below.

Something heavy was being dragged along the passage, accompanied by extraordinary sibilant sounds, resembling the swishing and hissing of an ostler rubbing down a horse. Both the girls seemed to recognise the sounds, for Waveney frowned and bit her lip, and Mollie said, in a troubled tone,—

"Oh, it is poor old 'Canute' come back;" and then they ran into the passage and looked over the balusters. Noel and a little fair man in a shabby velveteen coat were hauling a large picture between them, with much apparent difficulty. One end had got jammed in the narrow staircase, and Noel's encouraging "swishes" and "Whoa, there—steady, old man! Keep your pecker up, and don't kick over the traces," might have been addressed to a skittish mare. Then he looked up and winked at his sisters, and almost fell backwards in his attempt to feign excessive joy.

"Hurrah! three cheers! Here we are again—large as life, and as heavy as the fat woman in Mrs. Jarley's wax-works. But what's the odds as long as you are happy, as the lobster said as he walked into the pot."

"Hold your tongue, Noel," returned his father, good-naturedly. "It is your fault the confounded thing has got wedged. Keep it straight, and we shall manage it well enough;" and then he looked up at the two faces above him.

"There you are, my darlings," he said, nodding to them.

"You see I am bringing our old friend back; we will have him up directly if only this young jackanapes will leave off his monkey tricks." And then in a singularly sweet tenor voice he chanted,—

> "You hear that boy laughing? You think it is fun, But the angels laugh too at the good he has
> done. The children laugh loud as they troop to his call, And the poor man that knows him
> laughs loudest of all."

"Oliver Wendell Holmes," whispered Mollie; but Waveney made no answer; she only ran down a few steps and gallantly put her shoulder to the wheel, and after a few more tugs "King Canute" was safely landed in the studio, where Noel executed a war-dance round him, with many a wild whoop, after the manner of Redskins.

"Father, dear," whispered Mollie, in a delightfully coaxing voice, "sit down on Grumps while I make your coffee;" for the Ward family, being somewhat original, gave queer names to their belongings; and since they were children the old couch had been called "Grumps," tired hands and tired limbs and aching hearts always finding it a comfortable refuge.

"So I will, dear," returned Mr. Ward; and then both the girls hung about him and kissed him, and Mollie brushed back his hair, and put a rose in his buttonhole; but Waveney only sat down beside him and held his hand silently.

There was no difficulty in discovering where Noel got his good looks. In his youth Everard Ward had been considered so handsome that artists had implored him to sit to them; and for many years well-principled heads of girls' colleges feared to engage him as drawing-master.

And even now, in spite of the tired eyes and careworn expression, and the haggardness brought on by the tension of over-work and late hours, the face was almost perfect, only the fair hair had worn off the forehead and was becoming a little grey—"pepper and salt," Mollie called it. But the thing that struck strangers most was his air of refinement, in spite of his shabby coat and old hat; no one could deny that he was a gentleman; and in this they were right.

Everard Ward was a man who if he had mixed in society would have made many friends. In the old days he had been dearly loved and greatly admired; but just when his prospects were brightest and the future seemed gilded with success, he suddenly took the bit between his teeth and bolted—not down hill; his mother's sweet memory and his own dignity prevented that—but across country, down side roads that had no thoroughfare, and which landed him in bogs of difficulty.

For in spite of his soft heart and easy good-nature Everard was always offending people; his wealthy godfather, for example, when he refused to take orders and to be inducted into a family living; and again his sole remaining relative, an uncle, who wished him to go into the War Office.

"Life is an awful muddle," he would say sometimes; but in reality he made his own difficulties. His last act of youthful madness was when he left the Stock Exchange, where an old friend of his father had given him a berth, and had joined a set of young artistic Bohemians.

At that time he was supposed by his friends to be on the brink of an engagement to an heiress, he had seemed warmly attached to her, until at a ball he met Dorothy Sinclair, and fell desperately in love with her.

This was his crowning act of madness; and when he married her his friends shook their heads disapprovingly, and said to each other that that fool of a Ward had done for himself now. Why, the fellow must be imbecile to throw away a fortune and a good sort of woman like that, to marry a pretty little girl, without a penny for her dower!

And, indeed, though Dorothy was a lovely young creature, and as good and lovable as her own Mollie, she was the last woman Everard ought to have married.

The heiress would have made a man of him, and he would have spent her money royally and been the best of husbands to her; but Dorothy lacked backbone. She was one of those soft, weak women who need a strong arm to lean upon.

And so, when the children came, and the cold, cold blast of adversity began to blow upon them; when Everard could not sell his pictures, and poverty stared them in the face;—then she lost heart and courage.

"Everard, dearest, I have not been the right wife for you," she said once; for that long, fatal illness taught her many things. "Oh, I see it all so much more clearly now. I have disheartened you when you needed encouragement, and when our troubles came I did not bear them well."

"You have been the sweetest wife in the world to me," was his answer; and then Dorothy had smiled at him well pleased. Yes, he had been her true lover, and he was her lover to the last; and when she died, leaving three young children to his care, Everard Ward mourned for her as truly as any man could do.

Those were terrible years for him that followed his wife's death; his twin girls were only ten years old, and Noel a pale-faced urchin of five.

He never quite knew how he lived through them, but necessity goaded him to exertion. He worked doggedly all day long, coming home whenever it was possible to take his meals with the children. Sometimes some kind-hearted schoolmistress would tell him to bring one of his little girls with him, and this was always a red-letter day for Waveney and Mollie, for the poor little things led a dull life until Everard was able to send them to day-school; and after that they were quite happy.

He used to watch them sometimes as they went down the street with their satchel of books. Waveney would be dancing along like a fairy child, with little springy jumps and bounds, as though the sunshine intoxicated her, and Mollie would hurry after her, limping and lurching in her haste, with her golden brown hair streaming over her shoulders, and her sweet, innocent face lifted smilingly to every passer-by.

"My sweet Moll, she is her mother's image," Everard would say to himself, and his eyes would be a little dim; for, with all his faults and troubles and idiosyncrasies, no father was more devoted. His twin daughters were the joy and pride of his heart. When he came home at night, tired out with a long day's work, the very sound of their voices as he put the latch-key in the door seemed to refresh and invigorate him.

"Here's dad! here's dear old dad!" they would cry, running out to meet him; and then they would kiss and cuddle him, and purr over him like warm, soft young kittens. Noel would pull off his boots and bring him his slippers, and then "Grumps" would be dragged up to the fire, and Ann would be ordered to bring up the tea quick, and then they would all wait on him as though he were a decrepit old man; and Noel, who was a humorist even at that early age, would pretend to be a waiter, and say, "Yessir," and "No, sir," and "Next thing, sir," with an old rag of a towel on his arm to represent a napkin.

"I saw Ward the other evening," a friend of his said one day to a lady; "he teaches drawing at Welbeck College, where I take the literature classes, so I often see him; and one evening he took me home with him to Cleveland Terrace. Poor old Ward! he was not cut out for a drawing master; he was always a bit flighty and full of whimsies, and used to fly his kite too high in the old days; but he made a fool of himself, you know, with that unlucky marriage."

"Indeed," returned the lady, quietly.

"Ah, well! that is all ancient history. He has made his bed, poor fellow, and must just lie on it; but I do so hate seeing a man's career marred, especially if he is a good sort, like Ward!"

"And you went home with him?" observed his hearer, in the same quiet tone.

"Yes; and upon my word it was really a pretty little family picture. There was Ward, looking like a sleepy Adonis with his fair hair rumpled all over his head, and two sweet little girls hanging on each arm, and cooing over him; and that fine boy of his lying on the rug with a picture. I declare my snug bachelor rooms looked quite dull that night."

When anything ailed one of the twins, Everard's misery would have touched the most stony heart. When Mollie had measles, he nursed her night and day, and when Waveney and Noel also sickened, he was so worn out that if a kindly friend had not come to his assistance, he would soon have been on a sick-bed.

Happily it was holiday time, and there were no schools or classes; Miss Martin was a governess herself, but with the divine self-abnegation of a good-hearted woman she gave up a pleasant visit to a country house to help poor Mr. Ward—women were always doing that sort of thing for Everard Ward. But her little patients gave her a great deal of trouble.

Mollie cried and would not take her medicine from anyone but father, and Waveney was pettish; but Noel was the worst of all.

Miss Martin was plain-featured, and wore spectacles, and Noel, who inherited his father's love of beauty, objected to her strongly. "Go away," he said, fretfully; "we don't want no frights in goggles;" and he began to roar so lustily that Everard was roused from his sleep and came, pale and weary and dishevelled, to expostulate with his son and heir.

But Noel, who was feverish and uncomfortable, repeated his offence.

"We don't want no frights here, dad. Tell her to go."

"For shame, Noel," returned his father, sternly. "I am quite shocked at you. This kind lady has come to help us; and don't you know, my boy, that to a gentleman all women are beautiful?"

"Please don't scold him, Mr. Ward," returned Miss Martin, good-naturedly; but her sallow face was a little flushed. "Noel and I will soon be good friends; it is only the fever makes him fractious." And as tact and good temper generally win the day, the children soon got very fond of their dear Marty, as they called her; and as they grew up she became their most valued friend and adviser until her death.

It was Miss Martin whose sensible arguments overcame Everard's rooted aversion to the idea of his girls working.

"As long as I live I will work for them," he would say; but Miss Martin stuck to her point gallantly.

"Life is so uncertain, Mr. Ward. An accident any day might prevent you from earning your bread—you will forgive me for speaking plainly. Let them work while they are young." But though Everard owned himself convinced by her arguments, it was a bitter day to him when Waveney became Mrs. Addison's secretary.

"Father would cut the moon up in little bits and give them to us," Waveney had said to herself. And, indeed, to the fond, foolish fellow, no gift could have been too precious for those cherished darlings of his heart.

Everard always told people that he loved them just alike, and he honestly thought so; and yet, if Waveney's finger ached, it seemed to pain him all over; and all the world knows what that means!

CHAPTER IV.: THE WARD FAMILY AT HOME.

"And the night shall be filled with music, And the cares that infest the day Shall fold their tents like the Arabs, And as silently steal away." Longfellow.

As soon as Mollie had left the room, on household cares intent, Waveney lighted a small, shaded lamp that stood on the table. It was a warm evening, and both the windows were thrown up. The moon had just risen, and the vine-leaves that festooned the balcony had silver edges. As Waveney turned up the lamp she said, cheerfully, "Now we can see each other's faces," and then she sat down again and slipped her hand in her father's arm.

"Tell me all about it, dad, directly minute." And then a smile came to Mr. Ward's tired face, for this was one of the family stock jokes that were never stale, never anything but delightful and fresh, and whenever one of his girls said it, it brought back Waveney in her baby days, a tiny despot in red shoes, with a head "brimming over with curls," stamping her little feet and calling out in shrill treble, "Directly minute! Miss Baby won't wait nohow."

"There is nothing good to hear, little girl," returned Mr. Ward, with a strained laugh. "When you spell failure, spell it with a big F, my dear; that's all." But another skilful question or two soon drew forth the whole story.

He had had a harassing, disappointing day. The dealers who had sold one or two of his smaller pictures refused to give "King Canute" house-room. They could not possibly dispose of such a picture, they said; it was too large and cumbersome, and there were serious defects in it. One or two of the figures were out of drawing; the waves were too solid, looking like molten lead. There was no finesse, no delicacy of execution, the colouring was crude; in fact, the criticism had been scathing.

"They were so rough on me that my back was up at last," went on Mr. Ward, "and when Wilkes said I might leave it if I liked, and he would try and get a customer for it, I saw he was only letting me down a bit easier, and that he did not believe it would sell, so I just called a cab and brought it back."

Waveney winced. All this cab hire could not be afforded. And then, what were they to do? But the next moment she was stroking the worn coat-sleeve tenderly, and her voice was as cheerful as ever.

"Dad, it is a long lane that has no turning—remember that; and it is no use fretting over spilt milk. To-morrow we will get Noel to hang up dear old King Canute in that blank space, and if the stupid, cantankerous old dealers will not have anything to say to him, Mollie and I will admire him every day of our lives. Molten lead, indeed!" jerking her chin contemptuously.

But Mr. Ward, who had been too much crushed to revive at once, only shook his head and sighed. In his heart he knew the dealers were right, and that the work was not really well done. The stormy sunset looked blotchy and unreal, and the solidity of the water was apparent, even to him. The whole thing was faulty, mawkish, amateurish, and futile. He had been in a perfect rage against himself, the dealers, and all the rest of the world as he clambered into his cab.

He had had a rap upon the knuckles once too often. Well, he had learnt his lesson at last; but what a fool and dunce he had been!

"Take your punishment, my boy," he had said to himself, grimly. "Write yourself Everard Ward, U.A., unmitigated ass; and wear your fool's cap with a jaunty air.

"You wanted to paint a big historical picture! to be something better than a drawing-master. Oh, you oaf, you dotard, you old driveller, to think that you could set the Thames on fire, that you could do something to keep your memory fresh and green. Go back to your water-colour landscapes, to your water-wheels and cottages, your porches smothered in woodbine; you are at the bottom of your class, my lad, and there you will be to the end of the chapter." And then—for his imagination was very vivid—he saw himself, an elderly man, in his shabby great-coat, going out all weathers to his schools—a little shrunk, a little more hopeless, and his girls, his twin blessings—but here the hot tears rose to his eyes, and he bit his lips. Oh, it was hard, hard—and it was for their sakes he had worked and toiled.

Just then Mollie came with a little tray. There was a tall, curious old china cup on it which was known in the family as "Dives," and was considered one of their choicest treasures. When any one was ill, the sight of Dives, filled to the brim with fragrant coffee or delicious chocolate, would bring a smile to pale lips. As she placed the tray beside her father, Mollie's face wore a triumphant air, as though she would have said, "If any one could beat that cup of coffee or make better toast, I should like to see her, that's all."

"Thanks, dearest," returned her father, gently; "but you have scorched your face, my sweet Moll."

"Oh, that is nothing," returned Mollie, hastily, putting up her hands to her hot cheeks; she had been through all sorts of vicissitudes during the last half-hour. The water would not boil, or the fire burn properly, though she and Noel had put a whole bundle of sticks into it, and at every stick he had asked her a fresh conundrum.

"Have you told dad about Monsieur Blackie?" she asked; and then Waveney smiled.

"No, but I will, presently, when father has had his supper. Come out on the balcony a moment, Mollie. Is not the moonlight lovely!"

"Yes, I do love these 'white nights,'" returned Mollie, ecstatically. "We used to call them silver nights when we were wee children. Those roofs look as though they were covered with snow. And just see how nice our shabby old courtyard looks; those privets are quite grand. What an old dear the moon is, Wave! She covers up all little defects so nicely, and glorifies all common things."

But Waveney did not hear this little rhapsody, neither had she called Mollie out to watch moonlight effects.

"Moll, just listen to me a moment: you must not say a word to father about Harley Street—not one word."

Mollie looked at her blankly.

"And why not, Wave?"

"Oh, dear, not for worlds," returned Waveney, earnestly. "He is so low, so unlike himself to-night; he had so set his heart on that poor old thing being a success, but they have all been throwing stones at him, and he is so hurt about it. Don't you know what Noel always says: 'You must not hit a man who is down.' Those are school ethics, but it is true. Dad is just like the brere rabbit to-night,—'him lies low,'—and we must just talk to him and make him laugh."

"But Wave, surely"—and Mollie, who was nothing but a big, beautiful, simple child, looked quite shocked—"surely you cannot mean to see that lady without speaking to father!"

"But I do mean it, Mollie. Of course I want to tell father—I always long to tell him everything,—but it would be rank selfishness to-night; it would be the last straw, that terrible straw that breaks the camel's back. And I know just what he would do; he would not smoke his pipe and he would not sleep a wink, and he would be like a wreck to-morrow when he goes to Norwood. No: when it is settled it will be time enough to tell him;" and, as usual, Mollie submitted to her sister's stronger will. "Waveney was the clever one," she would say; "she saw things more clearly, and she was generally right;" for Mollie thought nothing of herself, and was always covered with blushes and confusion if any one praised her.

So Waveney had her way, and as Mr. Ward smoked his pipe she told him all about Monsieur Blackie; and then Noel shut up his lesson-books and came up stairs, and the three young people sang little glees and songs unaccompanied. And presently Mr. Ward laid down his empty pipe and joined too.

And the girls' voices were so fresh and clear, and the man's tenor so sweet, that a passer-by stood for a long time to listen.

Every now and then an odd boyish voice, with a crack in it, chimed in like a jangling bell out of tune. "Oh, Noel, please do not sing so out of tune; you are as flat as a pancake, and as rough as a nutmeg grater, isn't he, Moll?" and then Waveney made a face at the unfortunate minstrel.

"Don't come the peacock over me," began Noel, wrathfully, for any remark on his cracked voice tried his temper. "Hit one of your own size, miss."

"Hush, hush, Noel!" observed his father, good-humouredly. "You will do well enough some day. 'Drink to me only with thine eyes'—let us sing that, my pets." And then the voices began again, and the listener underneath the window smiled to himself and walked on.

It was late, and Mollie was yawning before the little concert was over; but when Mr. Ward went to his room that night the weight of oppression seemed less heavy. Yes, he had been a fool, but most men made mistakes in their lives, and he was not so old yet—only forty-four, for he had married young. He would leave off straining after impossibilities, and take his friends' advice—paint pot boilers in his leisure hours, and devote his best energies to his pupils. "Cincinnatus went back to the plough, and why not Everard Ward?" And then he wound up his watch and went to sleep. But long after the heavy-footed Ann had climbed up to her attic, breathing heavily, and carrying the old black cat, Mrs. Muggins, in her arms, and long after Mollie had fallen into her first sleep, and was dreaming sweetly of a leafy wood, where primroses grew as plentifully as blackberries, a little white figure sat huddled up on the narrow window-seat, staring out absently on the moonlight.

Waveney could see the dim roofs of the Hospital; the old men were all now asleep in their cabin-like cubicles—some of them fighting their battles over again, others dreaming of wives and children.

"After all, it must be nice to be old, and to know that the fight is over," thought the girl, a little sadly. "Life is so difficult, sometimes: when we were children we did not think so. I suppose other girls would have said we had rather a dull life; but how happy we were! what grand times we had that day at the Zoological Gardens, for example! and that Christmas when father took us to the pantomime! I remember the next day Mollie and I made up our minds to be ballet-dancers, and Noel decided to be a clown;" and here Waveney gave a soft little laugh. "Dear father, it was so good of him not to laugh at us. Most people would have called us silly children, but he listened to us quite seriously, and recommended us to practise our dancing sedulously; only he would not hear of shortening our skirts—he said later on would do for that. Oh, dear, oh, dear, was it not just like him? And of course by the next Christmas we had forgotten all about it."

But even these reminiscences, amusing as they were, could not long hinder Waveney's painful reflections. The idea of leaving home and going out into the world was utterly repugnant to her; she had told Mollie in playful fashion that it was the rack and the thumb-screw and the faggots combined; but in reality the decision had cost her a bitter struggle, and nothing but the strongest sense of duty could have nerved her to the effort.

Waveney's nature was far less emotional than Mollie's, but her affections were very deep. Her love for her father and twin sister amounted to passion. When she read the words, "Little children, keep yourselves from idols," she always held her breath, made a mental reservation, and went on.

"If only people liked Father's pictures!" she sighed, and then another pang crossed her, as she remembered his tired face, how old and careworn he had looked, until they had sung some of his favourite songs, and then his eyes had become bright again.

"Dear old dad, how he will miss me!" But when she thought of Mollie the lump in her throat seemed to strangle her: they had never in their lives been parted for a single night.

"And yet it is my duty to go," thought poor Waveney. "We are growing poorer every day, and it will be years before Noel can earn much. I am afraid the schools are falling off a little. Oh, yes; there is no doubt about it, and I must go;" and Waveney shed a few tears, and then, chilled and depressed, she got into bed; and Mollie turned over in her sleep and threw out her warm young arms.

"It was delicious," she murmured, drowsily; "and oh, Wave, why are you so cold, darling? What have you been doing?" But Waveney only shivered a little and kissed her.

The next morning both the girls rose in good time to prepare the early breakfast. Noel always left home at half past eight—long ago an unknown friend of Mr. Ward's had offered to pay his son's school fees, and, acting on advice, he had sent the boy to St. Paul's. He was a clever lad, and in favour with all his masters; he liked work and never shirked it. But his pet passion was football; he was fond of enlarging on his triumphs, and gloried in the kicks he received. It was understood in the family circle that he was to get a scholarship and go to Oxford; and of course a fellowship would follow.

"'The veiled Prophet' will expect it, my dear," Mollie would say, at intervals, when she was afraid he was becoming slack; for under this figure of speech they always spoke of their unknown benefactor. The whole thing was a mystery. The solicitor who wrote to Mr. Ward only mentioned his client vaguely—"an old friend of Mr. Ward's is desirous of doing him this service;" and in succeeding letters, "My client has desired me to send you this cheque;" and so on.

The girls and Noel, who were dying with curiosity, often begged their father to go to Lincoln's Inn and see Mr. Duncan—the firm of Duncan & Son was a good old-fashioned firm; but Mr. Ward always declined to do this. If his old friend did not choose to divulge himself, he had some good reason for his reticence and it would be ungrateful and bad form to force his hand.

"He is a good soul, you may depend on that," was all they could get him to say; but in reality he secretly puzzled over it. "It must be some friend of Dorothy's," he would say to himself. "There was that old lover of hers, who went out to the Bahamas and made his pile—he married, but he never had any children; I do not mention his name to the youngsters—better not, I think; but I have a notion it is Carstairs; he was a melancholy, Quixotic sort of chap, and he was desperately gone on Dorothy."

"Dad's a bit stiff about the Prophet," Noel once said to his sisters, "but if I am in luck's way and get a scholarship, I shall just go up to Lincoln's Inn myself and interview the old buffer;" and this seemed so venturesome and terrifying a project that Mollie gasped, and said, "Oh, no, not really, Noel!" and Waveney opened her eyes a little widely.

"You bet I do," returned Noel, cocking his chin in a lordly way. "I shall just march in as cool as a cucumber, and as bold as brass. 'I have come to thank my unknown benefactor, sir,' I would say with my finest air, 'for the good education I have received. I have the satisfaction of telling you that I have gained a scholarship—eighty pounds a year—and that, with the kind permission—of—of my occult and mysterious friend, I wish to matriculate at Balliol. As I have now attained the age of manhood, is it too much to ask the name of my venerable benefactor?'"

"Oh, Wave, is he not ridiculous?" laughed Mollie; but Waveney looked at her young brother rather gravely.

"Don't, Noel, dear; father would not like it." But Noel only shrugged his shoulders at this. He had his own opinions about things, and when he made up his mind it was very difficult to move him. Never were father and son more unlike; and yet they were the best of friends.

Mr. Ward always had a hard day's work on Tuesday. He had two schools at Norwood, and never came home until evening. The girls always took extra pains with the breakfast-table on the Norwood days, and while Mollie made the coffee, boiled the eggs, and superintended the toast-making, Waveney made up dainty little pats of butter and placed them on vine-leaves. Then she went into the narrow little slip of garden behind the house and gathered a late rose and laid it on her father's plate.

Waveney was in excellent spirits all breakfast-time. She laughed and talked with Noel, while Mollie sat behind her coffee-pot and looked at her with puzzled eyes.

"How can Wave laugh like that when she knows, she knows!" she thought, wonderingly; but at that moment Waveney looked at her with a smile so sweet and so full of sadness, that poor

Mollie nearly choked, and her eyes brimmed over with tears.

CHAPTER V.: FAIRY MAGNIFICENT.

"Leave no stone unturned." Euripides.
"What is useful is beautiful." Socrates.

"Wish me good luck, and do not expect me until you see me," were Waveney's last words, as Mollie stood at the door with a very woe-begone face. "Cheer up, Moll. Care killed the cat, you know;" and then she waved her hand and vanished.

It was still quite early in the afternoon when she reached Berkeley Square. In spite of her assumed cheerfulness, her courage was at a low ebb. The imposing appearance of the houses awed her; she knocked timidly, and the butler who opened the door looked like a dignified and venerable clergyman.

He received her affably, as though she were an expected guest. Miss Harford was out driving, but would be back shortly; his mistress, Mrs. Mainwaring, had desired that Miss Ward should be shown into the drawing-room.

Waveney never felt so small and insignificant in her life. For the first time she was conscious of a wish to be tall, as she followed him down the corridor. Then the thickness of the carpets distracted her, and the cabinets of china. Then a door was opened, and she heard her name announced, and a soft little voice said, "Certainly, Druce. Show the young lady in."

For one moment Waveney hesitated. The owner of the voice seemed invisible. It was a beautiful room, grander than anything that the girl had ever seen, and it was full of sunshine and the scent of flowers. Tall palms were everywhere, and china pots with wonderful Japanese chrysanthemums, and there were screens and standard lamps, and a curtained archway leading to an inner room; and here Waveney at last discovered a tiny old lady, half buried in an immense easy chair. She was the prettiest old lady in the world, but as diminutive as a fairy; her cheeks were as pink as Mollie's; and she had beautiful silvery curls under her lace cap. A mass of white, fleecy knitting lay on her satin lap, and the small, wrinkled fingers were loaded with costly brilliants.

"Fairy Magnificent," Waveney named her when she was retailing the account of her visit. She looked up with a pleasant smile, and pointed to a chair. "You have called to see my niece, Miss Harford—oh yes, she is expecting you, but she was obliged to pay a business visit; my nieces are busy women, Miss Ward—perhaps you will find that out for yourself some day." Waveney began to feel less shy; she looked round the room that she might describe it properly to Mollie. How Mollie revelled in that description afterwards; it was like a page in a story book—flowers and statues and palms, and that beautiful old lady in her satin gown.

Fairy Magnificent was evidently fond of talking, for she rippled on, in her soft voice, like a little purling brook, knitting all the time.

"Oh, we all have our gifts, my dear, but I am afraid in my day girls were terribly worldly; it was not the fashion to cultivate philanthropy or altruism, as they call it. I recollect a young man asking one of my nieces if they went in for 'slumming.' I wonder what we should have thought of such a question when I was young."

"Does Miss Harford do that sort of thing?" asked Waveney, with something of her old animation. She was such a dear little old lady—like a piece of Dresden china.

"Oh, not slumming exactly—they are too sensible to take up every passing craze; but they do an immense deal of good. They have a Home for governesses and broken-down workers very near them at Erpingham, and they have a room in the garden where they do all sorts of things. They have Thursday evenings for shop-girls, regular social evenings—tea, and music, and talk; and the girls are as nicely behaved as possible."

"Oh, what a grand idea!" and Waveney's eyes began to gleam and sparkle. "I have always been so sorry for shop-girls. I think they have such a hard, pushing sort of life. The poor things are often so tired, but they have to look pleasant all the same."

Mrs. Mainwaring looked amused at the girl's energy, but before she could reply there were quick, decided footsteps in the outer room, and the next moment a tall, dark woman in walking-dress entered.

When Waveney rose from her chair, the lady looked at her with extreme surprise.

"Miss Ward, I suppose;" and her manner was a little brusque. "Please sit down again, and I will speak to you directly. Aunt Sara, may I have the carriage, please. Morris says the horses are quite fresh. I find the letter that I expected is at the Red House, so it will be better for me to talk it all over with Althea."

"Do as you like, Doreen," returned Mrs. Mainwaring, tranquilly; "but you must attend to this young lady first, you know;" and then Miss Harford took a seat near Waveney.

The girl was suffering from a sense of painful disillusion. Mrs. Mainwaring's talk had given her a favourable idea of Miss Harford, but when she saw her, her first thoughts were "What a grievous pity that such a good woman should be so plain!" But the next moment she added, "Plain is too mild a term; she is really quite ugly;" and it could not be denied that Dame Nature had treated Miss Harford somewhat churlishly.

Her figure was angular, and a little clumsy, and not even her well-cut tailor-made tweed could set it off to advantage. Her features were strongly marked, and her complexion sallow, and her low forehead and heavy eyebrows gave her rather a severe look. She could not be less than forty, probably a year or two over that, but there was no affectation of youth, either in dress or manner.

Perhaps the only point in her favour was a certain frankness and sincerity in her expression that, after a time, appealed to people; and yet her eyes were a light, cold grey. Strangers seldom took to her at first—her quick, decided manners were rather too brusque, and then her voice was so harsh and deep; but they soon found out that she was to be trusted, and by-and-by they grew to love her.

Doreen Harford always spoke of herself as the "ugly duckling," who would never change into a swan in this world.

"I never do anything by halves," she would say, laughing, and her laugh was as fresh and ringing as a child's, though, perhaps, a little hard. "I am as ugly as they make them, my dear,"—for she was too happy and busy a woman to fret over her lack of beauty, though she adored it whenever she found it, and petted all the pretty children and animals.

"There's Aunt Sara," she would go on, "is she not like one of Watteau's Shepherdesses? Did you ever see anything so fine and pink and dainty?—and she is seventy-three. She has had lovers by the score, and she was only a young woman when General Mainwaring died; but she would never marry again, bless her!"

When Miss Harford sat down she pulled off her gloves in rather a disturbed manner.

"I was sorry to keep you waiting, but I had to go out on urgent business. You are very young, Miss Ward—younger than I expected, and than Miss Warburton led me to suppose."

She spoke in a slightly aggressive voice, as though Miss Ward were somehow to blame for her youthful aspect.

"That will mend in time, Doreen, my love," observed Mrs. Mainwaring, kindly. "I think Miss Ward seems a very sensible young lady." And then Waveney longed to hug her.

"I am nineteen," she said, looking Miss Harford full in the face. "That is not so very young, after all; and I have acted as secretary to a lady in Cheyne Walk. It was only a morning engagement, certainly, but Miss Warburton knows all about me, and she thought this situation would just suit me. I am fond of reading aloud, and I never get tired, and——"

"Doreen, if you do not engage this young lady, I think I shall." But Mrs. Mainwaring was only joking, as her niece knew well, for it would have been more than her life was worth to do such a thing.

For Fairy Magnificent had a faithful maid who simply worshipped her, and would have fought any woman who offered to do her service. Her mistress wanted no paid companion as long as she was in the house, she would say; and as Rachel ruled her mistress—and, indeed, the whole household, there was little probability of her indulging in this luxury.

Miss Harford's face brightened. She understood the purport of her aunt's little joke: she liked Miss Ward, and wished her niece to engage her.

"Althea will not mind her being young," she said, significantly; and then Miss Harford turned to Waveney.

"Miss Warburton will have given you some idea of the duties required"—and now her manner had decidedly softened. "We are very busy people, and we lead two lives, the working life and the social life; and as we are fairly strong, we manage to enjoy both. Unfortunately, my sister has had a little trouble with her eyes lately—the doctors say it is on the nerves. Sometimes when she reads or writes she has pain in them, and has to close her book, or shut up her desk. If she were to persevere the pain would become excruciating; it is certainly on the nerves, for sometimes she is not troubled at all."

"I understand," returned Waveney, in a low voice.

"Our doctor is an old friend and a very sensible man," continued Miss Harford, "and he proposed that my sister should find some young lady with a good voice and pleasant manner who would read to her, especially in the evenings, when nothing is going on, and to whom she could dictate letters."

"Oh, I am sure I could do that," returned Waveney, eagerly; and then Mrs. Mainwaring chimed in again.

"My dear, I am an old woman, so you may believe me. My nieces are the best women I know, and they make every one happy at the Red House."

"Now, Aunt Sara," returned Miss Harford, good humouredly, "how are Miss Ward and I to understand each other if you will keep interrupting us? You see, Miss Ward, the duties are very light, and you will have plenty of time to yourself. We want some one young and cheerful who will make herself at home and be ready for any little service. Are you musical?"

"I can sing a little but my voice has not been well trained."

"That is a pity. Now should you mind reading us a page or two?" And she handed her a novel that was lying open on the table.

Waveney flushed, but she took the book at once. For the first few minutes her voice trembled: then she thought of the new gown she wanted to buy for Mollie at Christmas, and then it grew steady.

"Miss Ward reads very nicely, does she not, Aunt Sara?" was Miss Harford's approving comment. "I think Althea will be pleased." Then turning to Waveney with a pleasant smile that lit up her homely features as sunshine lights up a granite rock, "I really see no reason why we should not come to terms. I do not know what we ought to offer you, Miss Ward, but my sister thought fifty pounds a year."

Waveney gave a little start of surprise. The terms seemed magnificent.

"Oh," she said, impulsively, "I shall be able to help father. What happiness that will be!" And then her face fell a little. "Will you tell me, please, is it very far to Erpingham?"

"Do you mean from here?"

"No, not exactly. I am thinking of my own home. We live in Cleveland Terrace, Chelsea." Then Miss Harford seemed somewhat taken aback.

"Is your father's name Everard Ward?" she asked, abruptly.

"Oh, yes,—have you heard of him?" returned Waveney, naively. "He is an artist, but his pictures do not sell, and he has only his drawing lessons. That is why I want to help him, because he works so hard and looks so tired; and Mollie—that is my sister—is a little lame, and cannot do much."

"Is that all your family? You do not speak of your mother."

Miss Harford was looking at the girl a little strangely.

"She is dead," returned Waveney, in a low voice; "she died when Mollie and I were ten years old, but there is a young brother, Noel."

Then Miss Harford turned to her aunt.

"Aunt Sara, I really think it would be best for Althea to see Miss Ward herself. You know I have to drive over to Erpingham now. It is quite early in the afternoon," she continued, looking at Waveney. "Can you not come with me? We shall be at the Red House in three-quarters of an hour. I could drop you at Sloane Square station by seven. It will be a pleasant drive, and the evenings are still light until eight."

Waveney hesitated. What would Mollie say to her long absence? But then, her father never returned home before eight on his Norwood days. The drive tempted her, and then, the idea of seeing Erpingham.

"If you are sure that I shall be back by seven," she said; and then Miss Harford rang the bell and ordered the carriage.

"Althea will give us tea. Come, Miss Ward." And then Mrs. Mainwaring held out her soft, little hand to the girl.

"Good-bye, my dear. You will be as happy as a bird at the Red House. Give my love to Althea, Doreen, and tell her to rest her poor eyes."

Waveney thought of Cinderella and the pumpkin coach as she stepped into the luxurious carriage. The novelty of the position, the enjoyment of the swift, smooth motion, and the amusement of looking out at the crowded street, completely absorbed her, and for some time Miss Harford made no attempt to draw her into conversation.

But presently she began to talk, and then Waveney found herself answering all sorts of questions about herself and Mollie—how they amused themselves, and why her father's pictures did not sell; and then Waveney, who was very girlish and frank, told her all their disappointment about "King Canute," and Miss Harford listened with such kindly interest that Waveney felt quite grateful to her.

"Father was so low and cast down about it last night, he said he should never have the heart to paint a picture again, because the dealers were so hard on him; and I am afraid he meant it, too. Oh, what a nice grey church! And actually, we are coming to a river. Oh, how picturesque those reddish-brown sails look in the sunshine!"

"This is Dereham," returned her companion. "It is not such a very long drive, is it? In little more than ten minutes we shall have reached our destination;" and then she began pointing out various objects of interest—another church, the shops in High Street where they dealt, then a high, narrow house, very dull and gloomy-looking.

"Some dear old friends of ours live in that house," she said. "It is not very inviting-looking, is it? Once they lived in such a beautiful place, until old Mr. Chaytor lost his money. I am always so sorry for them. I think troubles of this kind fall very heavily on some natures."

Waveney assented to this, but the subject did not much interest her. They had left Dereham behind now, and before them lay a wide, green common, with pleasant roads intersecting it. A little clear pool by the roadside rippled in the sunlight. Near it was a broad, grassy space shaded by trees. Two or three nurses sat on benches, and some children were dancing hand in hand, advancing and retreating, and singing in shrill little voices. "Here we go gathering nuts in May," they were chanting, and then one child fell down and began to cry. Across the common there were soft blue distances and a crisp wind, laden with the perfumes of firs and blackberries, fanned their faces.

Then they drove through some white gates. A lodge and a long, shady lane were before them, with long, parklike meadows on one side. It was all so sweet, so still, and peaceful, in the evening light, that Waveney was half sorry to find that their journey was at an end; for the next moment the carriage stopped, and the lodge-keeper opened some more gates, curtsying with a look of pleasure when she saw Miss Harford.

"I have not come home to stay, Mrs. Monkton," observed Miss Harford, with a friendly nod, and then the horses began frisking down a winding carriage drive. The shrubbery was thick, but every now and then Waveney had glimpses of little shut-in lawns, one with a glorious cedar in the middle, and another with a sundial and peacock. An old red brick Elizabethan house was at the end of the drive, with a long sunny terrace round it.

At the sound of the wheels two little Yorkshire terriers flew out to greet their mistress with shrill barks of joy.

"Oh, what pretty little fellows!" exclaimed Waveney.

"Yes, they are great pets. Fuss and Fury, that is what we call them," returned Miss Harford, smiling, "and I think you will allow that the names suit them."

CHAPTER VI.: QUEEN ELIZABETH'S WRAITH.

As they entered the large square hall with Fuss and Fury frolicking round them, a tall respectable-looking woman came forward to meet them.

"I suppose my sister is in the library, Mitchell?" asked Miss Harford, quickly.

"Yes, ma'am. Parker has just taken in the tea."

"Then will you please give this young lady some: take her into my room, and make her comfortable. I must ask you to excuse me for a short time, Miss Ward, as I have to talk over one or two things with my sister; but Mitchell will look after you."

"Oh, please do not trouble about me!" returned Waveney; and then she followed Mitchell down a long passage, full of beautiful plants, to a pleasant sitting-room with a deep bay window overlooking the lawn with the sundial; the peacock was strutting across the grass with the mincing, ambling gait peculiar to that bird, the peahen following him more meekly.

Through green trellised arches one looked on a tennis lawn, and beyond that was a large red brick cottage with a porch. When Mitchell brought in the tea-tray, Waveney asked her who lived there. The woman looked a little amused at the question.

"No one lives there, ma'am," she answered, civilly. "My mistresses built it, for their winter evening entertainments. There is only one room, with a sort of kitchen behind it. It is always called the Porch House."

Waveney longed to ask some more questions, but Mitchell had already retired, so she sat down and enjoyed her tea.

How happy she could be in this lovely place if only Mollie were with her! And then she thought of the fifty pounds a year. After all, Erpingham was not so far away. Perhaps they would let her go home once a week. If she could only have her Sunday afternoons and evenings to herself! And then her heart began to beat quickly. How delicious that would be! How Mollie and she would talk! And after tea they would sing their old hymns, and then they would all go to church together, and her father and Noel would walk to the station to see her off. And then she wondered if she should mind the long walk across the common; it would be rather lonely, she thought, on a dark winter's evening, and perhaps Miss Harford would not approve of it.

While Waveney indulged in these surmises and cogitations, Miss Harford had walked briskly across the inner hall, and, tapping lightly at a door, opened it and entered a beautiful long room fitted up as a library. It had a grand oriel window, with a cushioned seat, and a tiny inner room like a recess, with a glass door leading to the lawn with the cedar-tree.

A lady writing at a table in the centre of the room uttered a little exclamation of surprise.

"Why, Doreen, I was just writing to you; but it is the unexpected that always happens." And then the two sisters kissed each other affectionately.

"You can put away your letter and give me some tea instead," Doreen said, laughing; and then Althea smiled and walked to a little tea-table that had been placed in the window, with two inviting-looking easy chairs beside it.

"Sit down, Dorrie, do, and tell me what has brought you over like a flash of lightning on a summer evening," she said, as she took up the tea-pot.

Althea Harford was a better-looking woman than her sister, but she could never have been handsome. She was very tall, and her figure was decidedly graceful; she walked well, and carried her head with the air of an empress. Her eyes were expressive and even beautiful, but her face was too long and thin, and her reddish auburn hair and light eyelashes gave her rather a colourless look. She had a long, aquiline nose, and some people said that she reminded them of Queen Elizabeth, though it may be doubted whether that Tudor princess had Althea's air of refinement and gentleness.

She was evidently a year or two younger than her sister, but her dress, like Doreen's, was very sedate, and suitable to her age. She had a style of her own, which certainly suited her. When excited, or under the influence of some strong emotion, a faint pink colour would come to her cheeks, and a vivid light to her eyes; at such moments she would be almost beautiful.

The sisters were very unlike in disposition; but in spite of their dissimilarity they were the best of friends, and understood each other perfectly.

Doreen took life more lightly; she had a robust cheerfulness that seldom failed her. Althea had a greater sense of humour, and far more intellect; but there was a veiled melancholy about her, as though early in life she had suffered disillusion; and she would speak sometimes as though human existence were a comedy where the players wore masks and performed the shadow dance at intervals.

Both sisters were Ladies Bountiful, and gave nobly of their substance, but Althea could never be brought to acknowledge that she gave enough; she had scruples of conscience, and would sometimes complain that they were like Dives, and had their good things in this life.

"And as though we were not rich enough," she would grumble, "Aunt Sara is actually going to leave us her money"—for Mrs. Mainwaring had lately made another will in her nieces' favour. Doreen would have a large sum of money, but Althea, who was her favourite, would be the chief legatee, and Althea had groaned in spirit when she heard it.

"It is such a responsibility," she sighed; but Doreen would not listen to this.

"It is such an enjoyment," she retorted. "I do so love spending money, and so do you, Althea, in spite of your grumbling. And as to Aunt Sara's will, we need not make ourselves miserable about that, for she will probably live until she is ninety." And this view of the case cheered Althea greatly. Althea's temperament was by no means pessimistic, but like all deep thinkers she had to pay the penalty of her own acute perceptions. The unsolved problems of life saddened her, and at times disturbed her comfort. She envied Doreen her capacity for putting troublesome questions out of her mind. "I wish I had your mind, Dorrie," she said once. "It is such a comfortable, nicely padded mind. When disagreeable things happen, you just let down your curtains and keep yourself snug."

"Upon my word, Althea," returned Doreen, good-humouredly, "I am glad no one but myself heard that speech. You make me out a nice selfish sort of person."

"No, no, you are not selfish at all, you are far more ready to help people than I am. You are a good woman, Doreen, and you know I did not mean that."

"Then what did your riddle mean?"

"Well, just what I said. That you never worry and fret yourself over troublesome questions—social questions, I mean, difficult problems that meet one in this world at every corner; I often make myself quite unhappy over them, and go to bed with a heartache, but I do not believe that you ever lose an hour's sleep over them."

"I daresay not. In that sense I suppose I have a nicely padded mind; but, Althea, it is not that I do not realise the difficulty. But, my dear child, what is the good of sitting down before a mountain and waiting for it to open. Earthquakes of that sort won't happen. I put it by until I am grown up;" and as Althea stared at her she nodded her head. "Quite grown up, I mean; we are only children here, and we are not likely to get all our lessons perfect." And then, in a low voice, she said, a little solemnly, "'What I do thou knowest not now, but thou shalt know hereafter;'" and as Doreen said this her plain, homely features were transfigured and Althea looked at her with reverence; for in her simple faith Doreen had passed her and taken the higher place.

"Well, Doreen, what has brought you over this evening?" asked Althea, as she handed her sister a cup of tea. "I was thinking of driving over to-morrow to see you and Aunt Sara."

"Well, I wanted to see you about two or three things, Miss Ward amongst them. I have brought her over, and she is at present partaking of tea and cake in my room."

"Oh—do you think she will do?" asked Althea, quickly.

"Well, that is for you to decide. You shall see her presently and judge for yourself. At first sight I confess that I was not favourably impressed—she is such a childish-looking little thing, with fluffy, babyish hair curling over her head. But for her eyes, and expression, I should never have thought her grown up. She is rather like Laura Ridgway, only paler."

"Laura has very pretty eyes, Doreen."

"So has Miss Ward; they are quite out of the common. Aunt Sara took rather a fancy to her."

"Aunt Sara is a very good judge of character," her sister observed.

"Well, I liked her better myself after a time; her voice is deep, but I somehow admire it, and she read very nicely. She seems anxious to come to us. They are evidently rather poor. But——" Here Doreen hesitated in rather an embarrassed way.

"Out with it, Dorrie: there is something behind, I see."

"Well, it is for you to judge. I shall leave the decision in your hands. I think Aunt Sara is right, and that Miss Ward is a nice little thing; but she is Everard Ward's daughter."

Althea started; she was evidently quite unprepared for this. She changed colour slightly. "Are you sure of that, Doreen?" she asked, in a low voice. "You know how many Wards there are—dozens and dozens."

"Yes, and I never for a moment imagined that it could be Everard's daughter; but directly she mentioned her address—Cleveland Terrace, Chelsea—of course I recognised her. Wait a minute"—as Althea seemed inclined to interrupt her—"let me make it all clear to you. I put the question to her, 'Is Everard Ward your father?' That was plain enough, was it not? And when she said yes, I managed to glean two or three particulars, that we already know."

"Yes, but tell me, all the same;" and Althea's manner was a little eager.

"Well, she told me that her mother was dead—we knew that—and that she had a twin sister who was rather lame, and a brother Noel." Then, at the mention of Noel's name, Althea looked a little amused.

"What a strange coincidence!" she murmured.

"Strange enough, but rather embarrassing. Miss Ward was very naive and frank. It seems the poor man cannot sell his pictures; he has one on hand now. 'King Canute,' she called it, and none of the dealers will look at it. She says her father is very low about it, and that they want the money badly. Well, what now, Althea?" pretending to frown at her; for Althea's face was suffused with colour, and her eyes were very bright.

"Poor Everard!" she said, softly. "There is room for another picture in the Porch House." And then a queer little smile came to her lips. "It will be a valuable lesson to the girls."

Then Doreen shook her head at her.

"It could not be done, you foolish woman. You would be found out."

"We must discover another way, then," returned Althea, who was quite in earnest. "Perhaps Thorold will give it house room."

"But you must be prudent, dear."

"I will be discretion itself. The picture will not be purchased in my name, you can depend on that. I begin to think my nature is not straightforward, I do so love little plots, and underhand schemes. I should have made a good secret conspirator. Now about this girl: if she pleases me, I can see no objection to our engaging her. It is perfectly simple, Dorrie; they are poor, and the girls have to work. Fate, or rather—for it is no joking matter—Providence, has brought her to us. Is it too superstitious to say that I feel that I dare not refuse to take her. It may be another way of helping them."

"Yes, but in my opinion, Everard ought to know to whom he is sending her."

"Ah, I agree with you there, in spite of my subterranean and complicated schemes. I did not propose any fresh masquerade, as far as the girl is concerned. I am willing to be as open as the day. Now, as we have finished tea, shall I go to your room?" And Doreen smiled assent.

Waveney was standing by the window, crumbling some sweet-cake for the peacock. She turned round at the sound of the opening door.

The evening sun was shining into the room, and perhaps the light dazzled Waveney a little; but certainly she gave a very droll description of Althea to Mollie afterwards.

"The door opened, and a very tall woman in a grey gown seemed to glide in, for she walked so quietly that I could not hear a footstep; and lo and behold, it was Queen Elizabeth's Wraith."

"Oh, Waveney, what nonsense! And I do hate that horrid old Elizabeth."

"Well, so do I; but, all the same, Miss Harford is remarkably like her—such a long, thin face and nose, and reddish hair; and she had a sort of ruff of lace round her throat, and such a stately manner, it was quite queenly. And, I think, really, that I should have made my curtsy, only she came up to me in the kindest way and took my hand. 'I am so sorry that you have been alone all this time,' she said, in such a sweet voice, 'but my sister and I had so much business to discuss. She has told me all about you, so I am not going to trouble you with needless questions. You can just tell me anything you like about yourself. I have a great respect for workers, and always love to help them.'"

"It was nice of her to say that."

"Yes; it quite won my heart. I like both the Miss Harfords, Mollie; but Miss Althea—or Queen Bess, as I prefer to call her—is more to my taste. She interested me directly, and we had such a nice talk, just as though we were old friends; and she said at once that I could have my Sunday afternoons—think of that, sweetheart! I shall be with you every Sunday."

Althea's sympathetic nature had at once grasped the girl's trouble at leaving home.

"I think I could arrange for you to spend the greater part of your Sundays at home," she observed, "that is, if you are a good walker, for we never use our horses on Sundays, unless the weather is very bad. We dine early, for I always have a busy afternoon in the Porch House, and I could spare you easily."

"But the long walk back in the dark," faltered Waveney, who knew well that her father would make objections to this. Then Althea considered the point.

"Yes, you are right. You could not walk alone on dark evenings, and the winter is coming. There are houses, of course, but they stand so far back, and the gates are locked. Oh, no, my dear, that would never do. Neither my sister nor I could permit you to walk alone." Then her face brightened, and she continued with more animation, "I have an idea. My maid Peachy always goes to see her mother on Sunday afternoons; she lives near Victoria, and she always takes the same train back. We will find out which that is, and then you can walk up the hill together." At this the girl's joy was so evident that Althea had been quite touched.

Just at the close of the interview she had said a few words that greatly surprised Waveney.

"And now, my dear, I should like you to go home and talk things over with your people, and then you can write me a line saying whether you wish to come to us. We must not decide things finally until your father gives his consent. He will know our names." And, as Waveney seemed puzzled at this, "When we were young he visited at our house. Oh, not here; we lived in Surrey then."

"But when shall you want me," asked Waveney, anxiously. "Oh, I am sure father will give his consent. He is dreadfully unhappy at the idea of our working, but he knows it must be done."

"Still you must consult him," returned Althea, gently, and her manner was a little stately. "As for my wanting you, I shall be content if you could come to me in about ten days. Now I hear the carriage coming round. Good-bye. I think I will add au revoir;" and then she shook hands very cordially, and the next moment Doreen joined them.

There was very little conversation during the drive back. Miss Harford was busy with her letters and note-book, and Waveney leaned back on the cushions, and thought over her talk with Althea.

"How strange that father should have known them!" she said to herself. "He often talks of his old friends, but he has never mentioned their name. Harford—no, I am sure I never heard it until Miss Warburton spoke of them. If I go anywhere it shall be to the Red House—I have made up my mind to that. I like both of them—they are different somehow from other people; but I like

Queen Bess far the best."

CHAPTER VII.: A HUMOURIST AND AN IDEALIST.

"A merrier man, Within the limits of becoming mirth, I never spent an hour's talk withal." Act II.

While Waveney was doing her very best to make a favourable impression on the Misses Harford, an interview of a far different character was taking place at Number Ten, Cleveland Terrace.

Mollie, who was conscientious and strictly truthful, having been taught from childhood to abhor the very whitest of white lies, was trying laboriously to carry out a certain programme drawn up by Waveney. She was not to cry or to think of anything disagreeable, and she was only to look at the clock twice in an hour, and there was no need for her either to be always standing on the balcony and straining her eyes after every passer-by. It was sheer waste of time, and it would be far better to finish one of her pretty menu-cards; and Mollie, who was docile and tractable, had agreed to this.

"It shall have a spray of golden brown chrysanthemums," she said, quite cheerfully; and when Waveney left the house she arranged her painting-table and selected the flowers from Corporal Mark's nosegay.

But, alas!

"The best-laid schemes of mice and men Gang aft agley."

Scarcely had Mollie wetted her brush before Ann the heavy-footed came up with an inflamed face and red eyes.

"The pain was horrible," as she expressed it, "and was not to be borne. Would Miss Mollie spare her for half an hour, and she would get Mr. Grainger's young man to pull the tooth out?"

"Oh yes, Ann, certainly," returned Mollie, who was tender-hearted. But when Ann had withdrawn with a snorting sob, she mused with some perplexity over all the ills to which maids-of-all-work were liable.

Ann had looked so strong when they had engaged her, and yet she was always complaining of something. She was addicted to heavy colds in her head, and to a swollen face, sometimes diversified by an earache. She was a good-tempered, willing creature, but her infirmities were great, and more than once Waveney had advised Mollie to send her away.

"But she is so honest," Mollie would plead, "and she is so devoted to Mrs. Muggins," and so Ann had been suffered to remain. Noel took her off to the life. He would tie up his face with a wisp of flannel and sit hugging the cat for ten minutes at a time.

"Was it a poorty leddy, then, and did she want the poor little chickabiddies?" Ann would choke with suppressed laughter when she came in to lay the table. "Ain't it natural, Miss Mollie? and it is just what I did say to Mrs. Muggins."

Mollie was studying the chrysanthemum pensively when Annie put her head in again.

"The fire must not get low, Miss Mollie, because of the cake."

Then Mollie jumped up in dismay.

Ann was going out, and leaving that precious cake—Noel's birthday cake—and it was such a nice one! She had made it herself, and it had beautiful pink-and-white icing on the top. That her cake should be spoilt was a thought not to be endured for a moment. She knew what Ann's fires were   black, smoky concerns. As Mollie rushed into the kitchen the front door bell rang, and Ann, with her hat on, admitted a visitor.

"A gentleman, Miss Mollie, and I have shown him up in the studio." But Mollie, whose face was in the oven, did not hear this; her whole attention was absorbed by her cake—menu cards were forgotten. She stirred the fire, put on coals, and then sat down on the rug to watch the oven.

Meanwhile, the visitor walked briskly into the studio. He was a small, dark man, and his dress was somewhat Bohemian; he had a brown velveteen coat, and a yellow rose in his buttonhole, and he had bright, clear eyes, that saw everything worth seeing, and a good deal that ordinary folk failed to see—not that people always found this out. He had plenty of time for observation, and when he had grown a little weary of his solitude, he made a tour of the room. He stood for some time by Mollie's painting table. The menu cards struck him as very pretty and graceful in their design.

"My good little Samaritan is artistic, I see," he said to himself; "but there was no need for her to put on her best frock because a stranger called. But vanity and women are synonymous terms." And after this atrocious sentiment—which all women would utterly repudiate—he looked curiously at a framed picture standing on the floor.

"'Canute and his Courtiers.' Yes, I see; rather stale, that sort of thing. 'Canute' decidedly wooden, ambitious, but amateurish—wants force and expression." And then he shook his head. "Hulloa, what have we here?" and he stepped up to the easel.

It was a roughly executed sketch in crayon and was evidently a boy's work; but in spite of considerable crudeness, it was not without spirit.

A young lady was stepping down from an omnibus, and a queer little man in a peaked hat, and a huge moustache, was handing her out. He was grinning from ear to ear, and in his other hand was a sixpence.

"Your eternally obliged Monsieur Blackie," was written under the picture.

The visitor seemed puzzled; then a light dawned. Finally he threw back his head and laughed aloud. "We have a humourist here," he said to himself; and to restore his gravity, he began walking up and down the room; but every time he passed the easel he laughed again. "This is clearly not my little Samaritan," he said to himself. He had brought in a beautiful bouquet, and had laid it down on the round table. Every few minutes he took it up and looked at the door.

The household was certainly a peculiar one. An extraordinary young female, with her face tied up in flannel, had shown him upstairs after telling him that Miss Ward was in. He had been waiting nearly twenty minutes. Should he ring the bell? But there was no bell—not a semblance of one. Then he thought he would leave the flowers and the sixpence, with his card. Yes, perhaps that would be best. And then he hesitated. It was very absurd, but he rather wanted to see the little girl again; there was something so bright and piquant about her. Perhaps she was keeping out of the way on purpose. Perhaps Monsieur Blackie—and here he laughed afresh—was not to her taste. No sooner did this idea come into his head than, with manlike perversity, he determined to persevere.

He walked downstairs and into the dining-room. Here fresh amusement awaited him in the inscription, "Noel Ward, his Study."

"My friend the humourist again," he said softly; and then he pricked up his ears, for in some back premises he could distinctly hear a very clear, sweet girlish voice. He stole into the passage to listen.

And this is what he heard:—

"Here's to the maiden of bashful fifteen; Here's to the widow of fifty; Here's to the flaunting extravagant queen And here's to the housewife that's thrifty, Let the toast pass; Drink to the lass— I'll warrant she prove an excuse for the glass."

"School for Scandal," muttered the stranger. "A very good song and very well sung. I should like to clap. Let me see: that is what they used to do in the Arabian Nights entertainment—clap hands, enter beautiful Circassian slave, with a golden dish full of jewelled fruits. I will knock instead at the mysterious portal."

"Oh, is that you, Ann!" exclaimed a voice, cheerfully. "However did you get in? Fetch me some coals, please. And oh, I forgot your poor tooth. Was it very bad?"

"Pardon me," observed the young man, hurriedly. Then, at the strange voice, Mollie turned round.

Once, many years ago in a foreign gallery, Ingram had stood for a long time before a little picture that had captivated his fancy; it was the work of an English artist, and a very promising one, and was entitled "Cinderella." A little workhouse drudge was sitting on a stool in the chimney corner of a dark underground kitchen; a black, cindery fire was casting a dull glow; a thin tabby cat was trying to warm itself. The torn, draggled frock and grimy hands of the little maid-of-all-work were admirably rendered, but under the tangled locks a pair of innocent child's eyes looked wistfully out. A story book, with the page opened at Cinderella, lay on the lap.

Ingram thought of this picture as Mollie turned her head and looked at him, and, man of the world as he was, for the moment words failed him.

He was standing in a dull little kitchen—a mere slip of a place—looking out on a long straggling garden, very narrow, and chiefly remarkable for gooseberry-and-currant bushes; and sitting on the rug in front of the fire, like a blissful salamander, was a girl with the most beautiful face that he had ever seen.

Then poor Mollie, blushing like a whole garden full of roses in her embarrassment, scrambled awkwardly to her feet.

"Oh, dear! I thought it was our Ann. Will you tell me your name, please? Father is out, and we do not expect him home until eight."

"My business was with your sister," returned Ingram, regaining his self-possession as he saw the girl's nervousness. "Your servant let me in exactly five-and-twenty minutes ago, and as I thought the household was asleep I was endeavouring to discover a bell; and then I heard singing,—

"'Let the toast pass; Drink to the lass,'

Awfully good song that."

"Oh, dear," faltered Mollie—she would have liked to sink through the floor at that moment, to avoid that bright, quizzical glance; "that was father's song, not mine. Oh, I know now who you are. You are the gentleman whose pocket was picked yesterday."

"Exactly. Monsieur Blackie, at your service;" and then Mollie turned cold with dismay. Ann had let him in, and he had been in the studio, and Noel's absurd sketch was on the easel. He had recognised himself. And Mollie's confusion and misery were so great that in another minute she would have disgraced herself for ever by bursting into tears; only Ingram, fearing he had taken too great a liberty, hastened to explain matters.

"You see, Miss Ward, I was anxious to pay my debts, and thank your sister. If I remember rightly, I told her that I should call."

"Oh, yes; at least, Waveney was not sure that you would, and she had to go out."

"I should like to have seen her. Perhaps another time you will allow me——" Ingram reddened and hesitated.

"She may not be long. She has gone to Berkeley Square on business. Ah," as the bell rang, "that is Ann, so please will you go upstairs."

Mollie was not quite equal to the situation; she wanted to get rid of Monsieur Blackie, but he did not seem inclined to go; and Ingram took a mean advantage of her inexperience.

"I have left my hat upstairs," he said, hypocritically, "and there are some flowers which I brought for your sister, and I think they ought to be put in water." This appealed at once to Mollie.

"Oh, certainly," she said; and as she limped down the passage before him, a pained look came in Ingram's eyes.

"Oh, what a grievous pity," he thought, "that lovely face to be allied with such a cruel infirmity."

"Oh, what flowers!" exclaimed Mollie, burying her face in them; and then she glanced at the card shyly. "Moritz Ingram." What a nice name! Yes, he was rather nice, too. In spite of his droll looks, she liked his voice; but, all the same, if he would only go! He ought to go—and Ingram evidently shared this opinion, for he was hunting sedulously for his hat; and as his efforts were unavailing, Mollie was obliged to go to his help.

"I brought it upstairs," he kept saying. "'Manners makye man,' and I was always remarkable for my good manners. Why, even your sister took me for a Frenchman." And at this Mollie broke into a merry laugh, and Ingram's eyes twinkled sympathetically.

The next minute the door-bell rang again, and Mollie, who had just discovered the hat underneath the sofa—though how it got there, no one knew—was just going to dart to the door, when a cracked voice called out, "Cat's meat!" and the faint mewing of Mrs. Muggins was clearly audible in the distance and then Noel strolled in. He looked at Ingram in unfeigned amazement; then, being an acute lad, he grinned.

"Noel, this is Mr. Ingram, the gentleman Waveney saw in the omnibus yesterday."

"I recognised myself," returned Ingram, with an airy wave of the hand towards the picture, "though perhaps it is not a speaking likeness—a sort of cross between Mephistophiles and Daniel Quilp, with perhaps a soupçon of the Artful Dodger. I prefer to sit for my own portrait, don't you know."

Then Noel grinned again, rather sheepishly. For once he was reaping the just reward of his impudence.

"You are a humourist, my young friend," continued Ingram, blandly. "I am an Idealist. All my life—and I am exactly thirty seven—I have been seeking 'the impossible she.' That does not mean" (interrupting himself, as though he feared to be misunderstood) "any individual woman. Oh dear, no; originality is my favourite fetish."

Mollie looked bewildered, but she was rather impressed by this fine flow of words, but Noel's eyes brightened. "Was this not a man and a brother?"

"Women don't understand that sort of thing," he observed, confidentially; "they never laugh at the right jokes unless you label them;" and here Noel threw up his head and cocked his chin. "That is why I have taken to drawing—a picture pleases the poor things, and the funnier you make it, the more they like it."

"Indeed!" remarked Ingram, mildly. And then he looked at the handsome lad with unfeigned approval. "It is for your sister's benefit that you do these clever sketches? I am an artist myself—an embryo artist, I ought to say, for I have never sold a picture—but I recognise a brother in the art."

Then Noel, who detected irony in the smooth voice, looked a little sulky.

"It is not clever a bit," he growled; "it is beastly rot. I did it to get a rise out of Waveney—Waveney is the other one, you know."

"Did you say Waveney? I never recollect hearing the name before."

"No. It is a queer sort of name. Father had a great-aunt Waveney. When I want something short and handy, don't you know, I call her Storm-and-stress."

"Upon my word, Miss Ward, your brother is perfectly dangerous. If I stay here any longer I shall take the infection. I told you my special and particular fetish was originality. I seem to have met it here. Thank you"—as Mollie meekly handed him his hat—"I have trespassed on your kind hospitality far too long already. With your kind permission I will call again, in the hope of seeing your sister."

"What could I say?" asked Mollie, anxiously, when she related the account of the afternoon. The sisters were safely shut up in their own room—a large front room over the studio. Mr. Ward slept in the little room behind. "I could not say, 'No, please do not come, I am sure Waveney does not want to see you!'"

"Why no, of course not. You did quite right, Mollie dear. Did not dad say he showed his gratitude in a very gentlemanly way. And as for Noel, he has been talking about him all the evening."

"Yes, Noel took a fancy to him; and Wave, I do think he must be nice; he says droll things in a soft, sleepy sort of voice, and I am afraid I was rather stupid and did not always understand; but his eyes looked kind and gentle. I was not afraid of him after the first few minutes."

"Poor little Moll. Well, it was rather embarrassing to have to interview a live stranger all alone, and in the kitchen too!"—for Mollie had drawn a highly colored and graphic description of her first meeting with Monsieur Blackie.

Waveney had laughed mercilessly at first.

"Mollie Ward enacting the part of Cinderella or Cinder Maiden—enter the Black Prince with the glass slipper. Mollie, dear, I grieve to say it, but your feet are not as pretty as mine;" and Waveney, who was excited with her eventful day, kicked off her shoes, and began dancing in the moonlight, her tiny feet scarcely touching the floor.

And behold the spirit of mischief was in her; for, as Mollie sat on the bed and watched her with admiring eyes, she suddenly broke into a song; and this is what she sang:

"Here's to the maiden of bashful fifteen, Here's to the widow of fifty, Here's to the flaunting, extravagant quean, And here's to the housewife that's thrifty. Let the toast pass, Drink to the lass, I'll warrant she'll prove an excuse for the glass."

CHAPTER VIII.: MOLLIE'S BABY-HOUSE.

"Within 'tis all divinely fair, No care can enter my retreat; 'Tis but a castle in the air, But you and I are in it, sweet." Helen Marion Burnside.

It is necessary to retrace our steps a little; for it was not until much later that Waveney executed her pas-de-seul in the moonlight. Miss Harford had kept her word, and Waveney was deposited at Sloane Street Station punctually at seven; and before the quarter had struck she was walking quickly up Cleveland Terrace. Mollie, whose state of mind by this time baffled description, was on the balcony watching for her, and had the door opened before Waveney was at the gate; a few hurried questions and answers had been interchanged, and then they had heard their father's latch-key in the door.

"Oh, dear! oh, dear! Why is father so dreadfully early, this evening?" exclaimed Mollie, in a lamentable voice.

"Never mind," returned Waveney, philosophically. "We must just wait until bed-time; and then won't we make a night of it, Moll?"

"But father will hear us, and rap on the wall," observed Mollie, fretfully, "and tell us to go to sleep like good children."

"Oh, no, he won't, if we curl ourselves on the window-seat; it is a big room, and our voices won't reach him. Mollie dear, remember, nothing is to be said to father to-night; he is far too tired for fresh worries. To-morrow I will take him for a prowl, and talk to him severely. No;" as Mollie looked at her wistfully. "I must have him all to myself; I can manage him more easily so. Run down to him now, dear, while I take off my hat, and then I will join you."

Mollie did as she was told; and, thanks to Waveney's management, they had another merry evening. Monsieur Blackie was the leading topic. Waveney was quite touched when Mollie handed her the bouquet with a little speech; but Noel entirely spoilt it by croaking out in an absurd voice, "Your much and eternally obliged Monsieur Blackie."

"Hold your tongue, you young rascal," returned Mr. Ward, in high good-humour. "Mr. Ingram is a gentleman, and shows that he knows what good manners are."

"Manners make man," observed Mollie, slyly; and then Noel exploded again.

"He was the coolest hand I ever knew," he replied. "If he were his Grace the Duke of Wellington, he could not have lorded it better. 'You are a humourist, my young friend.' I should like to have given him one for his impudence! And then the cheek of telling 'the wobbly one' that he would call again."

Mr. Ward frowned.

"Noel, I will not have you call Mollie by that name. A jest is a jest, but it must not be carried too far."

"Pegtop, then," returned Noel, unabashed by this rebuke, for behind his father's back he winked at Mollie. "But he was not a bad sort of chap. He would be rather useful on an east-windy, dismal sort of a day—he would make you feel cheerful. I like a fellow who can take a joke without turning rusty over it"—and from Noel this was high praise.

Mollie thought the evening dreadfully long, and she fidgeted so much, and looked at the clock so often, that her father called her drowsy-head, and begged her to go to bed; but this made her redden with confusion. And then, when they were safe in their room, Waveney chose to be ridiculous and cut capers. But as soon as her little song was finished she produced an old shepherd's plaid rug, which was known in family annals as "the Lamb," and they both crept under it, and tucked up their feet on the window-seat, and felt cosy.

And if an artist could have drawn the picture, it would have made his fortune, for the rough old plaid set off Mollie's exquisite face and glorious golden brown hair to perfection, while Waveney's looked fair and infantine in the moonlight.

Waveney was the talker now, and Mollie was the listener, but every now and then there were little interjections of surprise and admiration. At the description of "Fairy Magnificent" Mollie drew in her breath and said "Oh!" Miss Harford's ugliness rather shocked her; she said "It was a great pity, and Waveney had never been used to live with ugly people"—which was perfectly true.

She thought Queen Elizabeth's Wraith a rather far-fetched description. She could not endure Queen Bess; she was such an unladylike person, and boxed gentlemen's ears. And if Miss Althea were like her——But here Waveney interposed.

"Don't be a little goose, Moll. She is like Queen Elizabeth, and you would say the same yourself if you saw her; but she is so nice and gentle that I am sure I shall soon love her. Well, let me go on. I want to tell you about the Red House." Then Mollie sighed with satisfaction, and composed herself to listen.

Mollie, with all her sweetness and goodness, was a little Sybarite at heart. She loved pretty things, fine house, gems, beautiful dresses. Mr. Ward had been almost shocked when he had taken her one day to Bond Street to look at the shops. It was impossible to get her away from the jewellers'; the diamond tiaras and necklets riveted her. "Who buys them, dad?" she had asked, in quite a loud voice; "dukes and earls, and those sort of people?"

"Yes, of course," returned Mr. Ward, a little impatiently, "and the Prince of Wales, I daresay;" for he was rather provoked at the attention the child was exciting. Two gentlemen who were passing, and had overheard Mollie's remark, smiled at each other.

"What a beautiful child!" observed one; he was a tall, old man, with a fine, benevolent face.

"You are right, Duke," returned the other, with a supercilious laugh. "Some little rustic come to town for the first time."

"Come, Mollie," observed her father, rather crossly, "we must not take up the pavement in this way or the Bobby will be telling us to move on;" and then Mollie had limped on until another shop-window attracted her.

Mr. Ward had felt a little perplexed by Mollie's unsatiable appetite for pretty things, and on their return home he unbosomed himself to Waveney.

"All girls like shops," he said, seriously, "and I knew Mollie would be pleased, but I never expected her to glue her face to the glass for half an hour at a time. She made herself quite conspicuous, and several people laughed at her."

"Mollie must be better behaved next time," returned Waveney, smiling. "Father, dear, I don't think it matters really. Mollie is young, and she leads such a quiet life, and sees so few things, that when she goes out she just loses her head. I think," she continued, calmly, "that she does care for pretty things more than most people,—she would love to be rich, and dress grandly, and have pictures and jewels and beautiful things. When we were tiny children she always would make me read the story of Cinderella; nothing else pleased her."

"Don't you care for pretty things, too, Waveney?" asked her father, a little sadly.

"Oh, yes, dad! All girls care a little, I think; but I am not always longing for them like Mollie. She makes up stories to amuse herself. Some one is to leave us a fortune, and we are all to be rich suddenly. She has actually imagined a house and fitted it up bit by bit; and just for the fun of the thing I have helped her—it is our play-house, you know. But Mollie thinks it quite real. If you say to her, 'Let us go down to Kitlands,' her eyes brighten, and she looks quite happy."

"You are foolish children," observed Mr. Ward, fondly. "Who would have thought that my sweet Moll had been such a little worldling at heart!"

"No, dad, you must not say that. Worldly people are selfish, and Mollie has not a selfish thought. It is just a pretty, childish fancy. I sometimes believe in Kitlands myself, we have talked about it so often. On windy nights I have seen the oaks tossing their branches in the park, and the deer huddling under them, and the west room where we always sit of an evening, with the bay window. And how the red firelight streams out on the terrace? And there is a delicious couch by the fire with a lovely Japanese screen behind it, and——" But here Mr. Ward put his hand over the girl's mouth.

"Do you think I am going to be entertained by a description of your baby-house?" he said, in mock wrath. "Tell Mollie she ought to be grown up by this time." But when he was left alone, he said to himself, "Now, why in the world should they have hit on that name Kitlands? Don't I recollect that sunny evening when I walked up the terrace, and the red light streamed from the west room!" He sighed, then roused himself. "Bless their dear, innocent hearts. Now if only their mother could have heard all that!"

Mollie was perfectly ravished with the description of the Red House, and as soon as Waveney paused to take breath, she said, "Why, it is almost as nice as Kitlands, only there is no park and no deer. But I wish I had thought of a peacock." Then she put her head on one side and reflected deeply. "There is the Italian garden, you know, Wave, a sundial would do very nicely there, and we could choose an inscription." But Waveney gave her a little push. "Don't be such a baby, Mollie. We are getting too old for Kitlands. We must put our play-house away with the dear old dolls. But, seriously, is it not perfectly delicious to think we shall be together every Sunday?"

"Yes, that will be nice, of course. But is it really settled, Wave?" and Mollie's voice was full of melancholy.

"I think so, dear; but, of course, I must talk to father. Darling, promise me that you will try and make the best of it. The week will pass so quickly, and then, when Sunday comes, we shall be together. I daresay I shall be with you by half-past three, just after father and Noel have started for their afternoon walk."

"I shall come to the station and meet you," interrupted Mollie.

"Will you? How nice that will be! And we shall have a cosy hour on Grumps, and you shall tell me all your worries—every one of them; and I will tell mine. Then, when father comes in, you and Noel shall get tea ready, and dad and I will have a little talk. And after tea we will sing all our favourite hymns, and then we will go to St. Michael's together, and I will have my old place by father."

"Yes; and then we will all go to the station with you. But oh, Wave, how I shall hate Monday mornings! I shall never feel cheerful until Wednesday is over;" but Waveney would not hear of this—she preached quite a little homily on the duty of cultivating cheerfulness; but her eloquence died a natural death when she saw Mollie nod, and ten minutes later they were both asleep.

It was a free morning with Mr. Ward, and he was not at all surprised when Waveney invited him to take a prowl.

"Won't Mollie prowl, too?" he asked, as he noticed her wistful expression. But Waveney shook her head.

"Mollie was an idle girl yesterday," she remarked, severely; "she must stay in and finish her menu card. There, you shall have the Black Prince's flowers to console you;" and Waveney placed them on the painting-table. "'Sweets to the sweet'—they are as much yours as mine, Mollie." Then Mollie blushed a little guiltily. More than once the thought had passed through her mind—how nice it would be if she had a Monsieur Blackie to bring her hot-house flowers. For Mollie was very human, and certainly

"A creature not too bright and good, For human nature's daily food,"

and she had her girlish weaknesses. Not that she envied Waveney her flowers; but, as she sniffed them delightedly, her imagination conjured up numberless bouquets for Miss Mollie Ward; only the donor must be tall and fair, not a little dark Frenchified artist like Monsieur Blackie.

Waveney chatted to her father quite gaily until they had crossed the lime avenue, and had reached the landing-stage. Then they walked a little way down the embankment, and sat down on a bench under a shady tree. It was still early, and there were few passengers; only now and then a river steamer passed, churning the blue water into light, foamy waves. Two or three children were bowling their hoops, followed by a panting pug.

Waveney cleared her voice rather nervously; then she slid her hand into her father's arm. Everard could see the worn little glove fingers on his coat sleeve; he stared at the white seams dreamily as he listened. He was a man who noticed trifles; there was a feminine element in his character. That little shabby grey glove appealed to him forcibly.

"Father, dear, I have something to tell you—that is why I did not want Mollie to come; it is so much easier to talk about difficult things to only one person." Waveney's voice was not as clear as usual. "Will you promise to listen, dearest, without interrupting me?" Mr. Ward nodded, but his face was a little grave. What could the child have to say?

Waveney told her story very fully. She gave her father a description of the Red House and Fairy Magnificent, but she never mentioned Miss Harford's name; she spoke of them vaguely as "the ladies."

"And you have settled all this without speaking to me?" and there was a hurt look on Mr. Ward's face. Then Waveney nestled closer to him.

"Father, dear, I wanted to tell you—I want to tell you everything; but you were so tired, and I thought it would be kinder to wait until I had spoken to the ladies."

"The ladies. What ladies? Have they no name?" he asked, irritably.

"Yes, dear, of course they have," returned the girl, gently. "Their name is Harford."

Then he turned round a little quickly.

"Harford. Oh, I daresay there are plenty of that name. I know Erpingham—Noel and I walked there one Sunday afternoon; but I do not remember the Red House."

"No; it stands in a lane. You have to go through some white gates. They have not always been at Erpingham; they used to live in Surrey." Then she felt him start slightly.

"I suppose you did not hear their Christian names?" he asked a little anxiously.

"Oh yes, dad, I did. The ugly one—she was very nice, but she is terribly plain—was called Doreen; and the pale, fair one, like Queen Elizabeth, was Althea." Then it was evident that Mr. Ward was completely taken aback.

"Doreen and Althea," he muttered. "It must be the same. With a singular coincidence! Waveney, my child, tell me one thing. Was the name of their house in Surrey Kitlands?"

"I don't know, father; they never told me. But stay a moment: there was a picture in Miss Harford's sitting-room of an old Elizabethan house standing in a park, and under it was written Kitlands Park. I meant to tell Mollie about that."

"It is the same—it must be the same," he returned, in a low voice. "The names are too uncommon. Yes, and it is true, Althea was a little like Queen Elizabeth. I would have given five years of my life that this had not happened. It is one of the little ironies of fate that my girl should have gone to them."

"Oh, why, father?" asked Waveney, piteously; her father's look of bitterness filled her with dismay. Why was he so disturbed, so unlike himself? He did not even hear her question. He got up from the bench quickly and walked to the railings. Another steamer was passing. Mr. Ward looked after it with vague, unseeing eyes.

Everard Ward was a proud man, in spite of his easy-going ways. He had had his ambitions, his aspirations, and yearnings. He had set his ideal high, and yet, for want of ballast, he had suffered shameful shipwreck.

At the beginning of life he had had his good things—health, good looks, talents, and friends. Doors had opened to him, kindly hands had been held out to him, and one of them a woman's hand; but he had turned away in youthful caprice, and had chosen his own path.

He had meant to have carved his own fortunes, to have painted pictures that would have made the name of Everard Ward famous; and he was only a drawing-master who painted little third-rate pot-boilers.

How Everard loathed his poverty! His shabby coat, and Mollie's pitiful little makeshifts and contrivances, were all alike hateful to him. Too well he remembered the flesh-pots of Egypt—the

Goshen of his youth, where he had fared sumptuously, when he had money to spend and the world smiled at him; and then, like a fool—the very prince of fools—he had flung it all away.

He had made a mess of his life, but he was not without his blessings; and in his better moments, when the children were singing their hymns, perhaps he would tell himself humbly that he was not worthy of them.

But as he stood by the river that morning, it seemed to him as though the cup of his humiliation was full to the very dregs. He had so broken with his old life that few ghostly visitants from the dim past troubled him; and now there had started up in his path the two women whom he most dreaded to see.

And one of them he had wronged, when, hot with a young man's passion, and tempted by Dorothy's sweet eyes and girlish grace, he had drawn back, suddenly and selfishly, from the woman he had been wooing.

Well, he had dearly loved his wife; but the disgrace of that shameful infidelity was never effaced from his memory. It was a blot, a stain upon his manhood, a sore spot, that often made him wince.

Would he ever forget that day they were in the old walled garden, gathering peaches, and Althea had just handed him one, hot with the sun, and crimson-tinted, and bursting with sweetness?

"You always give me the best of everything, Althea," he had said; but he was thinking of Dorothy as he said it, and of her love for peaches.

"I like to give you the best—the very best," Althea had answered sweetly, and her eyes had been so wistful and tender that he had felt vaguely alarmed. How he had made his meaning clear to her he never could remember. He had spoken of Dorothy, and perhaps his voice had trembled, for all at once she had become very silent, and there was no more gathering of peaches.

"I must go in now," she had said, suddenly, and he noticed her lips were pale. "Doreen wants me. Yes, I understand, Everard, and you have my best wishes—my best wishes." And then he had stood still and watched her, a tall, slim figure in white, moving between the fruit-trees and carrying her head proudly.

"And it is to Althea Harford that my daughter has applied for a situation," thought Everard, sadly. And again he told himself that he was draining the cup of humiliation to the very dregs.

CHAPTER IX.: ROSALIND AND CELIA.

"A hero worshipped and throned high On the heights of a sweet romance, A faithful friend who was 'always the same' Till the clouds grew heavy and troubles came. But this is life, and this is to live, And this is the way of the world." Gertrude Carey.

Waveney sat on the bench feeling very forlorn and deserted until her father came back to her. He had evidently pulled himself together, for he looked at her with his old kind smile, though perhaps his lips were not quite steady.

"Come, little girl, don't fret," he said, tenderly. "Least said is soonest mended, and we must just go through with it."

"But, father, are you sure you do not mind?" she returned, eagerly. "We are very poor, but I would rather please you, dear, than have ever so much money—you know that, do you not?"

Waveney's eyes were full of tears, and her little hands clasped his arm appealingly. Mr. Ward's laugh was a trifle husky.

"I know I have two good children," he returned, feelingly. "Look here, my child, things have got a little mixed and complicated, and I find it difficult to explain matters. It is my 'poverty and not my will consents,' don't you know—and we must just pocket our pride and put a good face on it."

"Do you mean that I am to go to Miss Harford? Are you very sure that you mean that, dad?"

"Yes, certainly"—but his face clouded. "Did you not tell me that Miss Althea suffered with her eyes, and needed a reader and companion? We were good friends once, so why should I put an affront on her by refusing her my daughter's services?"

Waveney sighed; she felt a little oppressed: her father took a reasonable and practical view of the case, but his voice was constrained; he was a proud man, and at times he chafed sadly at his limitations. He could not forget that he had come of a good old stock; he used to tell his girls to carry their heads high, and not allow themselves to be shunted by nobodies.

"Your mother was a gentlewoman," he would say, "and your great-grandmother had the finest manners I ever saw; she was a Markham of Maplethorpe, and drove in a chariot and four horses when she went to the county ball. It was your grandfather who ruined us all; he speculated in mines, and so Maplethorpe was sold. I saw it once, when I was a little chap: I remember playing on the bowling green."

Everard Ward thought he was doing his duty in teaching his girls to consider themselves superior to their neighbours, but sometimes Waveney would joke about it. She would come into the room with her little nose tip-tilted and her head erect, and cross her mittened hands over her bosom. "Am I like my great-grandmother Markham?" she would say. "Stand back, Mollie; I am going to dance the minuet;" and then Waveney would solemnly lift her skirts and point her tiny foot, and her little performance would be so artless and full of grace that Mr. Ward would sit in his chair quite riveted.

"Father, I wish you would tell me how you first came to know the Misses Harford?" asked Waveney, rather timidly.

Mr. Ward had relapsed into silence, but he roused himself at the question.

"It was in my Oxford days, child. I was quite a young fellow then. There were a good many pleasant houses where I visited, but there was none I liked so well as Kitlands.

"Mrs. Harford was alive then; she was rather an invalid, but we all liked her. I always got on with elderly women; they said I understood their little ways. I knew your Fairy Magnificent, too; she was a great beauty. We young fellows used to wonder why she had never married again."

"Oh, father, this is very interesting. My good little Fairy Magnificent."

Then he nodded and smiled.

"When Mrs. Mainwaring came down to Kitlands there would be all sorts of gaieties going on—riding parties and archery meetings in the summer, and dances and theatricals in the winter."

"Once we acted a pastoral play in the park—As You Like It. It was very successful, and the proceeds went to the county hospital. I remember I was Orlando."

"Was Miss Althea Rosalind?"

"No, your mother was Rosalind. She acted the part charmingly; it was her first and last appearance. Althea"—his voice changed—"was Celia; her sister Doreen insisted on being Audrey, because she said she looked the part to perfection."

"Then mother knew them, too?" observed Waveney, in surprise.

"Well, no, dear, one could hardly say that. We were in great distress for a Rosalind, and the Williams heard of our difficulty, and they said they knew a young lady who had studied the part for some private theatricals that had never come off. I had already met your mother at the county ball, and I was very glad to see her again. Rosalind"—he laughed a little—"and Orlando clenched the business."

"But, father, why have you dropped such nice friends?" It was evident that Mr. Ward had expected this question, and was prepared for it.

"Well, you see, my child, when I married your dear mother I was supposed by my friends to have done a foolish thing. It was difficult enough to hold our heads above water, without trying to keep in the swim. People quietly dropped us, as we dropped them. It is the way of the world, little girl." And then in a would-be careless tone, he quoted,—

"A part played out, and the play not o'er, And the empty years to come! With dark'ning clouds beyond and above, And a helpless groping for truth and love, But this is life and this is love, And this is the way of the world."

It was a habit of Mr. Ward's to quote poetry; he often read it to his children; he had a clear, musical voice. But Waveney was not content to have the subject so summarily dismissed.

"Father, dear, do you really mean to say that the Harfords gave you up because you were poor?" and her tone was a little severe.

"No, dear, it was I who gave them up. By the bye, Waveney, I wonder why they left Kitlands?" and as the girl shook her head, he continued, thoughtfully, "It was a big place, and perhaps they did not care to keep it up after their mother's death; they always wanted to live nearer town. Well, have we finished our talk?" and then Waveney rose reluctantly. He had not told her much, she thought regretfully; but, all the same, her girlish intuition went very nearly the truth.

There was something underneath; something that concerned Miss Althea. Why had her father looked so pained when she had mentioned the name? But with a delicacy that did her honour she was careful not to drop a hint of her suspicions to Mollie.

Mr. Ward thought he had kept his secret well. He was impulsive and reckless by nature, but his care for his motherless girls was almost feminine in its tenderness. They were too precious for the rough workaday world, so he tried to hedge them in with all kind of sweet old obsolete fashions, for fear a breath should soil their crystalline purity.

"Father would like to wrap us up in lavender, and put us under a glass case," Waveney would say, laughingly, and it must be owned that neither she nor Mollie were quite up to date. They did not talk slang; they were not blasé; and they had fresh, natural ideas on every subject, which they would express freely. Waveney was the most advanced; Mollie was still a simple child, in spite of her nineteen years.

Mollie was very curious on the subject of her father's intimacy with the Harfords, but Waveney managed to satisfy her without making any fresh mysteries.

"It is all in a nutshell, Mollie," she said, quietly. "When father was a young man he went to a lot of nice houses, and Kitlands was one of them. They were rich people and very gay, and gave grand parties, and he had quite a good time of it; and then he and mother married, and they were poor; and then, somehow, all their fine friends dropped off."

"Oh, what a shame!" interrupted Mollie, indignantly.

"Well, the Harfords did not drop him, but somehow he left off going there; and he has never even heard of them for twenty years. I think it upset him rather to have his old life brought up before him so suddenly; it made him feel the difference, don't you see!" and Waveney's voice was a little sad, she could so thoroughly enter into her father's feelings. What a change from the light-hearted young man of fashion, acting Orlando and making love to Rosalind in the green glades of Kitlands, to the shabby, drudging drawing-master, with shoulders already bowed with continual stooping.

Waveney wrote her little note of acceptance the next day. It brought a kind answer from Miss Althea; she was very glad that Miss Ward had decided to come to them. She and her sister would do their best to make her feel at home. Erpingham was so near, and they so often drove into town, that she could see her people constantly. "Please give our kind remembrances to your father, if he has not quite forgotten his old friends," was the concluding sentence.

Waveney handed the note silently to her father; he reddened over the closing words. What a kind, womanly letter it was. The faint smell of lavender with which it was perfumed was not more fragrant than the warm-hearted generosity that had long ago forgiven the slight.

Had he really wounded her by his desertion, or had her vanity merely suffered? How often he had asked himself this question. They had only met once, a week before his wedding, and she had been very gentle with him, asking after Dorothy with a friendliness that had surprised him; for, manlike, he never guessed how even a good woman will on occasion play the hypocrite.

"She is a kind creature," he said, giving back the letter; but his manner was so grave that even

Mollie did not venture to say a word.

The girls had a good deal on their minds just then. Waveney's scanty wardrobe had been reviewed, and Mollie had actually wept tears of humiliation over its deficiencies. "Oh, Wave, what will you do?" she said, sorrowfully. "And we dare not ask father for more than a few shillings!"

"No, of course not;" but Waveney's forehead was lined with care as she sat silently revolving possibilities and impossibilities.

What would the Misses Harford think of her shabby old trunk, that had once belonged to her mother? Then she threw back her curly head and looked at Mollie resolutely.

"Mollie, don't be silly. Life is not long enough for fretting over trifles. The Misses Harford know we are poor, so they will not expect smart frocks. I have my grey cashmere for Sundays, and I must wear my old serge for everyday. I will get fresh trimming for my hat, and a new pair of gloves, and——"

"And boots," ejaculated Mollie. "You shall have a pair of boots if I go barefoot all the winter; and your shoes are very shabby too, Wave."

"Yes, I know. I will talk to father and see what is to be done. If he would advance me a couple of pounds I could repay it at Christmas. Is it not a blessing that I have one tidy gown for evenings?"—for some three months before they had gone to some smart school party, and their father, being flush of money just then, had bought them some simple evening dresses. The material was only cream-coloured nun's-veiling, but Mollie had looked so lovely in her white gown that all the girls had been wild with envy.

The dresses had only been worn once since, and, as Waveney remarked, were just as good as new. "Shall you wear it every evening, Wave?" Mollie had asked in an awed tone; and when Waveney returned, "Why, of course, you silly child, I have no other frock. In big houses people always dress nicely for dinner; I found that out at Mrs. Addison's," Mollie regarded the matter as quite decided—her oracle had spoken.

Mr. Ward had advanced the two pounds without any demur, and the sisters made their modest purchases the following afternoon. As Waveney was re-trimming her hat, and Mollie painting her menu cards, Ann flung open the door somewhat noisily. "Mr. Ink-pen, miss," she announced, in a loud voice; and the next minute Monsieur Blackie entered. He looked trim and alert, as usual; his face beamed when he saw Waveney.

"It is the right Miss Ward this time," he said, shaking hands with her cordially. Then he looked at Mollie, and his manner changed. "Will you allow your maid to hang these birds up in your larder?" and he held out a superb brace of pheasants to the bewildered girl.

Mollie grew crimson with shyness and delight.

"Do you mean they are for us?" she faltered.

"Yes, for you and your sister, and your father, and my young friend the humourist. And please remember"—and now his smile became more ingratiating—"that they are from Monsieur Blackie. No, please do not thank me. They were shot by a friend of mine. I rather object to the massacre of the innocents myself, and I prefer doing it by deputy. By the bye, I find I have a new name—your maid is a humourist too. 'Ink-pen'—there is something charmingly original and suggestive about that. It makes Ingram rather commonplace."

"Oh, I think you have such a beautiful name!" returned Mollie, artlessly. "It is ever so much better than Ward."

Then Waveney nudged her.

"I think the pheasants ought to be hung up," she said, rather brusquely; and at this broad hint Mollie limped off, with very pink cheeks. "Whatever made you say that, Mollie?" was her comment afterwards.

"I don't think it is quite nice to tell gentlemen that they have beautiful names. I am sure I saw an amused look on Mr. Ingram's face."

But Mollie only looked puzzled at this.

"Ann is very stupid about names," remarked Waveney, as she took up her work again. "She always calls me Miss Waverley and Noel, Master Noll. Somehow she does not seem to grasp sounds."

"Was your sister christened Mollie?" he asked, quickly; and he looked at the menu cards as he spoke.

"Yes; it was mother's fancy, and I do so love the name," returned Waveney, in her frank way. "I daresay you would not guess it—people seldom do—but we are twins. Strangers always think Mollie is the elder."

"I should have thought so myself," returned Ingram; and then he took up one of the cards. Waveney thought he was a little nervous—his manner was so grave. "These are very pretty," he said, quietly. "I thought so the other day. The design is charming. May I ask if your sister ever takes orders for them?"

"Yes, indeed; a lady has commissioned Mollie to paint these. She is to have twelve shillings for the set."

"Twelve shillings!" and here Ingram's voice was quite indignant. "Miss Ward," he continued, turning round to Mollie, who had just re-entered the room, "it is a shame that you should be so fleeced. Why, the design is worth double that sum. Now there is a friend of mine who would willingly give you two guineas for a set of six. She is very artistic, and fond of pretty things, and if you are willing to undertake the commission I will write to her to-morrow."

Willing! Mollie's eyes were shining with pleasure. If she could only earn the two guineas! They should furnish sop for Cerberus—alias Barker. Waveney's earnings would not be due until Christmas, and the constant nagging of the aggrieved butcher was making Ann's life miserable.

"'Master says if meat's wanted it must be paid for, and he does not hold with cheap cuts and long reckonings.' Drat the man! I hates the very sight of him," remarked Ann, wrathfully, to her usual confidante, Mrs. Muggins—for with toothache, a swollen face, and an irascible butcher, life was certainly not worth living.

"Then I will write to my—to the lady to-morrow." Both Mollie and Waveney noticed the little slip. "I wonder if he is married," Waveney said to herself. But Mollie's inward comment was, "Very likely Mr. Ingram is engaged, but he does not know us well enough to tell us so."

Mr. Ingram was trying to regain his airy manner, but a close observer would have detected how keenly he was watching the two girls as he talked. Nothing escaped him—the new hat trimmings, and the faded hat; Waveney's worn little shoe, and the white seams in Mollie's blue serge.

Cinderella—he always called her Cinderella to himself—was no whit smarter than she had been the other day; her hair was rather rough, as though the wind had loosened it. And yet with what ease and sprightliness they chattered to him! Their refined voices, their piquante, girlish ways, free from all self-consciousness, delighted the young man, who had travelled all over the world, and had not found anything so simple, and artless, and real, as these two girls. It was Waveney to whom he directed his conversation, and with whom he carried on his gay badinage; but when he spoke to Mollie, his voice seemed to soften unconsciously, as though he were speaking to a child.

CHAPTER X.: "IT IS THE VOICE OF SHEILA."

"In the grey old chapel cloister I sit and muse alone, Till the dial's time-worn fingers Mark the moment when we twain Shall in paradisal sunlight Walk together, once again." Helen Marion Burnside.

There was no doubt that both Waveney and Mollie found their guest amusing. His views of life were so original, and there was such a quiet vein of humour running through his talk that, after a time, little peals of girlish laughter reached Ann's ears. It was Mollie who first struck the key-note of discord.

Mr. Ingram had been speaking of a celebrated singer whom he had heard in Paris.

"She is to sing at St. James' Hall next Saturday week," he went on. "They say the place will be packed. A friend of mine has some tickets at his bestowal if you and your sister would care to go." As usual he addressed Waveney; but Mollie's face grew very long.

"Oh, dear, how nice it would have been!" she sighed; "but Waveney is going away;" and her eyes filled with tears.

"Going away!" he echoed in surprise.

"Yes. She is going to be a reader and companion to a lady living at Erpingham, and she will only come home on Sundays;" and then a big tear rolled down Mollie's smooth cheek and dropped into her lap. "And we have never been apart for a single day!" She finished with a little sob.

"Dear Mollie, hush," whispered Waveney. "We ought not to trouble Mr. Ingram with our little worries. Erpingham is a nice place," she continued, trying to speak cheerfully. "Do you know it?"

"Oh, yes," he returned, quickly. "Most people know it. There is a fine common, and some golf links, and there are some big houses there."

"Yes; but the Red House is in Erpingham Lane."

Then Mr. Ingram started.

"I think some ladies of the name of Harford live there," he said, carelessly. "Two are very much given to good works."

"Oh, do you know them?" asked Waveney, eagerly; but it struck her that he evaded the question.

"We have mutual friends," he replied, rather stiffly. "They are excellent women, and do an immense amount of good. They have a sort of home for broken-down governesses, and they do a lot for shop-women. I have an immense respect for people who do that sort of thing," recovering his sprightliness. "I tried slumming once myself, but I had to give it up; it was not my vocation. The boys called me 'Guy Fawkes,' and that hurt my feelings. By the bye," as they both laughed at this, "I have never explained the purport of my visit. I understood from your sister," and here he looked at Waveney, "that Mr. Ward had a picture for sale. 'King Canute,' was it not? Well, a friend of mine has a picture-gallery, and he is always buying pictures. He wants to fill up a vacant place in an alcove, and he suggested some early English historical subject. He has an

'Alfred toasting the cakes in the swine-herd's cottage,' and a 'St. Augustine looking at the Saxon slaves in the market-place,' and it struck me that 'King Canute' would be an excellent subject."

"What lots of friends you seem to have!" remarked Mollie, innocently. "There is the one who shoots pheasant, and the one who buys menu cards, and now another who buys pictures."

Ingram looked a little embarrassed, but he was amused too.

"One can't knock about the world without making friends," he said, lightly. "Do you recollect what Apolinarius says: 'for I am the only one of my friends I rely on.' But the Chinese have a better maxim still: 'There are plenty of acquaintances in the world, but very few real friends.'"

"Is the picture friend only an acquaintance?" asked Mollie, rather provokingly.

"No, indeed," returned Ingram, energetically. "We are like brothers, he and I, and I have known him all my life. Well, Miss Mollie, do you think your father would be willing to let my friend have 'King Canute'? It is a famous subject, and brings back the memories of one's school days;" and then he walked to the picture and stood before it, as though he were fascinated; but in reality he was saying to himself, "Now, what am I to offer for this very mawkish and stilted performance?" And the question was so perplexing that he fell into a brown study.

Mollie looked at her sister. She was brimful of excitement. But Waveney shook her head.

"Would it not be better for your friend to see the picture first?" she said, in a cool, business-like tone; but inwardly she was just as excited as Mollie. Ten pounds would pay all they owe to Barber, and Chandler would wait. "I am sure that father would be pleased to see any one who cared to look at the picture," she finished, boldly.

Mr. Ingram regarded her pleasantly.

"You are very good, but there is not the slightest occasion to trouble you. I am my friend's agent in this sort of thing. I have been abroad a good deal, and have served my apprenticeship to art. I am an art critic, don't you know. Now, would you mind telling me, Miss Ward, how much your father expected to get from the dealers?"

"I don't know," returned Waveney, doubtfully. "There was no fixed price, was there, Mollie? Father told us that he would be content with ten pounds."

"My dear Miss Ward," returned Ingram, in a tone of strong remonstrance, "your father undervalues himself. Ten pounds for that work of art! Heaven forgive me all the fibs I am telling," he added, mentally, and then he cleared his throat. "I am no Jew, and must decline to drive a hard bargain. If Mr. Ward will let my friend have 'King Canute,' I shall be willing to pay, on his behalf, five-and-twenty pounds: I mean"—looking calmly at the girl's agitated face—"five-and-twenty guineas."

They were too overwhelmed with surprise and pleasure to answer him; and just at that moment—that supreme moment—they heard their father's latch-key.

Ingram described the little scene later on to a dear friend.

"It was Atalanta's race, don't you know. They both wanted to reach their father first; he was the golden apple, pro tem.

"The lame Miss Ward had long odds, but my little-friend of the omnibus beat her hollow. Can you fancy Titania coming down her ladder of cobwebs? Well, you should see Miss Ward number two, running downstairs—it would give you a notion of it. And there was the golden apple on the door-mat waiting for her."

"You are very absurd," returned his hearer, laughing, "but your description amuses me, so please go on."

"There is something very refreshing in such originality," he murmured, languidly. "I have an idea that Gwen would love those girls. Gwen is all for nature and reality. Conventionality might have suggested that it was hardly mannerly to leave a guest in an empty room, even for golden apples, but no such idea would have occurred to the Misses Ward. They even forgot that sound ascends, and that I could hear every word."

"Dear me, that was very awkward!" But the lady spoke maliciously.

"I could hear every word," he repeated, and then his eyes twinkled; but he was honourable enough not to repeat the little conversation.

"Father, Monsieur Blackie is upstairs!" and here Mollie giggled. "His real name is Ingram, but Ann calls him Mr. Ink-pen."

"All right, my pet; so I suppose I had better go upstairs;" but Waveney pulled him back.

"Wait a moment, father dear. What a hurry you are in! And your hair is so rough, and your coat is dusty. Give me the brush, Mollie. We must put him tidy. Dad, such a wonderful thing has happened. Mr. Ingram wants to buy King Canute 'for a rich friend who has a picture-gallery,' and he will pay you five-and-twenty guineas."

"Nonsense, child!" But from his tone Mr. Ward was becoming excited too. "Let me pass, Mollie; you are forgetting your manners, children, leaving a visitor alone;" and Everard Ward marched into the studio, with his head unusually high.

"The 'golden apple,' alias Ward père, was a shabby, fair little man with a face like a Greek god," continued Ingram. "He must have been a perfect Adonis in his youth. He had brown pathetic eyes, rather like a spaniel's—you know what I mean, eyes that seemed always to be saying, 'I am a good fellow, though I am down on my luck, and I should like to be friends with you.'"

It was evident that the two men took to each other at once. Ingram's pleasant manners and undisguised cordiality put Mr. Ward at his ease, and in a few minutes they were talking as though they were old friends.

The subject of 'King Canute' was soon brought forward again, and Ingram explained matters with a good deal of tact and finesse.

Everard Ward reddened, and then he said bluntly, "You are very good, Mr. Ingram, to offer me such a handsome price, but sheer honesty compels me to say the picture is not worth more than ten pounds. I have not worked out the subject as well as I could wish." And then he added, a little sadly, "It is a poor thing, but my own."

"My dear sir," returned Ingram, airily, "we artists are bad critics of our own work. My friends regard me as an optimist, but I call myself an Idealist. I am a moral Sisyphus, for ever rolling my poor stone up the hill difficulty." Then, as he noticed Mollie's puzzled look, he continued blandly, "Sisyphus was a fraudulent and avaricious king of Corinth, whose task in the world of shades is to roll a large stone to the top of a hill and fix it there. The unpleasant part of the business is that the stone no sooner reaches the hill-top than it bounds down again. Excuse this lengthy description, which reminds me a little of Sandford and Merton. But, revenons à nos moutons, I am ready, Mr. Ward, to take the picture for my friend at the price I mentioned to your daughters; and as I have the money about me"—and here he produced a Russian leather pocket-book—"I think we had better settle our business at once."

Everard Ward was only human, and the bait was too tempting. His conscience told him that the picture was a failure, and hardly worth more than the cost of the frame; and yet such is the vanity innate in man that he was willing to delude himself with the fancy that the stranger's eyes had detected merit in it. And, indeed, Ingram's manner would have deceived any one.

"It is the very thing he wants for the alcove," he murmured, stepping back a few paces, and regarding the picture through half closed eyes. "The light will be just right, and"—here he appeared to swallow something with difficulty—"the effect will be extremely good." And then he began counting the crisp bank-notes.

Waveney's eyes began to sparkle, and she and Mollie telegraphed little messages to each other. Not only the insolent Barker would be paid, but the much-enduring Chandler. When Mr. Ward went downstairs to open the door for his guest, Waveney threw her arm round her sister, and dragged her down upon Grumps.

"Oh, Mollie, I quite love that dear little Monsieur Blackie!" she cried, enthusiastically. "Think of ten whole pounds to spend! Father can have a new great-coat, and Noel those boots he wants so dreadfully, and you must have a new jacket—I insist on it, Mollie; I shall do very well with my old one until Christmas." But Mollie would not hear of this for a moment: if any one had the new jacket, it must be Waveney. What did it matter what a poor, little Cinderella wore at home? And they both got so hot and excited over the generous conflict that Mr. Ward thought they were quarrelling until he saw their faces.

"I like that fellow," he said, rubbing his hands; "he is gentlemanly and agreeable; he told me in confidence that, though he calls himself an artist, he only dabbles in art. 'If a relative had not left me a nice little property, I should long ago have been in Queer Street,' he said, in his droll way."

"Oh, then he is not poor as we are?" observed Mollie, in a disappointed tone.

"No, he is certainly not poor," returned her father, laughing. "I should think he is tolerably well-to-do, judging from appearances, and certainly he has rich friends. He has asked my permission to call again when he is in the neighbourhood;" and both the girls were pleased to hear this.

Waveney had not seen her old friends at the Hospital for more than a week, so one morning she went across to wish them good-bye. She had a little cake that Mollie had made for them, and some tobacco that she had bought with her own money.

It was a wet day, and most of the pensioners were in the big hall. One of them told Waveney that Sergeant McGill was in his cubicle with the corporal, as usual, in attendance. "They do say the sergeant's a bit poorly," continued her informant. And a moment afterwards she came upon Corporal Marks, stumping along the corridor with a newspaper in his hand. The little man looked dejected, but he saluted Waveney with his usual dignity.

"I hear the sergeant is not well. I trust it is nothing serious." Then the corporal shook his head, and his blue eyes were a little watery.

"Well, no, Miss Ward, not to say serious—we are none of us chickens, so to speak, and we have most of us cut our wisdom teeth a good many years ago. The sergeant has been poorly for a week now. He is down in the mouth, and I can't rouse him nohow. Would you believe it, Miss Ward, I was trying to argify with him this morning about that there Sepoy. 'For it stands to reason, McGill,' I said to him, 'that there could only be two of them;' and he fairly flew at me, lost his temper, and told me I was an infernal liar. Why, you might have knocked me down with a feather, I was so taken aback;" and the corporal's droll face was puckered up with care.

"Never mind, Corporal," returned Waveney, soothingly. "McGill was ill and not himself, or he would not have been so irritable with his old comrade. Look here, I have come to bid you all good-bye, because I am going away; and my sister has made you one of those cakes you like, and I have brought you some tobacco." Then the corporal's face cleared a little.

They found the old soldier lying on his bed, with a rug over his feet; his face looked drawn and pallid. At the sound of Waveney's light step he turned his sightless eyes towards her, and a strange expression passed over his features.

"There was only one step that was as light," he murmured, in his thick, soft voice, "and that was Sheila's, and hers hardly brushed the dewdrops from the heather." Then, as Waveney took hold of his great hand, "and it was her small fingers, too, the brown little hands that carried the creel of peat, and stacked it underneath the eaves; and it is Sheila that has come to me—Heaven bless her sweet face!—before I take the long journey."

"My dear old friend, do you not know me?" and Waveney looked anxiously at him. "It is not Sheila, it is Miss Ward who has come to wish you good-bye." Then the old man looked bewildered, and raised himself on the pillow.

"And are you ferry well, Miss Ward? And it is I who have made the mistake, like the old fool that I was. It may be I was dreaming—I was always clever at the dreams, as the corporal knows. But it seemed to me as though I could see the blue water of the loch, and the grey walls of our cottage, and the shingly roofs, and even the cocks and hens pecking in the dust. And there was Sheila coming up from the beach, with her bare feet, and red kerchief tied over her dark hair; and her smile was like sunshine, and her hands were full of great scarlet poppies. And if it was a dream, it was a good dream."

"Was Sheila your sister?" asked Waveney, softly. For she knew that Sergeant McGill had never been married, though the corporal was a widower. Then, at the beloved name, McGill roused to complete consciousness.

"No, Miss Ward. I had no sister, only six brothers, and Sheila was the lass of my heart; and when I had got my stripes we were to have married. But it was my fate, for when I came from the wars, there was the loch, and the purple moors, and the grey walls of the cottage; but Sheila, she would never come to meet me again with the poppies in her hand, and the wild rose in her cheek. She lay in the graveyard on the hillside, where the dead can hear the bees humming in the heather. But it is not the goot manners to be telling you of the old troubles, and very soon it is Sheila herself that I shall see."

"Tell Miss Ward the message that Sheila left with her mother, McGill."

"It was this that she said," he continued, in a proud tone, "'You must bid Fergus McGill not to grieve; he is a grand soldier and a good lad, and dearly I would have loved to have been his wife. But God's will be done. Tell him I will be near the gates; and that if the angels permit, that it is Sheila who will be there to welcome him.'"

"That message must have made you very happy," returned Waveney, tenderly.

"They were goot words, and I do not deny that they have given me comfort," replied McGill, solemnly. "But for years I had a heavy heart; for when a Highlander loses the lass of his heart, the world is a barren place to him. But it is the truth that Sheila has spoken, and it is herself that I shall see, with these dim old eyes."

He sank back a little heavily on the pillows. Waveney leant over him and spoke gently in his ear.

"McGill," she said, in her clear, girlish voice, "do you know you have hurt the poor corporal's feelings. You were angry with him this morning, and called him names."

Then there was a flush of shame on the grand old face.

"It was myself that was in fault, Miss Ward, for I lost my temper. But it is not the corporal who will quarrel with his old comrade. It was the liar that I called him, but it was I who disgraced myself."

"Never mind, old mate, I was wrong to argify, and so we are quits there. For it stands to reason," continued the corporal, "that when a man is poorly, he is not in a condition for fighting."

"Still, it was the bad manners to be calling any one a liar," returned Sergeant McGill. "But a Highlander's temper is not always under control. So I ask your pardon, Marks, but it was three Sepoys that I killed with my own hand, and I had the third by the throat."

"Dear Sergeant," interposed Waveney, softly, "Corporal Marks quite understands all that; and what does it matter?—a little difference between two old friends!" Then a strangely sweet smile lighted up the wrinkled old face.

"It is the voice of Sheila. And what will she be saying again and again: 'Blessed are the peace-makers'—and they are grand words."

"Shall I read to you a little?" asked the girl, timidly. Then the corporal took down an old brown Testament from the shelf, and Waveney read slowly and reverently, passage after passage, until the heavy breathing told her that McGill was asleep. Then she closed the book and went out into the corridor.

"He is very ill," she said, sorrowfully; "so feeble and so unlike himself." But the corporal refuted this stoutly.

"McGill is but poorly," he returned, so gruffly that Waveney did not venture to say more. "When he has taken a bottle or two of the doctor's stuff, he will pick up a bit; he sleeps badly, and that makes him drowsy and confused," and then he saluted, and stumped back to his comrade.

Waveney heard a different story downstairs.

"Have you seen McGill?" two or three said to her. "The poor chap, he is breaking fast. The corporal won't believe it, but it is plain as a pike-staff," and so on.

"Mollie, dear," observed Waveney, sadly, "I have such bad news to tell you: dear old Sergeant McGill is very ill, and I fear he is going to die; and what will the corporal do without him? And it is so strange;" she went on, "he thinks he is a lad again, in his Highland home, and that his sweetheart Sheila is coming to meet him. He calls her the lass of his heart, and it is all so poetical and beautiful;" and Waveney's voice was so full of pathos that Mollie's eyes filled with sympathetic tears.

CHAPTER XI.: "A NOTICEABLE MAN, WITH LARGE GREY EYES."

"As high as we have mounted in delight In our dejection do we sink as low." Wordsworth.

After all, Mollie had her way, and Waveney, in spite of piteous pleading and remonstrance, became the reluctant possessor of a warm dress and jacket.

Mr. Ward had put his foot down in a most unexpected manner; if Waveney would not buy her jacket he would go without his great-coat; Barker and Chandler had been paid, and there was sufficient money for everything. And when Waveney understood that any shabbiness on her part would be grievous in his eyes, she yielded at once.

"If father wishes it I will get the things," she said to Mollie; "but I never enjoy anything unless you share it."

But Mollie would not listen to this.

"What does it matter about me?" she said, gaily. "I am only a poor little Cinderella whose pumpkin coach has not arrived. My old jacket will do quite well until Christmas."

And then, when the purchases were made, Mollie was like a sunbeam for the rest of the day.

Waveney went twice to the Hospital before she started for Erpingham, but each time she found McGill more rambling and confused; and though he roused at the sound of her voice, he always thought she was Sheila. Corporal Marks looked more dejected than ever, but he maintained that the sergeant was doing finely. Waveney thought it was only the little man's natural pugnacity and habit of arguing, and that he did not really believe his own assertion; but though he pretended to grumble, he nursed his friend devotedly. "That there corporal never leaves him," one of the pensioners remarked to Waveney. "You would think they were brothers to see them—and fight they would, too, about those plaguey Sepoys, that you might have taken them for a pair of kilkenny cats. But bless you, miss, it was just for the fun of it."

The days slipped away all too fast; and one morning Mollie awoke with the thought that only one whole day remained before Waveney left home.

They were very busy all the morning, packing her box, and in the afternoon Waveney, who felt restless and rather low-spirited at the sight of Mollie's woe-begone face, proposed they should visit their favourite haunts, the lime avenue, old Ranelagh and the Embankment.

"It is so warm, and the house feels so stuffy!" she added; for Waveney loved air and exercise, and would gladly have been out of doors the greater part of the day.

Mollie willingly assented to this, but she was languid and out of spirits, and soon grew tired; so they sat down under an acacia in old Ranelagh and watched the children playing round them. It was one of those golden days of September, when the very air seems impregnated with strange sweet fragrance, when one thinks of waving corn-fields, and how the wheat ripples in the breeze like a yellow sea; and of deep, quiet lanes—with nut copses and blackberry thickets—or, better still, of a hillside clothed with purple heather, as though Nature had flung one of her royal robes aside. A day when the grand old earth seemed mellow and ripe for the sickle of old Time, and a soft sadness and sense of quiet brooding are over everything. "The summer is over," it seemed to say, "and the fleeting shows of youth, and the fruits of the earth are garnered in Nature's storehouse, and the feast of all good things is ready; so eat and enjoy, and be thankful."

The sisters were sitting hand in hand, and Waveney's small face looked pinched and long from inward fretting, for she was one who took the troubles of life with outward calmness, and chafed under them inwardly; but the sunshine, and the crisp, sweet air and the soft patter of red and yellow leaves, brought their message of comfort.

"Mollie," she said, trying to speak cheerfully, "I am thinking what a beautiful world it is, and how good life is, after all, in spite of worries. Here we are, making ourselves miserable because I have to go away to-morrow. Do you know, we are like those two foolish children we saw that day when father took us in the country. Don't you remember how they cried because their nurse wanted them to go down a lane—it was so dark and narrow, they said, and they were sure the wolves would eat them up; but the nurse knew there was that lovely open meadow beyond. Do you read my little parable, dear?"

"Yes, I think so," returned Mollie; but she spoke doubtfully. Waveney was rather prone to moralise when she found herself alone with Mollie. She called it "thinking aloud." Mollie was her other self. She could tell her things that she would not have breathed to any other creature.

"Well, you see," went on Waveney, "one has steep little bits of road now and then, like that poor King of Corinth—Sisyphus—was not that his name? We have to roll our stone up the hill Difficulty; but one never knows what may happen next. By the bye, Mollie, I rather fancy that Monsieur Blackie only pretends to play at things, and that he is really a clever man. There is something I cannot make out about him. He is mysterious. And then, why did he buy 'King Canute'?"

"Because his friend wanted a historical picture," returned Mollie, who always believed what people said.

"I know he told us so," replied Waveney, thoughtfully. "Mollie, I have a sort of conviction that you will often see him—that he means to turn up pretty frequently at Cleveland Terrace."

"Whatever makes you think so?" asked Mollie, much astonished at this. "What a ridiculous idea, Wave! when you told him yourself that you were leaving home to-morrow."

"But he does not come to see me," retorted Waveney; and then she added, hastily, "he is a friendly sort of person, and comes to see us all."

"Oh, yes, of course," returned Mollie, perfectly satisfied with this view of the case. "Then I daresay he will come sometimes when father is at home. He asked me very particularly when he was likely to be in, and if I went out in the afternoon, and I said, 'Oh, dear no, I always go out early to do the marketing, and then I am too tired to go out again.' Waveney, he did look so kindly at me, when I said that. 'Walking tires you, then. What a pity!' and he seemed quite sorry for me."

"He is a nice little Black Prince," replied Waveney, rather absently. The children had left the gardens with their nurses, and the place was now quite deserted. The next moment a gentleman crossed the lime avenue, and walked slowly down the path. As he passed their bench, he looked at the two girls in a quiet, observant way, and passed on.

As soon as he was out of hearing, Waveney said, a little wickedly, "Mollie, we have found him at last, 'the noticeable man, with large grey eyes.'"

For this was an old joke of theirs. They had been reading Wordsworth together one summer's day on this very bench, and when Waveney had come to this stanza she had laid down the book. "I like that description, Mollie," she had said; "it gives one a pleasant idea of a person. 'A noticeable man, with large grey eyes.' Now, I wonder if we shall ever see any one answering to that description."

Mollie laughed, and looked interested when Waveney said this; but a moment later she whispered, "Hush! he is coming back;" and then, to Mollie's alarm—for she was very shy and timid—he stopped and lifted his hat.

"Will you have the kindness to inform me," he said, addressing Mollie in a peculiarly clear, mellow voice, "if this path will take me to Dunedin Terrace. I am not well acquainted with Chelsea."

Mollie blushed and looked confused. Topography was not her strong point. "I think so. I am not quite sure. Do you know, Waveney?"

"Yes, but it is rather a roundabout way. Dunedin Terrace is quite half a mile away;" and then Waveney rose from the bench and considered her bearings, while the stranger quietly awaited her decision.

He was a tall man, and though his face was plain, there was something in his expression that attracted notice, an air of unmistakable refinement and culture. The keen grey eyes had already noted Mollie's lovely face; now they were fixed on the plainer sister.

"I think I can direct you properly now," observed Waveney, with her usual brightness; "but it is just a little complicated. You must go out of this gate, and cross Cleveland Terrace, take the second turning to the right, and the first to the left, and you will be in Upper Dunedin Terrace."

"Thank you very much;" and then he repeated her directions gravely and slowly; and then, lifting his hat with another "Thank you," walked quickly away.

"Yes, I was right," continued Waveney; "he is certainly a noticeable man; and what large, clear eyes." But Mollie shrugged her shoulders a little pettishly.

"I think he was rather ugly," she remarked, "and he is quite old—five-and-thirty, at least; and did you notice his shabby coat—why, it was almost as shabby as father's."

"No," returned Waveney; "I did not notice that. I was only thinking what a grand-looking man he was, and he spoke so nicely, too!" Then, as Mollie was evidently not interested, she changed the subject; and they sat talking until it was time for them to go home to tea.

It was a melancholy evening, in spite of all Waveney's efforts. Mr. Ward was tired and dull, and Noel was out of humour; but his sisters, who understood him thoroughly, knew that this was only his mode of expressing his feelings.

So he drew up his coat-collar and answered snappishly whenever Waveney addressed him; and grew red, and pretended to be deaf, when she alluded to her going away.

And when she was bidding him good-night, and her fingers touched his rough hair caressingly, he threw back his head with an annoyed jerk.

"I hate having my hair pulled," he said, crossly; "so give over, old Storm-and-Stress;" and then he whistled and walked out of the room with his chin in the air; but not before Waveney saw that his glasses were misty.

"Mollie, darling, remember I shall be home on Sunday, and it is Tuesday now," were Waveney's last words as she jumped into the train, and her father closed the door.

Waveney stood at the window until the dark tunnel hid them from her sight. Mollie's sweet face was swollen with crying, and her father's countenance was sad and full of care; the child whom he had cherished with peculiar tenderness was leaving his roof because he was incapable of providing for his household properly. He had been a failure all his life, and he knew it; but it was bitter to him that his old friend Althea should know it, too.

Waveney took a cab when she reached Dereham. The driver touched his hat when she told him to drive to the Red House, Erpingham.

"I know it," he said, as he took off his horse's nose-bag. "There ain't a cab-driver in Dereham that don't know the ladies at the Red House; they give us a supper in Christmas week, and there is another for the costers that use their donkeys well—and it is a rare spread, too;" and then he smacked his lips and jumped on the box.

Waveney looked out and tried to interest herself in the various objects they passed; but her head felt heavy as lead. The common looked lovely in the afternoon sunshine, and, as before, the children were dancing in and out the trees. Some little boys were sailing a boat on the pond, and a Newfoundland was swimming across it with a stick in his mouth. Some riders were cantering over the grass. Every one seemed gay and animated and full of life; dogs barked, children laughed, and the cawing of rooks filled the air.

As they drove in at the lodge gates the two little Yorkshire terriers ran out barking, and the elderly maid Mitchell came to the door.

"My mistresses are out, ma'am," she said, pleasantly, "but Nurse Marks has orders to make you comfortable. Will you please to go in, and I will see to the box and pay the cabman. No, ma'am," as Waveney timidly offered her some money. "Miss Harford always pays the cabmen herself."

"Aye, and pays them well, too," observed the driver, with a complacent grin. "No arguing with a poor chap who has to work hard for his living about an extra sixpence."

Waveney felt very strange and forlorn as she stepped into the hall, with Fuss and Fury barking excitedly round her, and then she saw a little old woman with a very long nose, and hair as white as snow bundling down the wide staircase to meet her; for no other word could describe Nurse Marks's rolling and peculiar gait.

"She is the most wonderful little old woman I have ever seen," wrote Waveney, in her first letter home. "If you were to dress her in a red cloak and peaked hat she would make an excellent Mother Hubbard, or the 'old woman who lived in her shoe,' or that ambitious old person who tried to brush the cobwebs from the sky. To see her poking that long nose of hers into corners is quite killing. She has bright eyes like a dormouse, and a cosy voice—do you know what I mean by that?—and she wears the funniest cap, with a black bow at the top. But there! you must see her for yourself."

"My ladies are out, dearie," she began at once, rather breathlessly. "Miss Doreen is at the

Home, and Mrs. Mainwaring has sent for Miss Althea unexpectedly, to go to some grand At Home; but she will be back to dinner, and she begged that you would excuse her absence, and I am going to take you to my room and give you some tea; for you are tired, dearie, I know;" and then Nurse Marks led the way upstairs, and Waveney followed, feeling as though she were the heroine of a fairy-story and that some benevolent fairy had her in tow.

"My ladies always calls this the Cubby-house," observed Nurse Marks, in a proud tone, "and to my thinking it is the nicest room in the house, though it is odd-shaped, as Mitchell says, and a trifle low."

It was oddly shaped indeed. One corner had been cut off, and the window, a wide one, had been set in an extraordinary angle, so that part of the room was insufficiently lighted. Here there was a large Japanese screen, which hid the bed and washstand.

A round table was in the centre of the room, and an old carved wardrobe and a nursery cupboard occupied the wall space. Some comfortable-looking rocking chairs, and a worn old couch, gave it a cosy aspect; but the chief feature of the room was the number of photographs and water-colour paintings that covered the walls, while framed ones stood by dozens on the mantelpiece and chest-of-drawers.

One of them at once attracted Waveney. "Why, that is the corporal," she said, in surprise. "Corporal Marks, I mean;" and she spoke in puzzled tones.

"Aye, that's Jonadab," returned Nurse Marks, complacently. "It is a grand picture, and his medals come out finely. Dinah thought a heap of that photo;" and then the bright dormouse eyes looked at Waveney, curiously. "Well, it beats me that you should know brother Jonadab. After all, the world is not so big as we think it."

"Of course I know Corporal Marks," returned Waveney, excitedly; but there was a lump in her throat, too, at the sight of the little corporal's familiar face, with its round, surprised eyes and shock of grey hair. "And I know Sergeant McGill, too."

Then, at the mention of McGill, Nurse Marks sat down and indulged in a hearty laugh.

"Well, now, if that is not like a book! And you are the young lady that Jonadab is always telling about! Is it not comfortable to know that 'their good works do follow them'? That's true, even in this world, for it stands to reason that things can't be hidden for ever. Sit down, dearie, and I will pour you out some tea. You are a bit homesick and strange, but that will pass, so keep up your heart, dear lamb;" and Nurse Marks poked her long nose into the tea-pot, for she was short-sighted; and Waveney watched her a little anxiously; but she need not have feared: Nurse Marks was a clever woman, and could always measure her distances accurately.

"Aye, he is a grand man, McGill," she remarked, as she cut some delicate bread-and-butter with a practised hand. "But he is not long for this world. Jonadab will miss him sorely, I fear; they are a queer pair to look at them, but they are just bound up in each other. They are like a couple of old children, I tell them; they quarrel just for the sake of making it up. But there, as Dinah used to say—poor thing!—her man was fine at argifying."

"Was Dinah your brother's wife?"

"Aye, dearie, and Jonadab thought a deal of her, and grieved sore when the dear Lord took her.

You will be wondering at his name, maybe, for it is out of the common, is Jonadab; but mother used to tell us that when the boy came, father was so proud and pleased that he went at once to the Bible for a name. And presently he came to mother, looking as pleased as possible, as though he had found a treasure. 'Rachel,' he says, in a loud voice, 'there is not a finer fellow to my thinking than Jonadab, the son of Rechab, and he was dead against the drink, too, and it is Jonadab that we will call him;' and so Jonadab it was," finished Nurse Marks, complacently.

CHAPTER XII.: THE PANZY ROOM AND COSY NOOK.

"There is rosemary, that is for remembrance.... And there is pansies that's for thoughts."
Shakespeare.
"That way madness lies; let me shun that." King Lear.

It was impossible for Waveney not to be amused by Nurse Marks' quaint tales; her sense of humour was too strong, and the atmosphere of the Cubby-house was so full of comfort that, in spite of herself, her sad face began to brighten.

"If you knew Sergeant McGill," she said, presently, "perhaps you knew his sweetheart, Sheila, too." Then Nurse Marks smiled and nodded, as she cut another appetising slice of bread-and-butter, and laid it on Waveney's plate—such sweet home-made bread and fresh, creamy butter!

"Aye, dearie, I knew Sheila McTavish well, for when I was a slip of a girl I had a bad illness, and my mother's cousin, Effie Stuart, took me back with her to the Highlands to bide with her for more than a year. The McTavish cottage was next to ours, and not a day passed that I did not see Sheila coming up from the loch-side with her creel, with her bare feet and red petticoat, and maybe a plaid over her bonnie brown hair. I was always a homely body, even in my young days, but never before or since have I seen a lovelier face than Sheila McTavish, 'the Flower of the Deeside'—that was what they called her."

"Was she engaged to McGill then?"

"Aye, my dearie. She had broken the sixpence with him, but he was away in India then. I remember one day, as I sat on the churchyard wall, Sheila came over the moor, and she had a sprig of white heather in her hand. She held it up to me with a smile. 'It is good luck, Kezia,' she said, and her eyes seemed full of brown sunshine, 'and this morning I have heard from Fergus McGill himself, and it is he who is the guid lad with his letters. He is coming home, he says, and then we are to be wed, and it is the white heather that will bring us luck.' Ah, dearie, before three weeks were over, Sheila, our sweet Flower of the Deeside, lay in her coffin, and they put the white heather on her dead breast; and when Fergus McGill came home there was only the grave under the rowan tree. There, there, it is a queer world," finished Nurse Marks, "and there is many a love-story left unfinished, for 'man' (and woman, too) 'is born into trouble,' and I know that the women get the worst of it sometimes; for it stands to reason," continued the old woman, garrulously, "that they think a deal more of a love tale. Now, as we have finished tea, shall I take you to your room, my dearie? It is called the Pansy Room, and is close to mine. Miss Althea is a grand one for giving names. All the bedrooms are called after flowers, to match the paper and cretonne. There is the Rose Room and the Forget-me-not and the Pink Room, and the Leafy Room, and the Marigold Room, where they put gentlemen."

"Which is Miss Althea's?" asked Waveney, quickly.

"Oh, the Rose Room. Miss Althea has a passion for roses. Miss Doreen sleeps in the Forget-me-not Room; everything is blue there. The other rooms are for their guests, but near the servants' quarters there are two pretty little attics called 'Faith' and 'Charity,' where they put shop-girls who have broken down and need a rest; and these are never empty all the year round. There is a little sitting-room attached, where they take their meals. There, they are crossing the tennis-lawn this moment from the Porch House. The tall one is Laura Cairns; she has had an operation and has only just left the hospital, and the little fat one is Ellen Sturt; there is not much the matter with her except hard work and too much standing."

"Oh, how good they are!" thought Waveney, as Nurse Marks bundled down the passage before her. "Every one seems to have something to say in their praise, even the cab-driver," and then she looked round the Pansy Room well pleased. It was so fresh, and dainty, and pretty, and, after her room at Cleveland Terrace, so luxuriously comfortable.

For there was actually a cosy-looking couch, and an easy-chair, and beautiful flowers on the toilet-table, and some hanging book-shelves full of interesting books.

The window looked over the tennis-lawn with the Porch House, where the girls were pacing arm-in-arm. One of them looked up at the window, and smiled a little as Waveney gazed down at her. Nurse Marks, who was already beginning to unpack, went on talking briskly.

"It was Miss Althea's thought, but Miss Doreen helped her to carry it out. It is always like that with my ladies, they are just the two halves of a pair of scissors, but they work together finely. What one says the other does. It is like the precious ointment, that's what it is, Miss Ward, my dear! and never a misunderstanding or a contrary word between them.

"The girls come for a month, and sometimes they stay longer; and if they are well enough they wait on themselves, or if not, Reynolds, the under housemaid, sees to them; and when the weather permits they are in the garden, or on the common the whole day long, and they have the run of the Porch House, too, and help themselves to books from the library; they are no trouble and fall in with our ways, and the blessing the Red House is to some of those poor things is past my telling. Now, dearie, shall I hang these things in the wardrobe for you—there is plenty of room and to spare. And then I will go back, and finish a bit of mending for Miss Althea."

Waveney was not sorry to be left alone; she wanted to begin a letter to Mollie. She had so much already to tell her. So she sat down at the writing-table, and her pen flew over the paper, until a quick, light tap at her door roused her, and Miss Althea entered.

Waveney gave a vivid description of her to Mollie afterwards. "She looked so grand and stately that I felt quite shy; but her dress was charming. It was a soft, cloudy grey, but it shimmered as though it were streaked with silver, and she had a close little bonnet that looked like silver too, and a ruff of fine cobwebby lace round her long neck. I fancy she always wears a ruff, and she looked more like Queen Bess than ever. Somehow she is oddly picturesque, and makes other people look commonplace beside her. But there, you must see her one day for yourself."

Althea came up to the writing table as Waveney rose, a little confused, and held out her hand to the girl with one of her winning smiles.

"I was so sorry to be out when you arrived," she said, kindly, "but my aunt, Mrs. Mainwaring, sent for me most unexpectedly. I hope Nurse Marks took good care of you."

"Oh, yes," returned Waveney, shyly, "she was very kind."

"Oh, my dear old nurse is the kindest creature in the world. She literally bubbles over with benevolence. Is not the Cubby-house delightful? Did you see the toy cupboard, where all our dear old dolls and toys are stored? Marks won't part with one of them; she is quite huffy if we propose to give them away. When children come to the house, she lets them play with them under her own eye. One day she came into the library with a long face to tell me that little Audrey Neale had broken Bopeep's arm;" and Althea laughed quite merrily; then she looked at the clock on the mantelpiece, and uttered an exclamation: "Half-past seven, and I am not dressed. What will Peachey say? I will come back and fetch you directly the gong sounds;" and then Waveney was left to finish her letter.

She did not see Miss Doreen until they entered the dining-room, and then she welcomed her very cordially. To Waveney the dinner-table was a revelation. She had never taken a meal out of her own home, and the soft, shaded lights, the hot-house fruits and flowers, the handsome silver, and the fineness of the damask, excited her wonderment. The servant moved so noiselessly over the thick carpets, and then she thought of Ann stumping round the table in her heavy boots.

Ah, they would be just sitting down to supper, and Mollie would be mixing the salad as usual; for Everard Ward had learnt to enjoy a salad in his Paris days, and would sup contentedly on bread-and-cheese or even bread-and-butter, if only he could have a handful of cress, or a stalk or two of endive, to give it a relish.

Doreen and Althea were quite aware that the forlorn little stranger was not at her ease. The small, childish face looked subdued and thoughtful, and the dark, spirituelle eyes were sad in their wistfulness; but with their usual tact and kindness they left her alone, and talked to each other in their cheerful way.

Althea gave a description of her afternoon party, which was full of gentle humour; and Doreen had a great deal to say about the Home. She had had tea with old Mrs. Wheeler—and as usual the poor old soul was full of her grievances against Miss Mason.

"She is a cantankerous, east-windy sort of body," went on Doreen, with a laugh, as she helped herself to some grapes, "and she leads poor Miss Mason a life. But there! one must not judge her, she has led a hard, grinding sort of existence. Althea, these grapes are unusually fine; don't you think Laura Cairns would enjoy some? Ellen likes pears better;" and then Doreen heaped up a plate with fine fruit and bade Mitchell take it to the Brown Parlour.

When the sisters rose from the table Althea touched Waveney's arm.

"Come with me to the library," she said, in a kind voice. "We shall sit there this evening. We do not often use the drawing-room—it is a very big room, and we always feel rather lost in it."

"I call this big, too," remarked Waveney, in rather an awed voice. She had never seen such a beautiful room in her life; it was better than any of the dream rooms at Kitlands.

The grand oriel window, with its cushioned seat; the carved oak furniture, and bookcases filled with handsomely-bound books; the fine engravings on the walls;—all excited her admiration. But when Althea drew back a curtain and showed her a tiny room hidden away behind it, with a glass-door opening on the terrace, she could not refrain from an exclamation of delight.

"Oh, what a dear little room!" she said, quite naturally.

"Yes, I call it my cosy nook. But it is not really a room, it is merely a recess." And Waveney thought how well Miss Althea's name suited it. There was a small writing-table prettily fitted-up, an easy-chair, and a work-table.

"I am so glad you have taken a fancy to it," went on Miss Althea—and she looked very much pleased—"because this is to be your little sanctum. You see, it would never do for me to have my reader and companion far away from me. And yet I imagine we should both find it irksome to be always together—even my sister and I could not stand that; but, you see, when the curtain is dropped, you will be quite private."

"And it is really for me!" and Waveney's eyes sparkled with pleasure.

Then Miss Althea smiled, and put her hand kindly on the girl's arm.

"I want you to be happy with us, my dear, and not to look upon us as strangers, because in the old days your father was a dear friend of ours. Last night an idea struck me. Do you think you would feel more at home with us if we were to call you by your Christian name? You have such a pretty name, and it is so uncommon."

"Oh, please do," returned Waveney, flushing with shy pleasure. "It was silly of me, but I was so dreading that 'Miss Ward;'" and somehow a load seemed lifted off her at that moment.

"She is such a little childish thing," observed Miss Althea afterwards; "and yet she has plenty of character. We are very unconventional people, Doreen, you and I; but I never could endure these artificial barriers. My dignity, such as it is, is innate; it does not need bolstering up. I could not be stiff and proper with Everard Ward's daughter;" and then a strangely sad look came into Althea's eyes, as though some ghost from the past had crossed her path; "no, certainly not to Everard Ward's daughter;" and Doreen smiled as though she understood her.

Doreen's world was inhabited by warm-blooded human beings; no ghostly visitants ever haunted her. "I am a woman without a story," she would say. "Most people have some sort of romance in their lives—even unmarried women have their unfinished idylls; but my life has been bare prose." But she always laughed when she made these speeches, for there was nothing morbid in Doreen's character.

Althea proposed, as the evening was mild and balmy, that they should take a turn in the garden.

"It will be very pleasant on the terrace, and in the kitchen-garden," she remarked, "but, of course, we must avoid the grass. Are not these shut-in lawns pretty? Through that arch, if it were light enough, you would have a glimpse of my flower-garden. I call it mine, because I give it my special supervision. Doreen takes more interest in the kitchen-garden, and when I boast of my roses and begonias, she is dilating on the excellence of her strawberries and tomatoes."

"I think I should care most for the flower-garden," observed Waveney. And then, of her own accord, she began telling Miss Althea about the pensioners' little gardens, and the corporal's flowers.

Althea listened with much interest, and then, little by little, her quiet questions and sympathetic manner induced Waveney to break through her shy reserve, and speak of her home. Althea soon found out all she wanted to know: the home that was so perfect in Waveney's eyes, the little warm nest that held all her dear ones, seemed meagre and bare to the elder woman, who had been used to luxury all her life, and had never had a want ungratified.

As the girl talked on in a naive way, all at once a vision rose before Althea's eyes of a brilliantly-lighted ball-room, and of a fair, boyish-looking man, with stephanotis in his buttonhole, standing before her with eager looks.

"It is our valse, Althea, and I have been looking forward to it all the evening." And then—and then——But she started from her reverie with a quick feeling of shame. Why had these thoughts come to her? He was Dorothy's lover, not hers. Had he ever cared for her really? "It was all a mistake. It was not he who was to blame, it was I—I!" and even in the September darkness she smote her hands angrily together. The love had been in her imagination; it had never existed—never. She had bartered her warm woman's heart for a shadow, and alas, alas! it was not in Althea's nature to change. "If I love once, I love for ever," she had once said in a bitter moment to Doreen. How she repented that speech afterwards! "No; you do not understand, neither do I; but I think it is my nature to be faithful."

When Althea roused from her brooding, she found that Waveney had become silent. "You were speaking of your sister, were you not?" she said, gently. "Some one told me," she continued, a little vaguely, "that she was very pretty."

"Oh, yes," returned Waveney, eagerly, "everyone thinks Mollie quite lovely. It is such a pity she is lame. It spoils things so much for her, poor darling! But people admire her just the same—in the street they turn round and stare at her; but Mollie never seems to notice them a bit. That reminds me of such a funny speech"—and here Waveney began to laugh. "An old Irishwoman who works for us sometimes, once said to her, 'It is my belief, Miss Mollie darlint, that the Powers above were after fashioning an angel, and then they thought better of it, and changed it into a flesh-and-blood woman. For the angel still laughs out of your eyes, mavourneen.' And would you believe it, Miss Harford, that Mollie only burst out laughing when Biddy said that, but I think it was beautiful."

"I must see your pretty Mollie," returned Althea, thoughtfully; "but we must go in now."

"I think I must tell Moritz that," she said to herself, with a smile. "'The angel still laughs out of your eyes, mavourneen.' How very like an Irishwoman!"

CHAPTER XIII.: CONCERNING GUARDIAN ANGELS AND ITHURIEL'S SPEAR.

"Though many a year has o'er us roll'd Since life's bright morningtide, I'm dreaming still the dream of old We once dreamt side by side." Helen Marion Burnside.

It had been a long, trying day to Waveney, and it was a great relief when she found herself again in the Pansy Room. It was still early in the evening; but as soon as the door had closed upon the girl Althea rose from her chair.

"I have had a tiring afternoon, Dorrie," she said, in rather a weary voice. "A well-dressed crush always flattens me—so many smart bonnets, and so few brains! Somehow society always reminds me of a trifle, all sweetness and froth."

"Aren't you a little mixed, Althea?" returned her sister, good-humouredly. "There is froth certainly, but in my experience there is plenty of richness and sweetness underneath, if you only dig deep enough."

"Oh, I daresay;" and then a droll idea came to Althea, and she laughed softly. "Don't you remember the gingerbread queens that we used to buy when we were children at the Medhurst Fair, and how angry I was when some one stripped the gilt off. I thought it was real gold—like Nebuchadnezzar's image. Well, some of those fine ladies reminded me of the gingerbread queens."

Doreen looked amused. "You are in a pessimistic mood, dear." Then she put her hands on her sister's shoulders and scrutinised her face a little anxiously.

"You are very tired. Are your eyes paining you, Althea?"

"No, dear, but I think I shall go to bed."

But when she had left the room Doreen did not at once resume her book. "I wonder what is troubling her," she said to herself. "I know her expression so well, and with all her little jokes, she is not at ease. I hope that we have not made a grievous mistake in engaging Miss Ward—and yet she seems a nice little thing! But there is a look in Althea's eyes to-night as though she had seen a ghost. When one is no longer young the ghosts will come;" and then Doreen sighed and took up her book.

Althea was very tired, but it was mental, not bodily fatigue, that had brought the dark shadows under her eyes. But it was not her habit to spare herself, or to shunt her duties.

So, instead of going straight to her room, she turned down the passage that led to the two little chambers where their humbler guests slept, and sat for a few minutes beside Laura Cairns' bed. The girl slept badly, and Althea's sympathetic nature guessed intuitively how a few cheering words would sweeten the long night; and she never missed her evening visit.

"It is better to lie awake in the country than in Tottenham Court Roads," she said, presently. Then Laura smiled.

"Oh, yes, Miss Harford; it is so heavenly, the peace and silence. But at first it almost startled me. In London the cabs and carts are always passing, and there seems no quiet at all; but here, one can lie and think of the birds in their nests. And how good it is to be free from pain! Oh, I am so much better, and it is all owing to your kindness, and this dear old place!" And here the girl's lips rested for a moment on the kind hand that held hers. "But you will not leave me without my message, Miss Harford?"—for it was one of Althea's habits to give what she called "night thoughts" to the sick girls who came to the Red House.

Althea paused a moment. For once she had forgotten it. Then some words of Thomas à Kempis came to her, "Seek not much rest, but much patience," and she repeated them softly. "Will that do, Laura?"

"Oh, yes—and thank you so much, Miss Harford. 'Not much rest, but much patience.' I must remember that."

"I must remember it, too," thought Althea; and then she went to the Cubby-house to bid her old nurse good-night, and to have a little chat with her.

Nurse Marks was loud in her praises of Waveney.

"I like her, Miss Althea, my dear," she said, eagerly. "She has pretty manners, and a good heart; dear, dear, just to think of it being Jonadab's young lady. He thinks a deal of her, does Jonadab. She will be a comfort to you, my dearie. But there, you are looking weary, my lamb, and Peachey will be waiting to brush your hair." And Althea was thankful to be dismissed.

She sent Peachey away as soon as possible, and then sat down in an easy chair by the window; her eyes were aching, but the darkness rested them. She was a good sleeper generally, but to-night she knew that no wooing of the drowsy god would avail her. Doreen was right, and the ghost of the past had suddenly started up in her path.

Althea's youth had been a very happy one, until the day when she and Everard Ward had gathered peaches together in the walled garden at Kitlands, and then it had seemed to her as though they were the very apples of Sodom—mere dust and ashes.

Everard had judged his own case far too leniently; he had been eager to clear himself from blame. "A young fellow has his fancies before he settles down finally," he would say, in his careless way. "Oh, yes, you are right, Egerton. I was sweet on Althea Harford—there was something fascinating about her; she was rather fetching and picturesque—you know what I mean. But Dorothy—well, it was love at first sight, the real thing and no mistake. I wanted to ask her to marry me that very first evening, only I could not do it, you know."

"I suppose not," returned his friend, dryly. "You are a cool hand, Everard, upon my word. I wonder what Miss Harford thought about it all. Perhaps I am a bit old-fashioned, but in my day we did not think it good form to pay court to one girl and marry another." But this plain speaking only offended Everard, probably because in his inner consciousness he knew the older man had spoken the truth.

Through the sweet spring days and the glorious months of summer Everard Ward had wooed the young heiress with the eager persistence that was natural to him. Althea's fascinating personality, her gentleness and bright intelligence, all dominated the young man, and for a time at least he honestly believed himself in love with her. He was not fickle by nature, and if Dorothy Sinclair had not crossed his path, and played Rosalind to his Orlando, in the green glades of Kitlands Park, he would to a certainty have married Althea Harford.

Hearts do not break, they say; but when Althea walked down the terrace steps that day, with her basket of peaches on her arm, she knew that the gladness and sweetness of her young life had faded, and that, if her heart were not actually broken, it was only because her unselfishness and sense of right forbade such wreckage.

"I shall live through it, Dorrie," she had said to her sister, in those early days of misery, "and, God helping me, it shall not make me bitter; but it has robbed me of my youth. One cannot suffer in this way, and keep young;" and she was right.

"If you could only hate him!" ejaculated Doreen. "In your circumstances I know I should loathe and despise him." But Althea only shook her head.

"How could I hate him, when I have grown to love him with my whole heart, when I have regarded myself as his." But here she stopped and hid her face in her hands, with a choking sob. "Oh, Dorrie, that is the worst of all, that I should have believed it, and that he never meant it; that he never really loved me."

"I think he was very fond of you, Althea," returned Doreen, eagerly. "Mother was saying so only last night."

"Yes, he was fond of me. We were friends; but I was not his closest and dearest. Dorrie, we must never talk of this again, you and I; a wound like this, so sore and deep, should be covered up and hidden. I must hide it even from myself. There is only one thing that I want to say, and then we will bury our dead. I cannot hate Everard—hatred is not in my nature—and neither can I ever cease to love him. Oh, there is no need for you to look so shocked"—as Doreen's face expressed strong disapproval of this. "There will be no impropriety in the love I shall bear him. If I could I would be his guardian angel, and keep all troubles from him." Then she sighed and put her hand gently on her sister's shoulder. "'Seek not much rest, but much patience;' that shall be my New Year's motto. We will bury our dead." Those had been her words, and for twenty years the grass had grown over that grave; and yet, on this September night, the ghost of her old love had haunted her, and the ache of the old pain had made itself felt.

Is there any grave deep enough to bury a woman's love? Althea Harford was nearly forty-one, and yet the memory of Everard Ward, with his perfect face, and boyish, winning ways, his gay insouciance, and light-hearted mirth, made her heart throb with quickened beats of pain. All these years—these weary years—she had never met any one like him—never any one whom she could compare with him. People had often told her that he was not specially clever, that his talents were by no means of a first-class order; but she had never believed them. To her fond fancy he was the embodiment of every manly gift and beauty; even Dorothy, with all her love for her husband, would have marvelled at Althea's infatuation.

And now Everard's daughter was under her roof, and the knowledge that this was so had driven the sleep from her eyes, and filled her with a strange restlessness. Waveney's smile, and the turn of her head, and something in her voice, recalled Everard. More than once that evening she had winced, as some familiar tone brought him too vividly before her.

Waveney's artless confidence had given her food for thought. She had long known the hard fight that Everard Ward was waging, in his attempts to keep the wolf from the door. On more than one occasion her secret beneficence had lightened his weight of care. If Everard had guessed who was the real purchaser of some of his pictures, he would not have pocketed the money quite so happily; but Althea kept her own counsel.

"If I could only be his guardian angel!" she had said, in her girlish misery; and no purer wish had ever been expressed by woman's lips; in some ways she had been Everard Ward's good angel all these years.

Still she had never realised the extent of his poverty until Waveney had told her about the purchase of "King Canute."

A friend of Mr. Ingram's wanted a historical picture, and it was so fortunate that he took a fancy to "King Canute!"—he had actually paid five-and-twenty guineas, and they had paid off the disagreeable butcher; and now father would have the new great-coat that he wanted so badly.

Waveney had said all this with girlish frankness, as she and her new friend had paced up and down the garden path in the September darkness; but Althea had made no answer. She only shivered a little, as though she were cold; and a few minutes later she proposed to return to the house.

"It is a beautiful evening, but we must not forget that it is September," she had observed. But her voice was a little strained.

No, she had never really realised until that moment how badly things had gone with him; that mention of the great-coat had effectually opened her eyes. And then, as though to mock her, a little scene rose before her—a certain golden afternoon spent in an old studio at Chelsea, where Everard Ward and a friend had established themselves.

How well she remembered it! and the balcony full of flowers overlooking the river, with a gay awning overhead.

It was summer time, and she had put on a white gown in honour of the occasion, and Everard had brought her a cluster of dark, velvety roses. "They will give you the colour you need," he had said, looking at her admiringly; what an ideal artist he had seemed to her in his brown velveteen coat! The yellow sunshine seemed to make a halo round his fair hair.

"You look like a glorified angel, Ward," his friend had said, laughingly. "What do you say, Miss Harford—would he not do for Ithuriel in my picture of Adam and Eve sleeping in Paradise, with the Evil One whispering in Eve's ear. Do you remember the passage:

'Him thus intent Ithuriel with his spear touched lightly.'

Look here, old man, you must sit for me to-morrow." But Everard had only grumbled and looked bored.

In those days great-coats had certainly not been lacking. And as this thought occurred to her, Althea had shivered and become silent.

About four-and-twenty hours later Mollie received the following letter, which she carried off to her bedroom and read over and over again. She had already had the note in which Waveney had described the Cubby-house and her Pansy Room, and Mollie had certainly not expected another so soon.

"My own Sweetheart.—Here I am actually writing to you again. But I know what a long, weary day this has been, and how my sweet Moll has been missing me; and I said to myself, 'A letter by the last post will send her to sleep happily, and make her think that we are not so far apart, after all!' Well, and how do you think I have been spending my first day of servitude? Why, all by myself on the common; and if you had been there it would have been simply perfect; the common is such a beautiful place, and it stretches away for miles. But you will be saying to yourself, 'Is this the way Miss Harford's reader performs her duties?' My dear child, I have not seen my Miss Harford to-day. At breakfast time, Miss Doreen told me that her sister had had a bad night, and that she was suffering great pain in her eyes. 'It is so severe an attack,' she explained, 'that she cannot bear a vestige of light, and reading would drive her distracted. Her maid Peachey is looking after her, and most likely by evening the pain will have worn itself out.' And then she advised me to take a book out of the library and sit on the common, as she would be absent the greater part of the day. It was rather a business choosing a book, but I took 'Ayala's Angel' at last, as it looked amusing, and angels always remind me of my Mollie. There, is that not a pretty speech?

"The two little Yorkshire terriers accompanied me—Fuss and Fury—they are such dear little fellows, and it was just lovely! There was a little green nook, with a comfortable bench, a little way back from the road, and there I spent the morning. Miss Doreen was still at the House, so I had luncheon alone, and afterwards I went out in the garden. The two shop-girls were there; they had hammock chairs under a tree. The tall, pale girl was working, and the other was reading to her. I stopped to speak to them, and then I found a delightful seat in the kitchen garden. It was so warm and sunny that you would have thought it was August. Mitchell came to tell me when tea was ready, and now I am up in my Pansy Room, writing to you. There is a pillar box quite near, and when I have finished it I shall slip out and post it." And then a few loving messages to her father and Noel closed the letter.

CHAPTER XIV.: THURSDAYS AT THE PORCH HOUSE.

"And touch'd by her fair tendance, gladlier grew." Milton.

When Waveney crossed the hall after posting her letter, the dressing-bell rang, and Mitchell, who encountered her on the stairs, informed her with quiet civility that both her mistresses were in the library, and had desired that she would join them as soon as she was ready.

It did not take many minutes for Waveney to brush out her curly hair and put on her white dress. It was almost severe in its simplicity and absence of trimming, but in hers and Mollie's eyes it was a garment fit for a princess; and when Waveney had pinched up the lace ruffles, and put in the little pearl brooch—which had belonged to her mother—she was innocently pleased with her appearance.

She had rather a shock when she entered the library. Doreen was not there, but Althea was sitting with her back to the light, with a green shade over her eyes. The pale tints of her gown— Waveney discovered she always wore soft, neutral tints—the pallor of her long, thin face, and the disguising shade, gave her a strangely pathetic look.

She held out her hand with a faint smile.

"I am so sorry, my dear, that this should have happened, and on your first day, too! It is the worst attack I have had for months, and no remedies seemed to have any effect. But the pain has gone now, and to-morrow I shall be myself again."

"Oh, I am so glad of that!"

"I am glad of it, too," returned Althea; "for I would not willingly miss one of our Thursday evenings. You will be surprised to hear that we have begun a course of Shakespeare readings. Some of the girls are so intelligent, and read so well! Our old friend, Mr. Chaytor, helps us. He is a barrister, but a very poor one, I am sorry to say; but he is wonderfully clever. He used to read to the girls. Then he got up an elocution class; and now he has started these Shakespeare readings, and the girls do so enjoy them!"

"It sounds very nice."

"I think you will say so. We have had Tempest and Twelfth Night, and to-morrow it is to be As You Like It. Mr. Chaytor is to be Touchstone and the melancholy Jacques. Rather contrasts, are they not?"

At this moment Doreen re-entered. She looked pleased as she noticed the animation in her sister's voice, and as the gong sounded, she said,—

"You will like Miss Ward to come and talk after dinner, Althea, while I write those letters." And Althea smiled and nodded.

"She looks very ill," Waveney said, in a low voice, as they walked down the corridor.

"Oh, yes," returned Miss Harford, "she always looks bad after one of these attacks; it is the pain, you see—my sister does not bear pain well; it wears her out."

Waveney felt relieved when dinner was over. Doreen was very kind and pleasant, but she was not a great talker, and hardly knew how to interest her young companion. "Girls were more in Althea's line," she said to herself, "Althea had such marvellous sympathy and understood them so thoroughly. She herself got on better with older women;" and once or twice she smiled in an amused way when she lifted her eyes from her plate and saw the little figure in white opposite her. "She reminded me of one of Moritz's pictures," she said, afterwards to Althea. "Whichever could it be? I have been puzzling myself all dinner-time. The white frock makes her look more like a child than ever; her eyes are lovely, but she is not pretty."

"Not exactly; but I like her face. I expect you mean that picture of Undine. Yes, she is wonderfully like it, only this Undine has her soul. By the bye, we have not seen Moritz for an age. I shall write to Gwendoline and tell her that her boy is up to mischief."

When Waveney returned to the library she found that one or two shaded lamps had been lighted, but that Althea was still seated in the darkest corner of the room.

She bade Waveney draw up a chair beside her. "My head is too confused to listen to reading," she observed; "so you shall just talk and amuse me. Tell me anything about yourself, or Mollie, or your brother; everything human interests me, and nothing in the world pleases me better than to listen to the story of other people's lives."

Waveney laughed; but she was a little embarrassed, too. "Shall I tell you about my dear old men at the Hospital?" she said, rather nervously; and Althea concealed her disappointment, and said, "Yes, certainly; tell me anything you like."

And so Waveney began; and as usual her narrative was very picturesque and graphic. But lo and behold! before many minutes were over she had crossed the green sward, and the lime avenue, and was standing in fancy before a certain high, narrow house, with vine-draped balcony, and an old courtyard; and as she talked her eyes were shining with eagerness. And now the beloved names were on her lips—father and Mollie and Noel. Althea almost held her breath as she listened. "Oh, we were so happy!" exclaimed the girl. "I think no one could have been happier—we were never dull, not even when Noel was at school and father away; but, of course, we liked the evenings best!"

"Oh, yes, of course," echoed Althea, softly.

"I think the winter evenings were best," returned Waveney, reflectively, "because we could make up such a lovely fire. Father was often cold and tired, but he always smiled when he saw our fire, and sometimes we would roast chestnuts—that was Noel's treat—and tell stories, and sing. Father has such a beautiful voice, and so has Mollie, and when they sing in church, people look round and wonder who they are."

"Your brother is happy at school, then?"

"Happy! I should think so! He is so clever—even his masters say so; and then, he never shirks his work like other boys. Oh, do you know, Miss Harford, he has set his heart on getting a scholarship; he is working for his examination now. If he gets it, we hope he will be able to go to Oxford, for he does so want to be a barrister."

"But, my dear, eighty pounds a year would not pay his expenses at any university." And then Althea bit her lip as though she had said more than she intended.

"Oh, we know that," returned Waveney, eagerly, "but we thought—at least, Noel thought—that perhaps the veiled Prophet——" And then she broke into a laugh. "How absurd I am! As though you could understand! But Noel is always so ridiculous, and gives such funny names to people! The veiled Prophet is that kind friend of mother's who has sent him to St. Paul's."

"A friend of your mother's, my dear?" Althea's tone was a little perplexed.

"Father always says it is some friend of mother's, but, of course, it is all guess-work. The lawyer, who pays his bills, tells us nothing;" and then, partly to amuse her hearer, and partly because it gave her pleasure to narrate anecdotes of the lad's cleverness and sense of humour, she told her how Noel intended one day to go to Lincoln's Inn and interview the old lawyer. And there was something so racy in the girl's manner, and she imitated Noel's voice so well, that Althea, who had been trying to suppress her amusement for some minutes, gave up the effort, and broke into a hearty laugh.

"My dear, you have done me good," she said, when they were serious again, "and my evening, thanks to you, has passed very pleasantly. But I am going to send you away now, as I must not talk any more." And then, as Waveney rose from her chair at this dismissal, she drew her gently towards her, and kissed her cheek. "I am your friend; remember that, Waveney," she said, in her quiet voice, and the girl blushed with surprise and pleasure.

The next morning Waveney was summoned to the library. She found Althea looking pale and weak, but she had discarded her shade. She was resting in a deep, easy-chair, and her lap was full of letters.

Waveney found that her work was cut out for her, and for more than an hour she was busily engaged in writing the answers dictated to her. One was to Mrs. Wainwaring, and Waveney felt great pleasure in writing it. She had not forgotten Fairy Magnificent. She had taken a fancy to the pretty old lady, and longed to see her again. When Althea had finished her correspondence, she put a volume of "Robert Browning's Life" into the girl's hand.

"I must not use my eyes to-day," she said, with a sigh, "so if you will be good enough to read to me, I will finish my jersey. Knitting and crochet are my only amusements on my blind days. We work for the Seamen's Mission." And then she added, brightly, "It is such a luxury having some one to read to me. We shall get through so many nice books, you and I."

The morning passed so quickly that both of them were surprised when the gong sounded. After luncheon Waveney was told to go out and amuse herself until tea-time, and she spent a delightful afternoon rambling over the common, with Fuss and Fury frolicking beside her. The little terriers evidently regarded her as a new playmate, and were on the friendliest terms with her.

On going up to her room to dress for dinner, which was always an hour earlier on Thursdays, she noticed a group of girls in the verandah of the Porch House. Some were sitting down, and others standing about with racquets in their hands. Through the open window she could hear merry voices and laughter. Laura Cairns and the other girl were with them. The young housemaid who waited on her volunteered an explanation as she set down the hot-water can.

"Those are the young ladies from the Dereham shops, ma'am. It is early closing-day with most of them, and they come up early to play tennis." Althea looked amused when Waveney repeated this speech.

"They are young ladies to Dorcas," she said, laughing. "But, indeed, some of these girls are so intelligent, and so truly refined, that one need not grudge them the term. One or two of them would grace any drawing-room; but, of course, we have our dressy smart girls, too. By the bye, Waveney, do you play tennis?" And as Waveney shook her head, "I thought not. The houses in Cleveland Terrace have only small gardens, and you would have no opportunity of practising; but I am a devout believer in tennis."

"Mollie and I always longed to play," returned Waveney, with a sigh. "But, of course, it was out of the question for Mollie."

"Yes, but it is quite possible for you, and if you like, Nora Greenwell will teach you; she is our crack player. Even my sister, who is severely critical, allows that she makes wonderful strokes; eh, Dorrie?"

"She plays exceedingly well," returned Doreen, looking up from a scrap-book she was making for a children's hospital. "But then, Miss Greenwell does everything well. She is to take Rosalind's part to-night, is she not?" Althea winced slightly as Doreen asked the question. To her dying day she would never hear Rosalind's part read or acted, without secret emotion. She had dreaded this evening ever since the play of As You Like It was decided upon, but none the less she had determined to be present.

"Yes," she returned, rather hastily, "of course, Mr. Chaytor selected that part for her, as Nora is certainly our best reader. Minnie Alston will be Celia." And then she turned to Waveney. "They are my two favourites. When my sister wishes to tease me, she calls them my two paragons. And, indeed, I am proud of them. Oddly enough, they serve in the same shop—that big haberdasher—Gardiner & Wells."

"Miss Ward has not passed the shop, Althea. She has yet to make acquaintance with Dereham."

"Why do you call her Miss Ward?" returned Althea, playfully. "It is far too stiff a name for her. Follow my example and call her Waveney."

But Doreen looked a little dubious at this. She was a kind-hearted woman, but an undemonstrative one, and her sister's pretty speeches and little caressing ways often filled her with envy.

Dinner that evening was rather hurried, and the moment it was over Althea took up a light wrap and invited Waveney to accompany her to the Porch House.

The girls had finished their tea, and were now arranging the room for their reading. Althea paused doubtfully on the threshold as she heard the commotion.

"We are a little early," she said; "and they never like me to find them in confusion. I will show you the kitchen, Waveney. Is this not a nice little place? And that room beyond is where the girls wash their hands and brush their hair. There is a store-room, too, where I keep my jams and cake."

A pale-faced young widow was washing up the tea-cups as they entered. She brightened up as Althea addressed her.

"That is my caretaker, Mrs. Shaw," observed Althea, in a low voice. "Come, they are fairly quiet now, and we may as well go in, as Mr. Chaytor is generally punctual."

Waveney felt a little shy as she followed Althea. The great room seemed full of girls. There were thirty or forty of them, but Althea shook hands with every one, and had a pleasant word for each.

"This is my friend, Miss Ward," she said, in her clear voice, to the assembled girls. "Nora," singling out a tall girl, with an interesting face, "I am going to ask you to teach Miss Ward to play tennis. The asphalt court behind the Porch House will soon be ready. Thanks to the early closing movement, some of you will be able to have a game before it gets dark."

"Yes, indeed, Miss Harford."

"And we can practise our skating, too," interposed a pretty, dark girl.

Waveney found out afterwards that it was Minnie Alston, and that she and Nora were great chums.

"That will be charming," returned Althea. She looked more like Queen Bess than ever, as she stood in the circle of girls, with the light shining on her ruddy hair and soft ruffles. "Now, girls, we must take our places;" and then she beckoned Waveney to a long, high-backed settle that stood by the fire. The room was large, and a little cold, so a fire had been lighted.

Waveney looked round with intense interest. The Recreation Hall, as it was called, was of noble dimensions, and evidently well-lighted, from the number of windows.

There was a platform at one end, with a piano; and two or three easels and half a dozen round tables, with gay, crimson cloths, occupied the centre of the room. These were at once surrounded by groups of girls, some with books in their hands. The floor was stained, and some warm-coloured rugs gave an air of comfort. A well-filled book-case, a few well-chosen prints, and a carved oak chair known as "Miss Harford's throne," comprised the remainder of the furniture.

This evening Althea had vacated her throne for the settle, and a few minutes later Doreen entered the room, and with a pleasant nod to the girls, she seated herself by her sister.

Althea looked pleased, but she was evidently surprised. Waveney discovered afterwards that it was not Miss Harford's habit to attend the Thursday meetings. The sisters had their different hobbies. Doreen's active energies found plenty of scope in her "Home for Broken-down Workers," and though Althea had contributed largely to it, and always visited it at least once a week, it was Doreen who was the head and main-spring of the whole concern. The committee of management, comprised of a few personal friends in the neighbourhood, were merely tools in her vigorous hands.

"I wanted to hear Miss Greenwell's Rosalind," she whispered. And then a man's step sounded in the little passage. There was a quick rap at the door, the girls all rose from their seats, and Althea went forward with a smile of welcome.

"You are punctual to a minute, Thorold," she said, as she shook hands. "Miss Ward, this is our old friend, Mr. Chaytor;" but as Waveney bowed demurely, a sudden gleam of amusement sparkled in her eyes; for lo and behold! it was "the noticeable man, with large grey eyes" who had enquired the way in Ranelagh Gardens.

CHAPTER XV.: ORLANDO TO THE RESCUE.

Macbeth. "If we should fail!" Lady Macbeth.   "We fail! But screw your courage to the
sticking place, And we'll not fail." Shakespeare.

Waveney was secretly piqued to see that there was no sign of recognition in Mr. Chaytor's eyes. He bowed as though to a stranger in whom he took slight interest, exchanged a few words with the sisters, looked at his watch, and then lifted his hand as a signal for silence, and the buzzing, girlish voices were instantly hushed.

The readers had already taken their places round the centre table. Miss Harford's throne and a reading-desk stood beside it. The rest of the girls had grouped themselves round the tables with their work. A few of them had a volume of Shakespeare in their hands. The moment after Mr. Chaytor's entrance one of the girls had left the room rather hurriedly, and a minute later Althea was summoned.

Mr. Chaytor was giving a few instructions in a low voice, and had not noticed the circumstance until Althea returned with a perturbed countenance.

"I am so sorry," she said, in a tone of vexation; "it is most unfortunate, but Miss Pierson has one of her giddy attacks, and is obliged to go home. She is in tears about it, but, as I tell her, it is no fault of hers."

Mr. Chaytor looked blank. His audience was impatient; already he had heard sundry thimbles rap the table, and his readers were eager to begin. But now there was no Orlando, what was to be done? Such failure was not to be borne. He frowned, considered the point, and then looked persuasively at Althea.

"If you will be so good——" he began; but Althea shook her head and turned a little pale. Not for worlds would she have read that part. To her relief, Doreen came to her aid.

"You must not ask Althea," she said, in her quick, decided way. "She was quite ill yesterday, and her head is not right to-day. I wish I could help you, but I am no reader, as you know. But there is Miss Ward; I think she would do nicely. You will help them, will you not?" turning to Waveney.

Poor Waveney was ready to sink through the ground. She grew hot and then cold. "Do try, dear," Althea whispered, coaxingly; and, to her dismay, she found Mr. Chaytor's grave, intent look fixed on her. The clear grey eyes were somewhat beseeching.

"It will be a great kindness," he said. "Your audience will not be critical, Miss Ward. Let me beg you to do us this favour."

"It is impossible. I should spoil everything," stammered Waveney, in great distress. "I have only once read As You Like It, and that was a long time ago."

But she might as well have spoken to the wind. Mr. Chaytor evidently had a will of his own. His only reply was to put a book in her hand and offer her a chair.

"I have promised that we will not be critical," he said, quietly. "You will soon get into the swing of it. To give you confidence, I will read Orlando's opening speech to Adam."

Then, as Waveney took her place, with hot cheeks and downcast eyes, a delightful clapping of hands welcomed her.

Althea looked anxious as she returned to the oak settle.

"Poor little thing, she is frightened to death," she whispered; "but Thorold was so masterful with her."

"I like men to be masterful," returned Doreen, in an undertone; "but I wish he would try it on with Joanna." And then they both smiled, and Althea said "hush!" as Mr. Chaytor's full, rich tones were audible.

Waveney's turn came all too soon. Her voice trembled, and was sadly indistinct, at first: but as one girl after another took up her cue, she soon forgot her nervousness, and entered into the spirit of the play. Several of the girls read well, but none of them equalled Nora Greenwell. Celia was passable, and Ph[oe]be certainly understood her rôle; but Nora read with a sprightliness and animation that surprised Waveney. The girl seemed a born actor. Her enunciation was clear, and the changes of expression in her voice, its mirth and passion, its rollicking, girlish humours and droll witcheries, were wonderfully rendered.

But it was Mr. Chaytor's reading that kept Waveney spell-bound. When as First Lord he narrates the story of the melancholy Jacques and the sobbing deer, the pathos of his voice brought the tears to her eyes; and as Touchstone his dry humour and clownish wit were so cleverly given that once Waveney laughed and was covered with confusion.

Twice the reading was interrupted by a charming little interlude, when three or four girls went up on the platform and sang "Under the Greenwood Tree" and "Blow, Blow, Thou Winter Wind." At the conclusion of the play, which was shortened purposely, Althea took her seat at the piano, and all the girls joined in an evening hymn.

Waveney did not sing, for her heart was full. The evening's performance had excited her, and her imagination, which was always remarkably vivid, seemed suddenly to grasp the full beauty and meaning of the scene. Was not this Christian socialism in its fairest aspect? she thought. Could any picture be sweeter or more symbolical than that group of young faces gathered round the two dear ladies; for Doreen was on the platform, too. Some of the faces were far from being beautiful—some were absolutely plain; and one or two sickly-looking girls with tangled hair, and decked out with cheap finery, were singularly unattractive. And yet, as Althea's long, slim fingers touched the notes, and the dear old tune that they had loved in childhood floated through the wide hall, each face brightened into new life.

"They are all workers," thought Waveney, as she watched them. "Some of them have hard, toilsome lives; they are away from their homes and amongst strangers, and, though they are so young, they know weariness and heartache. But when they come here, it is like home to each one, and it makes them happy. If I were a shop-girl at Dereham, I should look forward to my Thursday evening as I look forward to Sunday;" and then she said to herself, happily, "To-morrow I shall say the day after to-morrow, and how delightful that will be!"

Waveney was smiling to herself, when she suddenly raised her eyes and encountered Mr. Chaytor's amused glance. He had evidently been watching her for some time, for he was leaning back in the carved arm-chair, with the air of a man who felt he had earned his repose.

The next moment he came towards her. The hymn was over, but the girls were still gathered round Althea and wishing her good-night. Under the cover of their voices he addressed Waveney.

"I have not properly thanked you for your kind assistance, Miss Ward, but I assure you that I was most grateful. Miss Pierson's indisposition had placed us in an awkward dilemma, but you came to our help most nobly."

"I am afraid I acquitted myself badly," returned Waveney. She would have given much for a word of praise. People generally liked her reading, but she feared that Mr. Chaytor would be no ordinary critic.

"You did very well," he returned, quietly. "Indeed, considering you had only once read the play, I ought to give you greater praise. You see, Shakespeare is a sort of divinity to me. I think a lifetime is hardly long enough to study him properly. My reverence for him makes me unreasonable. Orlando did not suit you; you would have made a better Rosalind. If you were staying at the Red House, and liked to join my Thursday evening classes, I could give you a few valuable hints."

"I should like to join them," observed Waveney, colouring a little, "if Miss Harford could spare me." And as he looked a little perplexed at this, she added hastily, "I have come to the Red House as Miss Althea's reader and companion." And this explanation evidently satisfied him.

But the next moment, as Waveney was moving away, he stopped her.

"Will you pardon me, Miss Ward, if I ask if we have ever met before? I have a fancy that your voice,"—he was going to say eyes, but he checked himself—"is not quite unknown to me. I have been puzzling over it half the evening."

"Oh, yes, we have met before," returned Waveney, who was quite at her ease now. "It was in old Ranelagh Gardens, and you asked us to direct you to Dunedin Terrace. I hope you found it;" and he smiled assent to this.

"You were with your sister," he hazarded, and Waveney nodded; and then Doreen joined them, and Mr. Chaytor said no more.

Of course he recalled it now, and it was only last Monday too. But how was he to identify the little girl in her shabby hat with this dainty little figure in white?

True, her eyes had attracted him that day, but this evening he had not seen them fully until a few minutes ago. He recalled everything now; the beautiful face of the other girl, and the sweet, refined voices of both. He had wondered who they were, and why they were sitting hand in hand in the sunshine, and looking so sad; and it was only three days ago.

Doreen proposed that Waveney should come back with her to the house.

"My sister and Mr. Chaytor often stop behind for a little chat about the girls," she explained. And Waveney, glancing at them as she left the room, saw that she was right.

Althea had seated herself on the settle, and was holding up a small screen between her face and the firelight, and Mr. Chaytor was standing with one arm leaning against the mantelpiece looking down at her.

"I am so glad the reading went off so well," she said, when the door had closed after her sister and Waveney. "At one moment I was terribly afraid, until our little Orlando came to the rescue. She read very nicely, Thorold."

"Yes, very fairly, considering all things; but the part did not suit her. I hope you were proud of your pet protegée. I consider Miss Greenwell achieved a striking success to-night. I am not easy to please, but really once or twice I found myself saying 'Bravo!' under my breath."

"No; as a critic you are terribly censorious. Thorold—you will laugh at me—but Nora's cleverness and her undoubted talents almost frighten me. What is the good of her learning all this Euclid and French, and robbing herself of some of her rest to get time for her studies, if she is to spend her life in snipping off lengths of ribbon and tape from one end of the year to the other?"

"All the good in the world!" he returned, in a most energetic tone. "Why need the snipping of ribbon, as you describe it, interfere with the development of the higher life? Your argument is a weak one. You might as well say that cutting muslin by the yard for so many hours at a stretch interferes with the religious life; and yet I expect plenty of shop-women are good Christians."

There was a flash of amusement in Althea's eyes, though she pretended to be indignant.

"How absurd you are! But I will not believe that you have so misunderstood me. Let me explain what I really do mean. I am very proud of Nora, but I am so afraid that all this education and cultivation will make her discontented with her surroundings; no life can be perfect that is out of harmony with its environment. I know a dozen girls from Gardiner & Wells', and only one of them, Minnie Alston, is worthy of Nora's friendship. She is very lonely, and, as you know, her home is most unsatisfactory—a virago of a step-mother, and a lot of boisterous children. Her work does not suit her, but she dare not throw herself out of a situation."

"Yes, I see what you mean," returned Mr. Chaytor, gravely. "Increase of knowledge often creates loneliness, and one member of a family may move on a different plane, where his relations cannot follow him. But if they are sensible people they do not beg him to climb down to them, and leave off his star-gazing. I think we need not disquiet ourselves about Miss Greenwell; perhaps she may have good things waiting for her."

Mr. Chaytor spoke in an enigmatical tone—he was grave and reticent by nature, and some up-to-date people would have thought a few of his ideas antiquated. He had a great dislike to any kind of gossip, and never mentioned reports which reached him until they were actually verified. Some one had hinted to him that Nora Greenwell had found favour in the eyes of her employer's son. Robert Gardiner was well educated and intelligent, but his parents, who were very proud of him, wished him to marry well.

"I have saved my pennies, Bob, and when you think of taking a wife I shall buy a plot of ground in the Mortimer Road and build you a house." But as Mr. Gardiner said this he was thinking of his partner's only child—Annie Wells. She was a pretty, fresh-looking girl, and when her father died she would have six or seven thousand pounds—for Gardiner & Wells drove a flourishing trade in Dereham.

If Mr. Chaytor had mentioned this report to Althea it would have thrown a little light on a circumstance that had come under her observation.

There had been a mistake in her quarterly account with Gardiner & Wells, and one Thursday afternoon Robert Gardiner had walked up to the Red House to speak to Miss Harford.

Althea kept him waiting for ten minutes, as she was entertaining a visitor; but on entering the dining-room she found him standing at the window, so intent on watching a game of tennis that she addressed him by name before she could gain his attention.

"I beg your pardon, Miss Harford," he said, hastily; he was a fair, good-looking man, and almost gentlemanly in manner. "I was watching the game. You have a capital tennis-court."

"So every one says. Miss Greenwell is our best player."

"She plays splendidly. I never saw such strokes;" and all through the brief interview Althea noticed how his eyes were following the girl's graceful movements.

"If Nora and Minnie had not been playing, I think I should have invited him to have a game," she said afterwards to Doreen; "but I thought of Gardiner père, and was afraid I might shock his sense of propriety."

"It would not have been good taste," returned Doreen, sensibly. "You may depend upon it that Robert Gardiner has very little to do with the young ladies of the establishment." And then they both laughed.

"By the bye, Althea," observed Mr. Chaytor, when they had finished the subject of Nora Greenwell, "I am so glad you have taken your friends' advice, and have engaged a reader. I am sure Miss Ward will be a comfort to you."

"I think so, too. She is very bright and intelligent, and she talks in the most amusing way. She is so natural and unsophisticated."

"So I should imagine. Where did you pick her up?"

"Doreen applied to an agency in Harley Street. But Thorold," and here her voice changed, "what singular coincidences there are in life! Is it not strange that she should be Everard Ward's daughter?"

Mr. Chaytor was now sitting beside her, and as she said this he turned round and looked at her. He was evidently very much surprised.

"I had no idea of that," he said, in a low tone. "There are so many Wards. Such a thought would never have occurred to me." And then he glanced at her keenly. "Is it not a little awkward for you, Althea?" Then a faint flush came to her cheeks. She was five or six years older than Thorold, but they had been old playfellows and dear friends, and his brother had been one of Althea's lovers in the Kitlands days; and he knew all about the Ward romance, and, lad as he was, he had predicted its ending, as he watched Dorothy play the part of Rosalind in the pastoral play.

"I do not see why it should be awkward," she observed, quietly. "I have not met Mr. Ward for twenty years, but I should have no objection to do so to-morrow. He is very poor, Thorold, and I am afraid they are often in difficulties. His pictures do not sell well."

"Perhaps they are not worth much. I fancy Ward's genius is purely imaginary. None of his friends believed that he would do much as an artist. Well, it is getting late, and I am keeping you up, and then Doreen will scold me. Let me help you turn out the lights, and then I will walk with you to the house. It is a glorious night, and I shall enjoy my stroll home."

But as they stood in the porch a moment in the starlight, Althea touched his arm.

"How is Joa?" she asked, kindly.

"She is quite well!" he returned. "Joanna seldom ails anything; but she is no happier, poor soul. I sometimes think she never will be." Then his voice grew suddenly tired. "I do not profess to understand women, Althea. I suppose some natures are naturally depressed, and live in an atmosphere of worry; but they are scarcely pleasant house-mates. I am afraid that is hardly a brotherly speech;" and he laughed a little grimly as he shook hands.

"Poor Thorold!" Althea said to herself, as she crossed the hall. "Joa is the Old Man of the Mountains to him; she is a dead weight on him. And yet how seldom he utters a word of complaint!—scarcely ever, and only to me. But he can say what he likes to me; he knows I am a safe confidante."

CHAPTER XVI.: SIR REYNARD AND THE GRAPES.

"Her angel's face, As the great eye of heaven, shyned bright. And made a sunshine in the shady place." Spenser's Faërie Queene.

It is the opinion of certain wiseacres that enjoyment consists mainly in anticipation and retrospection, and that the actual pleasure is reduced to a minimum. But to Waveney her first Sunday at the Red House was simply perfect. Not the shadow of a shade crossed her path until she said good-bye to Mollie in the evening.

Even the weather was propitious, and when the morning mist had rolled off the common, another of those golden days, peculiar to Autumn, seemed to flood Erpingham with warm, mellow sunshine.

The rich brown and amber tints of the bracken excited Waveney's admiration as they crossed a corner of the common, on their way to church. It was the longest way, Doreen explained, but she had some business that took her to the upper end of the village. Then they walked slowly down the main street past the fountain and the Roman Catholic church, with its old lych-gate. On their way Waveney learned how the sisters spent their Sunday afternoons.

Doreen always went to the Home of Rest for Workers. One of the inmates had partially lost her sight, and Doreen generally read to her and wrote her letters. It was her custom to remain to tea; it gave the matron an hour's freedom, and made a change for the ladies.

The Porch House was always thrown open for the girls' use from two to six on Sunday afternoons. There was no meal provided, but some of them liked to come up for an hour or two's reading or study, or to meet their friends. In winter there was always a bright fire and plenty of light, and Althea, stealing down the dark garden paths, would peep, unseen, at the merry group of chattering girls gathered round the fire.

Althea's Bible-class was always held in the dining-room of the Red House. About twenty girls attended it. Waveney discovered later that Althea spent most of her mornings preparing for this class; but when she expressed her surprise at the amount of labour it involved, Althea only smiled.

"My dear, it is very necessary labour," she returned. "It is no easy matter, I assure you, to keep ahead of girls like Nora Greenwell and Alice Mitchell. I have to study for dear life, and sometimes their questions are so difficult to answer that I have to apply for help to our good Vicar.

"I am very fond of my Sunday work," she said, as she and Waveney walked slowly on until Doreen should overtake them. "Two or three of the girls always remain to tea. I give my invitations on Thursday evening; and as I make no distinction, and each one has her proper turn, there is no margin for jealousy. I limit the number to four, as I like my Sunday tea-parties to be cosy. We call them library teas, and Mrs. Willis is generally very liberal with her cakes. Well, dear, why do you look at me so?"

"I was only thinking how full your life is, and how happy you must be!" returned Waveney, simply; and a faint flush rose to Althea's cheek.

"All lives ought to be full," she said, gravely. "It always makes me angry when people talk of empty, blighted, or disappointed lives;" and her tone was so severe that Waveney felt vaguely surprised.

"But, Miss Harford," she observed, timidly, "a great many women are disappointed, you know."

"Oh, yes, of course, life is as full of disappointments as this bush is full of blackberries this morning. But, all the same, they have only themselves to blame if their existence is dull and colourless. There is too much mawkish sentiment talked at the present day," she went on. "I was only telling my girls so the other day. When trouble comes to a woman—and Heaven knows they have their share of suffering: I suppose, for their soul's good—it is no good creeping along the ground like a bird with a broken wing; they must summon all their pluck, and fight their way through the thorns. Of course, even the brave ones get a little torn and scarred, but they are too proud to show their wounds. Look, here comes my sister, and we will change the subject." And then, as Doreen joined them, they walked on quickly; but Althea's blue eyes had a strange glow in them.

When Waveney reached Sloane Square she found Mollie had kept her word, and was on the platform to receive her. She gave a little cry when she saw Waveney, and more than one passer-by looked round with kindly amusement as the sisters rushed into each other's arms.

"Oh, Mollie, how lovely you look! What have you done to yourself?" But Mollie only laughed. And then, like two children, they walked up the stairs hand-in-hand. And to Mollie it might have been the golden ladder that leads to Paradise. Her dearer self, her twin sister, was beside her, and the five blank days were over.

"Father and Noel have gone for a walk," she said, as they turned down King Street. "I shall have you to myself for a whole hour. Oh, Wave, how are we to talk fast enough!—so much has happened even in these five days! I wish I could write clever letters like you. But I am so stupid!"

"Nonsense, sweetheart. Why, I loved your letters, and always slept with them under my pillow."

"Did you, really? Oh, Wave, what a darling you are! But, of course, I did the same. And I was so amused at your meeting 'the noticeable man, with the large grey eyes.' Father heard me chuckling, and he insisted on my reading your letter to him; but he was quite startled when I came to Mr. Chaytor's name. I don't think he was quite pleased."

"What makes you think that, Mollie, dear."

"Oh, he frowned and bit his lip. You know his way. And then he took up the newspaper and cleared his throat. But I heard him mutter, as though to himself, 'Another of them. Now I wonder which of them it is.' But, as you only said Mr. Chaytor, I could not tell him."

"It was Thorold," returned Waveney. And then, as they came in sight of the house, she kissed her hand to it in a sort of ecstasy. "Oh, you dear old place, I have dreamt of you every night!" And then, as Mollie used her latch-key, Mrs. Muggins came to meet them, purring loudly, with uplifted tail.

"Dear me, I never noticed how steep and narrow the staircase is!" remarked Waveney, innocently. "And Mollie, dear, you really must cause father to get some new stair-drugget. Crimson felt would look so nice and warm, and would not cost much." But Mollie shook her head.

"We must wait for that, I am afraid," she said, sadly. Then she cheered up. "But, Wave, father has got such a lovely new great-coat, and he does look so nice in it; and Noel insisted on his getting a new hat, too. I tell father that he will be ashamed to walk with me, now he has grown such a dandy." And then Mollie broke off in confusion, and began to blush, for Waveney's eyes were fixed on the round table in the studio. A magnificent basket of hot-house grapes stood in the centre.

Waveney regarded it with the look of a cat that sees cream. There were three pounds at least, and the purple bloom of the fruit made a rich spot of colour in the room.

Waveney's expression was inscrutable. "Mollie," she said, at last, "the Black Prince has been here again."

"Yes, dear," stammered Mollie, with the air of a culprit discovered in a fault; "but I did not expect him—I told you so. I was on my knees darning the stair-carpets, because father caught his foot in a hole that very morning; and when Ann opened the door, there he was, and, of course, he saw me."

"Oh, of course, there is nothing wrong with Sir Reynard's eyes," muttered Waveney. "They are very good eyes, I should say." But this remark seemed to puzzle Mollie.

"Why do you call him Reynard, Waveney? He is not sly, not a bit of it. He was so funny. He wanted to help me with the stair-carpet—he said he was a good hand at darning; but I would not hear of such a thing, and, of course, I took him into the study."

"Well, child, what then?" and Waveney seated herself on Grumps, and patted the sofa gently as an invitation for Mollie to do the same. "And then Sir Reynard presented his grapes."

Mollie stamped her little foot.

"I will not have it, Waveney. You shall not call our nice little Monsieur Blackie by such a horrid name. Yes, he offered the grapes with such a droll little speech; but I can't remember exactly what he said, only that a friend of his had a splendid vinery, and he always sent him such quantities of grapes, and it would be a charity to help him to eat them, and so on."

"Yes, and so on. And you said, 'Thank you, my dear Black Prince. You are very generous to poor little Cinderella.'"

"Waveney, if you talk such nonsense I won't love you a bit. Of course I thanked him—and I must have done it nicely, for he looked pleased, almost as though he were relieved. 'That's right,' he said, heartily. 'What a sensible young lady you are, Miss Mollie! You take things naturally and as you ought—and I wanted to please you. You know I always want to please you.'"

Waveney caught her breath, and there was almost a look of fear in her eyes.

"Did he say those very words, Mollie?"

"Yes, dear," in a tranquil tone. "And I am sure he meant it, too. He did look so very kind. 'Do you know I wanted to please you the very first day I saw you,' he went on, 'and it has been the same every day since. I am such a lonely sort of fellow since Gwen left me. Gwen is my sister, you know.'"

"And that fetched you, of course?" But Waveney did not speak in her usual tone. And how she watched the bright, speaking face beside her.

"Yes, indeed, I thought of you, and I asked such a lot of questions about this Gwendoline, and I am sure he liked answering them. She is not pretty, Wave, not a bit—ugly, in fact; but her husband adores her. She is very tall and graceful, but he told me he would not show me the picture he had in his pocket, because plain people were not in my line. Wasn't that a funny speech? And then we had a quarrel; but he stuck to his point. He said he hoped that some day he would be able to introduce her to us, and that he would rather wait till then. But, Wave, what am I thinking about? I meant you to have some grapes." And then she jumped up from her seat and limped quickly to the table, and for a moment Waveney's eyes were a little misty.

"How innocent she is! What a child! But I dare not enlighten her," she said to herself. "I wonder what father thinks. If I can, I will just give him a hint. I think he ought to find out who Mr. Ingram really is; we know nothing about him. He may be in earnest—very likely he is; but he ought not to come when Mollie is alone."

The hour passed all too quickly, and just as Waveney was giving a full description of Thursday evening her father's voice made her start from her seat and fly downstairs; but there was no one that day to liken her to Titania. How Everard's face brightened at the sight of his darling! And even Noel "chortled in his joy," to use his favourite expression. He actually submitted to be kissed twice without making a wry face, though he immediately turned up the collar of his coat.

"It has been rather tropical lately," he observed, blandly, "but now old 'Storm-and-Stress' has come, we must look out for draughts." But Waveney was admiring the great-coat, and took no notice.

"It is father's turn," exclaimed Mollie, cheerfully. "Noel, you must come and help me get tea ready. We shall have it in the studio, of course;" and then she stumped off to the kitchen, and Waveney and her father went upstairs.

They had a little talk together. Everard asked a few questions about his old friends, and seemed much interested in all Waveney's descriptions.

"I think you have a good berth, dear," he said, presently, "and that you are likely to be very happy with the Misses Harford."

"Yes, father, and I am sure that I shall soon learn to love Miss Althea—Good Queen Bess, as I call her. But—but"—the colour rising to her face, as she squeezed his arm with her little hands—"I would rather be at home with my dad."

"I know that, darling, and dad has missed his little girl badly. By the bye, Waveney, there seems a plentiful crop of ghosts at the Red House. Mollie tells me that the other night you met a Mr. Chaytor."

"Yes, father, Mr. Thorold Chaytor. He seemed very nice, and he read so beautifully. Miss Althea says he is a barrister—but that, though he is so clever, he gets few briefs, and that he ekes out his income by doing literary work."

"He was always a clever fellow," returned Mr. Ward; "but I remember I liked Tristram best. Poor old Trist, he was a bit soft on Althea. I remember how angry he was when some one told him it was lad's love. Thorold was a cut above us, and we were rather in awe of him. I wonder what sort of looking fellow he is now."

"He is tall and rather distinguished looking. I mean, people cannot help noticing him." Then Mr. Ward's eyes twinkled mischievously.

"'A noticeable man,' eh, Waveney? 'with large grey eyes?'" Then Waveney blushed and laughed.

"What a perfidious Mollie! But, father, it is really such a true description! Mr. Chaytor is quite plain and ordinary-looking, and he is old, too,—five-and-thirty, I should say; but when he speaks you would never call him plain."

"No, I know what you mean. But his brother Tristram was a very handsome man."

"Did you know them well, father?"

"Very well, indeed. The Chaytors lived at the old Manor House—their grandfather had bought it. It was a fine old place, about two miles from Kitlands, and when I visited them they lived in good style and entertained largely. Old Chaytor, as we called him, was fond of life and gaiety; though we youngsters knew little about it, he kept racers, and about the time I married, his losses were so heavy that they could no longer afford to live in the old Manor House."

"Were there only those two brothers, father, dear?"

"No, there was a sister Joanna—Joa they called her—a pretty, fair girl; she and Althea were great friends. She was engaged to Leslie Parker. The Parkers were neighbours of theirs; they lived in a quaint old house in the village, called The Knolls, but I heard afterwards that, when the old Manor House was sold, and Mr. Chaytor died, the marriage was broken off. I never cared much for the Parkers; they were a mercenary lot. All the sons married women with money. But it was hard lines on poor little Joa."

"Oh, father, how dreadfully interesting all this is! I do so love ancient history."

"It was by no means interesting for the Chaytors," returned Mr. Ward, with a laugh. "Old Chaytor's love for the turf ruined them. When he died, his sons found that his affairs were hopelessly involved, and that he had left heavy debts. I had lost sight of them by that time; but I heard a year or two afterwards that Mrs. Chaytor was dead, too, and that Tristram had gone to New Zealand. Rumour said that he had turned out unsatisfactorily, and that his brother had shipped him off, but I know nothing more."

"Neither do I, except they are living in a dull-looking house in Dereham." And then Mollie limped in with the tea-tray, and Noel followed, carrying a huge plum cake on his head, like one of the black slaves in the "Arabian Nights." And then, as he made an obeisance like Lord Bateman's "proud young porter," it rolled to his feet; after which Mollie boxed his ears, and his father called him a young ass.

They had a merry tea, and then they drew round the fire and sang hymns; and church-time came only too quickly.

Waveney had her old place between her father and Mollie; and when the gas was turned down during the sermon, Mollie slipped her hand into hers.

And a dark young man, who was sitting a few pews behind them, watched them attentively through the service; and, when, in the dusk, he saw Mollie nestle up to her sister, a great softness came into his eyes, and he said to himself, "Poor little thing!"

But as Noel strutted beside his sisters on the way to the station to see Waveney off, he said a thing that surprised them.

"Did you see my friend the Idealist!" he asked, with his chin elevated. "My word, he looked quite the swagger gentleman in his new frock coat."

"Do you mean Monsieur Blackie!" asked Waveney; and she pressed Mollie's arm involuntarily. She had had no opportunity of giving her father that hint, and now she must wait for another week.

"Yes, Monsieur Blackie—Monsieur Blackie—Monsieur Blackie," returned the provoking lad, in a falsetto squeak. "Hold hard, father, you have nearly landed me into the gutter."

And then a little, dark gentleman, who was following them unperceived, gave a low laugh. "My friend the humorist at his tricks again," he murmured. "I wish Gwen could see that lad; she would love him."

CHAPTER XVII.: "LIKE SHIPS THAT PASS IN THE NIGHT."

One evening, about a week later, Thorold Chaytor walked quickly over the Dereham bridge on his way from the station. His day, as usual, had been spent in his dingy chambers in Lincoln's Inn; he had worked hard, and felt unusually weary, and the damp chilliness of the mists rising from the river made him shiver and button up his coat more closely.

A slight mizzling rain was now falling; the pavements were wet and greasy; the gas lights on the towing path seemed to waver and then flare up with windy flickers; the black hulls of the boats and barges moored to the shore loomed through the mist like vast monsters weltering in the mud; and the grey river flowing under the bridges washed silently against the piers in the darkness.

Mr. Chaytor's chambers in Lincoln's Inn were high up, and very small and inconvenient— "Chaytor's sky parlour," some of his friends called it, for in reality it consisted of only one room and a good-sized cupboard; but the view of chimney-pots from the window was certainly unique. To be sure, it was somewhat cold in winter, and at times the chimney was given to smoking, and in summer it certainly resembled the Black Hole in Calcutta; but these were trifles to be borne stoically, if not cheerfully.

In this den Thorold Chaytor did most of his literary work, and waited for briefs; nor did he wait wholly in vain.

Althea had spoken of him as a poor man, and this opinion was shared by many others. When old friends of the family, who had visited at the old Manor House, came down to the dull, shabby-looking house in High Street, where Thorold and his sister lived, they used to sigh and shrug their shoulders.

"It was grievous," they would say. "No wonder poor Joanna looked so old and careworn! And they only kept one servant, too;" and then they would talk, under their breath, of the wasteful extravagance at the old Manor House, and then of that racing establishment at Newmarket, to which the Chaytor fortunes had been sacrificed.

But if Thorold and Joanna practised rigid economy, and only kept one servant, it was because they stinted themselves of their own free-will.

Thorold Chaytor was not really poor; his literary work was successful, and his papers on social questions were so brilliant and versatile, so teeming with thought and sparkles of wit, that he was already making his mark as a clever writer.

And in his own profession he was not doing so badly. Quite recently he had distinguished himself in some case. "Chaytor is a clear-headed lawyer; he is sharp and has plenty of brains," his friends would say; "he will get on right enough, if he does not kill himself with work first."

Thorold loved his work. The hours spent in that grimy den were full of enjoyment to him; he was equally happy solving some legal problem or doing some of his journalistic work; his clear, strong brains delighted in labour.

He had one curious companion of his solitude—a small, yellow cat, who had only three legs, whom he had rescued from a violent death, and who refused to leave him.

Sisera was not an attractive animal, but his heart was in the right place; he adored his master, and when Thorold's step sounded on the stairs in the morning, Sisera would jump off the old coat on the shelf, where he was accustomed to pass the night, and limp with loud purrs to the door.

Sisera was as much a hermit as his master; he took his exercise among the chimney-pots, and never went downstairs, where unseen enemies lurked unnumbered for him. He had his pennyworth of milk, and his skewer of cats' meat, and a share of his master's frugal luncheon; and on Sundays the fat old housekeeper toiled up the stairs and deposited the rations for the day, grumbling as she did so.

But, although Thorold already earned a fair income, he lived as though he were poor, and both he and his sister were almost parsimonious in their habits; but not even Althea, who was their closest friend, did more than guess at the reason for all this thrift. Thorold had set himself an Herculean task—to pay his father's debts—and in this Joanna had willingly helped him; with all her faults and failings, she was a good woman, and her sense of honour was almost as strong as his.

Thorold was still at Oxford when his father died. His brother Tristram was three or four years older. He had been summoned in haste to the death-bed; but, to his relief, his father recognised him.

"It is a bad business, my boy," he said, faintly, as Thorold took his hand. "If I could only have my life again, I would do differently;" and a few minutes later, when they thought he was sleeping, he opened his eyes. "Never get into debt, Trist," he murmured. "It is hard for a man to die peacefully with a millstone round his neck." And Thorold was struck by the look of anguish that crossed his face.

"Father," he said, gently, for he was young and impressionable, and perhaps, in his wish to give comfort, he hardly knew what he was saying. "Father, you shall die in peace; and Trist and I will work hard, and pay your debts."

"Yes, yes," murmured Tristram, with a sob; "we will pay them, dad."

Then a wonderful smile came over the sick man's face.

"Good lads, good lads," he muttered. "God bless you both!" Those were his last words; but, even as he lay in his coffin, Thorold began to realise that the millstone was already round his own neck.

Those first few years that followed his father's death were very sad ones to Thorold. His mother's failing health, and Joanna's disappointment, embittered the peace of their home; and, worse than all, Tristram became a care to them. He had been brought up in expectation of a fortune; and, as far as work was concerned, his life at the university had been a failure.

"What does it matter whether I grind or not?" he would say. "I am having a good old time, and the governor will pay my debts." And when the evil days came, and George Chaytor's sons had to put their shoulders to the wheel and earn their bread, there seemed nothing that Tristram could do.

Again and again a berth had been found for him, but he had failed to keep it. Either he had been wanting in steadiness or application, or he had lost his temper and quarrelled with his employer. "He is not worth his salt!" one of them said angrily to Thorold.

In sheer desperation, Thorold went to an old cousin who had already shown him a great deal of kindness; and, with his help, Tristram was equipped and shipped off to New Zealand.

"Perhaps he will do better in a new world," Thorold said, when Joanna bewailed his departure rather bitterly. Tristram was her darling; she loved him far better than she did Thorold. Like many other prodigals, Tristram Chaytor was not without his endearing qualities. Women loved him, and he was good to them; but in character he was selfish and unstable as water, and very prone to fall into temptation. Already, as Thorold knew, he had become addicted to low pleasures. His friends were worthless and dissipated; but Joanna, who was mildly obstinate on occasion, turned a deaf ear to all Thorold's hints on this subject.

Tristram seemed to do better for a time in his new environment. Then he foolishly married some pretty, penniless girl who took his fancy, and after that they lost sight of him.

Thorold was thinking of him now as he walked over the wet bridge; although he was a ne'er-do-well, he was his only brother, and in the old days they had been close chums and playfellows.

"Dear old Trist," he said to himself. "I wonder what he is doing now, and if Ella makes him a good wife." And then, in the darkness, Tristram's handsome face and tender, humourous smile seemed to rise vividly before him. He could even hear his voice, clear and boyish, close to his ear—"Well played, old chappie—but it was a fluke for all that!"

"What on earth makes me think of Trist to-night?" Thorold asked himself, in some perplexity—but if he had only guessed the truth, he need not have puzzled himself: at that very moment, under the flickering, wind-blown gaslight, the brothers had passed each other without recognition, "like ships that pass in the night."

Thorold was trying to keep his umbrella steady, and took no notice of the passenger, who almost brushed his elbow—though he heard a small, childish voice say, "I don't like English rain, father." But the answer did not reach him.

"Aye, it is a bit saft, Bet—as the Scotch folk say. Creep under my Inverness cape, little one, and it will keep you dry." And then the little feet toiled on wearily and bravely in the darkness.

As Thorold let himself in with his latch-key, the parlour-door was opened hastily, and a woman's face peeped out anxiously. "Is that you, Thorold?" Then the man bit his lip with sudden irritation. Day after day, month after month, this was Joanna's never-varying formula—until "Is that you, Thorold?" seemed to be dinned into his brain like a monotonous sing-song.

"Who should it be" he longed to answer this evening. "What other fellow do you suppose would let himself in with my latch-key." But he controlled himself—Joanna had no sense of humour, and did not understand sarcasm. "Yes, here I am, as large as life," he returned, cheerfully. "But don't touch me, dear, for I am a trifle wet. Is supper ready? I will just change my coat, and be with you in a moment. Ah! Rabat-la-Koum," as a big, grey Persian cat rubbed against his legs, "so you are there, old mother of all the cats; and you are coming up with me, eh?"

"Don't forget to rub your feet, Thorold. There were marks on the landing carpet yesterday;" and then Joanna went back to pick up her knitting, feeling that she had properly welcomed her brother.

Joanna Chaytor had been a pretty girl, with that soft, rounded prettiness that belongs to youth; but at six-and-thirty she was faded and old-maidish. Doreen and Althea, who were several years older, scarcely looked their age, but Joanna had worn badly.

Disappointment and sorrow, and the small, carking cares of daily life, had washed away the pretty bloom from her cheeks, and had sharpened the lines of her face. Her brown hair was streaked with grey, and though her figure was still graceful and she dressed youthfully, strangers always thought she was at least forty-five.

Women are as old as they feel, people say, but in that case Joanna would have been seventy at least.

To her the drama of life had been wholly tragical. She had lost her father and the mother she adored, and the beloved home of her childhood. The man to whom she had given her young affections and whom she looked upon as her future husband, had basely deserted her in her adversity; and, as though this were not enough, her favourite brother was in exile, separated from her by the weary ocean.

If Joanna had married Leslie Parker, she would have made an excellent wife and mother; but her present environment did not suit her. She grew thin and weedy, as Althea once phrased it. Joanna was not a clever woman; she was dense and emotional, and her mild obstinacy and tenacity were powerful factors in her daily life. She had long ago shelved her deeper griefs; but a never-ending crop of minor worries furnished her with topics of conversation.

Thorold was fond of his sister, but she was no companion to him. His calm, self-restrained nature was the very antipodes of Joanna's fretful and nervous temperament. Manlike, he failed to understand why the dust and sweepings of the day should be brought for his inspection. Joanna had not toiled long hours in hard, strenuous brain labour, in a grimy attic, with a three-legged Sisera curled up at her feet; her work had been light, compared to his.

Sometimes, when he felt lonely and weary, and the need for companionship was unusually strong, he would try and interest her in his day's work; but it was always a failure. She would listen, and then her attention would fly off at a tangent, or he would see her trying to stifle a yawn.

There was something he wanted to tell her this evening; for the day had been eventful to him. If Althea had been his sister, he would have followed her into the sitting-room, wet as he was, and would have told her triumphantly that his foot was on the rung of the ladder at last, and that he had begun to climb in earnest. And he would have told her, too, that before long their father's debts would be all cleared off.

Thorold had not done this unaided. About eighteen months before, the old cousin who had come to his assistance with Tristram, died, and, with the exception of five hundred pounds to Joanna, left all his savings, amounting to several thousands, to Thorold.

Thorold never consulted any one; he asked no advice; he paid in twelve hundred pounds at his banker's, that it might be ready for a rainy day, and then he went around to his father's creditors, paying off each one by turn. The racing debts had been settled years ago, in his father's lifetime, by the sale of the old Manor House and the lands adjoining; but he had lived recklessly, and his creditors were many. He owed large sums to a carriage-builder in Baker Street, and to his tailor, wine merchant, and other tradespeople. One of them, a small jobbing carpenter, who lived in the village, stared incredulously at the cheque in his hand and then fairly burst out crying.

"It is for joy, Mr. Thorold," cried the poor fellow, rubbing his coat-sleeve across his eyes, "for I never expected to see a penny of the squire's money, and we have had hard times lately. Business has been slack, and my missis has been poorly and run up a doctor's bill, and God bless you, sir, for your honest dealing with a poor man, for I shall be able to keep the shop together now." And for that afternoon at least Thorold felt a lightening of the millstone round his neck.

Joanna looked at him a little tearfully when he showed her the receipted bills. She was not too dense to understand the grandeur of the action. How few men would have considered themselves bound by a few impulsive words gasped out by a death-bed!

"You have used all Cousin Rupert's money in paying father's debts," she said; and there was a queer look in her eyes.

"No, dear," he returned, gently, "I have not spent it all. I am keeping twelve hundred pounds for a rainy day. I thought that would be only right. But, Joa, there are only two bills left, and most of the things owing were for Tristram."

"Tristram!" in a startled voice. "Are you sure of that?"

"Yes—things that he wanted at Oxford and that father ordered; but three or four hundred will clear off the whole account."

"Thorold," returned his sister, plaintively—and now she was actually crying—"you do not expect me to help with my money?"

"No, of course not. What an idea!" he replied, hastily; but all the same he felt vaguely surprised. All these years Joanna had stinted herself of comforts, had scraped and saved and pared down every unnecessary expense with ungrudging cheerfulness, and with all her grumblings and worries she had never said one word of blame on this score. And now she was hugging her small fortune almost jealously.

"I am very sorry, dear, but I cannot give you my money," she went on quickly. "It is my own money, you know. Dear Cousin Rupert left it to me. I have helped you as well as I could all these years, but I must keep this for my very own."

"Of course you shall keep it," returned her brother; for Joanna was growing quite excited. "I suppose you will put it into the London & County Bank."

"Yes, that will be best; and then I can get it out easily."

"The consols would be better, perhaps," he continued, musingly; "and you would get more interest. Or you might buy some of those shares that Doreen was mentioning."

"No, no. I prefer the London & County," returned Joanna, obstinately. "Let me do what I like with my own money."

And Thorold said no more. But now and then he wondered if Joanna had drawn on her secret hoard. As far as he could see she had bought nothing fresh for the house, and certainly not for her dress, during the last eighteen months, and their bill of fare was not more luxurious.

CHAPTER XVIII.: JOANNA TANGLES HER SKEIN.

The house in High Street where the Chaytors lived was somewhat dingy and uninviting in its outward aspect, but inside it was not without its advantages.

A small paved court separated it from the street; and at night its front windows were illuminated by the flaring gaslights from the opposite shops. All day long the ceaseless patter of foot-passengers on the pavement, and the rumble and rattle of cabs, omnibuses, and carts, made the narrow windows shake in their frames. And it was far into the night before silence brooded over the old town.

On one side of the passage was a small room where Thorold kept a good many of his books and papers. It was called the study, but he never sat there. Joanna had long ago proved to him that with one servant and a limited purse, an extra fire would be quite a sinful extravagance. It was for this reason too that she so seldom used her drawing-room. It was a pretty room on the first floor, with a pleasant view of the garden, and in summer she liked to sit at the open window with her work, and watch Thorold digging and raking in the borders. Gardening was his favourite amusement, and he took great pride in his flower-beds. Sometimes, when she had leisure, Joanna would weed or water a little; but she always made much of these labours.

The room they mostly used was a large one on the ground floor. It extended from the front to the back of the house, and the two narrow windows at the farther end overlooked the shady old garden.

This part of the room was furnished as a study. The stained book-shelves were loaded with ponderous-looking books. A writing-table occupied one window, and two comfortable easy-chairs, and Joanna's overflowing work-basket, stood on either side of the fireplace. A book-stand and a reading-lamp were by Thorold's chair; the front portion of the room was used for their meals.

When Thorold came down that evening the room looked warm and cosy. The crimson curtains were drawn, and a bright fire blazed cheerfully. The supper was laid, and Jemima had just brought in a small, covered dish, and placed it before her mistress. Thorold was hungry, for his luncheon had been a light one. For a wonder, the chops were well cooked and hot; and as he helped himself to the nicely browned mashed potatoes, he felt disposed to enjoy himself. He would tell Joanna about his visit to Murdoch & Williams. She would be interested; and for once they would have a sociable evening. He even thought that he would ask for a cup of coffee, as he felt chilled and tired. And then, by way of making himself pleasant, he commended Jemima's cookery.

It was an unfortunate choice of subjects. Joanna, who had been tranquilly eating her supper, suddenly grew red and querulous.

"Ah, she can cook well enough if she chooses," she returned, "but there! she so seldom chooses to take pains. Thorold, I shall have to part with that girl; her wastefulness and extravagance are beyond everything. And then she is so self-willed, too—she will not mind anything I tell her. Again and again I have begged her not to put an egg in the rice pudding, but she does it all the same."

"I suppose she thinks the egg will make the pudding nicer," returned Thorold, mildly; and then, to change the subject, he said, boldly, "I have rather a headache this evening, dear. Do you think Jemima could make me a cup of coffee?"

"She could make it, but I doubt if you would care to drink it," she returned, fretfully. "And she wants to go out, too. She has got a young man, I know she has; I taxed her with it this very morning, and she was as impertinent as possible."

"My dear Joa"—for his sense of fairness was roused by this—"why should not the poor girl have a lover? She is very good-looking, and as long as she conducts herself properly I can see no objection to the young man."

"Yes, and she will be having him in, and giving him supper when we are out—not that I ever do go out, Heaven knows! I declare I quite envy you, Thorold, going out every morning to your work. Women's lives are far more dull and monotonous than men's;" here Joanna's voice waxed more plaintive than ever—it was naturally rather a sweet voice, but fretfulness and discontent had deadened the harmony. If, as they say, the closing of an eyelid will shut out the lustre of a planet, so, to Joanna, the small everyday worries seemed to obliterate the larger and grander interests of life. Jemima's good looks, her lover, her small impertinences and misdemeanours, loomed like gigantic shadows on her horizon. "If she could only learn the right proportion of things!" Thorold had said once to Althea, almost in despair.

When Joanna made her dolorous little speech, Thorold raised his eyes from his plate and looked at her. "Why do you not go to the Red House oftener?" he asked, gravely. "You know how glad they would be to have you. You stay at home too much, Joa, but it is your own fault, you know. Doreen and Althea are always sending you invitations."

"Yes, I know, and I am very fond of Althea. But somehow I never care to go to the Red House; it reminds me too much of the dear old Manor House. That room of Althea's makes me quite shiver when I enter it."

"Oh, I would not give way to those feelings, Joa," he returned, hastily. "In life one has to harden one's self to all sorts of things, and it is no use moping and brooding over troubles that cannot be altered. If Jemima wants to go out, perhaps we had better not wait any longer." And then he lighted his reading lamp, and unfolded his paper. In spite of the well-cooked chops, supper had certainly not been more festive than usual.

And then a strange fancy came to Thorold. How would it be with him if some younger, brighter face were to be opposite to him, evening after evening. Would not his home, humble as it was, be a very different place? He knew why he was happier in his chambers at Lincoln's Inn. To his reserved temperament, solitude was far preferable than uncongenial fellowship with this small human soul, this weary little pilgrim forever carrying her heavy pack of worries.

"Poor dear Joa," he said to himself, for his keen eyes had noticed the reddened eyelids. "Very likely she remembers that it is Tristram's birthday, and that he is thirty-eight to-day."

Jemima had cleared the table and vanished. He was still alone, and Rabat-la-Koum was curled up like a huge grey ball at his feet; the leading article was unusually clever, and absorbed him until a sudden fragrance pervaded the room, and there stood Joanna at his elbow with a steaming cup of coffee.

"I waited until Jemima went out, and then I made it myself. It is very strong coffee, Thorold, and it will do your head good." Joanna's voice was a little more cheerful as she said this, and the slight flush from her exertions made her look younger.

Thorold was quite touched; he put out his hand and patted his sister's arm caressingly. "How good of you to take so much trouble, my dear! I never thought of the coffee again. Sit down, Joa, and let us be comfortable. I have been wanting to tell you something all the evening."

"Have you, indeed?" and Joanna brightened. "Wait a moment. I want to wind some wool. I can hear you talk all the same. And yet I must mention one thing before you begin. The gas man called for his account, and you forgot to leave the cheque."

"Did I? I was in a hurry. But I will write it before I go to bed."

"Thank you. And there is one other thing, Thorold. If Jemima goes at her month, as she threatens, will she not forfeit her wages? You are a lawyer, so you ought to know."

"I am quite sure Jemima means to do nothing of the kind," he returned, impatiently. "Look here, Joa, she is the best servant we have had yet, and I would rather raise her wages than part with her. Take my advice for once, praise her a little more and find fault with her a little less; and if you are wise you will leave her young man alone;" and then he drank his coffee, moodily. Joanna had quenched his attempt at conversation again. Joanna pondered Thorold's advice as she unravelled her skein of yarn; it was somewhat tangled, and as she pulled it with nervous jerks, the yarn snapped and the ball rolled from her hand.

Thorold suppressed a forcible interjection as he groped under his chair for the ball. If ever he married, he determined that one of the first rules he would make for his wife's guidance would be that all wool-winding should be done by daylight.

Joanna had a tiresome habit of leaving a tangled skein for the comparative leisure of the evening hours. Thorold used to wonder sometimes if all her skeins were tangled. It got on his nerves sometimes and spoilt the enjoyment of his reading. Joanna's limp, nerveless movements, her jerky beginnings and abrupt endings, her brief spasms of energy, and the inevitable hunt for the unlucky ball, irritated him at times beyond endurance. It is quite ridiculous and almost derogatory to one's dignity to think how much daily life is marred by these small frets and torments. The buzzing of a bluebottle against the window-pane is certainly preferable to a brass band when the instruments are cracked, but the whizzing and fizzing of the insect may in time jar on the ear; and to thin-skinned people a midge's bite is fruitful of irritation.

Joanna was making up her mind slowly that her brother had given her good counsel, and that perhaps it would be well for her to follow it. Thorold was the master of the house, and if he wished to keep Joanna, of course the girl must stay. And when Joanna had arrived at this point, she broke the thread of her yarn again.

"I thought there was something you wanted to tell me, Thorold," she said, rather reproachfully, when she had found a new beginning. "I have brought my work and am ready to talk, but you do nothing but read." Then Thorold threw down his paper impatiently.

"I thought you were too busy with that work," he returned, rather curtly; "and, after all, it does not matter. It was only about my own business affairs."

"Oh, but I want to hear it," replied his sister, with much mild obstinacy. "It is seldom that you do care to talk to me, Thorold;" and here Joanna's voice was decidedly plaintive. "I sometimes think that if it were not for finding fault with Jemima I should almost lose the use of my voice."

Thorold was fast losing patience. Joanna was in one of her most trying moods; she was at once aggressive and despondent. She was at all times very tenacious of her sisterly privileges, and nothing offended her more than being kept in the dark. Well, he might as well get it over and be done with it; but he would be as brief as possible. "I only wanted to tell you that I have had a very satisfactory interview with Murdoch & Williams."

"Oh, indeed"—and here Joanna frowned anxiously over her skein. "They are solicitors, are they not?"

"Yes, but they are very big people. Joa, I think I am likely to get the brief. You see"—warming to his subject—"our last case was so satisfactory, and we got our client such heavy damages, that Murdoch & Williams were quite pleased. The junior partner made himself very pleasant, and said all kinds of civil things."

"And you think you will get it, Thorold?" and Joanna actually laid down her skein.

"I shall certainly get it;" and Thorold's eyes flashed with triumph as he spoke; at such moments his face was full of expression. "It will be a big case, Joa, and Sergeant Rivington will be leading counsel on our side." And then again he told himself that his foot was on the rung of the ladder, and that he had begun to climb in earnest.

"I am very glad, Theo;" and Joanna's blue eyes were rather tearful. She and Tristram had often called him Theo, but she seldom used the old pet name now. Thorold smiled a little sadly as he heard it.

"I knew you would be pleased, dear;" and his voice softened. "It will make a great difference to our income. Joa, I have made up my mind that the last of the debts shall be paid off before Christmas, and we will begin the New Year free and untrammelled. There shall be an end of all your small peddling economies. We shall not be rich, but at least we need not hoard our cheese-parings and candle-ends."

"I do not know what you mean, Thorold!" returned Joanna, in a puzzled tone. "We never use candles except in the coal cellar."

Then Thorold gave a grim, unmirthful laugh. If he ever married, the lady of his choice should have some sense of humour; nothing is more harassing and trying to the temper than to have to talk down to the level of one's daily companion. Althea once said, rather wittily, that Joa's brains were like a nutmeg-grater—one had to rub one's nutmeg very hard before the spicy fragments would filter through it.

"Perhaps we may have a better house soon!" he said, after a pause. "I should like to be out of the town and higher up the hill. The air is fresher, and it would be quieter."

"Oh, yes, much quieter!" Joanna smiled, and a pretty dimple came into view; at that moment she looked almost like a girl.

"We must wait for our good things a little," continued Thorold; "but there is no need for us to stint ourselves. And Joa," here he hesitated—"why should you not smarten yourself up a bit. Get one or two new dresses, or any fal-lals you require"—for his keen, observant eyes had noticed that the old lilac silk that Joanna always wore of an evening, a relic of the old Manor House days, was faded and darned, and of obsolete fashion. He was a man who was always keenly alive to the wants and wishes of his womankind. But even as he made the suggestion, he wondered why Joanna was hoarding her five hundred pounds, and why she should not use a few pounds to replenish her scanty wardrobe. He knew, and had been very angry when he heard it, that Althea had actually presented her with a beautiful dress, for church; because she said Joa was too miserly to spend a penny on herself.

Joanna blushed slightly when Thorold made his good-natured proposition. "You are very kind, Theo," she said, gently, as she folded her white, nervous-looking hands over her skein, "but I go out so seldom, that I do not require many new dresses. I have Althea's merino, and"—eyeing her lilac silk complacently—"there is plenty of wear to be got out of my old gown yet!"

"Well, you know best," returned Thorold, indifferently. If he had stated his opinion candidly, he would have suggested that the gown in question should be relegated to Jemima or the rag-bag. Well, he had done his part nobly; and now he might take up Guizot's Life. But the next moment Joanna's plaintive tones arrested him.

"Theo, do you remember what day this is?" And as he nodded, she continued, mournfully, "Trist is eight-and-thirty to-day; it is actually ten years since we have seen him—ten long years." And now a slow tear or two welled down Joanna's face. "What a weary time it has been! And he and Ella have never written—not a line, not a single word, since their little girl was born."

"He was going to Australia then, and he seemed to write in good spirits—we have his letter still, Joa. He was so pleased with his little daughter, and the prospect of the new berth offered him!"

"Yes, but that was eight or nine years ago. Oh, Thorold, why does he never write? Do you think he has ceased to care for us?"

"No, my dear, certainly not," replied her brother, kindly; for he was moved by her deep dejection. "But you know how casual and happy-go-lucky the dear old chap always was. Bad habits grow stronger as we grow older—remember that, Joa. Trist never liked making little efforts. He hated writing letters even in his school days—probably he hates it still. And yet, for all that, he may be flourishing on some sheep farm or other."

But this view of the case did not comfort Joanna, and during the rest of the evening she shed silent tears over her tangled skein. And all the time, not half a mile away, a man and a child sat hand in hand over a smoky little cindery fire; the child's shivering form wrapped in an old Inverness cape.

"Is it always cold in England, father? Why does not Mrs. Grimson make up a big fire?"

"Well, you see coals are dear, Bet, and the stove is a small one; but my old coat is warm and thick. Why, you look as snug as a robin in its nest, or a squirrel in its hole, or a dormouse, or anything else you like to name. I wonder what Aunt Joa will think of my little Betty when she sees her?" Then the child laughed gleefully.

"Shall we really find them, father?"

"Of course we shall find them, my girlie; but we must not tire those poor little feet too much. Put them up on my knee, darling, and dad will rub them and keep the chilblains away." And then, as he took the tiny feet in his hand, Bet's thin little arm went round his neck.

"Oh, father, I do love you so. It makes me ache all over to love you so hard;" and then Bet rested her rough, tangled head against her father's shoulder.

CHAPTER XIX.: A CHECK FOR THE BLACK PRINCE.

Before many days had passed Waveney had settled down happily at the Red House; and though she still missed Mollie, and had to combat frequent pangs of home-sickness, her environment was so pleasant, and her work so congenial, that it would have seemed to her the basest ingratitude not to be thankful for her advantages.

Sweet temper, and high principles, are important factors in a girl's happiness. Waveney knew she was walking in the path of duty, and that she had done the right thing in severing herself from the home life. A sense of independence and well-doing sweetened her daily duties, and at night, after she had prayed for her dear ones, she would sleep as calmly and peacefully as a tired child.

"I think Waveney is happy with us," Althea said, once, in a satisfied voice; and, indeed, at that moment the girl's clear notes were distinctly audible, singing to herself in the corridor, as she had been accustomed to sing in the old house in Chelsea. Waveney's duties were not very irksome. When Althea's eyes troubled her, her young companion would spend the morning and the greater part of the evening reading to her or writing from her dictation; and in this way Waveney gained a great deal of valuable information.

"It is a liberal education to talk to my dear Miss Althea," she would say to Mollie. "She is so clever, and knows so much, and yet she thinks so little of herself. I believe I love and admire her more every day."

"But you like Miss Doreen, too?" observed Mollie, tentatively.

"Oh, yes, I am quite fond of her, and she is always as nice as possible. But she could never come up to Queen Bess; she is more earthly and commonplace. But, there, I am not expressing myself properly. Miss Althea is human, too, but she is so much more sympathetic and picturesque."

"But the old ladies at the Home like Miss Doreen best," retorted Mollie.

"Yes, dear, old ladies are her specialities, and girls are Miss Althea's. You would think, sometimes, to hear her talk, that she was a girl herself, and knew exactly how they felt. Some of them almost worship her, and no wonder."

"I wish I could see her," sighed poor Mollie. "I love her, too, for being so good to you"—for her unselfish nature knew no taint of jealousy. When Althea's eyes were in good order, Waveney merely wrote a few letters, or copied some extracts neatly and then her duties in the library were over.

Sometimes she would walk across to the Home and read for an hour to the blind lady, Miss Elliot, or she would do little errands in the town for one or other of the sisters. Sometimes she would carry the weekly basket of flowers that Althea always sent to Joanna. But she never thoroughly enjoyed her visits. She told Mollie that Miss Chaytor was a rather depressing sort of person.

"I daresay she is good and amiable," she observed; "she must have virtues, or Miss Althea would not be so fond of her. But she looks as though she has been out too long in a bleak wind, and has got nipped and pinched. I think if she would only speak more briskly and cheerfully, that she would feel better; she wants prodding, somehow, like the old coster-monger's donkey;" and Mollie laughed at this.

Waveney certainly had her good times. Althea had presented her with a beautiful racket and a pair of tennis shoes, and on Thursday afternoons she and Nora Greenwell played tennis on the new asphalt court behind the Porch House. She also joined Mr. Chaytor's Shakespeare readings; they were to get up The Merchant of Venice next, and to her secret delight the part of Jessica was allotted her.

Mr. Chaytor took no special notice of her; she sat amongst the other girls, and listened to his instructions. Sometimes, when Thorold had finished some masterly declamation, he would look up suddenly from his book. Waveney's little pale face and curly head were just opposite to him; the deep, spirituelle eyes seemed glowing with golden light. Where was she? Not in the Recreation Hall, but on some marble steps belonging to a Doge's palace. The dark water was washing almost to her feet; gondolas were passing and repassing in the moonlight; grey-bearded men, in velvet doublets and ruffs, were standing in a group, under the deep archway; and Portia, in her satin gown, was walking with proud and stately step, followed by her train.

"It is your turn, Miss Ward," observed Thorold, quietly. And then, as Waveney started and flushed, he bit his lip with an effort to suppress a smile. He knew, by a sort of intuitive sympathy, where her thoughts had strayed. Her absorbed attention pleased and flattered him; he began to feel interested in so promising a pupil. "Miss Greenwell reads better," he thought; "but I doubt if she grasps the full meaning and beauty of a passage as Miss Ward does." And on more than one evening the little pale face, and dark, vivid eyes seemed to haunt him. Strangely enough he had used Doreen's comparison. "She is like Undine," he said to himself; and somehow, the name seemed to suit her.

Waveney's Sundays were always her happiest days; they were red-letter days and high festivals to her, as well as to Mollie; but each time she went home she thought Mollie looked lovelier, and on each occasion she found relics of the Black Prince.

The grapes had long ago been eaten, but a generous box of Paris chocolate had replaced them, and there were always fresh hot-house flowers in the red bowl. Mollie, who was becoming hardened, scarcely blushed as she pointed them out, and informed Waveney quite coolly that a hare or a brace of pheasants were hanging up in the larder.

"Sir Reynard at his tricks still," thought Waveney. And one evening she did give her father a hint. "Dad," she said, a little nervously, for she felt her task a delicate one, "Mr. Ingram is very kind to dear Mollie—he is always bringing her things, and of course she is pleased; but I do not think he ought to come so often when she is alone."

Everard started and looked at her. His little girl had plenty of penetration and sense, as he knew.

"No, dear; I suppose you are right," he said, slowly. "I will talk to Miss Mollie, and she must give Mr. Ingram a hint. The little Puss has encouraged him, I suppose." And then he frowned, and said, a little anxiously, "You don't think the fellow is making up to her, eh, Waveney?"

"Father, dear, how can we tell? Mollie is such a great baby in these sort of things; I think she fancies that she is not grown up yet, but she is nineteen. Dad, I think he must like her a little; but he ought only to come to the house when you are at home. Won't you try and find out all about him?"

But Mr. Ward shook his head; he hardly knew how that was to be done

"He is a gentleman," he returned, rather gravely, "and he is a good fellow—I am sure of that; and he has plenty of means. I like Mr. Ingram; he is a little eccentric, but he is honourable and straightforward. I would take my oath of that. Well, well, I will give Mollie a good strong hint." And Mr. Ward kept his word.

So a day or two later, when Mr. Ingram walked into the studio with some fresh flowers and a beautifully bound volume of Jean Ingelow's poems under his arm, that Mollie had innocently remarked that she longed to read, Mollie seemed hardly as pleased as usual to see him; she even turned a little pale when he presented the book with one of his joking speeches.

"Oh, thank you; you are very kind," she stammered, fluttering the pages. "And you have written my name in, too!" Mollie spoke hurriedly and breathlessly; she had not even asked him to sit down.

Mr. Ward's hint had certainly been a strong one.

Mr. Ingram looked at the girl a little keenly; then he took a chair and seated himself comfortably.

"What is it, Miss Mollie?" he said, gently. "You have something on your mind. Oh, you cannot deceive me," as Mollie blushed and shook her head. "I can read you like a book, and for some reason poor Monsieur Blackie is in disgrace."

"Oh, no, no!" protested Mollie, quite shocked at this. "You could not think me so ungrateful!"

"There can be no question of gratitude between you and me," returned the young man, gravely; and he looked a little pained. Then, as Mollie's sweet, wistful face seemed to plead forgiveness, he recovered himself with an effort.

"I am only troubled because I am afraid of hurting you," she went on; "and I am sorry, too, because I do so enjoy your visits. We know so few people, Mr. Ingram; but father said——" But here Mollie utterly broke down. And why ever was Mr. Ingram looking at her in that way? Was he angry or unhappy?

"You do not surely mean, Miss Mollie, that your father has forbidden my visits?" And now it was Mr. Ingram's turn to look pale.

"Oh, no, no!" gasped Mollie, "how could you think of anything so dreadful? Only father would like to see you sometimes and——" Then the stern look of gravity was no longer on Ingram's face.

"My dear Miss Mollie," he said, kindly, "please do not distress yourself so. Let me finish that sentence for you. Your father does not in the least object to my visits, but he would like me to pay them when he is at home, and he wishes you to tell me this."

"Oh, yes. Thank you; but how could you guess so cleverly?" and Mollie looked as though a world of care had rolled off her. But only an inscrutable smile answered her.

"Sir Oracle has spoken," he said, trying to resume his old manner. "Now, Miss Mollie, I may be an Idealist, but I can be practical, too. Will you kindly tell me on which afternoon I am likely to find your father."

"Only on Saturdays for certain."

"Very well, then, will you tell Mr. Ward, with my compliments, that unless his house be on fire nothing will induce me to ring his door-bell on Monday, Tuesday, Wednesday, Thursday, or Friday, unless by special invitation. But on Saturday I will do myself the pleasure of calling."

"Is that a message to father?" asked Mollie, a little puzzled at his tone. But Mr. Ingram only laughed and rose from his chair.

"I am rather a riddle to you, am I not?" he said, taking her soft little hand. And then his manner suddenly changed. "Miss Mollie," he continued, "do you remember the first time I saw you? You were sitting in the ashes, like Cinderella. I have called you Cinderella ever since."

"Oh, not really, Mr. Ingram! But, of course, I remember the day, for I was never so startled in my life. When the door opened I thought it was Ann, and, oh dear, how frightened I was for a moment!"

"It was like a picture," went on Ingram, and his eyes looked grave and intent. "The kitchen was a little dark, but a ray of sunshine was full on your face, and you were singing. Do you remember, Miss Mollie?" And Mollie hung her head, as though she were rather ashamed of herself.

"Oh, yes, that old song of father's." And then, rather pettishly, "But I don't want to remember that."

"I shall never forget it. I wish I were the Fairy Godmother instead of Monsieur Blackie. And then there is the Prince. What are we to do about the Prince, Miss Mollie?"

"Oh, I don't know," murmured Mollie, confusedly; for Mr. Ingram's manner was rather baffling that afternoon. But how amused he would be if he knew that Waveney often called him the Black Prince. "There never are princes in real life," she finished, demurely.

"Oh, I would not be too sure of that," he returned, coolly. "Life is full of surprises. Why, I heard of a fellow last year—he was only a dairy-man, and a rich uncle who had made his pile in Chicago, and was a millionaire, died, and left him all his money. He told me in confidence that for the first month he was nearly out of his mind with worry, for he and his wife had not a notion what to do with it. I gave him a lot of advice. I told him to give his children the best education possible, and to live comfortably without trying for grandeur; and he was a sensible fellow, and followed my advice. He has a good house, and a model farm, and his breed of Alderney cows is the finest in the country; and I have a great respect for him and his wife, and often go and see them."

Mollie was much impressed with this story; she was sorry when Mr. Ingram took his leave. He had paid such a very short visit, and she knew her father's message was the cause. But he had quite recovered his spirits, for, as he went downstairs, she could hear him singing to himself in a low, melodious voice:

"'Here's to the maiden of bashful fifteen,   Here's to the widow of fifty,   Here's to the flaunting, extravagant quean, And here's to the housewife that's thrifty. Let the toast pass, Drink to the lass, I'll warrant she'll prove an excuse for the glass.'"

Waveney was far happier in her mind when she heard from Mollie that Mr. Ingram's visits were always to be paid on Saturday afternoons; and even Mollie owned that she preferred this.

"You see, Wave," she explained, "it is a little awkward entertaining Mr. Ingram all by myself. If I were like you I should not mind it so much; but I never can talk properly, and he is so dreadfully clever."

"Well, he has travelled and seen the world; but he is not clever like Mr. Chaytor, Mollie. That man is a perfect well of knowledge." But this comparison did not seem to please Mollie.

"I think Mr. Ingram clever," she persisted, "and so does father. He said last evening that he was a thoroughly well-informed man. Oh, Wave, I forgot to tell you something. I asked him yesterday how long he meant to stay in Chelsea, and he looked quite surprised at the question. He said he had not been staying there for weeks, and that he was at his diggings as usual, but that he generally spent a night or two in town every week. 'When I am up in town, I always sleep at my club,' he said. Now, Waveney, is it not odd that he has never told us where he lives? And I did not like to ask him." And Waveney assented to this.

The following Sunday, when Waveney went home, she found Mollie in a state of great excitement.

It was a cold, November afternoon, and a dull moisture seemed to pervade everything. The pavements were wet and greasy, the horses' coats steamed, and the raw dampness was singularly penetrating. As the two girls hurried along, arm-in-arm, Mollie poured out her story breathlessly.

"Oh, Wave, you will never guess; such a wonderful thing is going to happen! Mr. Ingram has got a box at St. James's Theatre for Wednesday for Aylmer's Dream, and he has actually invited father, and Noel, and me; and father says we may go."

"Aylmer's Dream," returned Waveney. "I heard Mr. Chaytor talking about that to Miss Althea. He told her that she and Miss Doreen ought certainly to see it—that Miss Leslie's representation of the crazed Lady Aylmer was the most perfect piece of acting; and Mr. Sargent as Sir Reginald Aylmer was almost as fine."

"Yes, I daresay," interrupted Mollie, impatiently; for she had no wish to discuss the merits of the play beforehand. "But do listen to me, Wave, dear; Mr. Ingram will fetch us in a carriage, and he has promised to go early, so that I may see the curtain draw up. I shall wear my white dress. But what am I to do for a nice wrap?" Mollie's voice was a little troubled, and for the moment Waveney did not answer. She realised at once the difficulty of the situation.

"I shall not draw my salary until Christmas," she said, presently. "That will be a month hence; and we must not ask father for any money."

"No, certainly not."

"Well, then, we must just make the best of it," went on Waveney. "Your black jacket is impossible, and so is your waterproof. So there only remains 'Tid's old red rag of a shawl'"—a title they had borrowed from a charming tale they had read in their childhood.

"Oh, Waveney, dear, mother's old red shawl!" and Mollie's voice was decidedly depressed.

"What will Mr. Ingram say?"

"He will say—at least, he will think—that you look sweet. How could he help it, darling? Mother's shawl is warm, and in the gaslight it won't look so very shabby—you can throw it off, directly you get into the box. Father must buy you some new gloves; and, with a few flowers, you will do as well as possible." But though Mollie tried to take this cheerful view of the case, she did not quite succeed, and "Tid's old rag of a shawl" lay heavily upon her mind.

CHAPTER XX.: "DAD'S LITTLE BETTY."

"We have seen better days." Romeo and Juliet.
"Her little face, like a walnut shell, With wrinkling lines." Henley.

On Monday morning, when Waveney went into the library, Althea would always ask a kindly question or two about the previous evening, to which Waveney would gladly respond. But when the girl told her, with sparkling eyes, about Mollie's promised treat, and Mr. Ingram's kindness, she looked extremely surprised, and not a little amused.

Doreen, who had followed them into the room, and was hunting through the book-shelves for a volume she needed, turned with an exclamation. But Althea put her finger on her lip, with a warning gesture.

"Aylmer's Dream! Why, that is the very play that Thorold is so anxious for us to see," she observed, calmly. "Why should we not have a box, too? You are driving into town this afternoon, Dorrie, and you can easily go to St. James's. It will be a treat for Waveney—and you know we always intended to go."

"Yes, but not on Wednesday," returned Doreen, in a doubtful tone. But again Althea looked at her meaningly. As for Waveney, she was speechless with delight.

Althea sent her into the dining-room the next moment to fetch the Times and Doreen took instant advantage of her absence.

"Althea, are you serious? Do you really wish me to take a box for Wednesday?"

"Oh, yes," returned Althea, flushing a little; but there was a mischievous smile on her lips, "I am quite serious. Moritz is masquerading, and I want to find out his little game. My lord is too busy to call on his old friends. But I will be even with him. Hush! here the child comes, Dorrie. We will have a nice little drama of our own on Wednesday. I long to see pretty Mollie, and that 'lad of pairts,' Noel, and it will be a grand opportunity." Then, as Waveney returned with the paper, Doreen contented herself with a disapproving shake of the head. Althea was very impulsive, she thought, when she at last left the room. It was all very well to talk about Moritz, but she feared that she was putting herself in an awkward situation. Everard Ward would be there as well as Mollie and Noel, and they could hardly leave the theatre without speaking to him. But, old maid as she was, the idea of hinting this to Althea made her feel hot all over. "Althea would only laugh at me, and pretend not to understand," she said to herself; "and if she makes a plan, nothing will induce her to give it up."

In truth Althea was quite enamoured of her little scheme. "Now, Waveney," she said, in a mysterious voice, "you are not to say one syllable to Mollie, mind that!"

"Is it to be a surprise?" asked Waveney, opening her eyes as widely as the wolf in Red Riding Hood.

"Why, of course it is. We will all remain snugly hidden at the back of our box until the curtain draws up, and then they will be too absorbed to notice us. Think how delightful it will be to see Mollie's start of astonishment, when at last she catches sight of you!"

"Oh, what fun it will be!" exclaimed the girl, joyfully. "Yes, yes, it will be far better not to tell

Mollie; but I hope she will not call out when she sees me. Monsieur Blackie, too, and father and Noel. Oh, Miss Althea, how glorious it will be! There; I am forgetting your letters, and you wanted them written for the early post;" but Althea only smiled indulgently.

Waveney could settle to nothing properly that day; she had only been to the theatre twice in her life, and then only in the gallery. But to be in a box!—well, her excitement was so great that she took a long walk over the Common to calm herself.

Presently an unwelcome thought obtruded itself. Her white frock was losing its freshness with constant wear, but there was no possibility of buying a new one until Christmas, and she had no suitable wrap—not even "Tid's old red rag of a shawl." For a moment she was full of dismay, then, with her usual good sense, she determined to confide the difficulty to Miss Althea. She found her opportunity that very evening. Althea listened to her attentively. "My dear child," she said, very kindly, when Waveney had finished, "do you know the same thought occurred to me; but there is no need to trouble yourself. I have two or three evening cloaks that Peachy will not let me wear because she says they do not suit me, and of course you can have one. Oh, yes, there is a blue plush one that will just do." And Waveney thanked her delightedly.

There was nothing now to mar her enjoyment or to damp her anticipation. And the next morning a letter from Mollie gave her fresh pleasure.

"Oh, Wave, darling," it began, "it is so late, and father says I ought to be in bed; but I must write and tell you about such a wonderful thing that has just happened. I was mixing father's salad for supper and thinking how he would enjoy it with the cold pheasant when the door-bell rang, and the next minute Ann brought in a big box—one of those cardboard boxes that always look so tempting. It was from Marshall & Snelgrove, she said, and there was nothing to pay; and there was my name, 'Miss Mollie Ward,' written as plainly as possible. Oh, dear, how excited I was? But father would not let me cut the string, and he was such a time fumbling over the knots; and all the while he was laughing at me and calling me an excitable little goose.

"There were layers and layers of tissue paper, and then—oh, Wave, dear! never, never in all our lives have we seen such a cloak! I was almost afraid even to touch it. Father was right when he said rather gravely that it was more fit for one of the young Princesses of Wales than for his daughter.

"But I must try to describe it. It is a rich ivory silk, with a lovely pattern running through it that looks like silver, and it is so warm and soft, and lined with the faintest and most delicate pink, like the palm of a baby's hand—that was father's idea; and all round is the most exquisite feather trimming. And when I put it on, father said I looked like a white pigeon in its nest.

"Oh, Wave, do you think that our good little Monsieur Blackie sent it? There was no name, no clue of any kind. What am I to do? Ought I to thank him for it? But there is no one else who would do such a kind thing; and yet if he did not send it, how awkward that would be! You must think over it and help me, darling.

"Mollie."

Waveney did not long delay her answer.

"I am delighted about the cloak, sweetheart," she wrote, "and he is the very Prince of Black

Princes, to make my sweet Moll so happy; and now mother's old red shawl can go back into the cedar box.

"Why, of course it is Monsieur Blackie. Do you suppose any other person would do such a delightfully unconventional thing. It is like a fairy story; it is Cinderella in real life, the pumpkin coach and all. But Mollie, take my word for it, he will never own it.

"Perhaps if you get an opportunity you might tell him that you had been much mystified by receiving a beautiful present anonymously, and that you greatly desired to thank the kind donor, and then you will see what he says. Oh, he is a deep one, Sir Reynard, and I should not be surprised if he professes entire ignorance on the subject. If I could only peep at you on Wednesday! 'Oh, had I but Aladdin's lamp, if only for a day!' I have been singing that ever since I read your letter." And then Waveney closed her note abruptly, for fear she should say too much; but some subtle feeling of delicacy prevented her from telling Althea. That the cloak was Mr. Ingram's gift she never doubted for a moment; but though she had written jokingly to Mollie, and called him the very Prince of Black Princes, in reality she was secretly dismayed.

"If he loves her, why does he not tell her so?" thought the girl, anxiously, "instead of showering gifts on her in this Oriental fashion. Is it because Mollie is so unconscious and that she will not see, and this is his way of winning her? Mr. Ingram does nothing like other men; he is an Idealist, as he says. He is good and kind, but he is not good enough for my Mollie. She is worth a king's ransom; she is the dearest, and the loveliest, and the best;" and here Waveney broke down and shed a few tears, for her heart felt full to overflowing with mingled pride and pain.

Waveney had some errands to do in the town that afternoon, and amongst other things she had to take the usual basket of flowers to Miss Chaytor.

Waveney never cared for these visits. She liked Mr. Chaytor—he interested her more than any man she had ever seen; but his sister bored her. She told Mollie once that "she was as soft and damping as a November mist."

She found her this afternoon in one of her most depressing moods. She had been having an argument with Jemima, and, as usual, had retired baffled from the contest. Jemima was a clever girl, and had long ago taken her mistress's measure; and she had an invariable resource on these occasions.

"If I don't suit you, ma'am, I can leave this day month," she would say, crushingly; and then Joanna would hurriedly reply, "Please don't talk nonsense, Jemima. You suit me very well. But all the same you had no right to stand talking to the milkman for a quarter of an hour. Well, ten minutes, then," as Jemima, with some heat, protested against this; "and I will thank you to be more careful for the future."

Waveney heard the whole history of Jemima's misdemeanours. Joanna had taken a fancy to the girl, and often mentioned her to her brother. "She has such a pretty manner, and she is bright and sympathetic. She is just the person for Althea;" and Thorold had assented to this.

Joanna wanted her to stay to tea; but Waveney had had an excuse ready—she was only too glad to get out of the house. Her own vitality was so strong, and the interest of her own personality so absorbing, that she could not understand how any human existence could be so meagre and colourless as Miss Chaytor's seemed to be. "Is it because she is an old maid?" thought the girl, as she walked over the bridge. "If Mollie or I did not marry, should we ever be like that?" and then she added, piously, "Heaven forbid!"

What was it Miss Althea had said that first Sunday morning, as they walked through the village?—that it always made her angry when people talked of empty, blighted, or disappointed lives, and that it was their own fault if they did not find interests. "I wondered at the time what Miss Althea could mean," she said to herself; "it sounded a little hard. But I have thought it out since. We must fertilise and enrich our lives properly, and not let them lie fallow too long; there is no need that any life should be thin and weedy. I suppose Miss Chaytor has had her troubles, but she is not without her blessings, too. I daresay her brother is very good to her. Oh, yes, certainly, Miss Chaytor has her compensations."

Waveney had finished all her errands, but she meant to take a turn on the Embankment. The grey, November afternoon had a certain charm for her. It was not at all cold, and she wanted to sit down for a few minutes and watch the barges being tugged slowly against the tide. How mysterious they looked, emerging from the dark arches of the bridge! Already they were lighting the gas, and bright flickers were perceptible across the river. A faint wind was flapping the brown and tawny sails of some vessels that were waiting to be unladen; they reminded her of the tattered pennons in the chapel at Chelsea Hospital. And then she thought sadly of the dear old sergeant.

He had died peacefully in his sleep about a week after her visit, and his last conscious words had been about Sheila.

Mollie had seen the corporal two or three times, and one Sunday she and Waveney had gone over to the Hospital. The little corporal had looked aged and dwindled; but at the sight of Waveney he had brightened.

"Aye, he is gone," he said, in a subdued voice. "McGill is gone, and I am fairly lost without him. Ah! he was a grand man for argufying, and would stick to his guns finely. 'For it stands to reason,' says I, 'that a man with two eyes can see farther than a blind one'—not that McGill was blind then?—'and I'll take my oath that there were only two of those darned black niggers'; and then, how he would speechify and bluster, and there would be a ring round us in no time—and 'Go it, McGill!' and 'Up at him, corporal!' Ah, those were grand times. But the Lord gave and the Lord hath taken away"—and here Corporal Marks bared his grey head. "And must you be going, Miss Ward? Well, good-bye, and God bless you!" And now the slow tears of age were coursing down the corporal's wrinkled face.

"Aye, Jonadab frets sorely after his old comrade," remarked Nurse Marks, when Waveney told her about her interview with the corporal. "What is it we are told, my lamb?—'One taken and the other left'; and it stands to reason that the world is a poorer place for him."

Waveney was thinking about her old friends as she seated herself on a bench overlooking the river. At the farther corner a little girl was sitting. But there was no one else in sight.

Waveney was fond of children, so she smiled and nodded to the child in quite a friendly way.

"You must not sit long, or you will take cold, my dear!" she said.

"Oh, I am always cold," returned the child, in a plaintive little voice, "and I am tired, too, for I have got two bones in my legs, and they do ache so!"

Waveney looked at her curiously; she was not a pretty child—indeed, it was rather a singular little face, with oddly pronounced features. She had pathetic-looking eyes, and fair hair, which she wore in a long plait, and in spite of her shabby dress and worn boots her voice was refined and sweet. When she made her little speech, she sidled up to Waveney in the most confiding way.

"Do you have bones in your legs, too—but you are one of the grown-ups; grown-ups don't mind being tired. Daddie says when my legs grow longer they will leave off aching, and I suppose daddie knows."

"Poor mite!" thought Waveney, pityingly; and then she said, kindly, "Are you alone, little one? Is your home near?" But the child shook her head.

"Daddie and I have not got any home," she returned, wearily. "There aren't any homes in England, are there? We live with Mrs. Grimson in Chapel Road. I think she is a good woman," she continued, gravely, in her old-fashioned way; "she bathed my feet so nicely when I got wet. But I don't like her rooms; they are not like my own dear home."

"Where was your home, my dear!" asked Waveney, taking the little cold hand in hers; but the child hesitated.

"We had many homes, but they were all across the sea, a long, long way off. We came in a big ship, with such a nice captain. Daddie's gone to Hamerton to look for Aunt Joa, and Mrs. Grimson's Susan left me here. I never knew before that grown-ups could be lost, but we have been looking for Aunt Joa, till I have got the aches in my legs, and we have not found her yet!"

This was rather puzzling to Waveney, but she was one of those motherly girls who knew by instinct how to win a child's heart, so she only cuddled the cold little hands comfortably, and asked her if she had a pretty name. Then the little girl smiled, showing a row of white, pearly teeth as she did so.

"Dad and I think it nice," she returned, nodding her head; "but it is very short. Daddie says I am too small to have a big name. I am Betty," with an important air. "Dad's little Betty. But dad does always call me Bet. Is your name long or short?"

Waveney was about to answer this friendly question when a man's voice behind them made her start.

"Why, Bet," it said, "why are you perched up here, like a lost robin? And Susan has been looking for you half over the place."

"It is my daddie. It is my dear dad," cried the child, joyously, and the next moment she was running to meet a tall man, who was walking quickly towards them.

Waveney watched the meeting. She saw the man stoop and kiss the little one fondly; and then Bet took hold of his rough coat and drew him towards the seat.

"Susan was naughty, dad. She did tell me to sit there, and she would fetch me, and she did never come at all, but this young lady was very kind, so I did not cry."

"That's my brave little Bet." And then the man took off his hat to Waveney. "Thank you, very much," he said, heartily. "I was obliged to leave my little girl, and I am afraid they neglected her."

Waveney felt vaguely perplexed. The man's face, and even his voice, seemed strangely familiar to her, and yet she was sure she had never seen him before. He was a handsome man, though his face looked weather-beaten and somewhat worn. His clothes were rough and shabby, but his voice was unmistakably cultured; he had evidently seen better days.

"Susan is not always naughty," observed Betty. "She gave me a peppermint once, and it was very nice. Dad, dear, did you find Aunt Joa?" Then the man shook his head in rather a depressed way.

"No, Bet, and we are still down on our luck. There is no such name at Hamerton. Perhaps this lady may know it"—and then he looked a little eagerly at Waveney. "I am a stranger in these parts. Can you tell me if any one of the name of Chaytor lives at Dereham?"

"Why, yes," returned Waveney, surprised by the question. "Miss Chaytor and her brother live in High Street."

"And their names?—their Christian names, I mean?" asked the stranger, hoarsely.

"Mr. Chaytor's name is Thorold," returned Waveney, simply, "and his sister is Joanna." Then the man snatched up the child in his arms; he seemed almost beside himself. "Thank God, we have found them, Bet. My dear old Theo and Joa! Oh, what a fool I have been, going so far afield, and all the time they are actually at Dereham;" and then he sat down, and a few words cleared up the mystery.

About an hour later, as Joanna was drawing the crimson curtains over the window, Jemima threw open the door with a little fling.

"There is a child outside wanting to speak to you, ma'am. I would not let her into the passage, because she might have come to beg; but she said she wanted Miss Chaytor most particular."

"Very well, Jemima, I will go and speak to her;" and Joanna, who was very tender-hearted and never turned away a tramp unfed, went quickly to the door.

A little girl, a tiny creature, was standing there. She looked up in Joanna's face wistfully.

"Oh, please will you tell me if you are Miss Chaytor—Miss Joanna Chaytor," correcting herself with careful pronunciation.

"That is my name, certainly," returned Joanna, rather surprised at this. "And what do you want with me, my little girl?"

"Oh, please, Aunt Joa," returned the child, "I am Betty, dad's little Betty, and daddy is at the gate." And then, the next moment, a man's shadow was distinctly visible.

CHAPTER XXI.: A CHILD'S CREED.

Thorold Chaytor was not an imaginative man; he was neither emotional nor impressionable, and more than once lately he had puzzled himself over the singular persistency with which his long-lost brother Tristram haunted him. For the last two or three years he had hardly thought of him, but now, as he crossed the bridge of an evening, little tricks of speech and long-forgotten scenes would recur to his memory; but he never spoke of this to Joanna.

"Poor old Trist, I hope nothing has happened to him," he said to himself one evening, when the impression of his brother's presence had been so unusually strong that the familiar face had seemed as though it had been limned against the darkness. And then he thought sadly, and shuddered at the thought, how it was a well-known psychological fact that people at the point of death had often appeared, or rather seemed to appear, to some relative or friend.

"Of course, it is only animal magnetism—the transmission of thought—the influence of one mind over another," he thought—"a strong wave-beat of sympathy. But I should not have thought that I was the man for that sort of experience." And then he put this latch-key into the door, and let himself in.

As he hung up his hat on its accustomed peg, he was aware of an unusual silence in the house. The parlour door was not opened, and there was no Joanna, with her irritating question, "Is that you, Thorold?" Neither did he hear her soft, gliding footsteps overhead.

"Perhaps she has gone to the Red House after all," he said to himself. And the thought of an evening of blissful solitude pleased him well. But as he entered the sitting-room, he started. There were no preparations for the evening meal. The tea-things were still on the table, and, to his intense surprise, a child—actually a child—was fast asleep on the couch by the fire.

Thorold crossed the room softly, and contemplated the little stranger with puzzled eyes. "It must be one of Joa's waifs and strays," he thought—for he was aware of his sister's charitable propensities. And yet she hardly looked like a tramp's child.

"Very likely the poor little thing has lost her way, and Joa is taking her in for the night," he continued. "Poor child, she seems tired out." And then his eyes softened, as he noticed how carefully Joanna had wrapped her up in her old fur cloak.

The next moment he heard his sister's footsteps on the stairs, and went out into the passage to question her. But when he saw her face, he was struck dumb with astonishment.

Joanna was looking radiant. She was dimpling and smiling like the girl Joa of old, and her blue eyes were shining through happy tears.

"Oh, Thorold, why are you so late. We have wanted you so!" And Joanna's thin white hands grasped him almost convulsively.

"Who is that child?" he whispered, loudly. "Is it some one you have found in the street?" Then, in her excitement, she gave him an hysterical little push.

"You have seen her! Oh, Thorold, is she not like him? His little Betty! My darling Tristram's little Betty!" and as he stared at her, and turned pale—for a sudden prevision of the truth had come to him—she sobbed out, "Yes, yes, Tristram has come—he is upstairs; he is in your room,

Thorold. Go to him, dear, while I get your supper ready." And then Thorold drew a long breath, and darted upstairs. And Joanna, crying softly, out of sheer bliss and gratitude, busied herself in womanly ministrations.

Thorold was thankful to meet his brother alone. In spite of his reserve he was a man of deep feelings, and when he felt Tristram's mighty grasp of his hand, and heard his familiar voice say in broken accents, "Theo, dear old fellow!—dear old chap!" he was almost too moved to speak.

"Why have you not written to us all these years?" were his first coherent words; but Tristram shook his head—he had no excuse to offer. He had drifted from place to place, seeking work and not always finding it, and he did not wish his friends to know how hardly things had gone with him.

"I was always a proud beggar, Thorold," he said, with a sigh, "but my back is pretty well broken now, and there's Bet, you see."

"And Ella—where is your wife, Trist?" Then Tristram turned his head aside.

"Ella is dead. I buried her two years ago," he returned, sadly. "Poor dear Ella, she never had her good things in this life. 'You have taken me for better or for worse, but there has been no better in it at all,' I often said to her; but she never liked me to say it. Ah, she was the best wife a man could have, but she lies in the cemetery at Melbourne, and little Theo lies with her—I called him after you, old chap. But he never got over the fever. I think it was the loss of the boy that finished Ella, for she never seemed to hold up her head again."

Tristram evidently felt his wife's death acutely, and Thorold, with quiet tact, said a word or two of sympathy and then changed the subject.

Before their brief talk was over, and they went downstairs to join Joanna, Thorold found out that Tristram was utterly unchanged. The handsome ne'er-do-well, as Althea used to call him, was only a little older, and perhaps a trifle rougher, but he was the same irresponsible, happy-go-lucky, easy-tempered Tristram of old.

Shiftless and indolent, he had drifted wherever the tide of circumstance had carried him. Sometimes he had worked and at other times he had starved; but when any good Samaritan stretched out a helping hand and drew him out from the Slough of Despond, he would pull himself together and go on gaily, as though the sun of prosperity had always shone on him. Never were there two brothers so widely dissimilar. But Tristram was no evil-living prodigal, no black sheep, to be dreaded and shunned by all right-minded people; he had loved his wife, and had treated her well, and the poor woman had repaid him with the truest devotion; and now his sister had received him with tears of joy. His sins were the sins of a weak nature, a nature that disliked effort, and chose the softest paths for itself, and which landed him in strange places sometimes.

"I have made an awful muddle of my life," he said, when Thorold questioned him with kindly interest. "Don't you recollect the dear old governor said something of the kind on his death-bed? Upon my word, old chap, I think I am the unluckiest beggar that ever walked this earth. Nothing prospers with me. If I make a little money I somehow contrive to lose it. I am pretty nearly at the end of my tether, I can tell you that?"

"What made you leave Melbourne!" asked Thorold, in his calm, judicial way. Then Tristram shrugged his shoulders and seemed unwilling to answer the question.

"Well, I was a fool," he returned, presently; and he pulled his rough moustache a little fiercely. "The biggest fool out, if you will; but I got into a regular panic. There were two of them lying there, and Bet was seedy, and I got it into my head that the climate of Melbourne did not suit her; and then I thought what a fine thing it would be if Joa could look after her a bit. A child wants a woman's care; and as I smoked my pipe that evening I had such a fit of home-sickness that I was nearly crazy. I had a bit of money put by, and I took our berths the next day; and here we are, old chap, and you must just make the best of us;" and Tristram brought down his hand heavily on his brother's shoulder.

They went downstairs after this, and found Betty awake and sitting on her aunt's lap. The little one was chattering happily to her, and Joanna was fondly stroking the plait of fair hair. "So he says to me, 'You are dad's Betty, are you, my little Miss?' and I said, 'Yes, of course, Mr. Captain, that is what daddie does always call me,' and he laughed in his beard, oh! such a great laugh."

"Why, Bet, you chatterbox, are you talking about your friend the captain?" exclaimed Tristram. "Come here, you monkey, and speak to Uncle Theo;" and Betty came with ready obedience.

"I am very glad to see you, Uncle Theo," she said, gravely, slipping her little hand into his. And Thorold stooped down and kissed her cheek; then a little awkwardly he lifted her on his knee, and scrutinised the childish features. Bet's blue eyes opened rather widely; she was vaguely alarmed by her new uncle's solemnity.

"Daddie," she said, after a few minutes' silent endurance. "Does not Uncle Theo like me? He do stare so. And he has such big eyes." For, even to wee Betty, "the noticeable man, with large grey eyes" was a formidable being at close quarters.

They all laughed at this; and Thorold kissed her again, and told her to run to Aunt Joa and she would make her more comfortable. But to his astonishment Bet refused to leave him. Her nature was a curiously sensitive one, and she had got it into her small mind that her plain speaking had hurt him, and that she must somehow make it up with him.

"I don't mind big eyes if they are nice ones," she said, graciously; "and yours are pretty nice, Uncle Theo."

Bet was rather aggrieved when her flattering speech was received with fresh mirth. She was not so sure after that that she did not like Aunt Joa much the best.

When supper was over, Bet went to bed. Joanna had refused to part with her, and had carried her off to her own room. To the jaded, disappointed woman, the sight of Bet kneeling by the bedside and saying her simple prayers was very sweet and touching.

"God bless dear daddie, and my own dear mammie and dear little brother Theo, and Uncle Theo and Aunt Joa, too, for ever and ever.—Amen."

"Bet, darling," whispered Joanna, pressing the little white-gowned figure tenderly in her arms, "did father teach you those prayers?"

"Yes, he did teach me," returned Bet, sleepily; and then she roused up. "There was an old woman once, Aunt Joa, she was a silly old woman, and she did say to dad, 'Why do you let that baby pray for her mother? I am quite shocked,' and dad, he did say, 'I am sorry, ma'am, that you should be shocked, but I don't think the angels are a bit offended because my little girl asks God to bless one of the dearest of mothers.' Oh, I did laugh, I was so pleased when dad said that!"

When Joanna went downstairs, she found the two brothers talking over the fire. She sat down beside Tristram, but on this evening there was no tangled skein in her hands; they were folded placidly in her lap. It was occupation enough for her to look at Tristam's brown, weather-beaten face, and to listen to his voice. Now and then he looked at her with a kind smile.

"Trist, do you know that Thorold has nearly paid off father's debts?" she said, presently. Then Tristram regarded his brother almost with awe.

"Oh, you were always a fine fellow, Theo," he said, enviously. "You are the good elder brother, you know, and I am the prodigal." Here he sighed heavily. "Well, I am weary of my husks, I want to turn over a new leaf and settle down. You will find me some work, old chap, and I'll stick to it like a Trojan, I give you my word I will."

"Work is not so easy to find," returned Thorold, quietly, "but I will do what I can to help you. I am pretty busy myself, for I have to get up an important case. We will talk about ways and means to-morrow."

"Yes, and I must be going to my diggings now, or Mother Grimson will think I am lost. She's a decent body, Mother Grimson, and has been very good to my Bet." As Tristram rose from his chair, Joanna caught hold of his arm.

"Wait a moment, Trist—I want to ask Thorold something before you go. Why should not Trist and Betty come here?—at least for a time. There is plenty of room, and I could look after Bet— and Jemima is so fond of children. Do have them, my dear, it will make me so happy;" and Joanna timidly put her hand on Thorold's arm.

"No, no!" returned Tristram; but he spoke a little hoarsely. "You are a good creature, Joa, but I must not take advantage of your kindness. I have made my own bed, and it is a hard one, and I must lie on it." But he looked at his brother very wistfully as he said this.

There was no hesitation in Thorold's manner.

"Joanna is right," he said, calmly, "you had better come to us, Trist, at least for a time, while you are looking for a berth to suit you;" and Tristram accepted this offer with gratitude.

"Oh, Thorold, you have made us both so happy!" exclaimed Joanna, gratefully, when Tristram had left them. "Bet is such a darling, I could not bring myself to part with her." But Thorold only smiled at her without speaking.

When Joanna had gone up to her room, he sat down by the fire. He wanted to think over things quietly. The millstone that had been so long round his neck was slipping off, and now he must adjust his shoulders to a new burden.

The wanderer had returned, and he and his helpless child were to be received under his roof. Was he glad or sorry for this? Was the burden or the joy the greater? Would his home life be gladdened or still further depressed by these new inmates? Thorold could not answer these questions; his straightforward, sincere nature only grasped the one fact.

"It is my duty. With all his faults and follies, he is my only brother. God do so to me and more also, if I refuse to help my own flesh and blood!"

Althea was very much moved when Waveney carried home the news that evening. She drove down to High Street so early the next morning that Joanna was still doing her marketing. She found Tristram sitting by the fire, with Bet on his knee. He put down the child when he saw a stranger.

"Do you remember an old friend, Tristram?" she said, holding out her hand, and looking at him kindly. Then a sudden light dawned on him.

"Is it—can it be Althea?" he asked; and as she smiled he wrung her hands so energetically that she winced with pain. "Oh, yes, of course, I recognise you now. You are just the same, Althea. You are not a bit changed all these years."

"No, I have only grown older; we all do that, you know. And this is your little girl, Tristram? But she is not like you."

"No, Bet takes after her mother; but Ella was pretty, and Bet is not, bless her." Then Betty, who was snugly ensconced in Althea's arm, peeped out at her father with a protesting face.

"Did you want your little Bet to be pretty, dad?" she asked, rather sadly.

"No, my pet," he returned, laughing. "I don't want her any different."

"Oh, I am glad of that," returned the child; and then she frowned, anxiously. "You are quite sure, dad? I could try very hard, you know; every one can try hard to be pretty." And then, in a low voice, "And I could ask God to help me. Mother always did say, I might ask for anything I want; and I could just say, 'Dad wants his little girl to be real pretty, so please make me so for ever and for ever.—Amen.'"

Tristram looked at Althea with a smile; he was used to Bet's quaint speeches. He was surprised to see that Althea's eyes were full of tears.

"How beautiful it is!" she sighed. "The faith of little children, how it shames us poor worldlings!" But at that moment Joanna entered the room, and Bet, with a joyful exclamation, ran to meet her.

CHAPTER XXII.: BETWEEN THE ACTS.

"In all the humours, whether grave or mellow, Thou's such a touchy, testy, pleasant fellow,
Hast so much wit and mirth, and spleen about thee That there's no living with thee or without
thee." Addison (Spectator).
"The way is as plain as way to parish church."—As You Like It.

In all London there were no two happier girls than Waveney and Mollie Ward that Wednesday
evening; nevertheless, Mollie's cup of bliss lacked one ingredient to make it perfect. If only
Waveney were there!

If she had only known that at that very moment Waveney was peeping at her from the back of
the box opposite! "There is my dear Mollie," she whispered, excitedly; then Althea, much
perplexed, swept the boxes with her opera-glass.

She could not see the girl anywhere; but just opposite them, standing quite alone in the front of
a box, there was a young lady in a white silk cloak, and a pink shower bouquet in her hand, and
she had the sweetest and most beautiful face that Althea had ever seen.

"What a lovely girl!" she said to herself; and she was not surprised to see that opera-glasses
from all parts of the house were levelled in that direction; but the next moment she started—for
surely she recognized that dark, foreign-looking man who had just entered the box.

"Moritz!" she ejaculated. "Good heavens, could that exquisite young creature be Mollie Ward!"
and then Althea's colour changed as a slight, fair man joined them, followed by a tall,
aristocratic-looking youth with pince-nez.

"Father and Noel," whispered Waveney, in a voice of suppressed ecstasy; but only Doreen
heard her. Althea's lips were white and trembling; the lights were flickering before her eyes; the
tuning up of the instruments in the orchestra sounded harsh and discordant.

No, she had not expected this!—to find him so unchanged. It was twenty-one years since they
had met, and yet it seemed to her that it was the same Everard Ward whom she remembered so
well; he even wore the same white stephanotis in his coat.

He was a little older, perhaps, a trifle thinner, but it was the same perfect face. Distance and the
electric light softened down defects. Althea could not see how shiny and worn Everard's dress-
coat was any more than she could see the lines on his forehead and round his eyes, or the
threatened baldness; she only noticed that he stood in his old attitude, his head raised, and one
hand lightly twirling his moustache. Althea stifled a sigh. Well, she was glad to have seen him
again, very glad. When ghosts were troublesome it was well to lay them. And then, though her
woman's heart failed her, and she vaguely felt that Doreen had been wiser and more prudent than
she, she determined to pluck up spirit and play her little drama to the bitter end.

The curtain had now drawn up, and they were at liberty to seat themselves comfortably in the
front of the box. Mollie's and Waveney's eyes were fixed on the stage, but Mr. Ingram, who had
seen the play before, was not so engrossed. He had just discovered a picturesque little girl in a
sapphire blue cloak, and a curly babyish-looking head who reminded him of his little Samaritan;
he wanted to take another look at her, but he could only see her profile. And then Althea's long,

pale face and reddish hair came into view, and beside her Doreen's dark-complexioned features.

"Now what on earth has put it into my cousins' heads to come here to-night?" he said to himself, in a vexed voice. "It is not like Althea to spoil sport in this fashion. And they have brought little Miss Ward, too," and then he frowned and twisted his moustache fiercely, and growled under his breath, "Confound those women!" in quite irate fashion.

Any one who knew Mr. Ingram well—his mother, if he had one, or his sister—for there was certainly no wife en evidence—would have seen that he was greatly chagrined and perplexed; but, being a humourist and one of the most good-natured men living, he worked off his wrath harmlessly by parodying the well-known verse, and muttering it softly for his own refreshment:

"Oh, woman in our hour of ease A giddy flirt, a flippant tease, As aggravating as the shade By blind Venetian ever made. When pain and anguish wring the brow A veritable humbug thou."

And lo and behold! he was so pleased with his own cleverness that his exasperation died a natural death.

The first act was over before Mollie caught sight of Waveney, and then her delight and excitement were so great that her father had to gently admonish her that they were surrounded by strangers; and Noel, in a melodramatic whisper, threatened to take strong measures unless she behaved properly and left off kissing her hand like a crazy infant.

The next moment Mr. Ingram left his seat, and Althea, who guessed that he was coming across to them, went to the back of the box to receive him.

He looked at her gravely. "Et tu Brute!" he said, reproachfully, as he took her hand.

Althea laughed. "Oh, I was not spying on you, my lord," she returned, playfully; but he exclaimed,—

"Hush, for pity's sake!" in such an agonised tone that Althea nearly laughed again.

"That child does not hear us," she said, soothingly. "Shall we take a turn in the corridor?" And as he nodded assent, they went out together. Waveney had not even seen him enter the box; she was busily telegraphing to Mollie.

"Well, Moritz?" demanded Althea, in an amused tone, "you may as well make a clean breast of it. Why have you forgotten your poor old cousins at the Red House, and why are you masquerading in this mysterious fashion? They call you Mr. Ingram, these children, but you are not Mr. Ingram now; and though I am not curious—oh, not the least bit in the world!" as he smiled, provokingly; "I should like to know what it all means."

"What it means. Upon my word, Althea, you have asked a difficult question. One cannot always tell the meaning of things." And then Moritz pulled his moustache in a perplexed way. "Haven't you watched some boy throw a stone in a pond? It may be a mere pebble, but the circles widen and widen until the whole surface of the water is covered with intersecting circles?"

"Why, yes," she returned, coolly, "but we are not throwing stones just now, are we?"

"No, it was only a parable; I deal in parables sometimes. I was just flinging my little pebble for mere sport and idleness, when I called myself by my old name. I wanted to be incognito, to have no gaudy tag or bobtail attached to my hum-drum personality; only, you see, the play has lasted longer than usual."

"But why?" she persisted—but her tone was a little anxious. "Moritz, please do not think me disagreeable,—you were always a whimsical being, and only Gwen knows the extent of your eccentricities; but I am interested in these people." Here she caught her breath a little. "When Mr. Ward knows, he might not be pleased."

"Oh, I will take my chance of that," he returned, obstinately. But Althea had not finished all she had to say.

"We used to know him so well in the old days; he was constantly at Kitlands. No, I know you and Gwen never saw him there. You were living abroad those two years. But Thorold Chaytor knew him. I was thinking that all this masquerading might lead to awkward complications by and by."

"Nonsense!" he returned, quickly. "What makes you so faint-hearted? My dear cousin, there will be no complications at all." But Althea shook her head almost sadly.

"Listen to me," he went on, with increased animation. "It is a pretty little comedy in real life, and full of dramatic situations. I am enjoying my incognito immensely; it is the best bit of fun I have had since poor old Ralston died. In Cleveland Terrace I am Monsieur Blackie; I adore the name—it suits me down to the ground." Then, as Althea laughed, he took hold of her arm in a coaxing fashion.

"Althea, you are a good creature—you must promise to keep my secret for a little while. I have made all my plans and prepared my dénouement, and I shall want your help in carrying it out. No hints to Gwen, no treasonable correspondence! Gwen is a good girl, but her honesty is almost clumsy—it is yea, yea, and nay, nay, with her and Jack too. My masquerading, as you call it, would simply shock her. Now I have promised Miss Mollie to bring her sister to our box, and I must keep my word."

Perhaps Moritz's voice changed as he said this, but Althea looked at him rather earnestly.

"She is beautiful as an angel," she said, in a low voice. "Take care of yourself, Moritz." But only a flash of his eyes answered her. Certainly Althea looked very grave when she re-entered the box.

Mr. Ingram had warned Mollie that there must be no stage embrace, so she had to content herself by squeezing Waveney's hand at intervals.

The second act had already commenced, and until it had ended there could be no conversation between the sisters. But when the curtain fell for the second time Mollie dried her eyes—for she had been shedding a deluge of tears—sniffed daintily at her flowers, and then asked Waveney, in a loud whisper, if Miss Althea had given her that pretty cloak.

Waveney nodded. "Yes. Is it not sweet of her? She says I am to keep it. But, Mollie, dear, yours is almost too lovely. Do you know, Miss Althea would not believe you were Mollie Ward, because you were so beautifully dressed. Cinderella is turned into a princess to-night." And then she put her lips to Mollie's ear. "Did you find out anything from the Black Prince?"

"Yes—no—oh, please hush," returned Mollie, with a distracting blush, and a timid glance at Ingram. "No, dear, he will not own to it; but, of course, I know. There! the curtain is going up again, and we shall hear if that dear girl is really dead."

Mollie had made her little attempt while she was waiting for her father and Noel. Mr. Ingram had come early, but Mollie was already dressed, and limping up and down the room; for she was far too restless to sit still.

"I have brought you some flowers," he said, simply, as he handed her the magnificent bouquet. Then, as Mollie blushed and thanked him, she carefully rehearsed the little speech that she had prepared beforehand. He was looking at her cloak, admiring it. Yes, his eyes certainly expressed decided approbation.

"Mr. Ingram," she stammered—for tact and finesse were not strong points with Mollie, "do you know I have had a great surprise. I have had such a beautiful present. It came the other night, and there was no name and no address. And I do so want to thank the kind friend who sent it."

Mr. Ingram was arranging the flowers in his buttonhole. A leaf was awry, and he was the soul of neatness. Perhaps this was why he did not look at Mollie.

"Dear me," he said, quietly. "An anonymous gift! This sounds interesting. A little mystery always enhances the value of a thing."

"Oh, do you think so?" returned Mollie, rather nonplussed by his tone. "I suppose, being a girl, I think differently about that. I am sure that I should enjoy wearing my beautiful cloak a hundred times more if I could thank the giver."

"There now," observed Ingram, in a voice of supreme satisfaction, "I did not like to ask the question for fear you should think me inquisitive. And it is really that cloak that becomes you so well—that is the mysterious present—I congratulate you, Miss Mollie, I do indeed, for I never saw you look better in my life. Upon my word, if I were ordering an evening cloak for Gwen I would choose her just such another."

Poor Mollie. All this glib talk bewildered her, but she was far too grateful, and too much in earnest, to give up her point, so she only raised her lovely eyes to Ingram and said, very wistfully,—

"You could not help me to find out. I do so want to know." But Ingram only shrugged his shoulders: he even looked a trifle bored.

"You may ask me anything else, Miss Mollie, but I assure you I should make a bad detective. Why," he continued, airily, "I find it difficult enough to keep my own secrets, without finding out other people's. Oh, here comes our friend the humourist. And now may I beg to inform you that Monsieur Blackie's carriage stops the way."

Waveney did not return to her friends' box, and at the conclusion of the play they all met in the lobby. Waveney was hanging on her father's arm, but he disengaged himself hastily when he saw the sisters.

Althea, who had been nerving herself for this moment all the evening, was only a little paler than usual as she held out her hand to him.

"It is a great many years since we met, Mr. Ward," she said, with a grave smile.

"Yes," he returned, looking at her with equal gravity; but his eyes were sad. "More than twenty years, I think;" and then he shook hands with Doreen rather stiffly, while Althea spoke to Mollie and Noel.

"I should like you to come and see me, my dear," she said to the delighted girl. "Would next Tuesday suit you? Waveney shall come over in the carriage and fetch you. And perhaps your brother would join you, and take you back in the evening," And Mollie accepted this invitation with great readiness.

Everard, who had overheard this, came a step nearer.

"I must take this opportunity of thanking you for your kindness to my dear child," he said, with strong feeling in his voice. "It was hard to part with her, but you make her so happy that Mollie and I try to be resigned to her loss."

"You do not owe me any thanks," returned Althea, her lips paling with evident emotion, "for we love her for her own sake, and she is a great comfort to me. Ah, I see my cousin is beckoning to you, so I will wish you good-night."

Everard shook hands with her rather absently; but a moment later he came back to her side.

"Miss Harford, pardon me, but did you say, just now, that Ingram was your cousin."

Then Althea looked a trifle confused. How incautious she had been!

"Yes," she returned, guardedly, "Moritz is certainly our cousin—once removed. When we were at Kitlands, his father, Colonel Ingram, lived abroad, so that is why you never met him. Did you not ever hear us speak of Moritz and Gwendoline."

"I think not—I am sure not." But Everard's eyes were downcast as he spoke. Then, without another word, he lifted his hat and turned away; the mention of Kitlands had been like a stab. Even Althea hardly guessed how this meeting had tried him, and how cruelly his pride had suffered.

Althea was very silent all the way home. She was tired, she said, and Doreen and Waveney must discuss the play without her; but as she leant back in her corner of the carriage, very little of the conversation reached her ears. Ah, she had noted all the changes now. The shiny dress-coat, the lines, the slight baldness, had all been apparent under the flaring gaslights in the lobby. She could see now that Everard was aged and altered.

The spring and brightness of youth had gone, and care and disappointment and ceaseless drudgery had given him the stoop of age. Already his shoulders seemed bowed, as though some heavy load lay on them; but the face, grave and careworn as it was, was the face of her old lover. The features were as finely chiselled as ever. No sorrow, no failure, no wearing sense of humiliation, would ever rob Everard Ward of his man's beauty, though perhaps an artist would no longer desire to paint him as Ithuriel.

"I am glad to have seen him again," thought Althea; but a dry sob rose in her throat as she said it. How coldly, how gravely he had accosted her! He had expressed no pleasure in meeting his old friends, had asked no single question about their welfare. A few stiff words of thanks for her kindness to Waveney, but nothing more, nothing more; and Althea's eyes grew misty with unshed tears in the darkness.

There were some lines by Miss Murdoch that Everard had once written in her album. She had read them so often that she knew them by heart; they were haunting her now.

"Forgotten! no, we never do forget; We let the years go; wash them clean with tears, Leave them to bleach out in the open day Or lock them careful by, like dead friends' clothes, Till we shall dare unfold them without pain; But we forget not, never can forget."

"It is my nature to be faithful," Althea had once touchingly said to her sister; and to forget was certainly not possible to her!

CHAPTER XXIII.: ACROSS THE GOLF LINKS.

"Learn to live, and live to learn, Ignorance like a fire burns, Little tasks make large returns."
Bayard Taylor.

"Sits the wind in that quarter." Shakespeare.

When Waveney went home the following Sunday, she carried with her a choice little piece of information, which she retailed with much gusto at the tea-table.

"Father," she said, in a mysterious voice, "I have found out something so interesting about our dear little Monsieur Blackie." Then Mollie, who was pouring out the tea, paused in her task to listen. "He is a relation of the Misses Harfords—their cousin once removed. Miss Althea told me so. His father, Colonel Ingram, was their own cousin."

Mollie's face wore an awed expression; she was evidently much impressed. But Mr. Ward looked a little perplexed.

"Ingram," he muttered, "I do not remember the name, and yet I thought I knew all their relations."

"No, father, dear," returned Waveney, gently. "Miss Althea said you had never seen any of them—they were living abroad, because Mrs. Ingram's health was so bad. There was only one daughter, Gwendoline, and she is married now, but I thought you and Mollie would be interested to know that he is a connection of the dear ladies at the Red House."

Then Noel solemnly rapped on the table with his knife.

"I propose Monsieur Blackie's health," he said, grandly; "he seems a respectable sort of party, and I am proud to have made his acquaintance. I regret—I may say I deeply regret—that I once made the unlucky observation that his head was like a scrubbing brush, and that his moustache was of the Mephistophelian pattern; but what are such trifles between friends?" And then his voice grew thin and nasal. "For I guess, and do calculate, ladies and gentlemen, that the party in question is boss of the whole show, and will boom considerable." And then he sat down and glared at Mollie through his pince-nez; but Mollie, who seemed a little flurried and excited, said nothing at all.

Only, as she and Waveney were putting on their hats for church, she said, in rather a subdued, quiet little voice,—

"Wave, dear, of course I am glad about Mr. Ingram; but it does not make any real difference, does it? for we always knew he was a gentleman. Father thinks he must be rich, he is so generous with his money; but he will never be too grand to be our friend, will he?" Mollie's voice was not quite steady when she said this. To her simplicity it seemed a surprising thing that their homely, kindly Monsieur Blackie should have such grand relations.

Mollie spent a very happy day at the Red House. Althea, who knew what girls love best, told Waveney to take her all over the house and show her everything, and left them alone together. She and Doreen had an engagement for the afternoon, but tea was served up as usual in the library.

When Althea returned she found them nestled together in the big easy-chair by the fire, "looking like a couple of babes in the wood," she said to Doreen afterwards. And it was so pretty and effective a picture that she forbade them to move; and then she sat down and talked to them in so sweet and friendly a way that Mollie's soft heart was soon won; and when Noel arrived, looking a little shy and awkward—after the fashion of boys—he found them all talking merrily together.

Both Althea and Doreen were charmed with Mollie. Doreen frankly owned to her sister that she had never seen so beautiful a face.

"If it were not for her lameness she would be perfect," she said, regretfully; and Althea agreed to this.

"It is a pity, of course," she returned, gently; "but there is something pathetic in it; and then her unconsciousness is so childlike. She is a sweet creature, and I love her already, but not so much as I love my little Undine;" for, somehow, both she and Doreen often called her by this name.

Waveney had not seen her little friend Betty again, but Althea and Doreen were constantly at the house in High Street, and she often heard them mention her name. Sometimes of an evening, when she was reading to herself, she heard them talking about the Chaytors; and as they never dropped their voices, she thought it no harm to listen.

"Joa is a different woman," Doreen once said. "I never saw such a change in any one. I always knew Tristram was her favourite. Thorold has to play second fiddle now; I am a little sorry for him sometimes."

"Your sorrow is wasted, Dorrie," returned her sister, with a smile. "Thorold is too big and strong for these petty feelings; he values Joa's peace of mind far too much to disturb it by paltry jealousy. He tells me that for the present Tristram and the child will continue to live with them, until Tristram can earn enough to keep a respectable roof over his head. It was very lucky, finding him that berth, and it really suits him very well. But Joa says that Betty misses her father terribly; she spends half her time at the window, watching for him."

Betty's name was perpetually on the sisters' lips; her queer little speeches, her odd ways, her shrewdness and intelligence, and, above all, her warm, childish heart, were favourite topics; and Bet's last was a standing joke with them.

Waveney began to wish to see her again, but Miss Althea never sent her now to the Chaytors. Once Joanna called and had tea at the Red House, but Betty was not with her; the child had a slight cold, she said, and she had left her with Jemima. But throughout the visit she talked of little else. Bet's lessons, her story-books, the new doll that Althea had given her, and the basinette that she was trimming for a Christmas present, were all discussed quite seriously.

Waveney listened eagerly in her corner. For once she found Miss Chaytor interesting. Her voice had lost its fretful strain; she spoke with animation, and as she talked there was a pretty dimple that Waveney had never noticed.

"She must have been very pretty when she was a girl," thought Waveney. "She is good-looking now, and her face is quite pleasant when she smiles." And then again she heard Bet's name, and composed herself to listen.

"The love of that mite for her father is quite wonderful," went on Joanna. "Even Thorold notices it. Quite an hour before Trist is due, Bet will be gluing her face and flattening her nose against the window; and nothing will move her. And all the time she is humming to herself, like a little bird—such funny little scraps of tunes. And then, when he crosses the road, she is out of the room like a dart. And to hear all her old-fashioned questions to him in the passage! Oh, it almost makes me cry to listen to her! 'Are you very tired, father dear? Have you had a hard day? Does your head ache? and are your feet cold? But Aunt Joa has made up such a big fire!'—something like that every night."

"Bless her little heart," observed Doreen, sympathetically; but Althea only smiled.

"And then she brings him in and makes such a fuss over him," went on Joanna. "Just as though he were some feeble, gouty old gentleman. But Tristram lets her do it. I think he likes to feel her little fingers busy about him. She fetches him his warm slippers, and a footstool, or a screen if the fire is hot; and when he is quite 'comfy,' as she calls it, she climbs up on his knee and gives him an account of the day."

When Joanna had taken her leave, Althea stood looking into the fire with a grave, abstracted look. But when Doreen returned to the room, she changed her attitude slightly.

"Joa seems very happy, does she not, Dorrie? She has not worn so bright a face since the Old Manor House days!"

"No, indeed! And it is all Bet's influence. She is like a hen with one chick; it almost makes me laugh to hear her."

"I felt nearer crying, I assure you. But, Dorrie, is it not beautiful to see how love effaces self. 'And a little child shall lead them;' do you remember those words? Already Bet's tiny fingers have smoothed out the lines on Joa's face, and taught her to smile again."

Waveney only saw Mr. Chaytor on Thursday evenings at the Porch House. The Shakespeare readings were still in full swing, and she still sat beside Nora Greenwell. She sometimes thought that Mr. Chaytor spoke less to her than to the other girls, though he was always careful to point out any fault of punctuation; now and then, when she was a little weary of following the text, she would raise her eyes from her books; and more than once it had given her an odd shock to find at that very moment Mr. Chaytor was quietly regarding her; then some sudden shyness made her eyelids droop again.

Mr. Chaytor took no apparent notice of her. When the reading was over he always joined Althea, and a grave bow, or perhaps a pleasant "good-night," when Waveney left the room, was all that passed between them.

It was strange, then, that as Thorold Chaytor walked down the hill in the wintry darkness, a little pale face and a pair of dark, spirituelle eyes should invariably haunt him. Never in his life had he seen such eyes, so soft and deep and magnetic.

And then that babyish crop of brown, curly hair—he wondered why she wore it so, it made her look so childish; but he liked it, too—it struck him that she was lighter, and more sprightly and full of grace and lissomeness, than any girl he had seen, and that his name of Undine suited her down to the ground. He remembered well her sister's lovely face, but of the two he preferred his little Undine.

Once, when he had entered the Recreation Hall, and the seat beside Nora Greenwell was vacant, a troubled look came into his eyes; but Waveney, who had only gone across to the house for a book Althea wanted, re-entered a moment later; and Thorold's brow cleared like magic as her light, springy step passed by his chair.

"I hope I have not disturbed you," she said, rather timidly, as he rose from his seat and wished her good-evening; "but Miss Harford had forgotten her Shakespeare."

"Not at all; but we will begin now." Then, as Waveney opened her book, she wondered at Mr. Chaytor's grave, intent look.

About ten days before Christmas, Waveney, attended by her little companions, Fuss and Fury, started off for a walk over the Common.

It was one of those ideal afternoons in December, when all young creatures feel it is a joy to be alive. There had been a heavy frost in the night, and the bright, wintry sunshine had not yet melted it. The Frost King had touched the saplings with his white fingers, and even the bare blackberry bushes were transformed into things of beauty. The vast common seemed to glitter with whiteness under the pink glow of the winter's sky.

Waveney had turned her steps towards the golf links. The wind blew more bleakly there, but the wide stretch of open common, with the black windmill in the distance, always gave her a pleasant sensation of freedom. She loved to watch the sun sinking into his bed of bright-coloured clouds. But when the pink glow faded, and the sky-line became a cold, steely blue, she shivered a little, as though she had stayed too long at some pageant, and set her face homewards.

She had walked too far, and she knew the darkness would overtake her long before she reached the Red House, and then Miss Althea would gently admonish her for her imprudence.

The little dogs were tumbling over each other, and wetting their silky coats in the frosty grass. Waveney called them sharply to order. If no one were in sight she thought she would race them across the Common; but the next moment she heard footsteps behind her.

Involuntarily she quickened her own steps. It was rather a lonely part of the Common. There was no one to be seen, only the gaunt, black arms of the windmill seemed to stretch into the darkening sky.

The rapid, even footsteps behind her made her nervous, and gave her the feeling of being in a nightmare. If she could only look around! And then, to her intense relief, a familiar voice pronounced her name.

"Mr. Chaytor!" she gasped, for her heart was beating so fast that she could hardly speak. "Oh, how glad I am! It was very foolish of me, but I never can bear to be followed in a lonely place."

"I was afraid I frightened you?" he said, coming to her side, "but you were walking so fast that I found it difficult to overtake you. Forgive me, I know I have no right to lecture, but at this hour the golf links is far too lonely a place for a young lady."

"Yes, you are right," returned Waveney, touched by this kind interest in her welfare, "and I must never walk here again so late. But"—with a sigh of regret—"I do love it so."

"Do you?" returned Mr. Chaytor, quickly. "I wonder why." But with his habitual reserve he forbore to add that it was his favourite walk.

"It is so wide," she replied, in her earnest voice. "All this space with nothing between you and the sky makes one feel so free and happy. The sunsets are always so beautiful here, and if it were not for the loneliness I should love to watch the darkness, like a big black ogre, swallow up all the lovely light."

It was a pity Waveney could not see Mr. Chaytor's smile.

"Shall we stand and watch it now?" he said, indulgently. "You have a safe escort, so we need not fear your ogre. Only you must not take cold." But Waveney only thanked him, and said that she was late already, and that they had better go.

What a walk that was! and how Waveney remembered it afterwards! If Mr. Chaytor had laid himself out to please and interest her, he could not have succeeded better. Books, pictures, accounts of his old summer wanderings! And yet not for one moment did Waveney feel that he was talking down to her level. It seemed the spontaneous outpouring of a well-bred, intellectual man, glad to impart information to a congenial companion. But if Waveney was charmed and interested, certainly Mr. Chaytor was gratified. Miss Ward's bright intelligence, her racy and picturesque remarks, her frankly confessed ignorance, were all delightful to him; since the old Manor days he had seen so few girls, and none of them had attracted him in the least. There was something unique, out of the common, about Miss Ward; he felt vaguely that he would like to know more of her.

Perhaps it was this feeling that made him say presently "I am afraid you have forgotten your little friend Betty"—for he knew all about that meeting on the Embankment. Betty had given him a most realistic and graphic account. "And the little lady did warm my hands so, Uncle Theo,"—and here Bet rubbed away at his hands until she was red in the face—"and all the time she did talk, and her great big eyes were laughing at me."

"Bet has a good memory for her friends, and she often talks about you!" continued Thorold. "She is a fascinating little person, even to me, though I do not profess to understand children. She is full of surprises. You never get to the end of her. My sister fairly worships her!"

"Yes, I know," returned Waveney, softly; "and I am so very glad—glad for your sister, I mean. I should love to see Betty again. I am not like you, Mr. Chaytor; I have been a child-worshipper all my life. Oh, I know they are naughty sometimes, but they are so much nearer the angels than we are, and they are not such a long way off from heaven."

"'Heaven lies about us in our infancy!' Are you a student of Wordsworth, Miss Ward?" But she shook her head.

"I have read some of his poems," she returned, modestly. "But I am afraid I know very little good poetry."

"That is a pity; but one can always mend a fault. At Easter I propose having a course of reading from Tennyson and Mrs. Browning. Ah, here we are at the Red House."

"You will come in and have a cup of tea after your long walk," observed Waveney. "Miss Doreen is in town, but I know Miss Althea is at home." Then, after a moment's hesitation, Mr. Chaytor assented and followed her into the house.

"My dear child, how late you are!" observed Althea, rather anxiously, as Waveney opened the library door. "I was getting nervous about you!"

"I am afraid I am rather late," confessed the girl; "but, fortunately, I met Mr. Chaytor, and he has come in with me for some tea." Then there was no lack of welcome in Althea's face and voice. Fresh tea was ordered, and another supply of hot buttered scones, a big pine-log thrown on the fire; and as Thorold sat in his luxurious chair, with a glass screen between him and the blaze, with his little walking companion opposite him, and Althea's warm smile on them both, he had never felt himself more comfortable, or at his ease.

CHAPTER XXIV.: "LOST, STOLEN, OR STRAYED!"

"Rainy and rough sets the day— There's a heart beating for somebody; I must be up and away,
Somebody's anxious for somebody." Swain.

Mr. Ingram had once compared the English climate to unregenerated womanhood, and had declaimed on this subject in his own whimsical fashion at Cleveland Terrace, much to the delight of his young friend the humourist.

"It is womanhood pure and simple, and unadulterated by civilisation," he continued, blandly, as he twisted his Mephistophelian moustache. "It is the savage mother, and no mistake, with all her crude grand humours. Sometimes she is benevolent, fairly brimming over with the milk of loving kindness. She has her sportive moods, when she bubbles over with smiles and mirth—a May day, for example—when she walks through the land as meekly as a garlanded lamb."

"Hear, hear!" observed Noel, sotto voce; but Mollie, who was deeply impressed, frowned him down.

Mr. Ingram paused, as though for well-deserved applause. He felt himself becoming eloquent, so he took up his parable again.

"But the savage mother knows how to sulk and frown, and her tear-storms and icy moods are terribly trying. There is no coquetry about her then; it is the storm and stress of a great passion." And with this grand peroration Mr. Ingram gave his moustache a final twist, and, as Noel phrased it, brought down the house.

Waveney thought of Monsieur Blackie's parable—for of course it had been duly retailed to her in Mollie's weekly budget—when the weather changed disastrously before Christmas. The Frost King no longer touched the earth with his white fingers; the wintry sunshine had faded from the landscape; the skies were grey and threatening, and the raw cold made one's flesh creep. "Hardly Christmas weather," Althea observed, regretfully, as she looked out from the library window at the blackened grass and sodden, uninviting paths. Only under the wide verandah of the Porch House a crowd of birds were feeding. Waveney was, as usual, watching them.

"I am afraid it will rain before evening," returned Doreen. "The barometer is going down fast. I do so dislike a wet Christmas." And to this Althea cordially agreed.

But no amount of impending rain could damp Waveney's pleasurable expectations, for she had a delightful programme before her. That year Christmas day fell on Saturday, and as Althea and Doreen always dined with Mrs. Mainwaring, Althea proposed driving her to Cleveland Terrace.

"Aunt Sara would be delighted to see you, dear!" she said—"indeed, you were included in the invitation. But I told her that you would far rather be with your own people."

"Oh, thank you, thank you," returned the girl, gratefully. But her joy was unbounded when Althea suggested that she should not return to the Red House until Tuesday afternoon. "I shall need all my helpers then," she finished, smiling; and Waveney understood her. The Christmas programme had been duly unfolded to her. There was to be a grand tea and entertainment for Althea's girls at the Porch House, a festive evening at the Home for Workers, a supper for the Dereham cabmen, and another for the costermongers; and on Twelfth Night the servants at the

Red House always entertained their relations and friends in the Recreation Hall. "In fact," as Doreen expressed it, "no one would have time to sit down comfortably until the feast of Epiphany had passed." But, though Doreen spoke in a resigned tone of a weary worker, it might be doubted if any one enjoyed more thoroughly the bustle and preparation.

The day before Christmas was a busy one for all the inmates of the Red House. Doreen was at the Home all day superintending the Christmas decorations, and Althea spent most of her time at the Porch House, where a band of voluntary helpers were making garlands of evergreens, and framing Christmas mottoes in ivy under her skilful direction.

Waveney would willingly have helped in the work, but Althea had other employment for her. Some of her pensioners lived on the other side of the river, and Waveney, who often acted as her almoner, went off early in the afternoon to order parcels of groceries and other good things, and to carry them to two or three old women who lived in the almshouses.

The old women were garrulous, and detained her with accounts of their various ailments, so it was quite dark before the little gate of the almshouse garden closed behind her. For some time she had heard the pattering of the rain against the window-panes, and knew that she would have a long, wet walk home.

"Aye, but it is a wild night," observed Mrs. Bates, lugubriously, as she stirred her bright little fire afresh, "and it makes one shiver to one's very bones, that it do."

"But your warm shawl will be a comfort," returned Waveney, cheerfully. "Well, I must go now. 'A happy Christmas to you,' Mrs. Bates, and I hope your rheumatism will soon be better." And then Waveney unhasped the upper half of Widow Bates's door, and peered out into the darkness.

It was not inviting, certainly. The cold, sleety rain was falling in torrents. A wild night, assuredly, and one that meant mischief. But Waveney wore a stout waterproof cloak that Althea had lent to her, and thought she would be proof against any amount of rain or sleet. True, her umbrella was just a little slit, but she would soon have it re-covered.

A narrow, winding passage, resembling a cathedral close, led to High Street. A few old-fashioned houses fronted the garden wall of the Vicarage. Here it was so dark that Waveney was rather startled when she heard a child's voice close to her elbow.

"Oh, please, I am quite lost, and will you take me home?"

There was something familiar in the voice, but in the darkness it was impossible to see the child's face; but Waveney's ear was never deaf to any childish appeal.

"Oh, you poor little thing," she said, kindly, "where do you live, and what is your name?"

"I am dad's little Betty," returned the child. She spoke in a tired, dreary little tone, "and I live across the water, past the church, with Uncle Theo and Aunt Joa." Then, in spite of the wet, Waveney stooped down and put her arm round her.

"Why, it is my little friend, Betty," she said, in a puzzled tone. "Why are you out alone this dreadful night? Oh, you poor darling, your frock and jacket are quite soaking. Come, come, we must go home as fast as possible. Give me your hand, dear, and come closer to me, so that my umbrella may shelter you."

"Is it my little lady?" asked Betty, in a perplexed voice. "She did speak to me so kindly once on the seat by the river; but I have never, never seen her again."

"But we shall see each other presently, when we get to the shops," returned Waveney, cheerily. "Betty, darling, tell me, why are you out by yourself?"

"I wanted to meet dad," returned Betty, with a little sob. "Aunt Joa was out, and I was so lonely all by myself, and Jemima was busy and told me to run away, and I was aching dreadful because it was Christmas Eve and dad did not come; and I thought"—and Bet sobbed afresh—"it would be such fun to see him pass me, and then I should call out loud, 'Here's Bet, dad, and I have come to meet you;' but there was no dad at all."

"Yes; and then you missed your way?"

"It was so dark," returned Bet, plaintively, "and there were trees, and I fell down and hurt myself, and then I got frightened. Are you frightened in the dark, too?"

"No; I am only frightened of doing wrong things, Betty dear. I am afraid you have been very naughty, and that poor Aunt Joa will be anxious. Can you walk faster, darling?" But Bet, tired and miserable, felt as though her poor little legs were weighted with lead. But for the umbrella Waveney would have carried her; it hurt her to hear the child sobbing to herself quietly in the darkness. It was a cruel night for any child to be out. Mr. Ingram's "savage mother" was in her fiercest mood, and seemed lashing herself up to fresh fury.

There was scarcely a foot-passenger to be seen on the bridge, but a few shivering men and women were in the town making their Christmas purchases.

Bet cheered up a little when the bridge had been crossed. "We shall soon be there now," she sighed. "Do you know my home, little lady?"

"Yes, dear; and I know your Aunt Joa, too, and your Uncle Theo."

"And dad?"

"No, darling, not dad. But I daresay I shall know him some day. See how pretty all those lights look! Yes, this is the house," as Betty pulled at her hand. And the next moment they were standing on the doorstep.

To Waveney's surprise, Mr. Chaytor opened the door. He regarded them with amazement. Waveney's old umbrella had not fulfilled its mission, and the velvet on her hat was soaking, and so was her hair. But she was nothing to Betty. In the lamplight she looked the most abject little child possible. She was splashed with mud from head to foot, and her plait of fair hair was so wet that Mr. Chaytor hurriedly withdrew his hand.

"Why, she is wet through!" he said, in a shocked voice. Then Waveney hurriedly explained matters.

"I am afraid Betty has been rather naughty," she said, quickly. "She went out by herself in the hope of meeting her father. And then she lost herself, and got frightened. She was just by Aylmer's Almshouses when she spoke to me."

"Aylmer's Almshouses, across the river!" he exclaimed, quite horrified. "Why, I thought she was with my sister! What are we to do, Miss Ward?" looking at her with all a man's helplessness. "Joanna may not be back for an hour, and Jemima has gone to the General Post-Office. And the child is dripping with wet from head to foot."

Waveney was quite equal to the emergency.

"I think, if you will allow me, I had better take her upstairs," she returned, quietly, "and get off her wet things. And if you could get her something hot to drink—milk, or tea—anything, so that it is hot." Then Mr. Chaytor looked relieved.

"I could make her a cup of tea," he returned, "if you are sure that will do. The kettle is boiling now."

"Thank you, very much," was all Waveney answered. "Now, Betty dear, will you show me the way to your room?"

"I sleep in Aunt Joa's room," replied Betty, making brave efforts to restrain her tears. Her poor little lips were blue with cold, and her teeth were chattering. And her fingers were so numb that they could not turn the handle of the door, and Waveney had to come to her help.

It was a large, pleasant room, furnished simply, and a bright fire gave it an air of comfort. A child's cot stood beside the bed. There were some fine old prints on the walls, and the silver and ebony brush on the toilet-table, and the quilted silk eiderdown on her bed, spoke of better days.

Waveney took off her dripping waterproof and hat, and then she set to work, and in five minutes Betty's wet things lay in a heap on the floor, and she was wrapped up in her aunt's warm flannel dressing-gown, and ensconced in the big easy-chair. Then Waveney sat down on the rug and rubbed the frozen little feet.

"Betty," she said, coaxingly, "I do wish you would be a good child and go straight to bed." But Betty puckered up her face at this, and looked so miserable that Waveney did not dare to say more.

"It's my dad's birthday, and Christmas Eve," she said, in a heart-broken voice. "Dad would not enjoy his tea one bit unless I buttered his toast and gave him his two lumps of sugar."

"Well, then, you must tell me where to find you some dry, clean clothes," returned Waveney, with a disapproving shake of her head. But just then there was a tap at the door, and when she said, "Come in," to her surprise, Mr. Chaytor entered with two large cups of steaming tea in his hands.

"Jemima is still playing truant," he said, apologetically, "so I was obliged to bring the tea myself." And then he set down the cups on a little table, piling up Joanna's small possessions in a most ruthless fashion, to make room for them.

Perhaps the novelty of the situation bewildered him, or something in the little fireside scene appealed to him; for he stood beside Betty's chair for two or three minutes without speaking. Betty, in her scarlet dressing-gown, was certainly a most picturesque-looking little object, but Thorold's eyes rested longer on the girlish figure on the rug, at the busy ministering hands, and the damp, curly hair, still glistening with wet.

"Do please drink your tea, before it cools," he said, pleadingly. "When Jemima comes back, I shall send her up to help you, and clear all the wet things away." And then he went downstairs, and set on the kettle again to boil; and all the while the memory of a bare little foot resting on a girl's soft, pink palm, haunted him. "It is the eternal motherhood," he said to himself, "that is in all true women. No wonder Bet loves her. How could she help it?—how could she help it?" And then the door-bell rang, and Jemima entered with profuse apologies at her tardiness.

She was sent upstairs with a supply of hot water and towels, and as soon as Betty had finished her tea, her face and hands were washed, her hair dried and neatly tied with a ribbon. Then she was dressed in clean, fresh garments.

"I have got my best frock on, and I feel quite nice, and like Christmas Eve," exclaimed Betty, with a quaint little caper. "Oh, I am sure dad must have come, and Aunt Joa, too. Do let us go downstairs."

"Let me wash my hands first, darling," pleaded Waveney. "And oh, dear, how untidy I look!" and Betty stood by the toilet-table watching with critical eyes while Waveney tried to bring the unruly locks into order.

"Aunt Joa has such long, long hair," she observed. "When she sits down it almost touches the floor. But yours is nice baby hair, too—it is like little rings that have come undone; but it is pretty, don't you think so?"—feeling that Waveney must be the best judge of such a personal matter. Jemima giggled as she picked up the little muddy boots.

"Law, Miss Bet," she said, reprovingly, "how you do talk! No little ladies that I ever knew said such things. There's your pa, he is downstairs and a-waiting for his tea." But Bet heard no more.

"Come, come," she said, pulling Waveney by the dress. "Dad is downstairs, and the curls don't matter one bit." Then Waveney reluctantly followed her; her hat and gloves were drying; she could not possibly put them on for another half-hour, and she could hardly stay ruminating in Miss Chaytor's bedroom.

Joanna had not yet returned; she was evidently weather-bound at some friend's house, but a good-looking, weather-beaten man, in a rough grey coat, stood with his back to the fire. Bet ran to him at once.

"Oh, dad, I did so want to be ready for you, but I got wet and the little lady was helping me to dress up again."

"Yes, I know, Bet;" and then her father kissed her a little gravely, and held out his hand to Waveney.

"I am very grateful to you, Miss Ward. My brother has been telling me of your kindness to my little girl; she has been a very naughty child, I am afraid." Then Bet looked up in his face, and her lip quivered.

"Was it really bad of me to go out and meet you, dad?—really and truly?"

"Yes, darling, really and truly." And then Tristram took her on his knee. "What would dad have done without his little Betty?—and she might have been lost or run over."

"Oh, I would have found my way back," returned Bet, with a wise little nod of her head. "But I won't never do it again." And then her little arms went round his neck, and she rested her head against the rough grey coat; for her childish heart was full to the brim. "Miss Ward," observed Thorold, in rather a pleading voice, "as my sister is absent, may I ask you to pour out the tea." Then Waveney, blushing a little at the unexpected request, took her place quietly at the tea-tray.

CHAPTER XXV.: A WET NIGHT, AND A DIFFERENCE OF OPINION.

"I am Sir Oracle, And when I ope my lips, let no dog bark!" Merchant of Venice.
"Beggar I am, I am even poor in thanks." Hamlet.

What a strange Christmas Eve it was! Waveney felt as though she were in a dream, as she sat there demurely pouring out the tea, with Betty beside her, counting the lumps of sugar in each cup.

"Two for daddie, and one big one for Uncle Theo? Oh, that is not big enough, is it, Uncle Theo? And oh, dear!"—in a reproachful voice—"you did put in the milk first."

"I shall know better next time," returned Waveney, smiling; and then she watched Betty spreading her father's toast with butter. The child's concentrated earnestness, her absorbed gravity, amused her; but Tristram evidently took it as a matter of course. What a cosy room it was! Waveney thought. The crimson curtains were drawn, and a bright fire burnt in both the fireplaces—an unwonted extravagance—in honour of Christmas Eve; the circle of easy-chairs round the farthest fireplace looked snug and inviting.

Thorold did not talk much during tea-time—he left the conversation principally to his brother; but he often looked at the little figure that occupied Joanna's place. His fastidious eyes noticed the neat, dainty movements and the changes of expression on the bright, speaking face, and the lovely dimple when Waveney smiled or laughed. A man could hardly be dull with such a companion, he thought; and then, at some sudden suggestion, some overwhelming possibility, a dull flush rose to his temples, and he went to the window to inspect the weather.

"I am sorry to say that it is still raining, Miss Ward," he said, quietly, "and I am afraid we are in for a wet night; but I will get you a cab——"

"A cab!" interrupted Waveney, in a dismayed tone. "Oh, no, thank you, Mr. Chaytor, you must do nothing of the kind. I am as strong as a lion, and I never take cold—at least, scarcely ever. And what does a little rain matter?"

"You are a Stoic," he returned, somewhat amused at this; but she seemed so horrified at his suggestion that he said no more—being a man of deeds, not words. So when Waveney took possession of an easy-chair, and Betty brought her her baby doll to admire, she felt comfortably convinced that she would be allowed her own way; but she had reckoned without her host.

Waveney chatted happily to the child, while Tristram watched them with the lazy enjoyment of a tired man; and she never wondered why Mr. Chaytor was absent so long until he re-entered the room in his ulster.

"The cab is here, Miss Ward," he said, coolly; "and you will find your things in my sister's room. Jemima says they are quite dry."

Then Waveney only flashed a look of reproach at him, and walked meekly out of the room.

Of course he was right, she knew that, and that the idea of the long, lonely walk, in the pelting rain, was absurd in the highest degree. But as Waveney went upstairs she was not sure that she liked the quiet way in which Mr. Chaytor asserted his will; it made her feel like a little school-girl in the presence of a master. He had not taken the trouble to argue the point with her, or to prove to her that she had made a mistake, but had just gone out and brought the cab; and so Waveney, who, in spite of her sweet temper, was a trifle self-willed and obstinate, felt secretly aggrieved, and even offended. And she entered the parlour with so dignified an air that Thorold, who could read her face, smiled to himself.

Betty ran to her with a sorrowful exclamation.

"Oh, must you go, Wavie, dear?" she said, dubiously.

"Why, Bet," observed her uncle, rather shocked at this familiarity, "aren't you taking rather a liberty with your kind friend?"

"She told me her name," returned Bet, in eager defence, "and she did say that I might call her what I liked. I know it was Wavie, or something like it."

"Very like it, indeed, darling," replied Waveney, kneeling down and putting her arms round the child; "and it is prettier than Waveney, and I shall always want you to call me so. Now good-night, my little Betty." And then, as Betty clung to her and kissed her, Thorold looked at them rather gravely.

"I am ready now," observed Waveney, resuming her stiff manner. "I suppose it will be no use telling you, Mr. Chaytor, that I can very well go by myself."

"No," he returned, looking at her with very keen, bright eyes. "I am afraid your words would be wasted. You see, Miss Ward, I have a conscience, and my conscience tells me that I ought to see you safe in Miss Harford's hands." But to this Waveney vouchsafed no reply. She jumped into the cab and settled herself in her corner, and left Mr. Chaytor to dispose of himself as he would; and when he placed himself opposite to her, she only looked out intently at the lighted shops.

Even the rain could not quite damp the festivity. The snow-white turkeys and geese, garlanded with holly, made a brave show; and the butcher's shop was full of shabby customers. Waveney's soft heart yearned as usual over the babies and little children. Then she turned her head, and met Mr. Chaytor's amused glance—it was so kind, it spoke of such complete understanding, that she felt a little ashamed of herself.

"Miss Ward, have you forgiven me yet for doing my duty like a man?"

Waveney struggled with a smile, but she had not quite recovered herself, so she said, rather coldly,—

"I don't see that my forgiveness matters a bit!"

"Is not that rather crushing?" he returned. "Especially as it matters very much to me. I wish you would be friendly enough to tell me the real cause of offence. You could not reasonably expect that I should let you swim through this"—the rain beating an accompaniment to his words. "I would not have let my sister do it"—his voice softening into involuntary tenderness. Never had she seemed so lovable to him, even though her childish waywardness was making him smile.

"It was not the cab I minded so much," stammered Waveney, tingling with shame and confusion to her finger-ends, and glad of the darkness that hid her hot cheeks; "only you did it without telling me"—Waveney did not dare say what she really thought: that he had managed her like a child—"and it makes me unhappy, it does indeed, Mr. Chaytor, to bring you out this dreadful night, when you are so tired and have been hard at work all day."

"I never felt less tired in my life! And you are giving me great pleasure, in allowing me to perform this little service for you." Then Waveney blushed again, but this time for pleasure, for Mr. Chaytor's voice convinced her that he was speaking the truth, the whole truth and nothing but the truth.

"Now we have had our first and last little difference," he went on, cheerfully, "and shall be better friends than ever." And there was no outward dissent to this; only a mutinous sparkle in Waveney's dark eyes showed a silent protest.

"Would it be their last difference?" she thought; for she was a shrewd, sensible little woman, and had her own opinions on most things; but at least she had the grace and honesty to own that on this occasion she had been in the wrong.

What a short drive it was, after all! Almost before Waveney had seen that they were at the top of the hill they were driving through the lodge gates.

Althea came out into the hall to meet them in her heliotrope velveteen and lace ruff. She looked more like Queen Bess than ever.

"My dear child, I have been so anxious about you! But of course I hoped you had taken shelter. Thank you for bringing her home, Thorold. Will you come in, or is your cab waiting? We have our usual mulled wine and Christmas cake, which you ought to taste for the sake of the old lang syne."

"May I give the cabman some? Poor old fellow, he is so cold!" But it was a mere form of words. He need not have asked the question. On Christmas Eve not an errand boy or a carol singer left the Red House without being regaled with Christmas fare—"cakes and ale," as Althea and Doreen called it.

Thorold carried out a great mug of hot spiced wine and a mighty wedge of cake to the driver; then he took his by the hall fire, as he said he was too wet and dirty for the library. Waveney found him there alone when she came downstairs. Fresh pensioners were claiming the sisters' attention. He looked warmed and refreshed, and recommended her to follow his example.

"See what a treat you have given me, Miss Ward!" he said, smiling. "There is no mulled wine like this anywhere. The flavour brings back my dear old home to me."

"Do you mean the old Manor House?" she asked, softly.

"Yes," he returned, dreamily. "It is the season for old memories, is it not? At Christmas and New Year's Day the ghosts of the past stalk out of their dim recesses; but they are dearly loved visitants, and we do not fear them. Do you know what the Germans call 'heimweh?' Have you ever experienced it?"

But he need not have asked, for at the unexpected question the girl's head drooped to hide her tears. How could he know, how could any one know, how that brave young heart ached ceaselessly for her home and Mollie. Mr. Chaytor was quite shocked at himself.

"Dear Miss Ward," he said, gently, "you must forgive me again, you see; but I spoke without thinking."

Then Waveney shook her head and looked at him with a touching little smile.

"You have done nothing—it is only I who am silly to-night; but oh! I am always so wanting father and Mollie. But I shall see them to-morrow. Mr. Chaytor, I must go now; but thank you so much for all your kindness and for bringing me home. I am not ungrateful, really." And Waveney's wet eyes looked so sad and beautiful as she raised them to his face that Mr. Chaytor thought of them all through his drive home.

When Waveney woke the next morning she found the rain had ceased; but it was still too dark to discover anything further. They drove to church for the early service, and the warm, lighted church, with its Christmas decorations, and crowded with worshippers, reminded her of the dearly-loved church where she and Mollie had knelt side by side for so many years.

Breakfast was ready for them on their return, and they had the usual noisy welcome from Fuss and Fury. But Waveney was a little perplexed when Althea told her, with a smile, that she must eat her breakfast as quickly as possible, as they had plenty of business before them. "It is a comfort the rain has stopped," she continued, with an irrepressible shiver, "for we cannot possibly have the carriage out again, until we drive to town. How thankful I am that Aunt Sara gave me that fur-lined cloak last Christmas!" she went on, addressing her sister. "It keeps out the cold as nothing else does. I feel as cosy as that robin does in his red waistcoat."

Waveney ate her breakfast a little silently; she was wondering why there was no greeting word from home. Perhaps the postman had not come.

"Have you finished, Waveney?" asked Doreen, a little abruptly. "By-and-bye, if you have, we may as well go to the library, or we shall never get our parcels undone before it is time to start for church."

Waveney opened her eyes rather widely at this; but when she entered the room, she stared in amazement. The centre-table seemed a mass of plants, and brown paper parcels of every size and description were heaped on every available space.

To her surprise Althea quietly drew back the curtain of Cosy Nook, and motioned her to enter.

"You can amuse yourself there for a little while," she said, brightly, "while Doreen and I open our parcels. You will see Aunt Sara has not forgotten you." And then, with a kindly nod, she withdrew.

It was a pity that no interested observer saw the girl's start and blush of delight, for there, just opposite her, was a dress, flung across a chair, and a paper pinned on one sleeve. "Waveney, from her loving friend, Althea Harford."

Althea had pleased her own taste in the choice of that frock. It was a dark sapphire blue velveteen of the same shade as the cloak, and was perfectly plain, except for a dainty little ruff of yellowish lace; and nothing could have suited Waveney's pale, little face better.

She stood for a long time with folded hands, in mute admiration of that marvellous garment; she knew now why her white dress had disappeared so mysteriously for a day or two. It wanted doing up, Nurse Marks told her. But when it had been returned, Waveney could see very little difference. The poor, little frock looked sadly frayed and shabby; no wonder Miss Althea thought she needed a new one. But the kindness and the generosity of the gift were beyond everything, and there was a lump in Waveney's throat as her fingers touched the soft pile of the velveteen.

Doreen's present was a box of handkerchiefs, with Waveney's initials prettily embroidered by one of the workers at the Home, and Mrs. Mainwaring, with characteristic kindness and good taste, had contributed a beautiful little muff.

But Waveney's pleasure reached its climax when her eyes discovered a neat, little umbrella, with a note from Mollie attached to the ivory handle. "Please do not think me extravagant, darling," it began, "because I really can afford to give myself a big treat this year. The menu-cards have sold splendidly. Mr. Ingram says his sister has given him a commission for three more sets, so I shall be quite rich. I have bought myself a new jacket and hat, and father says that he certainly means to get me a tweed dress for Christmas, so I shall be as smart as you. He is only sending you gloves, but I know you will like them.

"And I have bought the umbrella out of my own earnings. You cannot think how proud I am of that! The poor old Gamp you were using would not keep a sparrow dry, it was so worn out, and I could not bear to think of you getting wet through. A happy Christmas to you, my darling! and no more at present from your loving Mollie."

Noel's present was wrapped up with the gloves; it was only a small manuscript book, neatly bound with blue ribbon, and in Noel's flourishing school-boy hand was written,—

"The further adventures of Monsieur Blackie, by a Humourist, and dedicated with the author's compliments to old Storm-and-Stress."

Ten minutes later, when Althea peeped through the curtain, she found Waveney still hugging her umbrella, while she looked over the pen-and-ink sketches with eyes twinkling with amusement. "Do you think it will fit?" she asked, softly. Then the girl started to her feet, her face crimson with emotion.

"Oh, Miss Althea, how am I to thank you?" she exclaimed. "You are too kind, oh, far too kind to me." And then, almost tearfully, "I have nothing to give you in return."

"Nothing! I thought I saw a pretty penwiper among my parcels, but I suppose I must have dreamt it; and I had an impression that Doreen showed me a needle-book."

"Oh, but they were only trifles."

"My dear, no gift, however small, from one who loves us, is a trifle, and I shall value your present. We have all we want, dear child, and the kindness of our friends almost embarrasses us. When you come back I must show you the beautiful things some of the girls have made for me, but there is no time to look at them now, for the church-bells are ringing." And then, as they went upstairs, Waveney laden with her treasures, the crowning touch was put to her day's pleasure. "I am so glad you like your frock, dear," remarked Althea; "it is certainly seasonable for winter evenings. You will find a parcel in your room directed to Mollie; it contains a similar dress for her." And the flash of joy in Waveney's eyes certainly repaid her.

CHAPTER XXVI.: A WHITE VELLUM POCKET-BOOK.

"And there's pansies, that's for thoughts."—Hamlet.

"There'll be a comforting fire; There'll be a welcome for somebody; One in her neatest attire, Will look to the table for somebody." Swain.

It was in the gathering dusk of the afternoon when Waveney found herself in the neighbourhood of Cleveland Terrace. They had driven fast, and yet to the eager girl the way had seemed strangely long. As they approached the house, Althea shivered a little, as though her fur-lined cloak had suddenly lost its robin-like cosiness. The steely winter's sky, the raw dampness of the atmosphere, the gloom of the half light, which made all objects appear out of due proportion, and gave them a hazy indistinctness, made her feel depressed and uncomfortable.

As the carriage stopped, the door was quickly opened, though not by the footman, and a familiar voice in the darkness said,—

"Thank you, Miss Harford, a thousand times, for bringing the child home. Waveney, my darling, 'a happy Christmas to you!' Run out of the cold, dear, it is beginning to snow." But Waveney kept her place.

"I must say good-night first, father. Were you watching for me? Do you know you have not wished the dear ladies a happy Christmas yet?" Then Althea's gentle, melancholy voice interrupted her.

"Dear child, there was no need to remind your father of an idle form. I am quite sure we have his good wishes for the sake of the auld lang syne. You are bareheaded, Mr. Ward. Do please go in;" and her slim, gloved hand was stretched out to him.

Everard bowed over it as he pressed it warmly.

"You will always have my best wishes," he said, very gravely. "Good-night, Miss Harford, good-night, and thank you, Miss Althea." And then he swung open the gate and went up the little courtyard, with Waveney clinging to his arm.

Althea looked after them with wistful eyes. What a stream of light met them! What did the narrow passage and steep, ladder-like stairs matter, or the frayed and dingy druggetting, when that starlight glow of home radiance beamed so brightly. And indeed, when Waveney felt Mollie's arms round her neck, and her warm cheek pressed against hers, her heart was comforted and at rest.

"Where are you taking me, sweetheart?" she asked, softly, as Mollie dragged her past the studio door.

"You must come upstairs and take off your things first," returned Mollie, panting from her exertions. "We shall have tea in the dining-room to-night, because there are muffins and crumpets, and I must see to them." Then Mollie threw open the bedroom door, and stood still in silent enjoyment to see Waveney's start of surprise at the sight of a splendid fire burning in the grate.

"Oh, Mollie!" she said, quite shocked at this extravagance, "have we ever had a fire here before, except when we had the measles?" Then Mollie laughed and shook her head.

"I daresay not, but I was not going to let you sleep in this cold vault for three nights when you have been used to a lovely fire in your Pansy Room. Why, Wave, you absurd child, how grave you look! Father won't have to pay one penny for it. I put two shillings into the housekeeping purse out of my own money, and we will just have a beautiful fire every night; and won't we enjoy ourselves!"

"It feels lovely," returned Waveney, kneeling down on the rug, for she was chilly from the long drive. "No, don't light the gas, dear, the firelight is so pretty." Then Mollie put down the match-box reluctantly.

"I wanted to show you something," she returned, in a low voice; "but perhaps if you make a blaze you will be able to see it. Oh, what is that?" as Waveney mutely held out a long brown paper parcel. "Is that another present? No, please don't open it; you must look at this one first." And then Mollie, with outward gravity, and much inward excitement, laid a beautiful Russian leather writing-case on the rug for Waveney's inspection.

Never had Waveney seen such a case, so dainty, so complete, so perfectly finished. The initials "M. W." were on everything—the silver paper-knife and penholders, and on the tiny card-case and inkstand; and every card and sheet of paper was stamped with Mollie's address.

Waveney was silent from excess of admiration, and also from a strong feeling of emotion. Only a lover, she thought, could have planned all those pretty finishes and details. Surely, surely Mollie's eyes must be opened now!

"Mollie, dear, I really don't know what to say," she answered, at last, when the silence became embarrassing. "It is really too beautiful for any one but Cinderella." Then a little conscious smile came to Mollie's lips, and her cheeks wore their wild-rose flush; and yes, certainly, there was a new wistfulness in her eyes.

"Was it not splendid of Mr. Ingram!" she said; but her voice was not quite steady. "It was so kind that I could not help crying a little, and then father laughed at me. I can't understand father, Wave. When I asked him if I ought to write and thank Mr. Ingram, he got quite red, and said that I must know my own feelings best. It was so odd of father to say that."

"Did Mr. Ingram write to you, Mollie?"

"No," returned Mollie, with her cheeks a still deeper rose. "There was only a slip of paper, with Monsieur Blackie's good wishes. But Wave, he is not coming back for a long time—he told me so. He said society had claims on him, and that he had a house-party impending, and other engagements; but I did not like to question him."

"Well, then, I suppose you had better write—only just a short note, Mollie; and pray, pray do not be too grateful. If he gives you presents, it is to please himself as well as you. But you do not know his address, you silly child."

"No," returned Mollie, with a sigh; "that is one of his mysteries. He calls himself a nebulous personage. 'If you ever want to write to me,' he said, the last time he came, 'if your father breaks his leg, for example, or my friend the humourist plays any of his tricks and requires chastisement, and the strong arm of the law, you can ask my cousin Althea to send on the letter for you.' Is that not a funny, roundabout way?"

"Rather," returned Waveney, drily, feeling as though she were on the edge of a volcano. "I think, Mollie dear, that under these circumstances it would be better not to write, but just wait and thank Mr. Ingram when he comes." And though Mollie looked a little disappointed at this decision, she agreed, with her usual loyalty, to abide by it.

When the new dress had been duly admired and Miss Althea praised to Waveney's entire satisfaction, they went downstairs to begin their Christmas merry-making in earnest.

Noel, who was always the Lord of Misrule on these occasions, had insisted with much severity on the usual programme being carried out.

So they had snapdragon in the dark dining-room after tea, and Mollie as usual burnt her fingers, and then they went up to the studio and acted charades and dumb Crambo to an appreciative audience—Mr. Ward, who occupied the front row, and Ann and Mrs. Muggins, who represented the pit.

"Laws, miss, ain't it beautiful and like-life?" observed Ann, the heavy-footed, for the twentieth time. But Everard's eyes were a little misty. If only Dorothy could have seen them! he thought. And then his imagination flew off at a tangent to his old friend, Althea Harford. All the evening her soft, melancholy voice had haunted him. "For the sake of auld lang syne" she had said, and her tone had been full of pathos. "She has never forgotten. I think she is one of those women who never forget," he thought; but he sighed as he said it.

To Waveney those three days were simply perfect, and every hour brought its enjoyment. On Sunday afternoon a snowstorm kept them prisoners to the house, and there was no evening church, so they sang carols by the fire instead, and Ann sat on the stairs with Mrs. Muggins on her lap, and an old plaid shawl of her mother's to keep her warm, and listened as devoutly as though she were in the vestibule of heaven.

"Which is my opinion, Miss Waveney," she observed afterwards, "as the Sadducees and Pharisees could not have sang more sweetly, not with all their golden harps neither."

Waveney looked puzzled for a moment; but Ann's idiosyncrasies were too well known in the household, and after a moment of silent reflection she said,—

"I see what you mean, Ann. You were thinking of the cherubim and seraphim, and it is a fine compliment you are paying us." And then she went off to share the little joke with Mollie and Noel; and the peals of laughter that reached Ann's ears somewhat perplexed that stolid maiden.

On Monday they woke to a white world, and then there was snow balling in the back garden, and then a long walk down Cheyne Walk and across the bridge to Battersea Park. And Mollie went with them, on her father's arm; and when she got tired, which she did far too soon, Noel took her home, grumbling at every step, and Waveney and her father went on. It was Everard's greatest pleasure to walk with his girls, but no companion suited him like Waveney; her light, springy step hardly seemed to touch the ground—and then she was so strong and active, and nothing seemed to tire her. Mollie's sad limp always made his heart ache.

As they stood looking at some floating ice in the river, Everard asked a little abruptly if Mollie had written to Mr. Ingram.

Waveney shook her head. The question rather surprised her.

"Why, no, father," she replied, slowly; "we do not know Mr. Ingram's address, so I persuaded Mollie to wait until he calls."

"Well, perhaps you are right," returned Mr. Ward, doubtfully. "But Waveney, child, I am getting a little bothered about things. I like the fellow, I like him better every time I see him—he has real grit in him, and he is a gentleman; but I never saw a girl courted after this fashion."

"What do you mean, father?" asked Waveney, a little timidly; for she and Mollie were not at all up to date, and their shyness and reticence on this subject were quite old-fashioned.

"Why, any child can see that Ingram worships the ground Mollie walks on," returned Mr. Ward, with a touch of impatience in his voice. "When she looked at him, with her big, innocent eyes, he stammered and changed colour more than once. Oh, the man is in earnest, I would take my oath of that; it is Mollie's side of the question I want to know; she ought not to encourage him by taking his presents unless she means to have him."

This was plain speaking, but Mr. Ward was getting desperate. His motherless girls had no protector but himself. It was pretty to see how Waveney blushed on Mollie's account.

"Father, dear," she stammered, "I can't be quite sure but I think Mollie is beginning to care a little for Mr. Ingram. She certainly misses him; he is very keen and clever, and I fancy that he understands her so well that he will not hurry things. I mean"—explaining herself with difficulty—"that he will not speak until he is certain that her heart is won."

"That is my opinion, too," returned her father; and then he looked at her with tender curiosity. "Where did you gain your knowledge of men, little girl?" But Waveney had no answer ready for this question.

That night, as they sat on the rug in the firelight, like two blissful salamanders, Mollie said, in a flurried and anxious voice,—

"Wave, darling, I want to consult you about something, and you must give me all your attention; you know," clearing her throat, as though it were a little dry; "we have decided that I had better not write to Mr. Ingram."

"Oh, yes, Mollie, we decided that long ago." Waveney spoke in a calm and judicial voice, but Mollie only grew more flurried.

"But I must do something to please him," she returned, in quite a distressed tone. "Think of all the pleasure he has given me, Wave. I have got such a lovely idea in my head. I have finished the menu-cards, and I want to paint one of these white velum pocket-books for Mr. Ingram—a spray of purple pansies would look so well on it. And I will have it all ready for him when he comes next. Don't you think he would be pleased, Wave?"

"Of course he would be pleased, sweetheart; he would carry it next to his heart, and sleep with it under his pillow." But this nonsense was received rather pettishly.

"I wish you would be serious when a person asks advice," returned Mollie, with a little frown. "You would not like any one to say those silly things to you." Then Waveney was on her best behaviour at once, and the naughty, mischievous sparkle faded out of her eyes.

"Don't be cross, Mollie darling," she said caressingly. "I do think your idea very pretty, and I should think Mr. Ingram will be very pleased, he does admire your painting so. Why have you selected pansies, I wonder?" Then, at this very simple question, Mollie looked a little confused. "They are his favourite flowers," she almost whispered; "he says you can never have too much heart's-ease in this world." And this answer fully satisfied Waveney.

The next morning they started off to Sloane Street to purchase the pocket-book, and Mollie expended the last of her earnings; and the moment Waveney left her, to return to Erpingham, she sat down to her little painting table and worked until the short winter's afternoon closed in.

Waveney did not see it until it was finished, and then her admiration fully satisfied Mollie. It was a charming design, and a pansy with a broken stalk, dropping from the main cluster, had a very graceful effect.

"Father likes it; he says I have never painted anything better!" observed Mollie, with modest pride; and Waveney cordially endorsed this.

Privately she thought the dainty pocket-book was more fit for some youthful bride. "Mr. Ingram could not possibly use it," she said to herself; "he will put it under a glass case, or lock it up in a drawer. And if Mollie ever writes love-letters to him, he will keep them in his pansy-book." And then she smiled to herself as she thought of his delight when Mollie, with many blushes and much incoherence, should hand him the book; she could almost see the flash of pleasure in his eyes. But as her lively imagination pictured the little scene, she was far from guessing under what different circumstances Ingram would receive his pansy-book.

CHAPTER XXVII.: AN IDEALIST IN LOVE.

"Whatever we gain, we gain by patience." S. Teresa.

"Faith, thou hast some crotchets in thy head now." The Merry Wives of Windsor.

About three weeks after Christmas Althea was sitting alone in her library.

The great room felt strangely empty that morning. There was no curly head to be seen bending over the writing table in Cosy Nook; no girl secretary to answer the silver chiming of Althea's little bell. Waveney and Doreen had gone up to town for a day's shopping, leaving Althea to enjoy the rest that she so sorely needed.

The severe round of Christmas feastings, the lavish dispensing of cakes and ale, would have tried a robust constitution, and even Doreen complained of unwonted fatigue; but Althea, highly strung and sensitive, had to pay the usual penalty for over-exertion by one of her painful eye attacks, which lasted for three or four days, leaving her weak and depressed.

It is strange and sad how mind and body react on each other in these attacks. A grey haze, misty and impalpable, seemed to veil Althea's inner world, and blot out her cheerfulness. The free, healthy current of her thoughts was checked by dimly discerned obstacles. A chilling sense of self-distrust, of rashly undertaken work, made her heart heavy.

"It is brain-sickness," Doreen would say, to comfort her. "It will pass, my dear."

"Yes, it will pass," returned Althea, with passive gentleness. "I know that as well as you do, Dorrie; but for the time it masters me. Althea ill and Althea well seem two different persons. Is it not humiliating, dear, to think we are at the mercy of our over-wrought nerves? A trifling ailment, a little bodily discomfort, and, if we are at heaven's very gate, we drop to earth like the lark."

"Into our nest," returned Doreen, with a smile. "You have chosen too cheerful a simile. Larks soar perpetually, and they sing as they soar."

"I think I am more like a blind mole at the present moment," replied Althea, pushing up her shade a little, that she might see her sister's face. "Dorrie, I am ashamed of myself. I deserve any amount of scolding. I try to count up my blessings, to think of my girls' happy faces, but I am fast in my Slough of Despond, and not all your efforts will pull me out."

"Very well, then, we must leave you there," returned Doreen, composedly; but she gave Althea's hand a loving little squeeze as she said this. Her heart was full of tenderness and sympathy, but she was too sensible to waste words fruitlessly.

These sick moods were purely physical, and would yield, she knew well, to time and rest. They were trials to be borne—part of Althea's life-discipline—the cloud that checkered their home cheerfulness; for these melancholy moods seemed to pervade the whole house.

Althea felt much as usual that morning, though she had not quite recovered her looks. Her face seemed longer and more sallow, and there were tired lines round her eyes. When a woman has passed her youth, mental suffering leaves an indelible mark; and Althea looked old and worn that day, and more like Queen Elizabeth's Wraith than ever.

"I am very idle," she was saying to herself, "but I feel that not one of the books that ever were written would interest me to-day. I have no spirit or energy for travels, history is too full of war and bloodshed, and biography would weary me; a novel—well, no I think not; I am not in the mood for other people's love-stories. I wish some one would write a novel about elderly people," she went on—"middle-aged, prosaic people, who have outlived their romance. How soothing such a book would be! I could almost write it myself. There should be plenty of incident, and very little moralising; and it would be like one of those grey winter days, when the sunlight is veiled in soft vapour, and every window one passes is red with the firelight of home."

The fancy pleased her, and she smiled at her own conceit; but it faded in a moment when the door-bell rang.

"A visitor at this time in the morning!" she thought, and a little frown of annoyance gathered on her brow; but it vanished when Mitchell threw open the door and announced Lord Ralston.

"Why, Moritz!" she exclaimed, and her voice was full of surprise and pleasure, "this is indeed a welcome sight. How long is it since you last honoured our poor abode? Draw that chair up to the fire and give some account of yourself. Even Gwen seems to have forgotten our existence since baby Murdoch made his appearance!"

"Ah, you may well say so," returned Moritz, with a dismal shake of his head. "Gwen is incorrigible. I give you my word, Althea, that the beatitude of that young woman is so excessive and so fatuous that it resembles idiocy. She fairly drivels with sentiment over that infant, and he is as ugly and snub-nosed a little chap as Gwen was herself. He has even got her freckles; and she calls them beauty-spots;" and Lord Ralston's voice expressed unmitigated disgust.

Althea laughed.

"I do not suppose that Madam endorses these sentiments. I should like to hear Mrs. Compton's opinion of her grandson."

"Well, she vows he is a fine child, and he has got Jack's eyes. But, all the same, I heard her tell Gwen that a plain baby often became a handsome man. So we can make our own deductions from that. 'Murdoch has his good points,' she went on, 'and he will improve.' And, would you believe it? that idiotic Gwen became as red as a turkey-cock.

"'There is no improvement wanted,' she said, indignantly. 'My precious baby is perfect. He is beautiful in his mother's eyes, whatever his cross old grandmother chooses to say!' And then she hugged the little chap and cried over him, and all the time Madam sat beaming on them both, with her fine old face tremulous with happiness.

"It is Ruth and Naomi over again," finished Moritz. "Madam still finds fault with Jack sometimes, but never with Gwen, and the way Gwen toadies her passes belief."

"Gwendoline is very happy, certainly. Never was there a better-matched couple than she and Jack Compton." Althea spoke in a tone of warm interest. She had forgotten her distaste for other people's love-stories at that moment, and the thought of her young cousin's happiness was pleasant to her. "Dear Gwen, I am so fond of her. I am glad that one man had the sense to fall in love with her, in spite of her plain face; but you know, Moritz, that I always thought Gwen's ugliness quite charming."

"Yes, but I could not have done it in Jack's place," returned Moritz, rather thoughtfully. "I am too great an admirer of beauty." And then he changed the subject a little abruptly. "Jack and Gwen and their son and heir have been staying with me at Brentwood. I had a house-party for Christmas and the New Year, and I wanted Gwen to play hostess. It was an awful bore, and I got pretty sick of it, but they had both been lecturing me on the duties I owed to my fellow-creatures. Well, I have played my Lord Frivol long enough, and now I am plain Mr. Ingram again."

"What, still masquerading? Isn't it time for you to unmask?" But he shook his head.

"No, not yet; but there is method in my madness. We have not quite completed our little comedy, but I think the closing scene will be effective." He shut his eyes as though to picture the scene, and then opened them abruptly. "I have not been to Cleveland Terrace for an age. In fact, I only came up from Brentwood this morning, and on my way up here I passed Doreen and Miss Ward."

"Oh, then you knew I was alone?"

"To be sure I did. That is why I appear in my true character. I suppose"—his voice changing perceptibly—"that Miss Mollie and her father and my friend the humourist are well?" But Moritz did not look at Althea as he put this question, and so did not see the little smile on her lips.

"They were quite well when Waveney went home on Sunday. She said Mollie was a little pale and tired; but then, she had been taking too long a walk. She spent a night here on the evening of our girls' entertainment. It was quite amusing to see how they all admired her. She was the May Queen in one of the tableaux. It was the prettiest thing imaginable."

"I wish I had seen it;" and Lord Ralston's eyes were dark and bright. If Althea had not guessed his secret long ago, she would have guessed it now. With one of those sudden impulses which were natural to her, she put her hand gently on his arm.

"Moritz," she said, in her sweet, womanly way, "does Gwen know. Have you made her your confidante?"

Just for a moment Moritz drew himself up a little stiffly—as though he resented the question; but the kindness in Althea's eyes disarmed him, and perhaps his need of sympathy was too great.

"There was no need to tell her," he returned, in a low voice; "she found it out for herself. Gwen is very acute about such things."

"And she approves?"

"Oh, we have not come to that point yet"—speaking in his old, airy manner—"but she was very much interested, and as good as gold. She laughed at me a little for what she called my fantastic chivalry; but, all the same, she seemed to like it."

"But, Moritz, why are you so afraid of appearing in your true colours? I do not see that Viscount Ralston is a less interesting person than Mr. Ingram."

"Perhaps not," he returned, drily; "but we all have our whims. I am an Idealist, you must remember that, and I have a wish to stand on my own merits as a man, and not to make myself taller by posing on my pedestal of thirty thousand a year. It may be a foolish whimsie, but it is a harmless one, and affords me plenty of innocent amusement."

Althea smiled, but she knew it was useless to pursue the argument. Moritz and Gwendoline were both utterly unmanageable when they had a crotchet in their head. They cared nothing about the world's opinion, and as for Madam Grundy, or any other madam, they had simply no regard for them. Already Viscount Ralston was considered a most eccentric person, and sundry matrons had admonished their daughters on no account to contradict him. "He is a little odd, certainly," one of them remarked, "but I am told he is really clever and original, and that sort of thing wears off after a time. Your father is very much taken with him, so you may make yourself as agreeable as you like to Lord Ralston."

"And when may I ask him to marry me?" returned the daughter, to whom this Machiavellian speech had been addressed; for Lady Ginevra had plenty of spirit, and was clever enough to read between the lines. "Mother was terribly put out," she informed her younger sister afterwards. "She lectured me for ten minutes on what she called my coarseness and vulgarity; but, as I told her, I prefer vulgarity to hypocrisy. 'You and father want me to marry Viscount Ralston,' I told her, 'because he has Brentwood Hall and a fine house in town and thirty thousand a year, and it does not matter one bit if I care for him or not; if he holds out the sceptre to me I am to touch it.' But, thank heavens, Jenny, these are not the Dark Ages, and though mother frowned and stamped her foot, there was no 'Get thee to a nunnery!'" And Lady Ginevra laughed and went off to put on her habit, for it was the hour when she and her father rode in the park.

Althea had a word to say before she let the subject drop.

"At the theatre you spoke of needing my help, Moritz. I hope you will let me know when my assistance is wanted."

"Oh, I was going to speak to you about that," he returned, quickly. "You see, my dear cousin, that there are circumstances in which a man is bound not to be selfish. Miss Mollie"—how his voice always softened as he said the name!—"is so simple and childlike; she knows so little of the world, and her life has been so retired, that I dare not hurry matters. She must learn to know and trust me before I can venture to make my meaning plain."

"Yes, I can understand that."

"Gwen quite agrees with me, but all the same I think—at least, I hope—that Monsieur Blackie's probation will soon be over, but Gwen and I have all our plans in readiness. What do you say to a picnic party at Brentwood about the middle of next month?"

"My dear Moritz, are you crazy? Really, an Idealist in love is a terrible being. A picnic in the middle of February! Do you want the three grim sisters, snow and hail and frost, to be among your guests?"

"Pshaw! nonsense!" he replied, impatiently. "There are lovely spring-like days in February. Besides, with the sort of picnic I mean, weather will not signify. You had better hear my programme first, Althea."

"Oh, go on," she returned, in a resigned voice. "I will try to forget my common-sense while I listen to you."

But he only twirled his moustache triumphantly.

"The party will be small and select; just you and the two Misses Ward and Gwen and myself."

"And not Noel?" in some surprise.

"Noel! Oh, dear, no! My friend the humourist would be decidedly de trop. He is too acute and wide-awake a youth, and Monsieur Blackie would be found out in a moment."

"But I thought Lord Ralston was to be our host!" Althea spoke in a puzzled tone. Then Moritz patted her in a soothing manner.

"Keep calm, I entreat you," he said, gently. "In the presence of great thoughts we should always keep calm. Lord Ralston is my intimate friend, please understand that. We are like brothers, he and I, and it is for the corner of his picture-gallery, at Brentwood, that King Canute was bought; Miss Ward and her sister will be interested to see it again. And as Brentwood Hall, with its Silent Pool, is a show place—a picnic there will be the most natural thing in the world."

"And the master is absent."

"Yes, he is absent—but he may return at any moment;" and here there was a strange glow in Moritz's eyes. "We must leave town early," he went on, briskly, after a moment's pause—"and I think we could reach Brentwood by midday. Gwen has promised to meet us at the Hall, and we shall have plenty of time to see the picture-gallery, and more of the rooms before luncheon. I shall coach the servants carefully, so there will be no contretemps. After luncheon there will be the conservatories and the Silent Pool, and then tea in the blue drawing-room; it will be light until half-past five, so you may as well tell Doreen not to expect you home until eight. Oh, I forgot one important part of the programme: Gwen means to carry you off to Kingsdene, either before or after tea, to see baby Murdoch and Madam; she is staying with them at present."

It was evident, from Althea's amused look, that the picnic at Brentwood would meet with her approval, and she was just about to give a cordial assent when Mitchell entered to tell her that luncheon was ready; and at the same time she handed her a telegram.

"It is for Miss Ward, ma'am," she said; "and the boy is waiting."

"Then I suppose I had better open it," returned Althea. "There was some talk of their going to Cleveland Terrace to have tea with Mollie, if they finished their shopping in time. Perhaps this is to say that she is out or engaged." And then Althea opened the yellow envelope. But her countenance changed as she read the telegram.

"Do not come," was all it said. "Mollie is ill—will write." It was from Everard Ward.

CHAPTER XXVIII.: "BUT YET THE PITY OF IT."

"For this relief much thanks."—Hamlet.

When Althea had read the brief message, she told Mitchell very quietly that there was no answer required, and that she might give the boy some refreshment and send him away; and then, as the maid left the room, she handed the telegram to Moritz.

It troubled her kind heart to see the pain in his eyes as he read it. He was quite pale, and his lips twitched under his moustache.

"What does it mean?" he asked, in rather a stifled voice. "I thought you said that she was well. If she is ill, why is her sister to be kept away? You see what he says: 'Do not come.'"

"Yes, I see," returned Althea, very gravely. "It must be something sudden; but I hope, for poor dear Waveney's sake, that it is nothing infectious. Let me think for a moment—one cannot grasp it at once. This is Wednesday, and on Sunday Mollie was well—only a little pale and tired; and yes, I remember, she had a slight headache, and so Waveney persuaded her not to go to church."

"A headache and pale and tired! Good heavens, Althea, it is clear as daylight! She was sickening for something." Moritz's tone was so tragical, and he paced the room so restlessly, that, in spite of her very real anxiety, Althea could hardly repress a smile.

"Dear Moritz," she said, gently, "there is no need to take such a gloomy view. Our pretty Mollie is human, and must be ill sometimes like other people. Perhaps it is a bad cold or influenza, or it might even be measles—they are very much about."

For Moritz's "unregenerate woman" had been singularly captious since the New Year, and close muggy days had paved the way for all kinds of ailments to which flesh is heir.

There was a great deal of sickness at Dereham, and Althea had been both wise and careful in refusing to allow Waveney to go as usual amongst her pensioners.

"Of course it may be anything," returned Lord Ralston, impatiently,—for even his easy temper was not proof against the bitterness of his disappointment,—he had so hungered and thirsted, poor fellow, for a sight of Mollie's sweet face. All these weeks he had been doing his duty nobly, and now he had looked for his reward. "Absence makes the heart grow fonder," he had said to himself that very morning. Would "this bud of love" which he had been nurturing so tenderly, have blossomed into "a beauteous flower" when they met again? Over and over again he had asked himself this question; but Mollie was ill, and all hope of an immediate answer was over.

"It may be anything," he repeated. "But who is to look after her? There is only her father and that half-witted maid-of-all-work. There used to be some friend who nursed them when they were ill, but she is living somewhere in the country with an invalid lady. We must get a nurse. Do you know where their doctor lives?"

But Althea shook her head.

"No; but we can find out. Moritz, I think the best plan will be for me to go over to Cleveland Terrace, and then I can tell Waveney exactly how things are; I will leave a line for Doreen and beg her to say nothing until my return." Then a look of intense relief crossed Moritz's face.

"It is a good idea," he said, eagerly; "and I will go with you." And Althea made no objection to this.

"It is a pity the carriage is out," she said, regretfully; "but George shall get us a cab. Now we will go and have some luncheon, and then I will get ready." But with both of them the meal was a pretence. Apprehension and worry deprived Moritz of all appetite, and Althea was so nervous and fluttered at the idea of encountering Everard in his own home, that she could scarcely eat a morsel.

She rose as soon as possible, and left Moritz to finish his repast; but he preferred pacing the room. In spite of his vivacity and gaieté-de-c[oe]ur, his jaunty airs and cheerfulness, he was easily depressed. Any form of illness that attacked those he loved, preyed on his mind. When Gwendoline's little son was born, he was so anxious and despondent that Jack Compton, in spite of his own natural solicitude for his young wife's safety, laughed at him and told him "that he looked as melancholy as a gib cat." "The old chap was in the doldrums and no mistake," he said to Gwen afterwards. "I tell him I played the man twice as well as he. But he is a good old sort, too." And then, with awe and wonder, the young father regarded the small and crumpled and exceedingly red morsel of humanity, lying snugly within Gwen's arm.

As they drove up to Cleveland Terrace they saw an unmistakable doctor's brougham before the door of Number Ten. Lord Ralston's swarthy complexion turned rather livid at the sight, but Althea only remarked, with composure, that they had come just at the right time.

Noel opened the door to them; he had seen them from the window; his face brightened perceptibly. "Father has gone up with Dr. Duncan," he said; "but they will be coming down directly; you had better come up into the studio. There is a fire there." And Noel led the way. Althea glanced quickly round the room as she entered. It was shabby, there could be no doubt of that, but there was an air of comfort about it. And then she subsided wearily into a corner of the big, cosy-looking couch; but Moritz marched off to the inner room and stood with his back to them, gazing at poor Mollie's little writing-table with an aching heart.

"Noel, what is the matter with your sister?" asked Althea, in a low voice; but Noel could not tell her. She had seemed queer and feverish the previous day, he explained, and his father had advised her remaining in bed. She had had a bad night, and her throat was painful, and he had been forbidden to go near her. This was Dr. Duncan's first visit. They had sent for him in the morning, but he had been unable to come until now.

It was evident that Noel could not enlighten them much, so Althea forebore to question him further, and waited silently until they heard footsteps descending the stairs; but as they passed by the studio door Althea heard the doctor say,—

"I will look in later and see what you have done about the nurse."

Noel heard it, too, for he looked rather startled.

"A nurse!" he muttered. "Poor old pater, that will bother him a bit." And then Everard came quickly into the room.

"Noel, I want you!" he said, rather sharply. "Duncan says——" but here he stopped in sudden surprise as Althea's tall figure rose from the couch.

"Mr. Ward," she said, quietly, "Waveney was out, so I opened your telegram, and I have come to see if there is anything I can do for Mollie. My cousin, Lord—I mean Mr. Ingram, has brought me." Then Everard, with rather a sad smile, held out his hand to the young man.

"You are both very kind," he said, simply, "but there is nothing you can do for the dear child. Mollie is very ill, and Dr. Duncan wishes her to have a good nurse at once. I am going to send Noel off to the Institution. He has given me the address—it is diphtheria, and her throat is in a dreadful state, and there is no time to be lost."

"Let me go," returned Moritz, earnestly. "I will take a hansom and be there in no time. Mr. Ward, I shall esteem it as a favour and a mark of true friendship if you will send me instead of Noel." But before Everard could reply to this urgent request, Althea's gentle voice interposed.

"Mr. Ward, please listen to me a moment. I know what this illness means—I have had it myself—Mollie will need two nurses; there would be no one to take care of her by day while the nurse rests, and any neglect would be an awful risk. Please let Moritz go and settle the business. There need only be one to-night, but the day-nurse must relieve her to-morrow morning. Let him have the address, and Noel can go with him; and then you must let me go up and see Mollie." And then Everard, in a dazed fashion, held out a folded piece of paper.

"Two nurses! I shall be in the workhouse," they heard him mutter. But no one took any notice.

"Althea, you are a trump," whispered Moritz, as she followed him into the passage. "Tell me anything she needs, and I will get it. Two nurses!—she shall have a dozen nurses. If the doctor approves, we will have a second opinion; we will have the great throat doctor, Sir Hindley Richmond, down." But what more Moritz would have said in that eager, sibilant whisper, was never known, for Althea gave him an impatient little push.

"Go—go; there is no use in talking. I shall not leave until the nurse arrives." And then she went back into the studio.

She had forgotten her nervousness now, her reluctance to enter Everard's house; her face glowed with kindly, womanly sympathy, as she approached him.

"I am so sorry for you," she said, gently; "and I am sorry for dear Mollie, too, for it is such a painful complaint. But with good nursing I hope she will soon be well. Is Dr. Duncan a clever man?"

"Oh, yes, I believe so," returned Mr. Ward, dejectedly; "but his charges are very high. Miss Harford, I am afraid we must manage with one nurse. I have not the means. I am a poor man." But Althea turned a deaf ear to this. It was far too early in the day to proffer help. He must not be told yet that he had good friends, who were only too thankful to be allowed to bear his burdens. For Mollie's sake, for Waveney's sake, and for poor Moritz's sake, there must be no indulgence of false and misplaced pride. He must be managed adroitly and with finesse and female diplomacy—no masculine blundering must effect this.

"How did Mollie catch it?" she asked, to turn his thoughts from the question of expense. But Everard could not answer this question. Mollie had not seemed well since Sunday, he said; she had been restless and irritable, and complained of feeling ill. She had been so feverish in the night that he thought it must be influenza, and he had sent for Dr. Duncan; but, early as it was, he had already started on his rounds, and had only just come. He would pay another visit later in the evening. Althea listened to this in silence; then she said, rather gravely,—

"Mr. Ward, what are we to do about Waveney? It will break her heart to be kept from Mollie; and yet——" Then he turned upon her almost fiercely, and there was an excited gleam in his eyes.

"I will not have it. Tell Waveney that I forbid her to come near the house. Good heavens! would she add to my troubles? Is it not enough to have one child ill?" Then his eyes filled with tears, and the hand he put on Althea's arm shook a little. "Dear Miss Harford, be my friend in this; keep Waveney safe for me." And something in his tone told Althea that, dearly as Everard loved all his children, this was the one who came closest to his heart.

"Do not fear," she returned, tenderly. "You can trust me, and Waveney loves you far too well to disobey you; but"—here she sighed—"it will certainly break her heart. Mollie is her other and her dearer self."

"Yes, poor darling, I know that; but she must be brave. Tell her, from me, please, that I will write twice a day if that will comfort her. She shall know everything. There shall be nothing hidden from her."

"Yes, I will tell her," returned Althea, sorrowfully. "And when my cousin returns, we will arrange about Noel; he must not stop here." Then there was an unmistakable look of gratitude in Everard's eyes.

"You think of everything," he said, in a broken voice. "I was troubling sadly about the poor lad. Now I am afraid I must leave you, as Mollie has no other nurse." But he was both touched and surprised when Althea rose, too.

"Let me go with you," she said, quickly; "I am not the least afraid. I had the complaint very badly myself before we left Kitlands."

"I fear we are both doing wrong," returned Everard, hesitating. "Your sister will be very angry with you." But Althea shook her head very decidedly at this, and he was too bewildered and miserable to argue the point.

The sick room looked bare and comfortless to Althea's eyes, in spite of the bright fire burning cheerily in the grate. The big iron bedstead, with its old and obviously patched quilt; the dark stained wood furniture, and the narrow window seats, with faded red cushions, were hardly a fit shrine for Mollie's dainty beauty. Mollie lay uncomfortably on her pillows; she looked flushed and ill, and her beautiful eyes had a heavy, distressed look in them. She held out her hands rather eagerly to Althea, but the next moment she drew them back.

"Oh, I forgot," she said, in a thick voice; and it was evidently a great effort to speak. "You must not come near me: Dr. Duncan said so. Tell my darling Wave that she must keep away if she loves me, and ask her not to fret. Oh, I cannot talk;" and here poor Mollie flung herself back on the pillows, and her hot, restless fingers tried to put back the heavy masses of rough tangled hair.

How Althea longed to brush it out and sponge the fevered face and hands! But at her first hint Everard frowned and looked anxious. "Not for worlds," he said, decidedly. "The nurse will be here directly. The Institution is hardly a mile from here, and Ingram will take a hansom." He spoke in a low voice, but Mollie heard him.

"Oh, father, is Mr. Ingram here?" she whispered. "How sorry he will be to hear I am ill!" And then a sudden thought struck her, and she beckoned to Althea rather excitedly. "Miss Harford," she said, in her poor, hoarse voice, "will you do something for me? In that small right-hand drawer behind you, you will see a little parcel; it is directed. Please give it to Mr. Ingram from me."

Althea secretly marvelled at this, but held her peace. When the dainty white parcel was in her hand, she said, gently,—

"Yes, dear Mollie, he shall have it directly he returns. But now your father does not wish me to stay. Good-bye. God bless you, my child." And Althea's tone of faltering tenderness arrested Everard's attention.

"It would not be safe. I dare not let you do anything for her," he said, very softly, as he opened the door. "I will stay with her until the nurse comes. But please, go down and rest." And Althea, who was trembling with some strange emotion, obeyed him without a word.

CHAPTER XXIX.: BARMECIDE'S FEAST, AND A BROWN STUDY.

Althea was glad of a few minutes' quiet to recover herself, for she felt agitated and shaken. The sight of that comfortless sick-room, and Everard's worn face and haggard eyes, oppressed and saddened her.

A perfect passion of pity for him and his motherless girls swept over her as she closed the door. She had left the room in answer to a wistful, pleading look from him; her presence there evidently troubled him, and he was unwilling for her to run any risk. It was kind, it was friendly of him, she thought. Everard always had a good heart; but at that moment her impulsive, highly wrought nature only yearned to show her sympathy in action. In spite of her sensitive nerves, she was constitutionally brave, and had no fear of any form of illness. "We shall only die when our time comes," was a favourite saying of hers, and neither she nor Doreen shirked anything that met them in their daily path of duty.

Mollie was very ill, there was little doubt of that, and she would probably be worse. The sight of the sweet, flushed face, and the remembrance of the poor, thick voice would haunt her, she knew; and there was Waveney——But at this point the sound of a hansom driving up rapidly dispersed her gloomy thoughts, and the next moment Lord Ralston entered the room.

"We have got her!" he said, triumphantly,—"Nurse Helena, the best and cleverest nurse in the Institution; and she will be here in ten minutes. I saw the matron, and there is another one coming at eleven to-morrow. I shall go round to Dr. Duncan's house presently, and have a talk with him. We must have Sir Hindley Richmond down, I am determined on that."

"Why not wait for to-morrow?" returned Althea, quietly. "You are so impetuous, Moritz. There is no need for you to see Dr. Duncan to-night. Poor dear Mollie is very ill—I have just seen her; but good nursing and the proper remedies may do wonders. Wait until to-morrow—it will be far better; and tell me what has become of Noel."

"He is up in his room putting up his things. I am going to take him round to Eaton Square directly. I shall stay there myself for the next week or two. And you really saw her, Althea? Is she—does she look very bad?" Moritz's anxiety was so intense he could hardly bring out the words.

"She is evidently in great pain," she returned, slowly. "It is impossible to judge at this stage. But she was able to speak to me. Moritz, she asked me to give you this; it was put away in a drawer, and she told me where to find it!" and Althea handed him the little white parcel.

"For me! are you sure it is for me?" he asked, breathlessly. But Althea, with a faint smile, only pointed to the direction, for, in Mollie's sprawling handwriting, was very lightly inscribed: "Mr. Ingram, with Mollie Ward's good wishes." Nothing could be more correct or proper. Then why did Lord Ralston's eyes brighten so strangely, and why did a sudden smile of tender amusement come to his lips? Because his keen scrutiny had detected something that Althea had not perceived—two half-obliterated letters before the "good": "lo"—he could make that out plainly. "With Mollie Ward's love"—that was what she had meant to write, until her maidenly scruples, and perhaps some sudden self-consciousness, induced her to change the inscription.

Moritz walked off into the inner room with his treasure. Would Mollie guess how her lover's heart beat almost to suffocation as he looked at the white vellum book with its clustering pansies?

"Little darling," he kept saying over and over to himself, "she must have known they were my favourite flowers." And then he looked at the first page and saw his name prettily illuminated. "Pansies, that's for thoughts," was the motto under it; and one or two pansies were drooping loosely underneath.

It was a dainty remembrance. Mollie had evidently not spared either time or thought for her friend. It was to be a token of her gratitude for all the pleasure Monsieur Blackie had given her, and for all his lavish gifts. But even Mollie could not guess, in the faintest degree, the intense joy that pansy pocket-book gave Ingram.

As he replaced it in its cover his eyes were dim, and his honest heart was recording its vows. If Mollie lived, her life's happiness, as far as human power could effect it, should be his task and joy. "My own darling, you are beginning to love me," he thought; "and now——" and then there was a stab of pain through the young man's heart, for how could he tell how long it would be before he saw "the angel laughing out of Mollie's eyes" again? When he went back into the other room he found Noel there. The nurse had arrived and had gone up to see her patient. And presently Everard came down to them.

He seemed a little surprised when Althea told him that Noel was going to stay with her cousin. "Moritz wants him, and they will be company for each other," she said. "It will be easier for him to go from there to St. Paul's by-and-bye." And as this was reasonable, Mr. Ward offered no objection. Then, at her suggestion, he sat down and wrote a few tender, urgent words to Waveney.

Althea took her leave after this. She had made another fruitless attempt to dissuade Moritz from going to Dr. Duncan; he was utterly unmanageable. "I mean to make a clean breast to him," he said, recklessly. "If he is a sensible man, he won't want any explanation. I shall tell him that Mr. Ward has influential friends, and that they wish a second opinion. Why, good heavens, Althea"—working himself up to a pitch of nervous excitement, "how do we know what that poor child needs, and that only money can buy?" And then Althea, with a vivid remembrance of that bare, dingy-looking room, wisely held her peace.

As she drove off she wondered vaguely, but without much interest, how Moritz was to keep up his masquerading at Eaton Square. Noel was a sharp-witted lad, as he had himself said, and there had been no opportunity of coaching the servants. An old retainer of the family, who had been the old viscount's butler, took care of the house when it was not occupied, and his wife and one or two maids kept a few rooms always in order. Moritz, who was a thorough Bohemian, had a habit of running up to town for a night or two as the fancy seized him, and he seldom announced his intention beforehand. More than once Mrs. Barham had been at her wits' end to make his lordship comfortable, but she soon got used to his odd ways, and now, when Moritz arrived at his town house, he was sure of finding his dining-room and library and a couple of bedrooms in first-rate order. Althea need not have wondered if she had listened to the brief conversation that took place between Moritz and Noel on their way to Eaton Square.

It was rather late, for Moritz, like an obstinate man, had had his way; he had left Noel in the cab and had seen the doctor alone. Though Dr. Duncan was a sensible man and no toady, he was much impressed by Lord Ralston's impetuous generosity. He could not deny, he said, that there were many things that his patient required, though he had forborne to name them, as he knew Mr. Ward had small means. Sir Hindley Richmond! Oh, certainly, he had no objection to meet him; but there was no need for that at present. He would keep it in mind; and Mr. Ward must be consulted. And then, after a little more talk, and a promise on the doctor's part to respect his confidence, the interview ceased. Moritz felt a little happier when he jumped into the hansom again. He thought Dr. Duncan had spoken hopefully of the case; and then, as he looked at the list in his hand, he foresaw a delightful morning's work before him.

To rush from shop to shop, to pay the highest price possible for each article, to order in fabulous quantities of the needed commodities, would be purest joy to him. If Mollie recovered she would find herself stocked for a year or two with eau-de-cologne and other good things.

"What an age you have been!" grumbled Noel. The poor lad was too cold and hungry and miserable to mind his manners. "Wasn't the old chap in?"

"Oh, yes, he was in," replied Ingram, vaguely. And then he pushed up the little trap-door and told the man to drive to Number Fourteen, Eaton Square. "I hope Mrs. Barham will be able to give us something to eat," he continued. "You see, she does not expect us, and there may be nothing in the house."

Noel's face grew rather long at this.

"Is it your house? Do you live there?" he asked, curiously.

"Yes," returned Ingram, "It is my house, but I am not often there. I have another house in the country." And then, rather abruptly, "Noel, lad, can you keep a secret—honour bright, you know, and all that sort of thing?"

Then Noel looked up in his face a little suspiciously, and there was a knowing twinkle in his eyes.

"Mum's the word," he said, quickly, "but I know what you are going to say. Your name isn't Ingram."

"Oh, yes, it is," returned the other, rather amused at this, "only I have another. It is the family name. My father was Colonel Ingram, and until eighteen months ago I was plain Mr. Ingram."

"And now?" and there was growing excitement in Noel's voice.

"Well, the only difference is an old cousin died, and so I became Viscount Ralston. Why, my boy," with a little chuckling laugh, "I was as poor as a church mouse before that—poorer than your father. I painted bad pictures that would not sell, and lived in a tin shanty, hold hard—don't interrupt me, for we shall be at my diggings directly. I want you to understand that for the present, at Cleveland Terrace and at the Red House, I am still Mr. Ingram. I have my reasons, and some day you shall know them; but I want you to promise that you will not betray me." Then Noel, feeling utterly bewildered, and not a little mystified, nodded an assent to this, and the next moment they stopped before one of the big, gloomy-looking houses in Eaton Square. A tall, grey-haired old man admitted them.

"I have taken you by surprise, Barham," observed Lord Ralston, carelessly; "and you see I have brought a friend."

"Yes, my lord," returned Barham, tranquilly. "And I am glad to say there is a fire in the library; but there is something wrong with the dining-room chimney, and the workmen have been there."

"All right. Just pay the cabman." And then Lord Ralston led the way to the library. It was a large room, and the firelight played fitfully over the carved oak furniture and red morocco chairs. The next moment the soft electric light enabled Noel to see his surroundings more plainly. Since his visit to the Red House his views had been considerably enlarged, and he at once told himself that this room beat Miss Harford's library hollow. Lord Ralston left him for a few moments. When he returned he said, with something of his old whimsical dryness,—

"I have just been interviewing my worthy housekeeper, and have left her metaphorically tearing her hair in the larder. She tells me that there is literally nothing in the house, so I suppose we may expect Barmecide's feast."

Noel nodded. He was well acquainted with the story of "The Barber's Sixth Brother," and quite understood the allusion. But the youthful pangs of hunger were so overmastering that he murmured something about bread-and-cheese, and then coloured up to the roots of his hair, fearing that he had taken a liberty.

"Oh, Mrs. Barham is a woman of resources; she will do better for us than that," was the indifferent reply. "But we must exercise our patience. I will take you up to your room now."

And Noel presently found himself ensconced in a most luxurious chamber, with a bright fire, and everything prepared for his comfort.

"It is like the 'Arabian Nights,'" muttered the lad, when his host had left him. "To think of my cheek—Monsieur Blackie, indeed!" And then Noel sat on the edge of the chair and chuckled. "A viscount! Great Scott! Lord Ralston! My word, how the pater and old Storm-and-Stress will open their eyes! To think that 'the wobbly one' will be my lady some day!" And here Noel gave a long, low whistle, proving that, in spite of that vulgarity, inherent in the English school-boy, the embryo barrister had his wits about him. "It does not take much eyesight to see a blank wall— especially when it is painted white, and the sun shines," he had observed once to Waveney. "Any fool can see that chap is dead nuts on Mollie"—which was forcible if a trifle coarse.

When Noel found his way back, with some difficulty, to the library, he saw a charming little dinner-table laid in readiness. Mrs. Barham evidently knew her business well. The fish and cutlets, and sweet omelette, were all excellent; and a wonderful dessert followed.

Lord Ralston was most kind and hospitable, but he was hardly as good a companion as usual; he seemed absent, and was continually falling into a brown study. When dinner was over, and coffee had been brought, he gave up all attempt to be sociable. He even invited Noel to help himself to a book, and for the remainder of the evening Lord Ralston sat in silence, with his eyes fixed on the beech-logs, which were burning and sputtering so merrily.

It was nearly dinner-time at the Red House when Althea reached home. Doreen, who was already dressed, was waiting for her in the library. Waveney was still upstairs.

There was a short and hurried explanation on Althea's part, and a few ejaculations of pity from Doreen. Then she followed her sister upstairs and sent Peachy away.

It was one of their pretty sisterly ways to wait on each other occasionally, and Althea, who was accustomed to this loving ministry, took it calmly and as a matter of course. Doreen wanted to talk to her, that was all.

"I am so sorry you had such a wretched afternoon," observed Doreen, affectionately. "Poor dear, you were hardly fit for it. How was Mr. Ward? I am afraid he will be dreadfully anxious."

"Anxious! I should think so from his looks. I should say he had had no sleep. Do you know, Dorrie, I have discovered something to-day; dearly as Everard loves all his children, it is Waveney who is the apple of his eye."

"He loves her better than his pretty Mollie? Oh, no, Althea."

"Yes, dear, I am sure of it, and I cannot say I am greatly surprised. Mollie is a dear, sweet child, but Waveney is more human and spirituelle, her nature has greater depth. Oh, there is the gong. Please help me to arrange this ruff. Dorrie, you must do all the talking at dinner. Waveney must have no hint of anything until we have finished—there is the shopping and your purchases; you must make the most of those."

"So you went out, after all?" was Waveney's first remark, when grace had been said; and her voice was rather reproachful. "And you promised that you would have a day's rest!"

"It hardly amounted to a promise, I think," returned Althea, with a forced smile. "One never knows what may turn up in the day's work, and I had to go out on an errand of charity. Well, how have you enjoyed your shopping expedition?" And this question launched Waveney at once into a lengthy description of all their purchases.

"It was too late to think of going to Cleveland Terrace," she finished, regretfully, "so we had tea at Fuller's instead. The cakes were delicious. Oh, how I longed for Mollie to be with us! She does so love buying pretty things."

"Oh, I forgot;" interposed Doreen, abruptly. "Mrs. Craven was at Marshall & Snellgrove's, buying things for Augusta's trousseau. We had quite a long talk, in the mantle department. I have ordered a nice waterproof cloak, Althea; it is Harris tweed, and your favourite grey." And so on, discussing the merits of each article purchased until dinner was over, and, with an unmistakable look of relief, Althea rose from the table.

CHAPTER XXX.: SUSPENSE.

"Down thou climbing sorrow! Thy element's below." King Lear.
"Till now thy soul has been All glad and gay: Bid it awake, and look At grief to-day."
Adelaide Anne Procter.

As Althea walked into the library, she was aware that Waveney was following her closely. Doreen had made some excuse and had gone off to her own room, probably to write letters.

"Do you want me to read to you to-night?" asked Waveney. She looked wonderfully bright and animated this evening. As she spoke she slipped her hand into Althea's arm, in a coaxing, girlish way. "Dear Miss Harford, I am not a bit tired. I feel as springy as possible"—this being a favourite word in the Ward vocabulary to express latent and superfluous energy.

"No, my child, not to-night," returned Althea, gravely. "Waveney, dear, I am afraid I have rather bad news for you. You were out when the message came, so I went over to Cleveland Terrace to inquire."

Then a troubled, almost a scared look, came into the girl's eyes.

"A message!" she gasped. "Did they send for me? Is any one ill—father? or——" But she did not finish the sentence, as Althea quietly handed her the telegram.

"What does it mean?" she asked in a bewildered tone; but her lips were trembling. "Mollie ill! But she is never ill. Except when we had the measles, she has never been in bed a single day for years. What is it? Why do you not tell me?" and Waveney spoke in a tone of intense irritation.

"I am waiting, dear, until you can listen to me," returned her friend, soothingly. "My cousin Moritz was with me when the telegram came"—here Waveney started—"and I thought—we both thought—that the best thing would be for me to go over to Cleveland Terrace. Moritz went with me. We saw your father, and I went up to Mollie. It is diphtheria—no one knows how she has caught it. She is ill, and her throat is very painful, but she could speak to me. She sent her love, and said that you must not think of coming to her."

Then an incredulous smile crossed Waveney's face.

"Mollie said that, but of course she did not mean it; the idea is too absurd. If I were not so miserable I could laugh at it. Not go to my Mollie when she is ill and in pain! Has father sent for Dr. Duncan, and have they given her a fire?—the room is so cold!" Then, interrupting herself with sudden impatience, "Why do I stop to ask these questions when it is getting late? Oh, Miss Harford, you ought to have told me before dinner! What does that matter? But I will get ready now. And if you will be kind enough to send for a cab, I shall not be five minutes changing my frock"—for even at the supreme moment some instinct told the girl that sapphire blue velveteen was not quite suitable for a sick room.

Althea was quite shaken by Waveney's impetuosity. It was evident that her young companion had entirely forgotten her rôle; her sole idea was that Mollie was ill, and that nothing else mattered. She was actually half-way to the door when Althea called her back in a tone that arrested even her attention.

"Waveney, my poor child, what are you doing? Did you not understand the telegram? Your father will not allow you to go home—he told me so himself; and here is a note he has sent you." Then Waveney, without a word, took the letter.

When Waveney had finished the letter, there was despair in her eyes.

"He is cruel. Every one is cruel," she said, in a choked, unnatural voice. And then, with a dry sob, "Oh, why am I not lying there in her place!"

"Do not say that, dear child," returned Althea, gently; "for then Mollie would have to suffer." And at this Waveney winced.

"Where are you going?" Althea spoke rather nervously, for again the girl seemed about to leave her. "Oh, Waveney, surely you will not go against your father's wishes." But she need not have asked the question. The loyal little soul would have died sooner than grieve that beloved parent.

"No, I cannot disobey father," she said, in a dull voice; and her poor little face looked so white and rigid. "I am going to my own room now."

"Will you not stay and let me talk to you a little?" asked Althea, anxiously. "You are taking things too hardly, dear. Mollie may be better to-morrow."

But she spoke to deaf ears.

"No, no. Please do not keep me. I must be alone. There is no use in talking. How do you know, how does any one know about things?" and Waveney abruptly turned away.

Althea's eyes looked very sad as the door closed behind her. "I knew it," she said to herself. "I knew how she would suffer. Her nature is intense. Those who love much, suffer much. Mollie and she seem to have only one heart between them. It is not so with all twins." But the next moment her dreary moralising was interrupted; for Waveney came hastily back and stood by her.

"I did not bid you good-night," she said, huskily. "I am afraid I was rude and abrupt; but I did not mean it. And you are so kind, so kind."

Then Althea put her arms round the girl and kissed her tenderly. "My dear, do not trouble about that. I quite understand. May I come to you presently? I may be able to think of something to comfort you." But Waveney shook her head.

"No; please do not come. There is no comfort for me while my Mollie is ill and suffering;" and Waveney drew her cold hands out of Althea's detaining grasp. It was sad to see how her step had suddenly lost its springiness. To be alone—that was her one thought now, as it is the instinct of all sorely wounded creatures in God's free world.

Waveney never recalled that night of misery without a shudder. The sudden shock quite prostrated her. That Mollie should be ill, perhaps dangerously ill!—for every one knew that people died of diphtheria: Princess Alice had, and the butcher's little daughter, and one or two others that she and Mollie knew—that Mollie should be ill, and that her only sister should not be allowed to nurse her!—this was almost inconceivable to Waveney.

It was this separation that seemed so unnatural, and Waveney chafed bitterly against her father's restrictions. After those first unguarded expressions she did not blame him in words, but again and again in her heart she accused him of cruelty.

"Oh, father, how could you, how could you!" she said over and over again that night. "It is not right, it is not fair, that you should torture me like this. If I were only there I should not be so unnerved and frightened, but everything is worse when one is kept away."

Waveney was right from her own point of view. She would have been her brave, resolute little self at Cleveland Terrace, and Mollie would have had the tenderest and most cheery of nurses.

"I should not have taken it. I should have been careful and left the nurse to do things," she said later on. "It was just father's nervousness."

Dr. Duncan's opinion she treated with contempt. It was part of a doctor's duty to say these things.

More than once Althea crept to the girl's door; but she could hear nothing. Once she turned the handle, but the door was locked. Waveney, who was still sitting huddled up in the easy-chair, heard the soft, retreating footsteps go down the passage again. Her fire had burnt out, and she felt strangely chilled. "I may as well go to bed," she thought, drearily; but it was long before the deadly cold left her limbs. Even when she slept, her dreams troubled her, and she woke the next morning to see Althea standing beside her bed with a cup of hot coffee in one hand, and in her other a yellow envelope.

"Will you drink this, my dear? Doreen and I have had our breakfast, but there is no need for you to hurry. If you lie still Nurse Marks will bring you yours."

"Oh, no, I could not think of such a thing," returned Waveney, quite shocked. "I am not ill. I would rather get up, please. I am so sorry I have overslept myself; but I was late, and——" Then she looked at the telegram wistfully. "Is that for me, Miss Harford?"

"No, my dear, it is for me. Moritz sent over to Cleveland Terrace quite early this morning. You will see what he says.

"'Miss Ward not so well. A bad night. Shall wire for Richmond.'"

"What does it mean?" returned Waveney, faintly, and her head sank back on the pillow. "I don't understand it."

"It means that you and Mollie have a good friend," returned Althea, sitting down beside her, "a very kind and generous friend. Moritz wants to help you all. Sir Hindley Richmond is the great throat doctor. He is wonderfully clever, and some of his cures are marvellous; but his fees are immense, and of course Moritz knows that Mr. Ward could not afford to have him, so he is arranging it with Dr. Duncan."

"But we have no right—we have no claim on Mr. Ingram," stammered Waveney. "But he is doing it for Mollie's sake."

She said it quite simply. In her own mind it had long been an assured fact that Mr. Ingram was her sister's lover. How could any one mistake such devotion?

"Yes, he is doing it for Mollie's sake," returned Althea, with equal frankness. "Poor fellow! he is very unhappy about her, and his only comfort is to do her service."

And Althea smiled a little as she thought of that tender and fantastic chivalry with which Moritz was wooing his beautiful Mollie.

"I will get up now," Waveney observed, restlessly. Mollie was not so well. It would drive her frantic to lie still and think of that. She would dress and go out. Miss Althea was too kind to think of asking her to write and read. She could not sit still. She must have air and movement.

But though she said no word of this, Althea understood her perfectly.

"We must leave her alone," she said, rather sadly, to Doreen. "Her nerves are unhinged by the suspense, and she is not used to trouble.

"I shall drive down to Cleveland Terrace," she continued, "on my way to Aunt Sara. There may be some little thing Mollie requires, and Waveney will be glad of news." She spoke rather hurriedly, as though she feared Doreen might raise some objection. But Doreen, who could read her sister like a book, merely nodded assent.

So all the morning Waveney wandered about the common like a little lost spirit, until her limbs ached with weariness; and after luncheon Noel arrived.

Mr. Ingram had sent him, he said, bringing out the words rather sheepishly. They had been shopping all the morning, tearing up and down Regent's Street and Bond Street in a hansom, and they had had luncheon at the Army and Navy Stores. Then they had called at the door of Number Ten, and Noel had seen his father. Things were much the same, and he sent his love, and so on.

Althea had already started when Noel made his appearance, so it was too late to prevent her fruitless journey to Chelsea.

There was nothing Mollie wanted, Noel declared, bluntly, and he chuckled as he thought of all the things Ingram had ordered. "My word, there's no mistake about his being a viscount," he thought. "If he turned out to be a duke I should hardly be surprised."

Waveney was very fond of her young brother, but his society failed to give her comfort; and Noel, on his side, was so awed and depressed by her sad face and unusual silence, that he could find little to say. It was quite a relief when his visit was over, and he had to return to Eaton Square.

But one word he did say as Waveney followed him into the hall.

"I say, Wave, I suppose you will send your compliments or kind regards to Mr. Ingram"—and here Noel cleared his throat. "He is awfully cut up, you know, and all that."

"Oh, yes, you may give him my kind regards," returned Waveney, in a listless tone. Then her conscience accused her of ingratitude. "Yes, certainly, Noel, my kindest regards. I know how good he has been; he is actually going to have that great throat doctor down to see dear Mollie."

"I know that," replied Noel, mysteriously. "I know a thing or two that would make you stare. He is a good old sort; he is as good as they make them, and he deserves to turn up trumps." And with this peculiar form of blessing—which was nevertheless genuine in its way—Noel adjusted his pince-nez, and marched off with his head in the air as usual.

When Althea returned, she had very little to add to this. Mollie was no better, certainly, and Dr. Duncan was undoubtedly anxious about her; but she had excellent nurses, and Sir Hindley Richmond was to come the next day.

There had been some hitch or difficulty, and Moritz had been much put out. Althea was in the dark about it, for Mr. Ward had volunteered no explanation.

"Sir Hindley Richmond is coming to-morrow," was all he said. "Mr. Ingram insists on it. He wired for him to-day, but there was some difficulty, and Ingram fussed awfully about it. I am not allowed to put in a word," he continued, with a feeble attempt at a smile. "The doctor and nurses manage everything; all sorts of things come to the house. Of course Ingram sends them, and if I remonstrate, I am told that the doctor ordered them, or that Nurse Helena wished for it."

Althea was the bearer of another sad little missive from Everard. Waveney carried it off to her own room. She was still reading it with dry, tearless eyes when the gong sounded.

"Do not lose heart, my darling," it finished. "It is always darkest before day. We will pray to our Heavenly Father that our sweet Mollie may be spared." Waveney was repeating this sentence over and over again, as she sat at the dinner-table. And Althea, seeing that she ate nothing, told Mitchell to fill her glass with Burgundy.

"You must take that, my dear, and some of this nice light roll. If you make yourself ill, it will only give additional trouble."

Althea spoke with such quiet decision that Waveney was compelled to obey. As she sipped the wine a tinge of colour came into her lips. But the bread was sadly crumbled on her plate. As she rose from the table her knees trembled under her, and she almost tottered as she followed Althea.

Last night about this time she had told her. What a nightmare of horror these four-and-twenty hours had been!

No wonder she felt giddy—no wonder—but here Althea took possession of her with gentle force.

"Sit down, Waveney. Why, you foolish child, you have over-walked yourself, and eaten nothing, and of course you feel bad." And before Waveney could summon up sufficient energy to contradict this, she found herself lying on the library couch, with the softest of pillows under her head and a warm quilt over her.

"Doreen and I are going across to the Porch House," observed Althea, kissing her. "It is Thursday evening. But dear old Nursie will look after you."

"Thank you. But she need not trouble," returned Waveney, drowsily. "I am quite well, only tired."

Every one was very kind, she thought. And Miss Althea, how dear and good she was! After all, it was very comfortable to lie still. The silence, the firelight, the soft warmth, were so soothing. Why were the bees humming so? Beehives and libraries were surely incongruous. And there were white lilies, too, nid-nodding at each other. And the writing-table had gone, and there was a bed of pansies. "Pansies, that's for thoughts," she said to herself. For, little as she knew it, Waveney was fast asleep.

CHAPTER XXXI.: DOWN BY THE RIVER.

"Only upon some cross of pain and woe, God's Son may lie. Each soul redeemed from self and sin, must have Its Calvary." Anon.

"The Porch House Thursdays," as they were called, had become red letter days in Thorold Chaytor's life. Ever since that wet Christmas Eve when he had partaken of "cakes and ale" in the hall at the Red House, he had looked forward to them with an intensity that had surprised himself. Little had he thought, when he had generously given a few hours of his scanty leisure to help Althea in her good work, that such deep enjoyment would be the result, and that he would actually count the hours until he could see a certain curly head bending over the book. If only any one had guessed how his heart always leaped at the sight!

Thorold's life until now had been laborious and joyless. His home was utterly uncongenial to him. He loved his sister, but there was no real sympathy between them, and, as he would often say bitterly to himself, "Joa cares more for Trist's little finger than for me;" and he was right. Joanna was one of those women whose short-sighted tenderness makes them lavish their best affection on some prodigal, or black sheep.

Perhaps the fault might lie a little with Thorold. His calm, self-controlled nature was somewhat repressive; few people understood him, or guessed that underneath the quiet, undemonstrative surface, there was a warm, passionate heart. Perhaps only Althea knew it; and even she was in error about him, for she thought that his intellect dominated his heart; but in this she was wrong.

Thorold Chaytor was a keenly ambitious man; he loved his work for its own sake; but he was also desirous of success.

As he knew well, his feet were on the first rung of the ladder. His literary work was already meeting with appreciation, and now he held his first brief. The first cold breakers had been passed, and the bold swimmer had his head well above water. Poverty would soon be a thing of the past. But even as he grasped this fact gratefully, he was aware that fresh responsibilities fettered him.

Tristram and Betty were on his hands. It would be long, probably years, before Tristram would be able to provide a comfortable home for his child, and when they quitted his roof he clearly foresaw that Joanna would go with them. Nothing would part her from Betty.

But, for years to come, how was he to marry? Would any girl care to enter that incongruous household? Would he wish to bring her? He was a man who would want his wife to himself, who must have all or none. No one must interfere with his monopoly. And then, with a pang of proud sensitiveness, he told himself that the thing was impossible. Nevertheless, the Porch House Thursdays were his high days and festivals.

As he walked up the hill, in the darkness, some new, strange feeling was throbbing at his heart; a sudden yearning to know his fate. It was no use to delude himself with sophistries, or to cheat himself any longer. The first moment he had looked into the depth of those wonderful eyes he knew that he loved Waveney, as such men only love once in their lives; and he knew now, too, well, that he must win her for his wife, or for ever live solitary.

His mind was in a chaotic state this evening. A subtle form of temptation was assailing him. Why should it be hopeless? True, he could not marry for years; but what if he were to tell her that he loved her, and ask her to wait for him, as other women had waited?

He dallied with this thought a moment. "Give me a little hope," he would say to her; "it will strengthen my hands, and I shall fight the battle of life more bravely. Let me feel that I am no longer lonely." But even as the words crossed his lips, he chid himself for his selfishness. Why should he bind down that bright young life, and condemn her to years of wearisome waiting? Why should his burdens be laid on her young shoulders? How could he know what the years would bring? His health might fail. And then, in a mood of dogged hopelessness, he let himself into the little gate that led to the tennis-ground and the Porch House. Little did he guess, as he passed the lighted window of the library, that the objects of his thoughts lay there sleeping for sorrow.

But his first glance, as he entered the Recreation Hall, showed him that the chair by Nora Greenwell was empty, and his face was graver and more impassive than ever as he took up his book. But more than once that evening, as he heard the latch lifted in the adjoining room, he lifted his head, and his wistful look was fixed on the opening door. But no little figure in sapphire blue came lightly into the room.

As soon as his duties were over Thorold crossed the room to Althea.

"Where is Miss Ward?" he asked, quietly. And Althea, who knew he had personal interest in all his pupils, took the question as a matter of course.

"I thought you would have heard," she said, a little sadly. "The poor child is in great trouble." And then she gave him a brief account of the last two days.

Thorold's face paled a little. He was extremely shocked.

"Her twin sister—that beautiful girl I saw in Old Ranelagh gardens?"

"Yes," returned Althea, sorrowfully. "I really think Mollie Ward has the sweetest face I have ever seen. Oh, I do not wonder that Waveney loves her so. She is suffering cruelly, poor child; but her father will not allow her to go home."

"No, of course not," he returned, so quickly that Althea glanced at him. "He is right, quite right. Diphtheria is terribly infectious. She might be ill, too. Good heavens! No one in their sense would expose a girl to such a risk." And Thorold spoke in a low, vehement tone of suppressed feeling; but Althea was too much engrossed with her own painful train of thoughts to notice his unusual emotion.

"No; you are right," she replied. "They must be kept apart. But, Thorold, it makes my heart ache to see her, poor child! It is impossible for any one to comfort her. I can do nothing with her."

Then Thorold's firm lips twitched a little.

"I am sorry," he said, in a quick undertone; "more sorry than I can say. Will you tell her so, please? Good-night. I must go home and work." And then he went off hastily, forgetting that it was his usual custom to help Althea extinguish the lights, and to walk down the dark garden with her; but Althea, sad and pre-occupied, hardly noticed this desertion on Thorold's part.

The evening had seemed a long one to her; her thoughts were in poor Mollie's sick room. Down below a lonely, anxious man sat by his solitary fire. "God comfort him," she said to herself, softly, as she rose from her seat.

The next few days dragged heavily on—days so dim with fear and anguish that for many long years Waveney never willingly alluded to that time, when the mere mention of it drove the colour from her face. Even Mollie, suffering tortures patiently, hardly suffered more than Waveney.

Sir Hindley Richmond had paid his visit, but had spoken very guardedly about the case. There were complications. It was impossible to say. A great deal depended upon nursing. He would come again—yes, certainly, if Mr. Ingram wished it; and then the great doctor drove off.

Everard took the news to the Red House. Perhaps he needed comfort himself, and pined for a sight of his darling. But Waveney's changed looks and languid step filled him with dismay.

She came to him silently, and as he took her in his arms a sob burst from his lips. "Waveney, you will break my heart. Have pity on your poor father. I have but two daughters, and Mollie——" And here he could say no more. Waveney put her hands on his shoulders; they were cold as ice, and her eyes had the fixed, heavy look of one who walks in her sleep.

"Father, is Mollie dying?" Her voice was quite toneless. Everard started in horror.

"My darling child, no—God forbid that such sorrow should be ours; but she is very ill, and I am afraid Sir Hindley Richmond thinks very gravely of the case. There are complications; but he will come again. Ingram insists on it. They are nursing her splendidly. Everything depends on that." But it may be doubted if Waveney heard this.

"Father," she said, in the same dull voice, "I want you to make me a promise. If there is no hope, if Sir Hindley says so, promise me that I shall see her—before—before—you know what I mean."

"Oh, Waveney, my little Waveney, for God's sake do not ask me that!" and Everard shook with emotion.

"But I do ask it." And then her arms went round his neck in a sudden passion of pleading. "Father, I will be good—I will not go near or kiss her; but her dear eyes must see me—she must know that I am there. Father, if you love me, you will not refuse." And then, with a choking sob, poor Everard gave reluctant consent.

Very little more passed between them, when Everard said he must go; Waveney made no attempt to keep him. For the first time in her life her father's presence failed to comfort her, and instinctively he realised this.

"Take care of yourself for my sake," he said, as he kissed and blessed her; but she made no answer when he left her. She paced up and down the room restlessly. Movement—that was her sole relief; and bodily fatigue—that would make her sleep. Once she pressed her face against the window and looked out at the darkness. "Mollie is dying," she said to herself, "and perhaps the dear Lord will let me die, too;" and then she smiled at the thought, and resumed her pacing to and fro in the firelight.

As Everard stumbled out of the room, Althea opened the door of the library and beckoned to him. She had no need to ask him any question; one glance at his face was enough. "Mr. Ward," she said, in her soft voice, "I cannot let you go like this. Sit down by the fire, and I will give you a nice hot cup of coffee. You always liked coffee better than tea, I remember."

"You are very good," he returned, in a hesitating voice. "But I am anxious to get back to my poor child. Dr. Duncan will be coming at six, and Ingram will be round for news."

"Oh, I would not keep you for worlds," replied Althea, gently. "But you must drink this first; and there is no need to drink it standing." And then, with a half-smile, Everard yielded. The beautiful room, the soft lamplight, the quiet face and kindly ministering hands of his old friend, gave him a sudden feeling of warmth and repose. He felt like a tired child brought out of the cold and darkness. As he drank his coffee, the numb, strained feeling gave way.

"Miss Harford," he said, suddenly, "it makes me miserable to see Waveney."

"Ah!" she returned, quickly, "I was afraid you would say that. But the poor child is not herself. She is stunned with trouble. When we talk to her, she does not seem to hear what we say. Doreen spoke to her a little sharply, to-day," she went on. "She did it to rouse her; but, of course, I told her that it would be useless. When she had finished, Waveney merely looked at her, and then went out of the room. And Doreen was so afraid she had hurt her that she followed her to say something kind. Waveney seemed quite astonished. 'You have not hurt me, oh, no!' she said. 'It is I who am rude, for I did not hear half you said. When I try to listen, my head pains me, and I get confused. But I think nothing hurts me.'"

Everard sighed. "What are we to do with her?" he asked, in a despairing voice.

"Dear Mr. Ward," returned Althea, in her flute-like voice, "we can do nothing but love her, and pray for her. She and her dear Mollie, too, are in God's hands—not ours. Try to trust them both to Him." And then Everard looked gratefully in her face.

"She is a sweet woman," he said to himself, as he walked towards the station. "I wonder why she has never married?" But no suspicion of the truth entered his mind.

Moritz used to send Noel up to the Red House nearly every day. But he never came himself. He spent most of his time at Number Ten, Cleveland Terrace.

Everard took very kindly to his visits. Moritz turned up at all hours, with all sorts of excuses. He would send up messages to the nurses, and very often would waylay Nurse Helena in the road outside. Nurse Helena, who had a kindly, womanly nature, would smile a little sadly, as she walked on. "He does not know, poor man, that he has a rival," she said to herself. "There is a Monsieur Blackie. I have heard the name often. But, poor child, what does it matter?" And here Nurse Helena shook her comely head. For that day, dear, sweet Mollie was at her worst. And Moritz was like a man distracted.

That afternoon Thorold Chaytor came home unusually early. He was bringing his work with him. Joanna and Betty were spending the day with a friend at Richmond, and Tristram had promised to join them in the evening, so he would have the house to himself.

It was nearly four o'clock, but down by the river there was still light. The water had a cold, steely gleam on it, and the black hulls of the boats drawn up on shore, looked hard and forbidding. There was a touch of frost in the air, and as Thorold lingered for a moment on the bridge, he was surprised to see a solitary figure on the towing-path. The next moment he uttered an exclamation, and then walked rapidly in the same direction; his keen, far-sighted eyes had recognised the pedestrian.

Waveney's restlessness had amounted almost to disease that day; she simply could not sit still. All the morning she had been wandering over the common with the little dogs running beside her, and the moment luncheon was over she started off on an errand to the Model Lodging-house.

Her limbs ached with fatigue, but a streak of red sunset, casting a glow on the river, attracted her irresistibly, and though the light had long faded, and the air was chill and damp, she still paced up and down; but she started, and a sudden giddiness came over her, as a deep voice accosted her.

"Miss Ward, is this wise or right? Have you no regard for your health?" and Thorold's voice was unusually stern; but even in that dim light, the drawn pallor of her face frightened him. Could sickness and sorrow of heart have wrought this change in these few days?

"Perhaps I have walked too much," she returned, faintly. "I am so fond of walking, and the river is so beautiful, and there is nothing else to do." And then a sudden impulse of self-preservation made her catch at his arm. "I am so giddy," she said, in a tired little voice. "If I only could sit down a moment!"

"There is a seat near," he returned, quietly; "let me help you." And then his strong arm almost lifted her off the ground. The next moment she was on the bench; but his arm was still around her. She was not faint; her eyes were wide open and fixed on the water, but her strength had gone, and, as far as he could judge, she seemed scarcely conscious of her surroundings. She even submitted like a child when he drew her head against his shoulder.

"Do not try to speak. It will pass, and you will be better soon." And then he felt her pulse. The feeble beats spoke of utter exhaustion. Very likely she had eaten nothing all day. There was only one thing to be done. She must be warmed and fed, and then he must take her home.

"Do you think you could walk a little now?" he asked, when a few minutes had passed, and the cold breeze from the river seemed to pierce through him. "It is not safe to sit any longer. There is a frost to-night, and we have only such a little way to go. Will you try?—and I will help you."

"Oh, yes, why not?" returned Waveney, dreamily. "But it is not a little way to the Red House, is it?" And then she rose stiffly, and if Thorold had not held her she would have fallen. "Why am I like this?" she panted. "I have never been weary before."

"You have walked too far," was his sole answer, "and you are numb with cold." And then, half-supporting, half-carrying her in his man's strength, they reached the bridge.

Under the gaslight he saw she had revived a little, and then he made her take his arm. The town was lighted, and there were plenty of passers-by; but, happily, there was not far to go. More than once, even in that short distance, he was obliged to let her pause for a minute.

As he opened the little gate, she pressed his arm feebly.

"Oh, not here," she said. "I must go home. Please do not make me go in; please—please, Mr. Chaytor."

"My dear child, can you not trust me?" was all his answer. "Do not fear. I mean to take you home." And, somehow, his calm, authoritative voice seemed to control her at once.

CHAPTER XXXII.: "I WILL NEVER BE FAITHLESS AGAIN."

"Nothing begins and nothing ends That is not paid with moan, For we are born in other's pain
And perish in our own." Thompson.

"He had a face like a benediction." Cervantes.

In spite of her terrible exhaustion, Waveney instinctively dreaded the surprised looks and curious questionings which she feared awaited her. The idea of Joanna's pity and Betty's welcoming caresses seemed alike repugnant; and when Thorold opened the parlour door, she drew back as though afraid to enter; but he gently led her in.

"They are all out," he said, quietly; "but you can rest and get warm." And then he drew up an easy-chair to the fire and placed her in it, and brought her a footstool; the next moment, with careful hands, he removed her hat, and put a cushion under her head; then he drew off her gloves, and gently rubbed her benumbed fingers.

Waveney submitted to it all passively. The warmth and stillness soothed her, in spite of herself. When Thorold left the room to speak to Jemima, she rested her weary head against the soft cushion and closed her eyes. How kind he was!—how kind every one was! And then, all of a sudden, great tears welled up in her eyes. The little parlours, with their drawn crimson curtains and bright fire, seemed to fade from her sight. She was sitting on a bench in Old Ranelagh gardens, and Mollie was beside her. The sunlight was filtering through the limes, the children were flitting to and fro like butterflies. "Here he is—the noticeable man, with large grey eyes," she was saying; and she could hear Mollie's sweet, scornful laughter in reply.

"Dear Miss Ward, please drink this; it will warm you and do you good." Thorold spoke in a clear, persuasive voice. But as Waveney opened her eyes, the tears were rolling down her small white face.

"Why did you rouse me?" she said, with a little sob. "I was dreaming, and it was so lovely. I was sitting with my Mollie, and we were laughing and talking together. Oh, Mollie, Mollie!" And here a fit of bitter weeping seemed to shake her from head to foot. No power on earth could have hindered the flow of those tears.

For one moment Thorold almost lost his calmness.

"Waveney, my dear child, hush!" he said, hoarsely, "you will make yourself ill. Why are you so hopeless? It is often darkest just before the dawn." And then his hand rested for a moment lightly on her head. "How do you know that your sister's life may not be spared? and then all these tears may have been needlessly shed. Child, do not lose your faith. God may be dealing mercifully with you and yours."

He spoke in a voice of intense feeling; then he gently raised her from the cushions, and held the cup to her lips.

"You must drink this," he said, very quietly and gently. And Waveney checked her tears and obeyed him.

"There, you are better now," he said, in a tone of relief, when the cup was empty.

"Yes," she whispered. "Thank you, for being so good and patient. I ought not to have troubled you so."

"Troubled?" returned Thorold, in a low, suppressed voice, "when there is nothing on earth that I would not do for you, my darling!" The last words were scarcely audible. Then he bit his lip, and rose hastily. What was he doing? He had forgotten himself. The sight of her tears, the anguish in her beautiful eyes, had utterly unnerved him. For the moment he had been oblivious of everything but her suffering, and his great love; and words of tenderness had forced themselves to his lips.

Good heavens! what had he done? And here he paced the room in agitation; but a glance at the easy-chair reassured him. Poor child! she was so dazed, so confused, that probably the words had not reached her ears. If they had—and here he frowned, and stared at the fire in perplexity—if, fool that he was, he had betrayed himself! And then, in spite of his self-reproach, a gleam of joy crossed his face. What if she had understood him, and knew, without doubt, that she was the darling of his heart!

But he would not trust himself to be alone with her any longer. He sent for a cab, and then went up to Joanna's room for an old fur-lined cloak, that he knew hung in her wardrobe.

A few minutes later, when he returned to the room, the cloak was over his arm. Waveney was still in the same position, lying back on the cushions, with closed eyes, and listless hands folded on her lap. But at the sound of his step, she struggled into a sitting posture.

"Have you come for me? May I go, now?" she asked, in a weak little voice. But he noticed that the colour had returned to her lips.

"Yes," he said, quietly. "The cab is here. But you must let me wrap you in this cloak, for it is bitterly cold outside, and this room is so warm." Then she stood up without a word, and allowed him to put it round her; then, still silently, he drew her hand through his arm, and led her slowly down the little courtyard.

For some minutes no word passed between them.

Thorold pulled up the windows. Then he wrapped the old cloak a little closer round her, and stooped to bring it under her feet. As he did so she put out her hand to stop him.

"Oh, please—please do not trouble about me so," she said, in a distressed tone. "I am quite warm now. You are so kind, and I cannot even thank you?" Then, with a sudden impulse, he took her hand, and held it firmly.

"Do you know how you can thank me best?" he said, very gently. "By taking better care of yourself in future. Waveney, promise me that you will never act so recklessly again. Good heavens! what would have become of you if I had not found you! And even now——" Then, with an involuntary shudder, he checked himself.

"I was very wrong," she returned, humbly, "but I was so unhappy, and I wanted to tire myself; and somehow the river, and the loneliness, soothed me. And then all at once I seemed to lose myself, and you came. I think the cold numbed me; but I understand better now, and I am sorry."

She spoke in broken little sentences, and it was with difficulty that he could hear the words; they were just entering the Lodge gates at that moment, and he leant forward in the darkness and lifted the cold little hand to his lips. "Yes, you were wrong," he said, tenderly, as though he were speaking to a child, "but you will never be so foolish again. You will take care of yourself for the sake of those who love you." Then he dropped her hand as a gleam of light from the open door streamed across the shrubbery. And as the cab stopped he saw Althea standing in the porch, with a light, fleecy wrap thrown over her head.

"Oh, Waveney," she exclaimed, in an anxious tone, as Thorold lifted the girl out. "Where have you been?" Then, as she caught sight of Waveney's face, "My dear child, you look dreadful. What has happened?"

"Nothing has happened," returned Thorold, impatiently. "Miss Ward is not well; the cold has struck her. Please do not keep her standing here." And, unceremoniously putting Althea aside, he almost carried Waveney across the hall.

"Take her to Doreen's room. There is a nice fire there," Althea said, quickly. But she was too late, for Thorold had already opened the library door. As he did so, two people, sitting by the fire, rose hastily and looked at them. The next moment Waveney uttered a cry and freed herself from Thorold's supporting arm.

"Father," she exclaimed, in a voice of terror, "you have come—you have come to tell me——" Then her breath failed her, and she almost fell into Everard's arms.

"My darling, I have come to bring you good news," he said, pressing her almost convulsively to him. "Oh, such good news, my Waveney! Mollie is better; the danger has passed, and——" But here he stopped, as Waveney's head fell heavily on his shoulder.

"You have told her too suddenly," observed Althea, in an alarmed voice. But Thorold, without a word, took the girl from her father's arms and laid her on a couch.

"She has fainted," he said, briefly. "You had better bring some brandy and smelling-salts. The sudden revulsion has been too much for her." And then he helped Althea apply the remedies, while Everard stood helplessly by, too shocked and troubled to be of any use.

It seemed long before Waveney opened her eyes. She seemed rather confused at first. As Thorold put a glass to her lips, she looked at him a little wildly.

"Is it another dream?" she whispered. "Was not father here really?"

Then Thorold smiled at her.

"It was no dream," he said, quietly. "The good news is quite true. Mr. Ward, will you take my place, please?"

Then Everard knelt down by her couch. Waveney's weak arms were round his neck in a moment.

"Father," she said, pressing her cheek against his, "tell it me again. Mollie—my Mollie—is not going to die?"

Then Everard, in rather a tremulous voice, repeated the good news. There had been a change for the better early in the day, but he had waited until the afternoon for the physician's verdict. The danger that they dreaded was no longer imminent; the disease had run its course; everything depended now upon skilful nursing, with care and watchfulness; Sir Hindley hoped that Mollie would, in time, recover her normal strength; but in this insidious disease there was the danger of sudden collapse from exhaustion—indeed, there were other risks, but Everard did not mention this.

Waveney listened with painful attention; then her heavy eyes were fixed wistfully on her father's face.

"It is really true!" she murmured. "Thank God, oh, thank God! Father, dear, may I see her now?"

Everard frowned anxiously; he had dreaded this question, but he had to be firm, for the doctor's orders were stringent.

"No, dear," he said, sorrowfully, "you must not see her yet. It is for Mollie's sake as well as yours. No one must see her; the least excitement or agitation, in her weak state, might be fatal. You must be patient, my little Waveney, and I will promise you this, that you shall be Mollie's first visitor;" and then Waveney hid her face on his shoulder.

"Do not let her talk any more," observed Althea, gently; and then Thorold came forward to take his leave. As he pressed her hand, Waveney looked at him with a touching expression of gratitude in her dark eyes.

"You were right," she said, in a low voice, "and I was wicked and faithless; but I will never be faithless again."

But his sole answer was a smile so bright and reassuring that in her weakness it almost dazzled her, as though some sudden sunbeam had flashed across her eyes.

"Fear nothing," it seemed to say, "poor little tired child, rest and be still." And indeed, before Everard left the house, an hour later, the worn-out girl was sleeping peacefully, while Althea, with motherly eyes, watched beside her.

It was late that night before Althea retired to rest. Thorold's account had filled her with uneasiness; his description made her shudder. The dark, solitary towing-path, with the dense mist rising from the river; the exhausted little creature trying to walk off her sorrow and restlessness. No wonder that Althea's kind heart ached with pity.

"Oh, Thorold," she said, and her eyes were full of tears, "how do we know what that poor child may have to suffer for her imprudence? She may have rheumatic fever. Oh, one cannot tell what may be the result of such madness."

Then Thorold shook his head with rather a sad smile.

"You must not take such a gloomy view. Let us hope there will be no bad result. I confess Miss Ward's exhausted condition alarmed me at first. It was distressing to see her. And then there was so little one could do!"

Thorold's tone had a note of pain in it, but Althea looked at him with an affectionate smile.

"Don't undervalue yourself, Thorold. In any emergency or trouble I know of no one who could give more efficient help. So many kind-hearted people spoil everything by their fussiness."

"Oh, that is one for Joa!"

"No, no, I was not thinking of poor Joa. With all her goodness, she is the last person I should care to have near me in any sudden trouble. Perhaps it is unkind of me to say this, but I know we think alike on this point;" and though Thorold made no verbal response to this, it was evident that he agreed with her.

When Waveney woke the next morning, she was conscious of aching limbs and unusual weariness and lassitude, and it was almost with a feeling of relief that she heard Althea say she must remain in bed.

"You have been a naughty little child," she said, kissing her, "and Doreen and I are excessively angry with you; so we have agreed that you are to be punished by some hours of solitary confinement. I am going to light your fire, and then you are to eat your breakfast and go to sleep again."

Waveney smiled quite happily at this. She had no wish to dispute the point. It was a luxury to lie still in her soft bed and watch the pleasant firelight until her drowsy eyelids closed again. In spite of her weariness and aching limbs, there was a fount of joy in her heart. "Mollie is better. Mollie will get well." Those were the words she repeated over and over again, and more than once her hands were folded, and "Thank God!" came audibly from her lips.

At midday Althea brought a note that Moritz had sent by a boy messenger. It was written to her, but there was a message for Waveney. She read part of it aloud. Mollie had slept well, and the improvement continued. Both doctor and nurses seemed satisfied.

"If I had my way, Sir Hindley should have a peerage," wrote Moritz. "He is worth all the other doctors put together; and Miss Mollie would never have pulled through without him, I'll take my oath of that." But Althea kept the remainder of the letter to herself. It was too strictly private and confidential even for Doreen's ears.

All day long, in her waking intervals, Waveney was keeping one thought at bay. Deep down in her inner consciousness, she was aware of some strange and secret joy which she dare not face, but which seemed to distil some rare and precious aroma.

"Was it a dream?" she was continually asking herself; but the answer to this perpetually eluded her. All the events of the previous evening had resolved themselves into a sort of painful vision. The dark, sullen river; her restless anguish; those confused moments when, giddy and sick, she had sat on the bench with Mr. Chaytor beside her; the walk through the lighted streets; and then the warmth and comfort of that friendly refuge.

It was not until late in the afternoon, when the wintry dusk had closed in, and the Pansy Room was bright with firelight, that the power of consecutive thought and memory seemed to return to Waveney, when some sudden remembrance made her bury her face in the pillow. What were those words that, in spite of her weakness, seemed stamped on her heart and brain?

"Trouble? When there is nothing on earth that I would not do for you, my darling!" No, it was no dream. She had actually heard them. He had really said them. Would she ever forget his voice, or the smile that had seemed to steal into her weary heart like a benediction? Then, for a few blissful moments, Mollie was forgotten in the overwhelming consciousness that the man she most admired and revered, who seemed so far above her in wisdom and intellect, should stoop from his great height to care for her.

CHAPTER XXXIII.: A QUIXOTIC RESOLUTION.

"Thine were the weak, slight hands That might have taken this strong soul, and bent Its stubborn substance to thy soft intent." Watson.

For the first time in his life Thorold Chaytor's conscience felt ill at ease; and, though his nature was by no means introspective or over-scrupulous, he tormented himself and suffered keen twinges of remorse, for what he called his unpardonable want of self-control.

Thorold's sense of honour was exceptionally high; in spite of his cold, reserved manner, he was extremely sensitive; the thought that he had been over-mastered and carried away by passion, even though it had been momentary, humiliated and shocked him.

In some of his ideas Thorold was somewhat behind his generation, and different from other men. He held old-fashioned and somewhat obsolete views on the subject of love, and his reverence for women savoured of the old days of chivalry.

In his hard-working life he had been brought little into contact with them. He had no time for society. An evening at the Red House with his old friends, Althea and Doreen, was the only relaxation he had allowed himself. But, in spite of his self-repression, Thorold Chaytor was intensely human, and, like other men, he yearned for the joys of wife and child.

"Man is not made to live alone," he would say to himself, drearily, as he sat late at night by his solitary fireside; and, though no visionary, the thought of some fair young face would haunt him persistently. "I wonder if I ever shall have a wife?" he would say to himself, as he looked into the red, glowing caverns before him. "I shall be hard to please. I should like her to be a younger and prettier Althea. Oh, she is a noble creature, Althea! She would have been a treasure to any man, but I fancy—I have always fancied—that she gave away her heart to Everard Ward. Well, who knows what may happen, when I have earned my fortune?" And then he smiled a little bitterly, as he opened his books again. Thorold's strong, intense nature took nothing lightly. If he loved, it was with his whole heart and soul. Alas! for him, the small, pale face and dark, spirituelle eyes of his little Undine were now all the world to him. From the first he had recognised her sweetness and intelligence.

How he had longed to hold her to his heart, and comfort her with the assurance of his great love! How his nerves had thrilled with passionate tenderness as he ministered to her, as though she were a little helpless child! And all the time his heart had, with mute reverence, worshipped her.

"I must not think of myself or my own happiness," he said to himself, as he walked down the hill in the darkness that night. "My days have been always joyless, and what does a little more pain matter? It is of her I am thinking. God forbid that I should cloud her bright young life with any of my cares or perplexity. My little Waveney, I would suffer a hundred-fold more willingly than see you bearing my burdens."

Poor Thorold! In his generous self-renunciation he was making a grievous mistake, though he little guessed it; for woman's nature was terra incognita to him. Generosity and self-abnegation are not solely masculine virtues, and there are women to whom any form of self-sacrifice for the sake of a beloved object is simply joy and happiness; who care nothing for waiting and poverty, if they can only lean on some strong arm and be at rest.

But Thorold was not wise enough to know this, so he formed a singular resolution. He would see Waveney again. He would watch her closely. Ah! he loved her so dearly that he felt he could almost read her thoughts. If she received him with her old frankness of manner, if there were no trace of consciousness in look or tone, he would know that his impulsive speech had not reached her ear, and he would content himself with being more guarded for the future.

But if, as some subtle instinct told him, there should be some undefinable change in her, some new veil of shyness, he would be certain that she had heard him too well, and in this case it was his full intention to make her understand in some way the difficulty of his position. "It is impossible for me to marry for a great many years. I am too heavily handicapped." Some such words as these he would say, and then he would leave her, but not until he had apologized to her with all the humility of which he was capable. And when he had arrived at this quixotic resolution Thorold was more at peace.

They would not meet just yet, for Waveney was unable to leave her room for some days, and spent most of her time, as Althea informed Thorold when he came in one evening, in sleeping like a baby.

"And she looks like one," observed Doreen, who had just come down from the Pansy Room. "I was watching her just now before she woke up, and I never saw such a baby face. I think it must be her short, curly hair that gives one the impression. I wonder why it has never grown long? Mollie Ward has such lovely hair!"

"Waveney told me once that it had never grown since some childish illness," returned Althea, "but that she did not mind it, as it gave her so little trouble. Why, Thorold, you are never going?" as he rose from his chair. "What nonsense! You must stay to dinner. You have not dined with us for an age."

"Not this evening," he returned, hurriedly, "or I should have to sit up all night working. I am glad to hear that Miss Ward is better," he continued, rather formally; "but she seems very weak, still. I suppose you have had Dr. Hilton."

"Oh, no, it was not necessary," returned Althea. "Waveney is not really ill. She is only worn out, body and mind. A few days' rest and feeding up, and plenty of Nurse Marks' cosseting will soon put her to rights. And now her mind is at rest about Mollie, she will soon be her cheerful little self again."

"I hope so," was Thorold's sole answer. And then, seeing that he was in one of his grave, silent moods, Althea did not press him to stay—only accompanied him to the door, and bade him a friendly good-night.

"Poor old Thorold, he does not look quite happy," observed Doreen, as her sister re-entered the room. "I wonder if he has anything on his mind?" And though Althea made no reply to this, the same thought had crossed her mind more than once.

When Waveney heard that Thorold had called to inquire after her the previous evening, she merely observed that it was very kind. But an hour or two later she insisted on dressing herself, and making an attempt to go downstairs.

Althea remonstrated at first; but Waveney was so bent on trying her strength, that she thought it wiser to let her have her way, and actually forbore to triumph when Waveney, with rather a piteous face, subsided weakly on the couch.

"Perhaps I had better wait until to morrow," she panted; "dressing has tired me so." And then, as Althea brought her another pillow, and covered her up snugly, she continued in a weak voice, jestingly, "I feel as though I had the corporal's wooden legs, instead of my own. They do move so stiffly; but then, wooden legs don't ache. Never mind; anything is better than the heartache." And to this Althea cordially agreed.

Everard Ward paid them another visit while Waveney was still in her room. When he came again he found her cosily established in the library, and, though looking still rather weak and pale, in excellent spirits.

For every day the good news was verified, and Mollie made slow but steady progress to recovery. Only once had there been a return of anxiety, when, for one long half-hour, Mollie's weakness was so great that Nurse Helena feared sudden collapse. Everard did not tell Waveney this. But he kept her well acquainted with every little detail of the sick room—what nourishment Mollie took, and how many hours she slept, and even a speech or two, repeated by her nurses.

Once she sent her dear love to Waveney. And another time she asked if Mr. Ingram ever came to the house, and had looked both pleased and surprised when she heard he had been daily. "Twice or three times a day" would have been no exaggeration of the truth. But Nurse Helena wisely kept this to herself. For, of all things, she dreaded any agitation or excitement for her patient.

When Waveney grew stronger she drove daily with one or other of the sisters. And when the February sunshine tempted her, she took short strolls over the Common, with Fuss and Fury.

One Sunday afternoon, when Althea and Doreen were occupied as usual, Waveney put on her hat and went out. There had been rain the previous night, and the garden paths were damp. And at luncheon Althea had recommended her to take a little walk, in the direction of the golf links, as it would be higher and dryer there.

"Do not go too far, and tire yourself," had been her parting words. "Remember Thursday." As though Waveney could have forgotten it, for a moment! For that day she was to see her dear Mollie again.

It was a lovely afternoon. The air was soft and balmy, and full of the promise of spring, and thrushes and blackbirds were singing for joy, because the dark, wintry days were over.

Waveney could have sung with them, out of very gratitude and happiness. Oh, how sweet life was! After all, Mollie was getting well, and——But here Waveney flushed and walked on more rapidly; for there were certain thoughts that made her heart beat too quickly.

"I am very faithless," she was saying to herself, as she came in sight of her favourite seat. It was in a little hollow, and in the summer the larches and willows made a pleasant shade. There was a pond near, where children loved to sail their little boats, or throw sticks in the water for some excited dog.

In her letters to Mollie, she had called it "her green parlour."

She would have rested there for a few minutes, but she saw it was occupied by a gentleman, so she walked on slowly. The next moment, however, she heard her name pronounced, and Thorold Chaytor stood beside her.

"You are tired. You wanted to sit down," he said, abruptly, as they shook hands. "Please come back and rest a moment. It is so warm and sheltered in the hollow."

"I was not really tired," returned Waveney, nervously; but she avoided looking at him as she spoke. "It is rather a favourite seat of mine, and the view is so pretty."

"Yes, I was admiring it just now," replied Thorold; "but you will sit down for five minutes, will you not?" Then Waveney, shy and confused, accompanied him a little reluctantly across the grass. But as Thorold walked silently beside her, under his quiet manner there raged a perfect tempest of conflicting feelings.

His sudden and unexpected appearance had taken Waveney by surprise, and her startled blush, and confusion, betrayed her agitation at the meeting. Her new timidity, the faltering of her voice, and her avoidance of his eyes, all told the same tale to Thorold: she had understood, and she was not indifferent to him!

A spasm of joy shot through Thorold's heart at this thought; then he remembered his resolution, and crushed down his rising happiness.

"I must think of her, and not of myself," he said to himself, as he took the seat beside her.

"I am glad to see you are so much better," he began, after a long pause, that neither knew how to break. "But you are not quite strong yet; your step has lost its old spring." Then he interrupted himself, as though he feared to say so much. "But all that will pass."

"Yes, it will pass," she returned, trying to speak naturally, and looking at him for the first time. The soft brilliancy of her eyes almost dazzled Thorold. He nearly forgot his resolution, as he looked into their brown depths. "Do you know, Mr. Chaytor, that on Thursday I am actually to see my Mollie. I am counting the hours, and so is she."

"And that makes you very happy?" he asked, in a low voice.

"Oh, yes; so grateful and happy! Father has seen her, of course; and he says I must be prepared to find her very weak. Is it not a pity she has lost her lovely colour? But Nurse Helena says it will come back. She seems such a kind woman. When I send little notes to Mollie, she answers them so nicely, and gives all Mollie's messages."

Waveney had forgotten her nervousness in this engrossing topic; but Thorold's answer was a little vague.

"And you will never be faithless again?"

"No!" she returned, flushing at this; "I will try to be more trustful in future." And then, more kindly, "Mr. Chaytor, you were so good to me that miserable evening, I have so often wished to thank you, and tell you that I am not unmindful of your great kindness." Then he checked her.

"Miss Ward, you owe me no gratitude; any one would have done what I did. It is your forgiveness I ought to ask, for I am afraid that in my sympathy and pity I forgot myself."

He said this with such difficulty, and in such a constrained tone, that Waveney looked at him in astonishment. Then, as she saw his expression, her head drooped a little.

"I do not know what you mean," she said, under her breath.

"I cannot explain myself," he returned, hurriedly; "would to heaven that I could. But I think from your manner that you do not misunderstand me. Miss Ward, there is something I want to tell you about myself if you will pardon my egotism. We are good friends, I trust, and if possible I want you to think well of me."

Waveney listened silently to this, but she bit her lip to conceal a smile. Was it likely that she of all persons would think ill of him?

"I am unfortunately placed," he continued. "All my life circumstances have been too strong for me. Other men can please themselves, but I have never been free to choose my own path. Duties and responsibilities have crowded on me from mere boyhood. Fresh ones have come to me within the last few months."

Then Waveney understood that he was speaking of his brother and little Bet, and her attention became almost painful.

"I can see no end of it all," he went on—and there was despair in his voice. "It must be years—perhaps many years—before I can think of marrying. I ought to have remembered this—I ought not to have forgotten myself." Then he rose abruptly, and his face was very pale. "Miss Ward, you have been very good to listen to me so patiently, but I must not keep you here any longer; it will not be safe for you."

He was standing before her as he spoke, but for a moment she made no reply, only sat with bent head, and her hands folded tightly together in her lap. But as he stooped and put out his hand, as though to help her to rise, she suddenly looked up in his face.

"Thank you," she said, quite simply. "You need not fear that I should ever misunderstand one so good and kind;" and then she flushed up, and rose quickly from the bench. "It is too late to go on now, and Miss Harford will be expecting me. Please do not come any farther. There is no need to spoil your walk. Give my love to your sister and little Bet—dear little Bet."

"Are you sure? Do you not wish me to accompany you?" he stammered; but she shook her head with a semblance of gaiety.

"Oh, no. I shall be at the Red House in five minutes. Good-bye, good-bye."

Waveney was in such a desperate hurry that she forgot to shake hands. She almost ran down the little path between the furze-bushes.

The thrushes and blackbirds had ceased their songs, and the sunshine had faded from the landscape, but in Waveney's heart there was a strange, new joy.

"He loves me, he loves me," she was saying to herself, "though he will not tell me so for a long time. Oh, how good he is! how patient and self-sacrificing!" And then her eyes were dim as she remembered the suppressed pain in his voice. "I have never been free to choose my own path." Was that not true, absolutely true? and could any man have done his duty more nobly? And yet this hero, this king among men, actually loved her! And now Waveney's eyes were full of tears.

CHAPTER XXXIV.: "I HAVE WANTED MY OLD SWEETHEART."

"Our doubts and our fears we are leaving; Before us the future uprears, Where angels a rainbow are weaving Of smiles and of tears." Helen Marion Burnside.

During Waveney's indisposition Everard Ward had been constantly at the Red House, and these visits had been full of consolation to both father and daughter. Althea's kindly welcome and womanly gentleness had, from the first, put him at his ease. Both she and Doreen had cordially pressed him to repeat his visits, as they gave Waveney so much pleasure. Once, when the sisters were out, and Waveney was making tea for him in the library, she asked him suddenly why Mr. Ingram never called at the Red House.

"I do not think it is quite kind and cousinly," she said, rather seriously.

Everard seemed a little embarrassed by the question.

"Why, you see," he replied, in rather a hesitating way, "Ingram is so fully engaged. He is up at our place regularly every morning and evening. He does not seem able to exist away from it. Mollie ought to consider herself a lucky little girl," he continued, thoughtfully, "for I never saw a man more deeply in love. He is a fine fellow—Ingram—the best-hearted fellow I know; and I only hope"—and here he looked at Waveney rather searchingly—"that our dear Mollie values him as he deserves."

"I think Mollie is beginning to care for him," returned Waveney; "at least, I fancy so. But, of course, one can only guess at her feelings. You see, he has given her so much pleasure. And she has learnt to depend on him so much for companionship and sympathy, that it would be strange if she were to harden her heart against him, at last. But, father,"—her voice deepening with emotion,—"do you think he is quite good enough for our sweet Mollie? He is very kind and amusing—our dear little Monsieur Blackie, but——" Everard interrupted her abruptly.

"Pshaw, what a ridiculous name! I think it is quite time that you and Noel dropped it. Monsieur Blackie, indeed! Absurd! I cannot imagine why you have all taken such a liberty with him." Everard spoke in such a ruffled tone that Waveney stared at him in surprise.

"But, father, dear, he likes it. He is as proud of the name as possible. In his little notes to us he always signs himself 'Monsieur Blackie.'" And then she added, rather wickedly, "You know, dear, the name does suit him so perfectly. If he were tall, and handsome, and dignified, we should have found him quite a different name."

But this explanation did not seem to please Everard. "Nonsense, child!" he said, quite sharply. "What do looks matter? A good heart, and a generous nature, are worth far more. Some of the greatest men in the world were short of stature. Nelson and Napoleon—oh! and many others. But girls are so silly and sentimental, they prefer some Adonis six feet high, with an empty purse and head."

Waveney laughed merrily at this. Then a sudden thought came to her.

"Father," she said, rather gravely, "it is easy to see that Mr. Ingram will have no difficulty with you, and that you are his best friend. Has he"—and here she hesitated, and flushed—"has he spoken to you yet? I mean, has he told you that he loves Mollie?"

"My little Waveney, that is not a fair question," returned Everard, quickly. "But I suppose that there is no harm in telling you that I am most certainly in Ingram's confidence. Now, no more questions; he has begged me to respect his secret. Yes"—rising from his seat, and speaking with repressed excitement—"he has my best wishes for his success. Now I must go, dear child, for I have promised to dine with him and Noel."

When Everard had gone, Waveney sat down by the fire; the conversation had given her plenty of food for thought. Her father was in Ingram's confidence; it was evident that he fully approved of him as a prospective son-in-law—that Ingram's generosity and kindness of heart had won him over completely. "I like him," she said to herself, "and I think I could get fond of him as a brother; but in Mollie's place"—and here Waveney shook her head. The vision of a grave, strong face, with keen, thoughtful grey eyes, seemed to rise before her; a quiet, cultured voice vibrated in her ears. Well, Mollie was welcome to her Black Prince. To her there was only one man in the world, and his name was Thorold Chaytor.

This little talk had taken place two or three days before her interview with Thorold that Sunday afternoon. After that she thought less about Mr. Ingram. She was reading her own version of the old, old story, which most women read once in their lives; and though the opening chapter was headed "Waiting and Patience," it was none the less sweet and engrossing to the reader. There was something heroic to her in Thorold's silence and self-renunciation. "He is great because he has learnt to conquer himself," she thought. "Most men are dominated by their own passions and prefer inclination to duty." And then, like a true woman, she reverenced him the more.

It was the longest week that Waveney had ever passed, and it seemed as though Thursday would never come.

Althea had promised to have luncheon with Mrs. Mainwaring that day, so she proposed to drive Waveney over to Cleveland Terrace about noon. She had already made her preparations for the interview by sending Mollie the prettiest and daintiest blue dressing-gown. Mollie, who was still very weak, had shed tears over the gift; but Nurse Helena had only laughed at her, and made her try it on.

Everard was in the studio, touching up a picture that one of his pupils had painted, when Waveney entered. She was rather pale and breathless. How shabby and bare the dear old room looked to her, after her long absence! And yet, in spite of its dinginess, how she loved it!

"Oh, father, how nice it is to be here again!" she said, softly, as she stood near him. And Everard smiled and patted her cheek.

"Ingram left those flowers for you," he said, pointing to a charming bouquet on Mollie's little painting-table. "He was so sorry that he could not wait and see you, but he had to meet an old friend at his club." But before Waveney could make any reply to this, or look at her flowers, a pleasant-looking woman in nurse's garb entered. She had a gentle face, and kind eyes, and Waveney went up to her at once and took her hand.

"You are my sister's Nurse Helena," she said, quickly. "Thank you for all your care of Mollie. May I see her soon?"

"Certainly. Will you come with me now? Miss Ward heard the carriage stop, and she sent me down to bring you up at once. I need not caution you," she continued, as they went upstairs, "to be very quiet, as my patient is still weak. She is on the new couch that Mr. Ingram sent for her use, and I think you will say she looks very comfortable." Waveney was far too agitated to answer. As Nurse Helena opened the door, she heard Mollie's dear, familiar voice say, in weak accents, "Wave, darling, is it really you?" and the next moment she was kneeling by the couch, and she and Mollie were clasped in each other's arms, and Mollie's thin white cheek was wetted by her sister's tears.

"Wave, dear, you must not cry so," whispered Mollie, in a troubled voice. "I am better, and Nurse Helena says that I get stronger every day." Then Waveney, ashamed of her want of self-control, and remembering the nurse's injunction, brushed away her tears and tried to smile.

"I have wanted my old sweetheart so badly," she faltered, and with difficulty she repressed a sob; in spite of her pallor, Mollie looked lovelier than ever—almost too fragile and beautiful, Waveney thought, with that faint flush of excitement on her wasted cheeks, and the violet lines under the large eyes.

"Not more than I have wanted you, darling," returned Mollie, softly. "Wave, I want to see your dear face more clearly. Look, Nurse Helena has put that seat close to me, so that I can hold your hand, and we can talk comfortably. She is going to leave us alone for a quarter of an hour, and I have promised to be good and not tire myself." Then, as Nurse Helena closed the door, "Oh, Wave, it is almost worth all the pain and weariness, to have such happiness as this!"

"It is almost too good to be true," returned Waveney, tenderly. "Dear Mollie, it has been such a dreadful time. If I could only have borne the pain for you! But to know you were suffering, and that strangers were nursing you, and I could do nothing—nothing——" and a faint shudder crossed her as she remembered those days of anguish and suspense.

"Hush, darling," replied Mollie; but there were tears in her eyes. "We will not talk about that sad time now. Do you think I did not know what my Waveney was feeling? That night I was so bad, and I thought that perhaps I should die, I prayed that I might see you once more, and that we might bid each other good-bye. There, don't fret," for Waveney was kneeling beside her again, with her face hidden in the pillow. "I only want to tell you how good Nurse Helena was to me, and how she comforted me. I was very miserable the next day, though I believe I was really better; and when Nurse Helena asked me what was troubling me, I told her it was because I was so wicked that I felt I could not be happy in heaven, if my Waveney were breaking her heart about me here, and that with such feelings I was not fit to die. And she said, in such a comforting way,—

"'But you are not going to heaven yet, my child, so you need not trouble your head about leaving your sister. As for feeling wicked—well, we are none of us angels, but it is my belief that our Heavenly Father will not be angry with us for loving those He has given us to love.' Oh, she is such a sweet woman, Wave! If you only knew her you would like her as much as I do. Nurse Miriam was very kind, too, but she is not as nice as Nurse Helena."

"I love her already for being so good to my darling," returned Waveney; and then she tried to smile. "Mollie, dear, there is some one else to whom we owe gratitude."

Then a swift, undefinable change passed over Mollie's face.

"I know whom you mean," she returned in a low voice; "and father has told me how good he has been. It was Mr. Ingram who sent Sir Hindley down, and he made him come three times. Nurse Helena says his fees are tremendous, and that he is the greatest throat doctor in the world. And then he is paying for the nurses. I found that out the other day. And every day something comes—game, and wine, and fruit, and flowers, and yesterday this lovely couch. Oh, Wave, somehow it oppresses me to think of it all, for how is one to repay such kindness?"

"We will think about that, dear, when you are stronger. Oh, we shall have so much to talk about and to plan, so you must make haste and get well, for I cannot do without my sweetheart any longer."

Then Mollie smiled, well satisfied.

"Oh, dear, how nice it will be!" she said, in rather a tired voice. "Do you know, Wave, Miss Althea sent me a message by father the other day. She has promised to spare you to me whenever I want you, and when I go to the sea you are to come, too."

This was news to Waveney.

"I have heard nothing about it. Are you quite sure?" she asked, doubtfully.

"Quite sure," returned Mollie, decidedly; "but it was only settled last night. He—Mr. Ingram, I mean"—and here Mollie spoke rather hurriedly and nervously, "was talking to father. He said change of air was necessary after such an illness, and that the doctor wished it, and that I should never get strong without it. And then father gave in, and it was decided that I should go as soon as possible, and that you and Nurse Helena were to come, too. Oh, there she comes," as the nurse opened the door, "but I am sure our quarter of an hour is not up yet."

"It is just twenty minutes," observed Nurse Helena, composedly. "Just five minutes too long, I can see, by your face. Miss Ward, will you bid your sister good-bye, please? I should like her to be quiet for a little before her dinner."

"Yes, you must go, Wave," observed Mollie, with ready submission; "but you are to have dinner with father before you go back, and I am to see you again on Sunday." And then the sisters kissed each other silently. But as Waveney turned on the threshold for a last look, Mollie waved her hand. "Oh, it has been so nice," she said, feebly, "and I am so happy." But, almost before Waveney was downstairs, Mollie was asleep.

"Well," observed Everard, with a questioning smile, "have you talked Mollie into a fever?"

"I am afraid we did talk rather too much," returned Waveney, penitently, "for Mollie looked very tired when I left. But, father, how weak and thin she is! I could not help fretting when I saw her. But she looks sweeter than ever, dear thing, and Miss Althea's blue dressing-gown is lovely! She was quite a picture with that Indian silk rug over her feet, and all those beautiful flowers beside her."

"Ingram again," returned Everard, with a groan. "Do you know, he is actually going to Eastbourne next week to take lodgings for her and Nurse Helena, and nothing I can say will stop him."

"Mollie says I am to go, too," observed Waveney, anxiously.

"Yes, dear, Miss Harford proposed that, and I think she is right in saying that you need a change, too; you are looking thin and pale, my child."

"Oh, I am very well," she replied, hastily; and then Ann, the heavy-footed, came up to tell them that dinner was ready. After that, as Waveney was too restless to stay in the house, they went out for a walk, and strolled in Old Ranelagh gardens, and then down the lime walk and along the embankment to Cheyne Walk; and then, as it was growing dusk, they walked on quickly to Sloane Square, and Everard put her in the train.

"Good-bye until Sunday, father, dear," were her last words, as the train moved off. But that night, before Waveney fell asleep happily in her Pansy Room, Nurse Helena's homely words recurred to her.

"Well, we are none of us angels, but it is my belief that our Heavenly Father will not be angry with us for loving those He has given us to love."

"Thank God for that," she murmured, "and that it is no sin that I love my Mollie so intensely." And in the dying firelight Waveney folded her little hands together, and with a grateful heart said her Te Deum.

CHAPTER XXXV.: "WHAT AM I TO SAY?"

"So we grew together, Like to a double cherry, seeming parted, And yet a union in partition, Two lovely berries moulded on one stem." Shakespeare.

Although March set in fierce and blustering as a lion, it might have been as mild as any lamb to Waveney; for when one is young, and the blood courses freely in the veins, even a nipping east wind and grey skies are not the intolerable hardships that older people feel them, especially when a well-spring of joy is bubbling up in the heart.

Mollie was getting well—that was the key-note of Waveney's happiness. And though Althea shivered and looked depressed, as she gazed out at the uninviting prospect, and even Doreen shrugged her shoulders and made uncomplimentary remarks on the weather, Waveney only laughed and looked provokingly cheerful.

"I don't mind the long walk one bit," she returned, in answer to a pitying observation from Althea. "I shall walk as fast as possible and keep myself warm; and as for the dust, don't you know the old saying, that 'a peck of March dust is worth a king's ransom'?" But Althea smiled a little sadly as Waveney ran out of the room to put on her hat and jacket.

"How happy the child is!" she said, with an involuntary sigh. "After all, Dorrie, when one is growing old, it is pleasant to have a bright young creature about the house. Don't you remember when Aunt Sara first suggested that I should have a companion, that you looked rather blank, and said that our old cosy life would be quite spoiled?"

Althea spoke in rather a depressed voice, and Doreen looked at her anxiously.

"Yes, I remember," she replied, quietly. "The idea quite worried me. I was almost cross with Aunt Sara for mentioning it. But I am glad now that Waveney came to us," she continued, thoughtfully. "She is a dear little thing, and one can't help loving her; and then, you have found her such a comfort."

"Indeed, I have," was Althea's reply; "she is such a bright, intelligent little soul, and she has so much tact and sympathy. I am afraid I almost begrudge her to Mollie, especially as——" But here she checked herself.

"You are not feeling quite well, dear," observed her sister, affectionately. "I hope your eyes are not troubling you." But Althea shook her head.

"Not particularly. No, don't fuss, Dorrie, there is nothing really the matter; only the east wind is my enemy. How is one to feel happy without sunshine and warmth? Do you remember that March we spent in the Riviera, and those orange groves, and the bed of Neapolitan violets under our window? How delicious it was!"

"But, Ally, dear," remonstrated Doreen, "why do you speak in that regretful voice? You know Aunt Sara wanted you to spend the winter with her at Mentone, but you refused at once."

"Of course I refused," returned Althea, indignantly. "Do you think I was going to leave you alone all the winter? Besides, there was my work. What would have become of my Porch House Thursdays, and my classes and Library teas? Oh, no, Dorrie. What is the use of 'putting one's hand to the plough, and looking back?' Work has its responsibilities. As long as my strength lasts

I want to do my own little bit as well and as perfectly as I can." And then Mitchell came in for the coachman's orders, and Althea went off to read the letters in the library.

Waveney spent half her time at Cleveland Terrace. As Mollie grew stronger, she yearned incessantly for her sister's companionship, and, as Althea once remarked to Everard, "it seemed useless and cruel to keep them apart." And Everard fully concurred in this opinion.

"But you are very good to spare my little Waveney to us so much," he said, gratefully, "and we ought not to take advantage of your kindness. The child was here three or four times last week. I am afraid she is neglecting all her duties for Mollie." But though Althea was too truthful to deny this, she assured him that she was perfectly willing to spare her young companion.

"I don't think I ever saw two sisters so devoted to each other," she continued. "It is really beautiful to see their love for each other."

"It has always been the same," returned Everard, in a moved voice. "Even when they were mere babies, Mollie would refuse to touch her cake unless Waveney had half. Dorothy had to put them to sleep in the same cot, or Mollie would have cried half the night. It was the prettiest sight, she used to tell me." And then he broke up rather abruptly. "I am an old fool about my girls," he said, with a little laugh; "but, you see, I have had to be mother as well as father for so many years." But Althea made no answer to this. She only bade him good-bye very kindly. It was the first time he had mentioned his wife to her. Dorothy! How his voice had softened as he mentioned the beloved name.

That morning when Waveney made her little speech about a peck of March dust, she found a delightful surprise awaiting her at Cleveland Terrace.

Her father was not at home. She knew well it was his day at Norwood, so she went hastily past the studio door without peeping in as usual; but the next moment she saw Nurse Helena on the threshold beckoning her.

"Will you come in here for a minute, Miss Ward?" she said, rather mysteriously. And Waveney, with some surprise, retraced her steps, and then, as she followed her in, a little cry of delight broke from her, for there was Mollie pillowed up cosily on the old couch, and smiling at her in the most triumphant way.

"Oh, you darling!" exclaimed Waveney, in perfect ecstasy at the sight. "Do you mean that you have actually walked downstairs?"

"Yes, and all by myself, too," returned Mollie, proudly. "But do you know, Wave, I have been grumbling dreadfully. 'Grumps' is not a bit comfortable;" and she pinched the old moreen cushions rather pettishly. "But Nurse Helena promises that I shall have my lovely new couch down to-morrow. It will stand quite well in that corner between the window and fireplace, and I shall be able to see any one who comes to the gate. It is so stupid only to lie and look at the fire."

"Of course it is, you poor dear; but you will soon be watching the waves breaking on the beach, so cheer up, sweetheart." But it was evident that Mollie was not listening. Something else was occupying her thoughts. Her fingers played absently with Waveney's curly hair as she knelt beside her. Then she drew a note from under her pillow.

"Nurse Helena brought me this on my breakfast-tray," she said, flushing a little as she spoke;

"but I have not answered it yet. I want you to tell me what I ought to do." Then Waveney, who had recognized Ingram's handwriting, read it somewhat eagerly.

"Short and sweet," observed Waveney, smiling at the superscription; but Mollie was in no mood for trifling.

"What am I to say?" she asked, anxiously, and her eyes looked bright with excitement.

"My darling, that is for you to decide. Are you sure that you are quite strong enough to see Mr. Ingram? Shall we ask Nurse Helena what she thinks about it?"

"I have asked her," replied Mollie. "And she said that if I did not stay up too long, or tire myself with talking, that probably I should be well enough to see a visitor, the day after to-morrow."

"Well, dear, shall I write and tell him so? Shall I ask him to come in the morning, or the afternoon?"

"Oh, the afternoon, please. But Waveney,"—and here Mollie seemed on the verge of tears— "of course I want to see Mr. Ingram, but yet I do dread it so. What am I to say to him? And how am I to thank him, for all he has done? I feel quite overwhelmed by it all." And then, as Mollie was still very weak, one or two tears rolled down her cheeks; but Waveney kissed them away.

"Oh, you silly child!" she said, tenderly. "Fancy crying, just because a kind friend wants to come and see you! Why, it will do you all the good in the world! There is no one so amusing as Monsieur Blackie. Take my advice, Mollie dear. Be as kind to him as you like, but don't trouble your poor little head about making him grateful speeches. Wait until you are stronger. You may depend upon it," she continued, "that the Black Prince has simply been pleasing himself, quite as much as he has you. I expect generosity is just an amiable vice of his—a sort of craze, don't you know. He likes playing minor providence in other people's lives. It makes him feel warm and comfortable." But Mollie was quite indignant at this.

"You are very clever," she said, rather petulantly. "But you talk great nonsense, sometimes. An amiable vice, indeed! I should like father to hear that! Why, the other night he said, quite seriously, that Mr. Ingram had been a perfect godsend to us all. And Waveney"—and here Mollie's voice grew plaintive—"I do feel as though I owe my life to him. For if it had not been for Sir Hindley, and Nurse Helena, and Nurse Miriam I should never have got well—for father had no money, and what could we have done?" and here Mollie broke off with a sob.

"Darling, do you think I don't know all that?" returned Waveney, vexed with herself for her attempt at a joke. "I would not undervalue Mr. Ingram's kindness for the world. He has been our benefactor—yours, and mine, and father's, and Noel's. As for myself, I could grovel in the dust at his feet, out of sheer gratitude for all his goodness to my Mollie. What I meant to say was this: Mr. Ingram does not want our thanks. We are his friends, and he just loves to help us. So be as nice to him as you like, sweetheart, but don't embarrass him with grateful speeches, for you would certainly cry over them—and then he will get into a panic, and ring violently for Nurse Helena." And then Mollie laughed. And after that they talked with their old cheerfulness. Indeed, Waveney was quite wild with spirits. For Althea had told her, that morning, that she would give her a month's holiday, when Mollie went to Eastbourne.

It so happened that Waveney had promised to spend an hour at the Hospital with Corporal Marks on the very afternoon that was fixed for Mr. Ingram's visit. The old man was depressed and ailing. "Jonadab has never got over the sergeant's loss," as his sister used to say; and she reminded Mollie of this.

"It just fits in nicely," she observed; "for, you see, two is company, and three's none, and I should have been dreadfully in the way. But I shall be back in time to make tea for Mr. Ingram, and we will have a cosy little time together. Now I must go, dear, for I promised Miss Althea that I would not be late. So good-bye until the day after to-morrow."

"I wish it were to-morrow," whispered Mollie, feverishly. "I do so hate waiting for anything like that. I shall just think about it, and what I am to say, until I get quite nervous. There, don't talk about it any more;" and Mollie, who looked flushed and tired, pushed her gently away.

Waveney had promised to have luncheon with her father before she went to the Hospital, and when Wednesday came she went up to the studio to have a peep at the invalid.

"Why, Mollie!" she exclaimed, as she entered the room, "it is quite a transformation scene!"

And, indeed, the shabby old studio looked wonderfully bright and cosy. The round table had been moved to the other side of the room, and Mollie's pretty couch, and a low table that Ingram had sent for her use, were placed between the fireplace and window, and a bowl of Neapolitan violets was beside her. There were flowers everywhere, and as for Mollie,—"Oh, you dear thing! how sweet you look!" remarked Waveney, with a hug.

And, indeed, Mollie had never looked more lovely. Nurse Helena had fastened two little pink rosebuds in the lace at her throat, and their soft, delicate tint just matched Mollie's cheeks; she had a tiny gold vinaigrette in her hand, which she showed Waveney.

"It came this morning, with the flowers," she said, rather shyly.

Waveney looked at it silently. "M. W." was engraved on it.

"Is it not beautiful, Wave? But I wish—I wish he had not sent it."

When luncheon was over, Everard walked with Waveney to the door of the Hospital. He had a tiring afternoon's work before him. By tacit consent, neither of them spoke much of Ingram's visit.

"I hope it will not tire Mollie too much," was all Waveney said. And once Everard hazarded the observation that Ingram was sure to be punctual.

CHAPTER XXXVI.: "SEE THE CONQUERING HERO COMES!"

"That man that hath a tongue, I say, is no man, If, with his tongue, he cannot win a woman."
Two Gentlemen of Verona.
"Love looks not with the eyes, but with the mind, And therefore is wing'd Cupid painted blind." A Midsummer Night's Dream.

As Moritz drove to Cleveland Terrace, he carefully rehearsed his part, as he had already rehearsed it a dozen times before.

"I am going to see your sister this afternoon," he had said to Noel at breakfast that morning. "Miss Mollie, I mean; have you any message for her?"

"No; only my love, and that sort of thing," returned Noel, coolly, as he cut himself another slice of bread. And then, contrary to his custom, for he was one of the most talkative and sociable of men, Ingram relapsed into silence.

"Feels a bit grumpy, I fancy," thought Noel, with a suppressed grin. "If I ever have a young woman, I wonder if I should feel in that way. Why, the poor old chap has had hardly any breakfast." And Noel shook his head solemnly, and adjusted his pince-nez, and then helped himself liberally to the cold game pie.

Ingram's knowledge of invalids and sick-rooms was purely rudimentary. He had a theory that sick people must be treated like children. They must be coaxed, amused, and made as cheerful as possible; there must be no agitation, no bringing forward of exciting or perplexing topics, no undue warmth of expression and feeling.

"I must be perfectly cool and quiet," Ingram said to himself, as he came in sight of the house. "I must not let her see what I have gone through all this time; Monsieur Blackie must take no liberties—he must be just kind and friendly." But as the brougham stopped, Ingram looked a little pale, although he put on his usual sprightly air as he went up the courtyard.

Pride must have its fall, says the old proverb. And perhaps Ingram, who was an Idealist, relied a little too much on his theories and good intentions; as Noel would have said, he was too cocksure of himself.

Anyhow, when Ann, of the heavy foot, ushered him up to the old studio, where he and Everard Ward had passed so many hours of misery and suspense, and he saw Mollie's sweet face, flushing and paling with shy pleasure, Ingram found himself unable to say a word for the sudden choking sensation in his throat; he could only stand there like a fool, holding the thin little hand that Mollie had silently held out to him.

"Won't you sit down?" observed Mollie, faintly; but her lips trembled as she spoke, for Ingram's dumb emotion almost frightened her. It was so unlike her dear old friend, Monsieur Blackie, to stand there without a word of kindly greeting. Mollie's flower-like face grew painfully suffused. "Do please sit down," she faltered, with a growing sense of discomfort and helplessness.

Ingram did as he was bid, but he did not relinquish her hand.

"Mollie," he said, and his eyes were dim with a man's trouble, and the passionate tenderness, that he was trying bravely to repress, was so evident in his voice and manner that even Mollie, innocent and guileless as she was, thrilled in every nerve.

"Perhaps I had better go away," he stammered. "I shall tire you, agitate you, if I stay. I must not say what I think, and, by Heaven, I cannot talk platitudes, when you have come back from the very valley of the shadow of death. Mollie, shall I go? — for I cannot answer for myself, if I remain!"

"Why should you go?" returned Mollie, piteously. "I thought it would be so nice to see you, and I wanted you to thank you. You have done so much for me! Waveney told me that you would not like to be thanked; but indeed, indeed, I am grateful."

"Grateful to me!" returned Ingram, indignantly, and he dropped her hand. "Mollie, do you wish to pain me, that you say such things to me? Gratitude! when I would willingly give you everything I possess! Unsay those words, my darling," he pleaded, passionately. "Don't you know that I love you better than anything in the world? Oh, Mollie, dearest, if I had lost you I think I should have mourned for you all my life."

Ingram was certainly not acting up to his theory. Monsieur Blackie had utterly forgotten his rôle. He had promised himself to keep perfectly cool and collected, to be kind and friendly, and to avoid all emotion or excitement, but before ten minutes had passed he was pouring out his pent-up feelings.

"Oh, Mollie, dear Mollie!" he went on, in a broken voice—for Mollie, shaken and agitated, had hidden her face in her hands—"all this time I have been trying to win you. I want you to be my sweet wife, to give me the right to watch over you all my life. Darling, do you think you can care for poor Monsieur Blackie a little?"

"I do care," sobbed Mollie. "How can I help it, when you have been so good to me? I think"— but Mollie whispered this with her soft cheek pressed against his shoulder as he knelt beside her—"I think I have cared for you all this time." And perhaps that moment's ecstasy fully repaid Moritz for all the pain of the last few weeks.

Moritz behaved very well on the whole. When the first few minutes of beatitude were over, Mollie's pale cheeks and tearful eyes reminded him that she was an invalid, and he forbore to overwhelm her with his delight and gratitude. He sat beside her talking quietly, while Mollie lay back on her pillows in languid happiness, listening to her lover. He was telling her how proud he was of his sobriquet, and that no other name would ever be so dear to him as "Monsieur Blackie."

"I hope you will always call me by that name, Mollie, darling. To you I would always be Monsieur Blackie."

"But Moritz is so much prettier," she objected; "and Monsieur Blackie would be so long for daily use."

And then Ingram hastened to explain, in his eager way, that he had not meant that. Of course his wife—how Mollie blushed at that—must call him Moritz; but he never intended to lose his dear old title.

"Wave often calls you the Black Prince," returned Mollie, with a low laugh. "Oh, dear, how wonderful it all seems! Do you know"—very shyly—"I never imagined that any one would ever care for me, because of my lameness. Are you sure that you do not really mind it?" and here Mollie's voice grew anxious and even sad. "I am so awkward and clumsy. You know Noel often calls me 'the wobbly one.'"

"Noel will never call you that again," returned Ingram, quite sternly. "I gave him a good lecture the other day. Why, Mollie dearest, you are simply perfect in my eyes. I am afraid to tell you how lovely and dear I think you. The wonder is that you could ever bring yourself to care for me; for, as Gwen says, I am about as ugly as they make 'em," continued Ingram, in his quaint way. And then Mollie laughed again, though there were tears in her eyes of sheer joy and gratitude.

Mollie was very humble on the subject of her own merits; she had no conception how Ingram worshipped her sweetness and beauty. His crowning triumph had been that Monsieur Blackie, and not Viscount Ralston, had won her love.

"Gwen may laugh at me, and call me a fool," he thought, "but her sarcasm and smart speech will not trouble me in the least. I have played my little game, and got my innings, and the loveliest and dearest prize in the world is mine." And then he fell to musing blissfully on the surprise in store for his sweetheart. What would Mollie say when he showed her her future home? What would she think of Brentwood Hall, and the Silent Pool, and the big conservatory that Gwen had called their winter-garden, and the long picture-gallery, where, in an obscure corner, "King Canute" hung as large as life?

Moritz smiled happily to himself as he thought of the family diamonds, over which Gwen had gloated, and which he had vainly entreated her to wear.

"Jack would not like it," Gwen had answered, gravely. "They are for the future Lady Ralston, not for me."

How glad he was now that Gwen's unworldliness and good sense had been proof against the temptation! For in those days how was he to know that a certain sweet Mollie Ward would steal away his heart? When Mollie asked him, a little curiously, why he was smiling, Moritz returned, without a moment's hesitation, that he was merely thanking Heaven that she was not rich in worldly goods.

Mollie opened her eyes rather widely at this.

"I mean, dear, that I shall so love to give you all you want," he said, tenderly.

"But—but you are not really rich, are you?" asked Mollie. "Of course I know you are not poor, because of all the lovely things you have given me, and—and——" But here Mollie stopped; she had not the courage to mention Sir Hindley's fees.

"No, I am not poor," returned Ingram, quietly. "I have had a nice little property left me by a relative. We shall be very comfortable, dear, and when you are my wife you will not have to bother your poor little head with making ends meet." For once he had discovered Mollie shedding tears over her battered little housekeeping book, because she had exceeded the week's allowance. It was only seven-and-sixpence, or some such paltry sum, but Mollie was covered with shame at her own carelessness, and Ingram, who was, even in those early days, head over ears in love, longed to take her in his arms and kiss the tears away.

"Yes, I think we shall be very comfortable, darling," went on Ingram, somewhat hypocritically, as he remembered with secret glee his thirty thousand a year. Then, as even his inexperienced eyes detected signs of exhaustion in Mollie's increasing paleness, he somewhat quickly dropped the subject.

Mollie was not merely tired; she was dazed with the wonderful new happiness that had come to her. In spite of her love of pretty things, her little girlish vanities and harmless ambitions, she was far too simple-minded to be really worldly. If Moritz, in the old approved fairy-tale fashion, had suddenly filled her lap with diamonds and emeralds, they would only have dazzled Mollie's tired eyes. Later on, perhaps, these baubles and adjuncts of rank and wealth would gratify and delight her, but at this present moment she would have regarded them with indifference.

It was the man, Moritz Ingram, whom she wanted. It was Monsieur Blackie, with all his quaintness, his oddities, and eccentricities, his old-world chivalry, and true, manly tenderness, whom Mollie loved and honoured. Mollie, with all her simplicity and childliness, had been wiser than most women, in going straight to the root of the matter. It was nothing to her that her chosen lover was short of stature—a small, dark man, with a sallow skin, and closely-cropped hair that would have done credit to a convict. Mollie saw nothing but the kind, dear eyes, and pleasant smile, and she would not have exchanged him for any Adonis, though he stood six feet in his stockings.

Moritz's conscience was uneasy. More than once he had made an effort to go, but Mollie's soft little hand had kept him a willing prisoner. "Waveney will be here directly," she said. "She has promised to make tea for us." And at that very moment Waveney entered the room.

The lamp had not been lighted, and only the firelight threw a flickering, uncertain glow over the two faces before her. But something in Mr. Ingram's attitude, in the very atmosphere of the warm, flower-scented room, made Waveney's heart beat with quick, sympathetic throbs.

"Oh, what is it?" she said, stumbling a little in her haste. But, as she put out her hands to save herself, Ingram caught them in his own.

"My little Samaritan," he said, affectionately, "do you know, I am going to be your brother. Will you wish me joy, dear!" And then in his airy, foreign fashion, Moritz lifted her hand to his lips.

"My brother!" gasped Waveney. Well, she had expected it. But, all the same, she felt a little giddy. Mollie's Prince had come, as she knew he would, and would carry Mollie away.

"Darling, come here," and Mollie stretched out her arms almost piteously. "Wave, why do you stand there, as though you were turned to stone? Don't you want me to be happy?" she whispered, as Waveney, at this appeal, knelt down beside her.

"Oh, Mollie!" returned poor Waveney, "I know that I ought to be glad, and I am glad. But"—with a sob that would not be kept back—"But—but, I have lost my old sweetheart."

"Never!" returned Mollie, energetically, and her arms were round her sister's neck as she spoke. "Wave, dear, you must not say such things. Nothing, nothing, can ever come between us, or make our love less. Kiss me, darling," she went on, "and promise me that you will never say that again." And then, as Waveney stooped over her, she whispered in her ear: "After all, I have found out the best way of thanking him."

Perhaps it was as well that Nurse Helena made her appearance at that moment with the lamp, and so broke up the agitated little group. Waveney got up, feeling rather guilty, when Nurse Helena commented somewhat severely on Mollie's flushed and tired face.

"There has been too much talking," she said, in her quiet, authoritative voice. "Miss Mollie must have her tea, and go upstairs and rest." And then she regarded Ingram rather suspiciously. Nevertheless, when she went out of the room there was an amused twinkle in the nurse's grey eyes.

When Ann brought up the tea-tray Waveney was assiduous in her attentions to Mollie and her fiancé. She chatted to Ingram in her old frank way. Mollie was to rest and listen to them; she was to enjoy her tea and the delicate tongue sandwiches that Nurse Helena had cut so carefully. But Nurse Helena was right, and there must be no more talking. And then she amused them both by retailing to them the corporal's odd speeches.

Directly tea was over Ingram took his leave. "Before Nurse Helena turns me out," he observed, with a laugh. Waveney, who waited for him outside, was somewhat taken aback at the length of the farewell. "Parting is such sweet sorrow," she said to herself; but she sighed as she said it. Waveney, who was bitten with the same disease, was certainly not disposed to be hypercritical on the behaviour of the lovers.

She had a few words with Mollie before nurse came to claim her charge.

"Oh, Wave, I cannot understand it!" Mollie exclaimed, and her eyes looked bright and excited. "Fancy my being engaged before you! I, who never expected to have a lover of my own! Dearest, you must love him for my sake, he is so good. Oh, there is no one like him!" and Mollie seemed almost appalled at the magnitude of her bliss.

Waveney had promised to wait for her father; he was to put her into the train. And Althea had directed her to take a cab from Dereham station straight to the Red House.

Everard was somewhat later than usual, and they had only a little while together. He listened to the wonderful news with the air of a man who had fully expected it.

"I knew Ingram would steal a march on us," he said, rubbing his hands together. "I told him to wait until the child was stronger, and I thought he agreed to this; but you can never depend on a man when he is in love. And so Mollie really cares for him," went on Everard, in a pleased voice. "Well, she is a sensible girl, and does me credit. As for Ingram, he is a capital fellow, a son-in-law after my own heart," went on Everard, with a smile that perplexed Waveney, it was so mysterious and yet so full of amusement.

CHAPTER XXXVII.: A DEVOUT LOVER.

"A man he seems of cheerful yesterdays And confident to-morrows." Wordsworth.
"I do perceive here a divided duty." Othello.

When Waveney broke the news of Mollie's engagement to her friends at the Red House, the sisters only looked at each other with a meaning smile.

"So that is the end of the comedy," observed Althea, in an amused voice. "'All's well that ends well,' eh, Dorrie? Of course we all knew how it would end, that evening at the theatre."

"To be sure we did," returned Doreen, complacently.

Nothing ever ruffled her placidity. If people chose to be engaged or married, it was their affair, not hers. Doreen never envied them, never drew unfavourable comparisons between her friends' matrimonial bliss and her own single blessedness. She had walked contentedly "in maiden meditation, fancy free," all these years. "I was cut out for an old maid," she would say sometimes, laughingly, to her sister; "the rôle just suits me. You are different," she once added, looking rather wistfully at Althea as she spoke.

"Yes," replied Althea, frankly, "you and I are different people, Dorrie. You are the happiest and most contented woman I know; but"—a little pathetically—"I have not had all my good things." And, though she said no more, Doreen understood her.

"It is very odd to think that that pretty little Mollie Ward is to be a connection of ours," went on Doreen, when Waveney had bidden them good-night. Waveney's heart was so full that she yearned to be alone in her Pansy Room and think over the day's excitement. "Mollie will be our cousin." And as Althea assented to this with a smile, she continued, "I wonder what Gwen will think of her new sister-in-law?"

"My dear Dorrie, I think I can answer that. Given will be charmed with her. You know how much Gwen thinks of beauty, and where will you find a sweeter face than Mollie's? Then she is such a dear little unsophisticated thing. Ah, Gwen will lose her heart to her, you may depend on that. Upon my word," she went on, "I think Moritz has not chosen so badly, after all. Indeed, for an idealist, he has done very well for himself, and I shall write and congratulate him most cordially. Mollie will make a most fascinating little viscountess. She will have much to learn, of course; but she will be no faint-hearted Lady of Burleigh, sinking weakly under the burden of 'an honour into which she was not born,'" finished Althea, with a little laugh. And then, as the old grand-father's clock in the hall struck ten, Doreen rang the bell for prayers.

Althea did more than write her letter of congratulation. She drove down all the way to Cleveland Terrace a day or two afterwards, to see Mollie, and wish her joy; and she was so kind and sympathetic, she praised Moritz, and said so many nice things about him that Mollie was ready to worship her for her tact and gentleness.

Mollie's pretty bloom was returning to her cheeks, and on her left hand there was a splendid half-hoop of diamonds. She showed her ring to Althea, with a child's shy eagerness.

"It is far too beautiful," she said, proudly; "but he did not buy it for me—it belonged to that old relative who left him the property."

"Oh, indeed," returned Althea, with polite interest; but there was an amused gleam in her eyes. Of course the ring had belonged to old Lady Ralston, who had been a beauty and an heiress, and whose diamonds had been the envy of all the dowagers at the county ball. And then Moritz had come in and interrupted them. He was evidently taken aback at the sight of his cousin Althea; but her cordial welcome and her warm congratulations soon restored his equanimity, and he was soon chatting to her and Mollie in his old light-hearted fashion.

Mollie was to go down to Eastbourne the following week, and the two girls were to be chaperoned by Nurse Helena. Mollie was recovering her strength so fast that Nurse Helena's office was likely to be a sinecure. But when Althea pointed this out very gently to Moritz, he put his foot down very decidedly.

"Of course, Mollie was getting better," he said, with the air of an autocrat, and the sea-breezes would soon set her up. But how could his cousin Althea imagine that two girls could be alone at a place like Eastbourne? The very idea shocked him. As Mr. Ward could not leave town, except from Saturday to Monday, he had insisted that Nurse Helena should be put in charge. "I shall run down myself every few days," he finished, "and I suppose one has to study the proprieties." Then Althea very wisely held her peace.

Moritz went to the station to see them off. The girls were in high spirits, and Mollie, who knew that she would see him again before many days were over, could hardly summon up gravity enough to bid him good-bye. It was Moritz who looked melancholy; London was a howling wilderness to him without his darling. He had sent Noel back to keep house with his father, and he meant to go down to Brentwood Hall and seek consolation with Gwen and her boy. Gwen would give him all the sympathy he demanded; she was as romantic and unconventional as he was. Gwen dearly liked a lover; she would listen patiently to all his discourse on Mollie's perfections, and she would help him with the decorations, and the refurnishing of the rooms that were to be got ready for his young wife.

Moritz, who had been such a patient wooer, was now in hot haste to clinch his bargain.

Mollie, startled and protesting, had been carried away by his masterful eloquence, and had signed away her freedom. They were to be married in the middle of August, and to spend their honeymoon at his shooting box in the Highlands. The moorland air would be good for Mollie, he said, and they and the grouse would have it to themselves.

"I don't hold with rushing about from place to place, on one's wedding trip," he observed to Althea—for he had his theories on this subject also. "When Jack and Gwen were married, they went off to the Austrian Tyrol, and Heaven knows where besides. But I know a thing or two better than that. The Hut is a cosy little place, and there are some comfortable rooms in it. I will send down Murdoch—he is a Highlander and a handy fellow, too, and his wife is a capable woman—to make things ship-shape for a lady. We will have a few days in Edinburgh first, and show Mollie Holyrood and Arthur's Seat, and she shall feast her eyes on the shops in Princes Street"—for Moritz remembered, with lover-like accuracy, Mollie's girlish penchant for shop-windows. Moritz could be practical on occasion, and he somewhat astonished Althea, when he took her into his confidence, by his thoughtfulness for his young fiancée's comfort.

It was to his cousin Althea that Moritz entrusted the formidable but delightful task of ordering the trousseau. Gwen was too far from London to undertake such an onerous business; he had already talked the matter over with Mr. Ward, and had wrung from him a reluctant consent. Even Everard's pride and independence could not resist Moritz's urgent entreaties that a trousseau befitting Mollie's future rank should be provided at his expense. But before this could be done, Mollie must see her future home, and be made aware of her splendid position. And for this purpose it was arranged that, when the month at Eastbourne was over, she should pay a visit to the Red House; and then Moritz's long-deferred picnic to Brentwood should take place.

Althea had her own little plans, which she did not impart to Moritz, although she had already talked them over with Waveney.

"You know, my dear child," she had said, seriously, to her, the evening before Waveney started for Eastbourne. "I have been thinking a great deal of you and Mollie, and I have made up my mind to part with my dear little companion."

"What can you mean?" asked Waveney, in a startled voice; but she flushed uneasily. "I know I have been very little use to you lately, and that I have neglected my duties shamefully; but I was going to speak to you about that; I want you to give me less money—indeed—indeed," as Althea looked extremely amused at this, "I am quite serious. I have not earned my salary, and I cannot take it—it would not be honest;" and here Waveney drew up her slight figure, and looked very resolute.

"Why, Waveney, my dear child," remonstrated Althea, "surely you are not going to disappoint me after all these months! I thought we were such good friends, you and I, and that we understood each other thoroughly!" And as the girl looked at her in dumb questioning she continued, affectionately, "Dear friends do not differ for a trifle, or stand on their dignity. What are a few pounds, more or less, compared to all you and Mollie have done for me?"

"How do you mean, dear Miss Althea?" asked Waveney, quite taken aback at this. "I have done little enough, I know, and as for Mollie——"

"You have brought fresh interests into my life," returned Althea, quietly. "You have given me two more human beings to serve and love. Yes," she continued, but her voice was not quite steady, "I am very fond of you and your pretty Mollie, and it adds to my happiness to feel that I am any help or comfort to either of you."

"Comfort! What should I have done without you?" replied Waveney, with emotion. "My own mother could hardly have been kinder and more patient!" Then Althea flushed slightly.

"Well, then, you will be a good child, and let me finish what I have to say." And then, in her clear, sensible way, she explained her views about the future.

When Mollie married, Waveney would have to leave them. It was impossible for her father and Noel to do without her.

And Waveney, who had not taken this into consideration, felt a sudden thrill of pain at the idea of leaving the Red House.

As this was the case, went on Althea, she and Doreen both agreed that it would be cruel to part her and Mollie during the few months that remained to them. Mollie was coming to the Red

House for some weeks to do her shopping, but when she went back to Cleveland Terrace, Waveney must go with her. "That is why I say that you and I must part, my child," finished Althea, gently. "I shall miss my bright companion sadly—so sadly, indeed, that I never mean to have another. But, Waveney, your father has the first claim to your services. I dare not deprive him of your society when Mollie has gone. There, we will not talk any more," as she saw that Waveney's eyes were full of tears. "Think over what I have said when you are at Eastbourne, and take Mollie into your confidence. I know she will say that I am right."

And, indeed, when Waveney consulted her, Mollie, who was a very sensible little person, fully endorsed Queen Bess's opinion.

"Of course I could not do without you, darling," she remarked with decision. "Moritz"—she always said his name so prettily and shyly—"would not like me to be alone, and as for father and Noel, they would be too uncomfortable with only that stupid Ann to look after them." And then Waveney owned, with a sigh, that she and Miss Althea were right.

Waveney took herself to task severely for her reluctance at leaving the Red House. Was she guilty of loving the flesh-pots of Egypt? Was her home to be less to her because Mollie would not be there? Waveney cried "Shame!" to herself because the thought of Ann's clumsiness fretted her; while the meagre housekeeping, and all the pretty economies that had been Mollie's share, and were now to be shifted to her shoulders, filled her with a sore distaste and loathing. She had grown to love the Red House, and every room in it. The luxury, the comfort, the perfection of the trained service, the homelike atmosphere, the cultured society of the two sisters and their wide work and sympathies, all appealed strongly to Waveney's nature. Her life in the Red House had been a liberal education. How much she had learnt there! And then the Porch House Thursdays——But at this point in her reflections Waveney checked herself abruptly. Too well she knew where the sting lay, and why the pain of leaving Erpingham would be so sharp and continuous; only there could she enjoy the society of Mr. Chaytor, and she knew well that at Cleveland Terrace her Thursdays would be blank and sad.

"Wave, dear," exclaimed Mollie, on that first evening, as they were together in their comfortable sitting-room looking out on the Parade and the sea, while Nurse Helena was busy in the room above unpacking their boxes, "isn't this one of our dreams come true, that you and I should be at the seaside together?"

"It was your dream, not mine, Mollie," returned Waveney, in a teasing voice. "You were the dreamer in the old days. I was far more prosaic and matter-of-fact." And then she settled herself more comfortably against Mollie's couch. "There was your Kitlands dream, you know, and a hundred others."

"Oh, never mind Kitlands," replied Mollie, with a touch of impatience in her voice. "That was a dear dream, but of course it was too big and grand ever to come true. But how often we used to make believe that we were going to the seaside! Don't you remember, Wave, the little bow-window parlour over the tinman's in High Street that we were to take, and the sea-breezes that would meet us as we turned the corner, and how we were always to have shrimps for tea?" And then Mollie laughed with glee. "But this is much better, isn't it, dear?" and she looked at the big, cosy room that Ingram had selected for their use.

They were like a pair of happy children that evening. Mollie had insisted that she and Waveney should share the big front bedroom; and she was so wide-awake and excited that she would have talked half the night, only Waveney sternly refused to be cajoled.

"Nurse Helena has begged us not to talk," she said, "and I feel I am on my honour. No, Mollie, I will not be coaxed. I am a woman of my word, and I gave Nurse Helena my promise. There shall be no pale cheeks for the Black Prince to see on Saturday. Go to sleep like a good child." And then Mollie consented to be silent.

It was a happy month, and nothing occurred to mar their enjoyment. They spent delightful mornings on the beach or parade; in the afternoon, while Mollie had her siesta, Waveney and Nurse Helena wrote their letters, or enjoyed the books with which Ingram had provided them; after tea, when the evenings were fine and warm, they drove into the country, coming back to an early supper.

Moritz always came down from Saturday to Monday, and put up at the hotel close by. Once he brought Mr. Ward with him, and another time it was Noel; and then, indeed, Mollie's happiness was complete.

Only one thing troubled Mollie as the days went on. In spite of her high spirits, Waveney was not quite herself. She had silent fits at times. She was absent and distraite, and did not always hear what Mollie said to her; and more than once as they sat in the moonlight, looking at the silvery path across the dark sea, Mollie had heard a suppressed sigh.

"There is something on her mind, something she is keeping to herself," thought Mollie, anxiously, "and we have never, never had a secret from each other. It is not like my own Wave to hide anything from me, and I shall tell her so." And, indeed, Mollie was so tearful and pleading, so pertinacious in her questions, and so quick and clever in her surmises, that before they returned to the Red House Waveney's poor little secret—her unfinished story—was in Mollie's keeping. Mollie was full of tender sympathy. She cried bitterly over Waveney's description of that meeting by the river. She quaked and shivered,—was hot and cold by turns with excitement.

"Of course he cares for you, darling," she said, putting her arms round her sister's neck. "How can he help it? Oh, it will all come right," she continued, cheerfully. "One day you will be as happy as we are. What a pity he is so poor and proud! Men are so blind. It would be so much nicer to be engaged, and wait—oh, any number of years," went on Mollie, with womanly philosophy.

But to this Waveney made no answer. Perhaps in her secret heart she was glad Mollie knew. Never in their lives had they had a thought unshared by the other.

But when Mollie was alone she made a naughty little mouche.

"How can she care for that plain, old-looking man?" she said to herself. "Why, I should be frightened to speak to him, he looks so grave. Waveney is a hundred times too good for him. 'A noticeable man, with large grey eyes,' is not to my taste," went on Mollie, with a blissful remembrance of her own dear Monsieur Blackie.

CHAPTER XXXVIII.: MOLLIE'S PRINCE.

"And, while now she wonders blindly, Nor the meaning can divine, Proudly turns he round and kindly: 'All of this is thine and mine.'" The Lord of Burleigh.

"It is all arranged about the picnic," exclaimed Mollie, in a joyous voice, as she entered their bedroom, where Waveney was busy packing her own and Mollie's things. It was the last day before their return to town. Moritz had come down unexpectedly the previous evening, and had paid his usual morning visit; he had gone back to the hotel to write his letters, and had promised to join them on the Parade later on.

"What picnic?" observed Waveney, absently. She was at that moment regarding with great satisfaction the new spring dresses that had just come from the dressmaker's. They had been bought with her own money; and the pretty hats, and smart boots and gloves, had all been provided from her quarter's salary, and, although Mollie had at first refused to allow Waveney to spend her money on her, she was soon persuaded that any shabbiness on the part of his young fiancée would be distressing to Mr. Ingram's feelings. "You know he likes people to be nicely dressed," Waveney had remarked, rather severely, "so please don't be foolish, Mollie. Surely"— in a pathetic voice—"you won't begrudge me this last chance of buying clothes for my sweetheart?" And what could Mollie do after that, except hug her silently, in token of yielding?

"What picnic?" returned Mollie, indignantly. "Why, our long-promised visit to Brentwood Hall, of course, to see dear old King Canute in the picture. Moritz says he has arranged everything with Miss Althea. I am to have a day's rest at the Red House, and on Thursday we are to go."

"But Miss Althea is always engaged on Thursday," objected Waveney. "She has her Porch House evening."

"Oh yes, I know," retorted Mollie—she was fairly glowing with excitement and happiness— "but Miss Althea says she doesn't mind being absent for once. We are to drive down to Waterloo, and Moritz will meet us there, and it is only an hour's journey by train. Moritz says that his sister has promised to join us at luncheon. I was just a wee bit frightened when he said that; but he assured me that she would not be the least formidable. She is very tall, Waveney, and very plain—at least, strangers think her so; and she always calls herself ugly, but he was sure I should soon love her. 'Gwen is the dearest girl in the world,' he went on, 'and Jack just worships her. Jack Compton is her husband, you know.' Oh Wave, I do hope she will like me."

"Of course she will like you," returned Waveney, with comfortable decision. "I would not give a fig for Mrs. Gwen if she had the bad taste not to admire my Mollie. Well, I hope it will be a fine day for Moritz's picnic, and then we can wear our new dresses. But, Mollie dear, are we really to have luncheon at Brentwood Hall? I thought Moritz said his friend was away, and that only servants were there?"

"Yes, but he says he and Lord Ralston are such close friends that he has carte blanche to do as he likes. He is Viscount Ralston, and he is very rich. Moritz says he has over thirty thousand a year. He seems to have very grand friends," went on Molly, rather thoughtfully. "I am afraid they will look down on me, a poor little lame Cinderella."

But Waveney scouted this idea with energy. Mollie was well born and well educated; no one could look down on her. Moritz would not have to blush for her, even if his friends were dukes as well as viscounts. Mollie must hold her own, and not be too humble on the subject of her own merits. It was quite evident that Moritz thought her the dearest and sweetest thing in the world, and she ought to be satisfied with that. And then Mollie cheered up and forgot her fears, and they packed happily until it was time to go out. When the eventful day arrived, Mollie woke Waveney at an unconscionably early hour, to inform her that the weather was simply perfect, and that they might wear their new dresses without fear of a shower.

It was one of those typical May days, when Nature puts on her daintiest and fairest apparel, when the fresh young green of the foliage seems to feast and rest the eyes.

The air was sweet with lilac and may; and the tender blue of the sky was unstained by a single cloud. When Mollie came downstairs, in her pretty grey dress, with a little spray of pink may at her throat, Althea thought that she matched the day itself.

"Mollie has quite recovered her looks," she said to Doreen; "the dear child is a great beauty, and Gwen will be charmed with her." And, indeed, as they drove through there were many admiring glances cast at the pretty, blushing face.

Moritz was at the station to meet them. He had a white flower in his buttonhole, and looked jubilant and excited. Perhaps he was a trifle fussy in his attentions. Mollie must take his arm, he said; the station was so crowded, and there were a lot of rough people about.

Poor Mollie felt a little nervous and conscious. It was difficult to adapt her slow, lurching walk to Monsieur Blackie's quick, springy tread. Moritz might be as tender over her infirmity as a mother over some cripple child; but Mollie, who was only human, could have wept over her own awkwardness. Perhaps her limping gait had never given her more acute pain than now, when Ingram was trying so carefully and labouriously to adapt his step to hers.

Mollie's cheeks were burning by the time they reached their compartment; but when Moritz sat down beside her with a fond look and word, she forgot her uneasiness, and was her own happy self again.

The journey was a short one. When they reached Brentwood, Moritz hurried his party through the little country station before the stationmaster had an opportunity of accosting him.

An open barouche with a fine pair of bays was awaiting them. When Waveney admired them, Moritz remarked rather complacently that Ralston was a good judge of horse-flesh. And then he asked Mollie how she would like to drive herself in a low pony-carriage with a pair of cream-coloured ponies. And Mollie, thinking that he was joking, clapped her hands gleefully.

"How delicious that would be!" she returned. "But it is very naughty of you to tantalise me in this fashion. Oh, what a dear old village!" she went on. "And, Moritz, the people seem to know you." For Moritz was lifting his hat every instant in response to some greeting.

"Oh, they are always civil to people who are staying at the Hall," returned Ingram, evasively. But at that moment he met Althea's amused glance. "Very well done, my lord," she said, under her breath; and then she shook her head at him.

They were just turning in at some open gates, and before them was a shady avenue. At the end, some more gates, of finely wrought Flemish work, admitted them to the sunny gardens and terrace; while before them stood the grand old Hall, with its grey walls and quaint gables and oriel windows embowered in ivy and creepers.

"It is a lovely old place," murmured Althea; but Mollie and Waveney were speechless with admiration. To their eyes it looked like an enchanted palace, surrounded by shimmering green lawns. The great door was wide open, as though to receive them; but there was no sign of human life. When the carriage had driven away, Moritz took Mollie's hand and led her across the wide hall, with its pillars, and grand oak carvings, its mighty fireplace, and walls covered with curious weapons, with here and there a stag's antlers, or the head of a grinning leopard.

They only paused for a moment to admire the great stone staircase, that was broad enough for a dozen men to walk abreast. One of the Ralstons, in a mad frolic, had once ridden his gallant grey up to the very top of the staircase.

"I am going to show you everything," observed Ingram, as they walked down the softly carpeted corridor. "We call this the Zoo," he continued, "for if you look at the pictures, Mollie, you will see they are mostly of animals. There are some good proof engravings of Landseer, and the sculpture is rather fine; but the most beautiful groups are in the picture-gallery, upstairs. The fifth Viscount Ralston was a connoisseur of art, and spent a good deal of his income in pictures and sculpture. It was he who brought the Flemish gates from Belgium; they are considered very fine, and are always pointed out to visitors."

Mollie began to feel a little breathless; she wanted to linger in every room, but Moritz, who had his work cut out for him, hurried her on.

They went through the big dining-room, which was large enough for a banqueting-hall, and into a smaller one, where the table was already laid for luncheon; and then into the library and morning-room. When Mollie asked, with naive curiosity, if there were no drawing-room, Moritz laughed and told her to wait.

"These are Ralston's private quarters," he said, ushering her into a cosy sitting-room, fitted up for a gentleman's use. But when Mollie would have investigated, with girlish curiosity, the mass of papers on the writing table, he quietly took her arm, and marched her into the billiard-room adjoining. "Ralston would not like us to look at his papers," he said, gravely. "He is an untidy fellow, and his writing-table is always in confusion."

"Is Lord Ralston married?" asked Mollie, presently, as they went slowly up the stone staircase. Althea, who overheard her, was obliged to pause; she was shaking with suppressed mirth; but Waveney was far too busily engaged in admiring a painted window to notice her merriment. Ingram was quite equal to the occasion.

"He is not married yet, dear," he returned, quickly, "but he does not expect to be a bachelor much longer. Shall I show you the rooms that he has chosen for his future wife, or shall we go to the picture-gallery?" But Mollie's excitement was too great for fatigue, and she at once decided to see Lady Ralston's rooms.

To Mollie's inexperienced eyes they were grand enough for the Queen. She was almost indignant when Moritz explained that the boudoir and dressing-room were to be refurnished. It was shameful extravagance, she repeated, more than once; what did it matter if the furniture was a little old fashioned? Mollie was quite eloquent on the subject, as she stood in the wide bay window of the boudoir. It was a charming window. Mollie looked straight down the avenue to the great bronze gates. The rooks were cawing in the elms; some tame pheasants were pluming themselves on the lawn below; and a wicked-looking jackdaw was strutting up and down the terrace. The beds were full of spring flowers.

"Oh, how perfect it all is!" sighed Mollie; and then she said, in quite a decided tone, "I do think it will be wicked for Lord Ralston to refurnish this room."

"There, Gwen, do you hear that?" exclaimed Moritz. And Mollie turned hastily round. A tall young lady was standing in the doorway watching her. She was quite young, but Mollie thought she had never seen any one so tall; and certainly it was her opinion, that first moment, that Mrs. John Compton was the plainest person she had ever seen.

Mollie, who was a great admirer of beauty, felt a sort of shock at the sight of Gwen's frank ugliness; her small greenish-blue eyes crinkling up with amusement, the bluntness of her features, and her wide mouth, gave Mollie a pang. She had yet to find out her redeeming points,—her beautiful figure, the rich brown hair, and pleasantly modulated voice.

"Moritz, is this my dear new sister?" asked Gwen, with a smile so bright and warm that it quite transfigured her plain face. And then, with frank kindness, she put her arms round Mollie and kissed her. "Mollie, you must be very good to me," she went on. And now there were tears in her eyes. "Moritz is my only brother, and we have been everything to each other. Have we not, old boy?" And Gwen pinched his ear playfully, and then greeted Waveney and her cousin Althea in the warmest fashion.

There was a little hubbub of talking and laughter, and then Moritz drew Mollie's arm through his and led her away.

Probably Gwen had had her orders, for, instead of following them, she made room for Waveney on the wide window-seat.

"There is something Moritz wishes me to tell you," she said, quietly, "and that he is telling your sister now."

However important Moritz's communication might be, it had to be deferred until Mollie had exhausted her whole vocabulary of admiring terms at the sight of the noble gallery.

It was a drawing-room and ball-room as well as a picture-gallery. Three great fireplaces, with their cosy environment of luxurious lounges and easy-chairs, gave warmth to the whole room. And on the other side were windows with deep recesses, every one forming separate cosy nooks. In one was a low tea-table and a circle of easy-chairs. Another was fitted with an inlaid writing-table and cabinet. A third contained only a low velvet divan. It was in this last recess that Moritz at last contrived to detain Molly.

"Dear Mollie," he said, gently but firmly, "there will be plenty of time to look at the pictures and sculpture after luncheon; but I want you to listen to me a moment. I have to ask your forgiveness for a little deception." Moritz's face was so grave that Mollie regarded him with astonishment.

"My forgiveness! Are you joking, Moritz?"

"No, darling, I am quite serious. I have brought you here under false pretences. But I will tell you all about it by-and-by. Dearest, this is your future home. It is here that you and I are to spend our lives together. Moritz Ingram and Viscount Ralston are one and the same person."

Mollie's face grew white. The little hand he held trembled with emotion.

"Oh, no, not really?" she gasped.

"Yes, really, my sweet one. But I cannot have you look so pale and frightened." Then, as Mollie glanced shyly at him, he caught her suddenly to his breast. "My little blessing," he whispered. "You loved your old friend, Monsieur Blackie; but you will not tell me now, I hope, that Ralston is to be less dear to you."

"No, no!" stammered Mollie; "but I cannot understand. Oh, Moritz, why did you do it?"

"I will tell you, dear," he returned, quietly. "You know, at one time, Gwen and I were very poor. We lived in a pokey little house that we called 'The Tin Shanty.' You shall see it some day, and I think you will own that Ten, Cleveland Terrace, is a mansion compared with it. We were almost at the end of our tether when the death of a cousin made me Viscount Ralston and master of Brentwood Hall and thirty thousand a year."

"Oh, Moritz!" and Mollie shivered and hid her face.

"I was a lucky fellow, was I not, dear? and I was truly thankful for my good things. I was always very sociable, and fond of the society of my fellow-creatures, and when Gwen married I led rather a gay life. But after a time I got disgusted. Mothers with marriageable daughters made a dead set at me. Before the season was over I could have had my pick of half a dozen beauties. Viscount Ralston, with his thirty thousand a year, was considered a desirable parti. Mollie, dear, it fairly sickened me. You know I was an Idealist, and I never could make up my mind to move in the ordinary groove, like other people, and I registered a mental vow that, unless I was loved for myself, I would never marry. When I first met my little Samaritan I had no wish to disclose my title; but it was a mere freak at first to remain incognito, until—until I saw you, my darling. Oh, Mollie, do you remember that day, and how I heard you singing, and discovered Cinderella sitting on the hearth? Shall I tell you a secret, dear? When I left the house that day I said to myself, 'I will move heaven and earth to win that girl for my wife.'"

"Oh, Moritz, did you really?"

"Yes, love, and then and there I decided to be Mr. Ingram. I had no difficulty in preserving my incognito. I bound over my cousins to secrecy. It was only your illness that complicated matters. I found, then, that it was necessary to take your father and Noel into confidence; but you and Waveney were to be kept in ignorance. Gwen is telling her at this present moment. But now, Mollie, I have finished my confession, and I only want to hear from your lips that Monsieur Blackie is forgiven."

"There is nothing to forgive," she faltered. "I think I am glad that I did not know. But oh, Moritz, there is one thing that makes me sorry." And now there was a painful flush on Mollie's cheek. "You know what I mean. I wish for your sake that I was not lame."

"My poor little darling," he returned, compassionately. "But I think I love you all the more for your helplessness. Thank Heaven, my wife will never have occasion to tire herself. The cream-coloured ponies are in the stable, Mollie, and when we are married I mean to give you riding-lessons."

And then, for very joy and gratitude, Mollie burst into a flood of happy tears.

"Oh, it is too much, too much," she sobbed. "I do not deserve such happiness. Moritz, you must teach me everything. I want to be worthy of this lovely home and you." And then shyly, but with exquisite, grace she lifted the kind hand to her lips.

CHAPTER XXXIX.: EVERARD YIELDS THE POINT.

"Down on your knees, And thank Heaven, fasting, for a good man's love." As You Like It.
"He does it with a better grace, but I do it more natural." Twelfth Night.

It is given to few favored mortals to know such hours or moments of intense happiness, that their cup of bliss seems well-nigh overflowing. But such a moment had come to Moritz Ingram and Mollie.

When Gwendoline came to summon them to luncheon, two such radiant faces beamed on her that she smiled back at them with joyous sympathy.

"Come here and congratulate me, Gwen," exclaimed her brother. "Mollie has forgiven me for my little ruse; she knows an idealist must have plenty of scope, and that everything is fair in love or war." And as Mollie did not contradict this audacious statement, Gwendoline let it pass without rebuke.

"Moritz, she is just perfect," she whispered, as Mollie left them and went down the gallery, in search of Waveney. "Oh, I know," as they watched the pretty, girlish figure with its awkward, lurching gait. "It is a pity the dear child is so lame; but she is like a little stray angel for loveliness. There, she has found her sister; we must leave them for a few minutes together."

Mollie discovered Waveney standing in one of the window recesses, looking down on the terrace. At the sound of footsteps, she turned round.

"Well, Mollie," she said, trying to smile, but her lip quivered. "So the Prince has come, after all, and my sweetheart is to be a great lady."

"Are you glad, Wave?" asked Mollie, with a loving hug, "really and truly glad?"

Then Waveney's dark eyes filled suddenly with tears.

"Glad that my Mollie should have this beautiful home, and all these fine things? My darling, what a question! Don't you know that I love you better than myself? I could cry with joy to think that there will be no more dull, anxious days in store for you, no worrying over Ann's stupidity, and no fretting because sixpence would not go as far as a shilling." Then, as Mollie laughed and kissed her, "I wonder what the Black Prince would have said if he had seen that poor little housekeeping book, drenched with tears?"

"Don't, Wave—please don't remind me of my silliness. Oh dear, how unhappy I used to be! And now"—and here Mollie gazed with delighted eyes down the splendid gallery—"to think that I shall ever be mistress of this! It is just like a wonderful fairy story; for none of our castles in the air—not even Kitlands—came up to this."

"Of course not," returned Waveney, energetically; "only Cinderella could compare with it." And then, in a teasing voice, "Your ladyship will not need to glue your face against shop-windows any more. You will have diamonds and pearls of your own."

"Yes, and a pony-carriage, with cream-coloured ponies!" exclaimed Mollie, joyously. "And Wave, just think! Moritz is going to give me riding-lessons! Oh, his kindness and generosity are beyond words. Darling, you must love him for his goodness to your poor little Mollie; and Wave, remember, all this will make no difference. I think I care for it so much because I shall be able to help you and father."

They were interrupted at this moment. Moritz carried off Mollie, and Gwen proposed that they should follow. "For, while Moritz has been dramatising," she observed, "you two poor things have been starving." And Waveney could not deny that she was excessively hungry.

The old, grey-haired butler was in his place when they entered the dining-room. Moritz stopped to speak to him.

"Tell Mrs. Wharton that I shall bring Miss Ward to see her this afternoon," he said; and then they took their places.

Both the girls were a little subdued by the unwonted magnificence of their environment, but they struggled gallantly against the feeling.

As Mollie ate her chicken, and sipped her champagne, she wondered how soon she would get used to be waited upon by two tall footmen, and how she would feel when she was first addressed as "My lady." "I hope I shall not laugh," she observed to Waveney afterwards.

Waveney was wondering why she had never noticed that Moritz had rather an aristocratic look. Their old friend, Monsieur Blackie, had always had good manners; but now that he was in his own house, and at his own table, she was struck by his well-bred air and perfect ease.

"He looks like a viscount," she said to herself, "and yet he is perfectly his old self. Mollie was wiser than all of us, for she found out that he was worthy of her love." And then Waveney fell into a reverie over her strawberries. Her thoughts had strayed to a certain dull, narrow house in Dereham. Thorold Chaytor's grave face and intellectual brow seemed to rise before her. If she had his love, she would not envy Mollie her rank and riches; she would envy no one. Even now she had her secret happiness, for the words she had heard that sorrowful night were for ever stamped on her memory. "Trouble? when there is nothing on earth that I would not do for you, my darling!" How, then, could she doubt that she was beloved?

When luncheon was over, Moritz took Mollie to the housekeeper's room and introduced her to Mrs. Wharton. Gwen accompanied them; and then they went back to the picture-gallery, and Mollie and Waveney feasted their eyes on the pictures and sculpture. It was pretty to see the girls when they recognised poor old "King Canute." Mollie actually kissed the canvas. "You dear old thing!" she said, apostrophising it. Wretched daub as it was, crude in colouring and defective in execution, Moritz proudly termed it the gem of the gallery.

"It helped me to win my Mollie," he said to Gwen, who was regarding it dubiously. "I painted many a worse picture when we were at the Tin Shanty, eh, Gwen?" And her assent to this was so emphatic that Moritz felt decidedly snubbed; but he rose to the occasion nobly.

"Mr. Ward has not quite worked out his subject," he went on; "but his idea is good, and I shall always venerate it as the failure of a brave man. 'A gallery of failures.' Would that not be a happy thought, Althea? Suppose you and I start a hospital, refuge, or whatever you like to call it, for diseased works of art? We would buy them cheaply, at half-price, and the poor things should live out their time." And here Moritz looked round the company for approval.

"How about the survival of the fittest?" asked his sister, scornfully.

"Oh, that will be all right," he returned, easily. "Besides, we should have no very fit specimens, in a gallery of failures. They would be in all stages of disease. But just think, my dear, what an encouragement it would be to the artists! 'If my failure is remunerative,' the poor beggars would say to themselves, 'I must just try again, and do better next time.'"

"You are very absurd, Moritz." But Gwen looked decidedly amused. And Mollie, privately, thought it a clever idea.

When they had finished inspecting all the treasures in the gallery, Gwen summoned them to tea. The tea-table was in the prettiest of the alcoves, which was large enough to hold seven or eight people.

After this they went down to the gardens, and through a small fir-wood, to the Silent Pool. Here the carriage was to meet them.

Mollie and Waveney were enchanted with the Silent Pool. The still, green pool, surrounded by the dark firs, the beauty, the stillness, and the solemnity of the spot, inspired them with awe. To Althea it was a favourite and well-remembered place. She had visited it more than once, in the old viscount's time. For it had never been closed to the public. That still pool, with its dark, hidden depths, reminded her of her own life, with its calm surface, and troubled under-current. "There are so many lives like that," she thought, as she looked back at the solemn scene. And then she followed the others, down the winding path, to the little inn, which was known as the Brentwood Arms. Here Gwendoline bade them an affectionate farewell. And then they drove off to the station.

"It has been the most wonderful day that I have ever spent in my life!" exclaimed Molly, a little breathlessly.

"It has been a happy day to me," returned Moritz, in a low tone. "There can only be one day more perfect, and that will be our wedding day, Mollie."

When they reached Waterloo, Althea refused to allow Moritz to accompany them to the Red House. Mollie was tired and over-excited, and must rest. He was to come to them the following evening, to meet Mr. Ward and Thorold. There was to be a sort of friendly re-union. It was Noel's birthday, too. But there must be no more excitement for the present. And Althea was so firm and inexorable that Moritz had to yield.

"I think we are all tired," observed Waveney. "But it has been a lovely day." And then, in spite of Althea's advice to rest and be quiet, she and Mollie discussed their delightful picnic. Only, as they drove down High Street, and passed a certain house, Waveney became a little silent. The blinds were up, and the lamp was lighted. Waveney distinctly saw a tall figure standing by the window. Althea evidently recognized it, too. "Thorold has come back early from the Porch House," she said. And then she spoke on quite a different subject to Mollie.

The next few weeks were busy ones at the Red House. There were long mornings of shopping, and endless interviews with dressmakers and milliners; and the all-important business of the trousseau occupied the three ladies from morning to night.

Mollie took a child-like pleasure in it all. Prosperity did not spoil her. She was still the same simple, light-hearted Mollie of old, and the one drawback to her perfect happiness was the thought that Waveney could not have it too. "I wish I could give you half my trousseau," she said, quite piteously. But Waveney only laughed at her.

"Don't be a simpleton, Mollie," she returned. "Why, you foolish child, there are actually tears in your eyes! Don't you know that all these fine things—these satins and silks and laces—would be most incongruous in my position? What could I do with them at Cleveland Terrace?"

"But you will be at Brentwood half your time," retorted Mollie. "Moritz says he could not have the heart to separate us; and he is so fond of you, Wave."

"Yes, dear; but all the same, I must not expect to be as smart as your ladyship." And then Mollie made a face at her.

Moritz had not forgotten his little Samaritan, and Althea had her orders. Besides the beautiful bridesmaid's dress, a tailor-made tweed, and two pretty evening frocks were provided for Waveney; and then, indeed, Mollie was content.

There was so much to do that it was not until the beginning of July that Waveney and Mollie went back to Cleveland Terrace to spend the last few weeks with their father and Noel. The wedding was to be from the Red House, and it was already arranged that they were to return a week before the marriage.

All this time Moritz had haunted his cousin's house morning, noon, and night, and had refused to consider himself in the way. Every few days Everard dined there, and now and then Thorold was invited to meet him.

Everard was now quite at home at the Red House. Almost insensibly he had relapsed into the old intimacy with Doreen and Althea. He forgot he was only a poor drudge of a drawing-master. He forgot his shabby dress-coat, and pitiful little economies. Brighter days were in store for him; his little Mollie was to be the wife of a nobleman, and Waveney was coming back to him to be the light of his home; and there was little doubt in his mind that Noel would distinguish himself and pass his examination.

"I feel better days are coming," he said once to Althea. She was his old friend and confidant; he would often speak to her of his children's future, and her gentle sympathy never failed him.

It was Althea's advice that he sought, when Moritz told his future father-in-law that he intended to allow him an income. Everard, who was as proud as he was poor, was sorely perturbed in his mind when he heard this.

"What am I to do?" he said, in a vexed voice, when he found himself alone with Althea that evening. They were all in the garden together—Ingram, and Thorold Chaytor, and Joanna, as well as Moritz. They had broken up in little groups, and Everard and Althea had strolled down a side path behind the Porch House.

"I wish you would give me your advice," he went on, "for I am in a terrible fix. Ralston is the most generous fellow I ever met; he wants me to give up my teaching and accept an income from him. The fact is," continued Everard, rather bitterly, "he is unwilling that his father-in-law should be only a poor devil of a drawing-master. It is just his pride, confound him! But, as I tell him, I have my pride, too. I am afraid I hurt his feelings, though he was too kind to tell me so."

"Moritz is very sensitive," returned Althea; "in spite of eccentricities, he is very soft-hearted; his generosity amounts to a vice; he is never happy unless he is giving."

"Oh, that is all very well," replied Everard, in rather a huffy voice. "But if I do not choose to be indebted to my son-in-law, surely my feelings must be considered as well as his."

"True, my dear friend." But Althea smiled as she spoke. "But it seems to me, if I may speak frankly, that your pride is at fault here. Moritz wishes to be a son to you; he will be your Mollie's husband; he has more than he can spend—every year he is likely to grow richer, for, as you know, they have found coal on the Welsh property; he and Mollie will be rolling in money, and——" Here she hesitated.

"And Mollie's father will be out at elbows. Why do you not finish your sentence, Miss Harford?"

"No; I should not have put it that way," returned Althea. "But I think it will be rather hard on Moritz, and doubly hard on Mollie, if you refuse the gift that their filial love offers you. Mollie knows how you loathe teaching. It is the crown of her happiness that her marriage will enable her to help you and Waveney. Moritz intends to give her a magnificent allowance for her own private use, and directly they were engaged he informed her that he intended to settle an income on her father. Mr. Ward, you cannot be proud with your own children. Why not accept your son-in-law's kindness? I am sure you will not repent it." And then Everard yielded.

Mollie and Waveney were overjoyed when they heard that Althea's counsel had prevailed, and Moritz was excessively pleased; he was even disposed to encroach a little on his privileges, only Althea begged him to be cautious.

"You and Moritz must bide your time," she said, one day, to the little bride-elect; "you have both gained a victory, and you must be content with that for the present. Your father told Waveney the other day that nothing would induce him to leave Cleveland Terrace. Your mother died there," she continued, in a low voice, "and I suppose that is why he is attached to the house."

"Yes; but it is such a dingy, dull little place," returned Mollie, sadly, "and Moritz meant to buy such a pretty house, and furnish it so beautifully. But I suppose we shall have to wait."

"Indeed, you must. But cheer up, Mollie; new carpets and curtains, and light, tasteful papers will soon transform Number Ten, Cleveland Terrace, into a charming abode—indeed, I do not believe you will recognise it."

"And Ann is to be sent away? You are sure of that, Miss Althea?"

"Yes, and two good servants are to replace her. Waveney will have no trouble with her housekeeping. Now I hear Moritz's voice, and you know his lordship objects to be kept waiting!" And at this hint Mollie blushed beautifully and ran away.

CHAPTER XL.: THE VEILED PROPHET.

The evening before Waveney and Mollie returned to Cleveland Terrace there was a family gathering at the Red House. Everard Ward and his son and Lord Ralston dined there.

Waveney had secretly hoped that Mr. Chaytor would have been invited; but Althea, who was not aware of the girl's secret, had said, more than once, that no outsiders were to be admitted, and Waveney vainly tried to hide her depression. In spite of home-sickness and longings for the society of her twin sister, she had been very happy at the Red House. Her affection for Althea only had deepened with time, and the thought that she was no longer to minister to her comfort filled her with profound sadness.

Dereham and Erpingham had grown very dear to her, and the idea of separation from her kind friends made her heart heavy.

"You will often be with us," Althea said, trying to cheer her. "Do you think Doreen and I mean to lose sight of you? No, my dear, no. 'Once loved is always loved.' That is the Harford motto, and most certainly you are not losing your friends."

"No, but it will not be the same," returned Waveney, sadly. But the real cause of her depression was not the parting from her beloved Queen Bess. If she could only say good-bye to her other friend! If she could see him again and have some look and word to treasure up in her memory! On the last Porch House Thursday he had hardly spoken to her. It almost seemed as though he had avoided her, and certainly there had been no farewell. Most likely he would expect to see her on the following Thursday, and then Althea would tell him that she was gone.

Waveney tried to console herself with the thought that she would see him at the wedding, for both he and his sister were to be among the guests. But when one is in love even five weeks' absence seems like an eternity in prospect. And Thorold's silent influence and unspoken affection was already dominating Waveney's entire nature.

It was a sultry July day, and Althea had proposed to Doreen that ices and dessert should be served in the verandah of the Porch House, overlooking the tennis lawn; and when dinner was over she led the way to the garden. When they came in sight of the verandah, Lord Ralston expressed his approval with his usual frankness, but Everard looked at Althea rather meaningly.

"It reminds me of Kitlands," he said, in a low voice. "Don't you remember you often had dessert on the terrace?" And Althea smiled assent.

"Dorrie and I are very fond of these al fresco meals," she observed. "I think in summer we should like to have them all in the open air."

And then, as they seated themselves in the comfortable hammock chairs, Doreen came across the grass with some letters in her hand. She had intercepted the postman on his way to the house.

"They are mostly for me," she said, looking at the addresses. "One from Aunt Sara, and another from Laura Cameron, and Mrs. Bell's account. Yours will keep, Althea; it is only a business-looking document from Mr. Duncan. Correspondence with one's family lawyer is not particularly interesting," added Doreen, briskly.

"Is old Andrew Duncan still in existence?" asked Lord Ralston, casually, as he handed an ice to

Mollie.

Everard looked up quickly.

"Andrew Duncan & Son, of Number Twenty-one, Lincoln's Inn? I did not know he was your lawyer, Miss Harford."

But Noel suddenly broke in.

"Why, that is our Duncan, father!" he exclaimed, rather excitedly. "The veiled Prophet is his client, you know. That reminds me," he went on, with a glance at his sisters, "I am going to beard the old lion in his den, one of these days. The Veiled Prophet shall be unmasked, as sure as my name is Noel Ward."

"Noel is speaking of the unknown benefactor who is so generously educating him," explained Everard. "The silly children always speak of him as the Veiled Prophet——"

But here he stopped suddenly, as though he were shot. He had been addressing Althea, who was sitting near him; but at his first word, her pale face had become suddenly suffused with a painful flush, which deepened every moment. That scorching blush seemed burnt into her very soul as she sat with downcast eyes, unable to say a word.

"Will any one have any strawberries?" asked Doreen, hastily. Althea's confusion filled her with compunction, and she was anxious to atone for her carelessness. She handed some to Everard as she spoke, but he waved them aside with some impatience.

"Good heavens! was it you, Althea?" he asked, in a tone of dismay.

Then Noel sprang from his chair.

"It is Miss Harford!" he said, loudly. "By Jove! this is a surprise!" and the boy's face grew suddenly red. "All these years we have been talking of the Veiled Prophet, and it never entered into our heads that it was a prophetess."

"My friend the humourist has evidently hit it," observed Moritz, airily; but he was looking keenly at Althea. "Other people can play comedies," he said to himself; and then he twirled his moustache until it was perfectly ferocious-looking, and fell into a reverie.

Poor Althea tried to speak, tried to rise from her chair, but two pairs of white arms kept her a prisoner. Waveney and Mollie were kneeling beside her.

"Dear, dearest Miss Althea, was it really you?" asked Waveney, and the tears were running down her face, and Mollie was covering her hand with kisses. "How could we guess that you were Noel's unknown friend?"

"Hold your tongue, old Storm-and-Stress!" interrupted Noel, with boyish abruptness. "A fellow can't edge in a word with you women. It is for me to thank Miss Harford; it is for me——Oh, confound it all!" And here Noel, to everybody's surprise, and his own too, suddenly bolted.

"Let me go to him!" pleaded Althea, gently.

She had not said one word, or lifted her eyes to Everard's face. As she passed him, her dress almost brushing against him, he made no attempt to detain her. Doreen followed her; and then Moritz joined the agitated little group.

"My cousin is a good woman," he said, with solemnity, as though he had just discovered the fact. "She has noble purposes, and has the courage to follow them out. I admire especially the finesse and cleverness with which she has elaborated and carried out her beneficent scheme. It might almost be compared, in its grandeur of conception, and its marvellous diplomacy, with another drama of human life, in which I have played a part." And here Moritz looked at his young fiancée, and his humour changed. "Come and take a turn with me, Mollie darling," he whispered in the girl's ear; and then Waveney and her father were left alone.

No one ever knew what passed between Althea and Noel in the Porch House; but, for the rest of the evening, Noel was unusually grave and thoughtful. But as Althea was about to return to the verandah, where the lad had already betaken himself, she came upon Everard. He was standing alone in the porch, and was evidently waiting for her.

It was now late, and the moon had risen, and Everard's face was illuminated by the white light. At the sight of him, Althea's assumed calmness vanished; but she tried to speak in the old friendly way.

"Were you looking for me, Mr. Ward?" she asked, hurriedly. "Are they all in the verandah still?"

"Yes," he returned, curtly; "but I have come to ask you a question. Althea, why have you done this; why have you heaped these coals of fire upon my head?"

Poor Althea! The avalanche had fallen, and she had nothing more to fear; never again, as she told herself, would she live through such a moment of humiliation and shame. The purity of her motives and the absence of all self-seeking and consciousness, would make it easy to defend herself.

"Mr. Ward," she said, in her sweet, pathetic voice, "we are old friends, and to me the claims and responsibilities of friendship are very real and sacred. When your trouble came, when you lost your dear wife, I heard from a mutual friend that you were struggling in deep waters, and that, in spite of hard work, you found it difficult to make ends meet."

"That is true," returned Everard. "But——"

"Please let me tell you everything," she pleaded. "This mutual friend often spoke to me of your twin girls, but one day he mentioned Noel. 'He is a bright little lad,' he said, 'and very sharp and intelligent; but Ward frets sadly about his education. He has no means of sending him to a good school, and he is very down about it, poor fellow!' Those were his very words. I never forgot them. I know, from your own lips, what a bright happy boyhood yours had been. You had told me so many stories of your Eton days, and it seemed to me so grievous that your son should be robbed of his rightful advantages."

"You forget that it was his father who was to blame for that," returned Everard, with emotion. "My children must reap what their father sowed. When I married Dorothy, we made up our minds to renounce the good things of this life. Oh, I know the name of your informant, Althea; it was Carstairs! He was a good fellow, and he was in love with my Dorothy; but when I carried her off, he never turned against me. I remember that evening, and how low I was in my mind about the poor boy. But there! I am interrupting you, and you have not finished."

"There is not much to say," replied Althea, gently. "Mr. Carstairs' account troubled me greatly. I wanted to help you, but I knew, and Doreen knew, too, that any offers of assistance would have been indignantly refused. We Harfords are obstinate folk, Mr. Ward, and we love to get our own way, and then and there I concocted my little scheme, and my good Mr. Duncan helped me to carry it out. But for Doreen's unlucky speech, the Veiled Prophetess would have remained veiled." And then she tried to laugh; but the tears were in her eyes. "Everard, dear old friend, you are not angry with me?" and she stretched out her hand to him.

"Angry!" returned Everard, vehemently. "One might as soon quarrel with one's guardian angel, for Heaven knows you have been an angel of goodness to me and mine."

"No, I have only been your friend," returned Althea, a little sadly. "But now it is your turn to be generous, and do me a little favour. Will you let me finish my work? Noel is a dear boy, and I have grown to love him; he and I understand each other perfectly. It was always my intention to send him to Oxford. Mr. Ward, you will not refuse me this pleasure?"

But Everard shook his head.

"We will talk about that later on, when Noel has got his scholarship;" and something in his tone warned Althea to say no more. "She would bide her time," she said to herself; and then, after a few more grateful words from Everard, she made some excuse and returned to the house. But for some time Everard did not follow her. He lighted his cigarette, and paced up and down the garden path.

Coals of fire, indeed! They were scorching him at this very moment. Long years ago he had wronged this woman, and she knew it. He had inflicted on her the most deadly wound that a man can inflict. He had won her heart, and then in his fickleness he had left her; and now, in her sweet nobility, Althea had rendered him good for evil. Secretly and unsuspected, she had befriended him and his; but even now he little guessed the extent of her benevolence, and that, in the home for workers, many of his pictures had found a place. Althea had kept her secret well.

"Good God!" he said, almost with a groan. "Why are men so weak and women so faithful? I can never repay her goodness." And then he thought of his dead wife. Dorothy had been the love of his youth; she was the mother of his children; he had never ceased to regret her loss, and he had always told himself that no other could take her place. In his way he had been faithful, too, but he knew now, when it was too late, that he had built his happiness on the wrecked hopes of another woman's heart.

The next day the girls returned to Cleveland Terrace. Althea had driven them to the door, and then she left them. Everard was out, but as they stood in the old studio, hand in hand, Mollie's bright face clouded.

"I never thought it was quite so shabby," she said, rather dejectedly. "How bare and comfortless it looks!" Probably Waveney had thought the same, but she played the hypocrite gallantly.

"Nonsense, Mollie," she returned, energetically. "We are just spoiled and demoralized by all the comforts of the Red House. We will unpack our boxes, and then we will put the room in order. Moritz has sent in a cartload of flowers, and it will be such fun arranging them!" And then Mollie cheered up; but she had no idea, as Waveney chattered and bustled about, that her head was as heavy as lead. It was Thursday, and that evening Mr. Chaytor would look for her. But the place by Nora Greenwell would be vacant.

After the first day, things were better. Lord Ralston paid them daily visits, and Althea and Doreen drove over constantly from the Red House. Everard was generally absent. He had not yet given up his drawing classes. But the summer vacation would set him free. Waveney and Mollie contrived to amuse themselves; they sat in old Ranelagh Gardens with their work and books. Moritz often followed them there. Sometimes, when Mr. Ward had a leisure afternoon, he would organise some pleasure-trip. Once he drove them down to Richmond, and they had dinner at the "Star and Garter." And one sultry July day they went by train to Cookham, and spent the afternoon in the Quarry Woods. Indeed, Moritz was never happy unless he was contriving some new pleasure for his darling.

The wedding was fixed for the tenth of August, and on the third, Mollie and Waveney returned to the Red House. The trousseau was complete, but there were finishing touches that needed Mollie's presence.

When she tried on her wedding-dress, and Althea had flung over her head the magnificent Brussels lace veil that was one of Lord Ralston's presents, she and Doreen exchanged looks of admiration.

"She is almost too lovely," Althea said afterwards. "And then, she is so unconscious of her great beauty. 'I know I am pretty,' she once said to me. 'And I am so glad, for Moritz's sake.' I think I must tell Gwen that."

CHAPTER XLI.: THE TRUE STORY OF LADY BETTY.

"Man is his own star, and the soul that can Render an honest and a perfect man, Commands all light, all influence, all fate, Nothing to him falls early, or too late. Our acts our angels are, or good or ill, Our fatal shadows, that walk by us still." John Fetcher.
"They laugh that win." Othello.

Two or three days before the wedding there was another gathering at the Red House. Gwendoline and her husband were staying with Lord Ralston, and Doreen suggested that the Chaytors and Everard Ward should be invited to meet them. Althea made no objection. Only when her sister proposed dessert in the verandah, she gently, but decidedly, put her veto upon it.

"There are too many; we had better remain in the dining-room," she replied, with heightened colour. And Doreen, who, with all her bluntness, had plenty of tact, said no more.

Every one accepted. But at the last moment Joanna excused herself, on the plea of indisposition. But Tristram Chaytor accompanied his brother. Waveney and Mollie were dressed alike that evening, in soft, ivory-coloured silk. Only Mollie's spray of flowers were pink, and Waveney wore dark red carnations. Thorold, who sat by her at dinner, noticed a diamond bangle on her arm. Waveney saw him looking at it.

"It is a present from Lord Ralston," she said. "I am to be Mollie's bridesmaid, you know. Was it not good of him. I never had anything so lovely in my life before."

Thorold murmured some response. Then he addressed his next neighbour. Waveney was dangerously attractive that evening; her dark eyes were bright with excitement and pleasure, and in her white dress she looked more like Undine than ever. The conversation during dinner turned upon long engagements. It was Gwendoline who started the subject; a friend of hers, who had been engaged for eight years, had been married that very morning. Gwendoline brought down on herself a chorus of animadversion and censure from the gentlemen, for saying that she rather approved of long engagements, and a warm discussion followed. The gentlemen took one side of the argument, and the ladies the other; but Gwen stuck tenaciously to her opinion.

"Waiting never hurts any one," she said, oracularly. "Don't you remember Lady Betty Ingram, Moritz? Lady Betty was an ancestress of ours," she continued; "she lived when farmer George was king, and she was faithful to her love for more than twenty years."

"Five-and-twenty years, was it not, Gwen?" And then, as most of the party begged to hear the story, Gwendoline narrated it in her own charming way.

"Lady Betty had been for some time one of Queen Charlotte's ladies-in-waiting. But Court life was not to her taste; she was lively by nature, and she disliked all the etiquette and restraint, and she pined to be back with her parents in the old home. But before she left the Court she made the acquaintance of a certain Sir Bever Willoughby—at least, he was only Bever Willoughby then, the son of an impoverished baronet, and heir to heavily mortgaged estates.

"Lady Betty was no beauty, but she was considered fascinating by most people. She was very witty, and she danced beautifully, and handsome Bever Willoughby lost his heart to her when he saw her walk through the minuet; for she pointed her toe so prettily and curtsied with such exquisite grace, that Willoughby was not proof against her charms. One evening when they were at Ranelagh, and Lady Betty looked more bewitching than ever in her little quilted satin hood, Willoughby suddenly addressed her in an agitated voice.

"'My Lady Betty,' he said, 'the Court is not the place for a poor man. You have robbed me of my peace of mind, but no lady, however fair, shall rob me of my honour. I am going to win my laurels. To-morrow I sail for America. Fare you well—and God bless you—dear Lady Betty.' And then he bowed to her with his hand on his heart, and for four-and-twenty years she never saw his face again, though she heard of him often.

"It was then that Lady Betty returned to the old Hall. And there she lived a quiet life, cherishing her aged parents, and busy with her still-room and herb-garden, after the fashion of those days. She had many lovers, but she never married; for, as she once told her mother, she had never met any one to compare with Sir Bever Willoughby. 'He was a goodly youth,' she said, 'and when I looked on his countenance I bethought me of young David, playing his harp among his sheep; but he had one fault, and it has spoiled both our lives—he was too proud to owe his fortune to the woman he loved.'

"Lady Betty was in her comely middle age when she next saw Bever Willoughby. She had grown rather stout, but people said she was handsomer than she had been in her youth. She was dancing a minuet in the picture-gallery at Brentwood Hall, when a tall, soldierly-looking man, with his arm in a sling, attracted her notice. When their eyes met Lady Betty blushed like a girl, but Sir Bever turned very pale. When, a week or two later, Sir Bever asked her to marry him, Lady Betty looked him full in the face.

"'There is an old proverb, Sir Bever,' she said, 'that tells us that some things are better late than never; and methinks this wooing of yours is somewhat tardy.'

"'Say not so, dear Lady Betty,' he returned, passionately, 'for though I rode away without telling my love, I have had no wife or child, but have been your true lover at heart all these years.'

"Then Lady Betty dropped him a low curtsy; but he saw the sparkle of tears in her eyes.

"'You have not been more faithful than another,' she replied. 'You are a brave soldier, Sir Bever, but you had no right to break a woman's heart, as mine was broken that evening at Ranelagh.'"

"But she married him?" pleaded Mollie, rather piteously, as Gwendoline paused for a moment.

"Oh, yes, she married him, and they were very happy; but Sir Bever only lived ten years. As he lay dying he expressed his regret that their wedded bliss had been so brief.

"'Dear heart,' returned Lady Betty, 'your mannish, foolish pride kept my husband from me for nigh upon twenty-five years, but we will make up for it hereafter;' and then she fell on his breast weeping. 'Death cannot part true hearts,' she cried, 'and thou wilt be my own Sir Bever in heaven.'"

And here Gwen caught her breath, for Jack was looking at her; and actually Mollie, silly little Mollie, was crying.

"It is a lovely story, Gwen," observed Althea; and then she rose from the table. A little later, when the gentlemen had had their coffee, they all went out on the terrace, and Waveney found herself pacing the garden paths with Mr. Chaytor.

They talked on indifferent subjects—the beauty of the evening and the charm of a well-kept garden. And then they paused to listen to a nightingale in the shrubbery. Presently they sat down in the verandah at the Porch House, and watched the other couples passing to and fro below. Lord Ralston and Mollie, Gwen and Jack Compton, and Doreen and Tristram; the other three, Althea and Mr. Ward and Noel, had seated themselves on a bench outside the library window. The moon was rising behind the elms. Waveney's eyes were fixed on it, when Thorold suddenly broke the silence.

"What did you think of the true story of Lady Betty?" he asked. There was something inexplicable in his tone.

"I thought it beautiful," she returned; "though I did not cry over it as Mollie did. They were both so faithful; but Lady Betty was braver than Sir Bever."

"What do you mean?" remonstrated her companion. "Surely it was better for him to ride away without telling his love. You do not agree with me"—looking in her face. "You think Sir Bever was wrong to be afraid of his poverty."

"Yes, I think he was wrong," faltered Waveney. "I agree with Lady Betty, that he had sacrificed their youth to no purpose. You see, he gave her no chance of setting things right; he just rode away, and left her to bear her life as well as she could."

"You are severe," returned Thorold, eagerly. "You do not make an allowance for a man's pride, that will not stoop to take everything from a woman. I grant you the story was pretty, and that Mrs. John Compton told it well; she has a charming voice and manner."

"Oh, yes; and she is so nice. Mollie is quite fond of her already."

"I do not wonder at it; but, Miss Ward, I want to convince you that you ladies are not the only ones who set us an example of faithfulness. Men may be proverbially fickle, but there are exceptions to the rule."

"Oh, yes, of course."

"It is difficult to judge in some cases. There was a friend of mine——" Here Thorold hesitated and glanced at the girl's averted face. Something in her attitude—the shy droop of the head, the hands clasped so tightly on her white gown—excited him and quickened his pulses. There was a tremor in his voice as he went on. "My friend was deeply in love with a girl. She was very young. He was much older, and weighted with many cares and responsibilities, and he was poor—oh, far too poor to take a wife."

Again he paused, but Waveney made no comment, only her hands were clasped more nervously.

"He did not exactly ride away, as Sir Bever did," he went on; "but he made up his mind that the most honourable course would be to lock up the secret of his love in his own breast, and not burden that bright young life with his troubles. No!"—with strange emphasis—"he loved her too well for that. Dear Miss Ward, surely you will own that my friend was right."

Waveney would have given worlds not to answer. Her little pale face grew rigid with suppressed emotion. Though she never raised her eyes, she was conscious that he was watching her keenly; his strong will seemed to compel her to speak.

"My friend was right, was he not?" he repeated, slowly, and as though he were weighing each syllable.

"No," she returned, abruptly; "he was wrong. He was as mistaken as Sir Bever." And then she grew crimson. Oh, if she could only escape! If she could bring this conversation to an end! She was tingling from head to foot with sheer nervousness.

"So I begin to think myself," returned Thorold, coolly. And then his voice deepened with sudden tenderness. "Waveney, my dear one, tell me the truth. Would you wait for me?"

Gwendoline always boasted that she had made the match. "For you know, Jack," she would say, "if I had not told that story about Lady Betty, Mr. Chaytor would never have mustered up courage to speak to Waveney that night, and they might have been pining for each other for years."

After all, it had come about quite naturally. Perhaps Thorold had read something in Waveney's eyes, as she listened to that old love-story, that made him change his purpose of silence. But he never repented it.

"We may have to wait for years," he said to her, when the first agitation of their great joy had calmed a little. But Waveney only gave him one of her radiant smiles.

"Faithfulness has not gone out with powder and patches," she said, in her quaint way. "I would rather wait through a lifetime, knowing without doubt that you loved me, than have to exist through years of chilling silence." And in his heart Thorold agreed with her.

Everard Ward gave his consent very willingly when Thorold, in rather an embarrassed voice, told him that he feared they could not be married for perhaps four or five years. He received the news with profound satisfaction.

"Chaytor is a son-in-law after my own heart," he said to Althea. "He will not rob me of my little girl for the next five years. 'My dear fellow, I am delighted to hear it,' I said to him; but he looked at me rather reproachfully."

"I hope they will not have to wait quite so long," returned Althea, gravely.

But Everard would not endorse this. Lord Ralston had robbed him of his Mollie, and he could not spare his little Waveney.

Perhaps Althea was the most astonished at the news. Thorold and Waveney had kept their secret so well that she had never guessed it; but when her first surprise was over, she rejoiced heartily in their happiness.

"Thorold has grown years younger since his engagement," she said one day to Joanna. "He is not half so grave and sober now." And Joanna assented to this.

"I am getting very fond of Waveney," she replied. "Tristram likes her, and so does Betty."

But Joanna spoke without enthusiasm. Her brother's choice had greatly surprised her, and privately she thought his engagement to a penniless girl was an act of pure folly. "If he had only married a girl with money!" she would say to Tristram sometimes.

But Althea, who had not outlived romance, approved thoroughly of the engagement. She saw that Waveney entirely satisfied Thorold—that she was the light of his eyes, and the desire of his heart. "My lonely days are over," he once said to her. And it was true. Waveney's bright intelligence enabled her to take interest in all his work, and he could share all his thoughts with her.

When Mollie and Lord Ralston plighted their vows in the old church at Erpingham, Thorold was making silent vows in his heart, and looking at a little white figure with worshipping eyes. And Waveney was repeating her Te Deum.

"Oh, Mollie, I don't think you are happier than I am," she whispered, when they were alone together for a moment.

But Mollie looked just a trifle dubious. Thorold was very nice and clever, and she meant to be quite fond of him; but he could not be compared to her Moritz.

"Oh, Wave, do you know what I heard as we came out of church just now?" she said, merrily. "Somebody near me said, 'The lame bride is a real beauty, and they say she is a ladyship now.'" And then Mollie laughed gleefully, and gave her satin train a little fling. "Wasn't it funny? But I don't think Moritz quite liked it. And Wave"—and now Mollie's dimples were in full play— "somehow I could not feel quite grave when Colonel Treherne called me Lady Ralston."

CHAPTER XLII.: "WOOED, AND MARRIED, AND A'."

Mir. "Here's my hand." Fer. "And mine with my heart in it." The Tempest.
"There's a divinity that shapes our ends, Rough hew them how we will." Hamlet.

It was arranged that Waveney was to remain at the Red House while painting and papering were being carried on at Number Ten, Cleveland Terrace.

Ann, the heavy-footed, was dismissed with a month's wages, and Mrs. Muggins accompanied her. A competent caretaker was put in charge. And Althea had already engaged two capable maids, to come in when the work of renovation was complete.

It was the first time Doreen and Althea had ever spent August in town; but Mrs. Mainwaring's sudden illness had detained them, and, as soon as she was fit to travel, they had promised to stay with her at Whitby.

While Waveney remained with her friends, Everard Ward and his son went down to a farm-house in Yorkshire, that Lord Ralston had recommended, where they would have excellent accommodation, at a very moderate price, and very good fishing. It was the first real holiday that Everard had enjoyed for years, and Noel wrote ridiculously illustrated epistles, retailing sundry ludicrous adventures. "His revered parent," as he informed Waveney, "was becoming fatter, and more plebeian, every day." And here there was a spirited pen-and-ink sketch of Everard in a huge straw hat, fishing on a boulder, with a briar-wood pipe in his mouth, and several small fishes winking at him as they frisked harmlessly by. "Caught nothing since Friday week," was written underneath the picture.

In spite of her happiness, Waveney could not reconcile herself to Mollie's absence. The parting had tried them both. No one forgot the bride's tear-stained face, as Lord Ralston lifted her into the carriage. "Oh, do take care of my Wave," were her last words to Althea, as they drove away.

Waveney shed many a tear in her Pansy Room. But she cheered up when Mollie's first letter came. And after that she wrote almost daily. She was very happy, she said, and Moritz was so good to her. But of course it was strange, being without her Wave. It was such a lovely place, and the cottage was so cosy. They were out all day, fishing, or wandering over the purple moors. Sometimes Moritz had a day's shooting with the keeper, and then she and Donald, the gamekeeper's son, drove down with the luncheon. They had dinner at eight—quite a grand dinner, and Donald waited on them. "I have given up pinching myself hard, to be sure that I am not dreaming," she wrote once, "but for all that I am leading a story-book existence. Oh, I am so happy, darling! I can hardly say my prayers without crying for sheer thankfulness. My dear Moritz spoils me so dreadfully. He says he hates me to be out of his sight for a moment, and if I were to believe half he says I should be as conceited as possible. It is just his blarney, I tell him. And then he pretends to be affronted."

When Althea showed Waveney the improvements she and Doreen had effected in Number Ten, Cleveland Terrace, the girl could hardly believe her eyes. New papers, and carpets, and curtains, had quite transformed the dingy old house. The stairs were covered with crimson felt, and the studio, and the bare, ugly room, where the sisters had slept, looked perfectly charming.

"A little money and a good deal of taste do wonders," observed Althea in a matter-of-fact tone. But Waveney wasn't so sure about the money. Moritz had evidently given his cousins carte blanche, and though there was very little new furniture in the studio, the fresh cretonne and flowering-plants gave it an air of finish and refinement.

It was a pleasant life they led there. Never since his wife's death had Everard been so content and happy. Mollie's brilliant marriage gave him great satisfaction, and he had no fear of losing his little Waveney for many a year to come. He was set free from the drudgery he hated, and he and Waveney were always together. Thorold spent his Sundays with them, and he came one evening in the week beside. They had made this rule at the beginning, and he never infringed on it.

Every fortnight or so they dined at the Red House, and Althea often had tea with them when she drove into town. She and Everard had resumed their old friendliness; neither of them had forgotten that scene in the verandah of the Porch House, but, by mutual consent, the subject of Noel's education had been dropped for a time.

At the beginning of October the newly married pair returned to town, and spent a week at Eaton Square, and Mollie and Waveney were together every day.

"Why, Mollie, I declare you have grown an inch taller," were Everard's first words to her; and privately he thought that young Lady Ralston was even handsomer than Mollie Ward had been. Both he and Waveney agreed that happiness and prosperity had not spoilt their darling; she was the same simple, light-hearted creature, thinking as little of herself, and rejoicing over her pretty things as a child might have done.

Perhaps there was a little veil of shyness and reserve when she spoke of her husband. Moritz was evidently perfect in her eyes; but only to Waveney did she dwell on his good qualities.

"People do not know him," she said once—"they think him eccentric; but it is just his way of talking. He is so true, Wave; Gwen says that she is sure that he has never told a lie in his life, and he is so unselfish, he is always wanting to make people happy. When he was so poor he would deprive himself of a meal if a beggar looked hungry; and now he is always planning some generous gift or other. He lends his shooting lodge to poor artists or curates. Oh! I cannot tell you half of the things he does. He calls me his little blessing; but I feel I can never, never, repay his goodness." And here such an exquisite blush tinged Mollie's cheeks, that it was a pity Lord Ralston did not see it.

Mollie was naturally anxious to see her beautiful home, and the lovely rooms that Moritz had refurnished for her. But her regret was so great at leaving Waveney that Lord Ralston, who could refuse nothing to his sweet Moll, suggested that she should pay them a visit in November. He had already arranged that the whole Ward family were to keep their Christmas at Brentwood Hall; but there was no reason why Waveney should not spend a week or two with them in November.

It was impossible to refuse so tempting an invitation; and when Waveney reached Brentwood Mollie and the cream-coloured ponies were at the station. Mollie was in a perfect glow of pride and satisfaction as she drove Waveney through the village.

Waveney's first act after unpacking was to find the portrait of Lady Betty in the picture-gallery. Mollie pointed it out to her. Lady Betty simpered down on them from the faded canvas. She had a round face and powdered hair drawn up under a lace cap, and one slim hand held a bunch of roses. Her yellow brocade looked as stiff as buckram, and her white arms were veiled with rich lace. "Lady Betty Ingram, in her twenty-fifth year" was written in the catalogue.

Never had Mollie or Waveney spent such a Christmas as they spent that year at Brentwood Hall. Thorold Chaytor was with them. Lord Ralston kept Christmas in the old style. There were mummers and carol-singers on Christmas Eve, and "cakes and ale" ad libitum in the housekeeper's room.

The John Comptons came over from Kingsdene, and the day after Christmas Day there was a ball for the servants; and on New Year's Eve there was a festive gathering, to which people came ten miles round, and there was dancing in the picture-gallery. Madam Compton was there, looking queenly in black velvet and point lace, and she and Jack were delighted when after supper Gwen danced a minuet with her brother. Gwen was looking her best that evening. She wore a cream-coloured satin gown, cut somewhat quaintly, and her beautiful neck and arms were bare of ornament. As Gwen moved down the picture-gallery, Mollie vowed that not even the renowned Lady Betty could have curtsied with such grace. "Oh, how beautifully she dances!" whispered Mollie; and Jack heard her, and beamed with delight.

When the clock struck twelve they all joined hands, and Lord Ralston made them a little speech. Then the band struck up and they all sang "For Auld Lang Syne."

Mollie sat enthroned like a little queen all the time the dancing went on. The diamonds she wore were hardly brighter than her eyes. Once, when her husband said, a little sadly, "How he wished his sweet Moll could dance, too!" Mollie's lip quivered for a moment; then she said bravely,—

"It does not matter, dear. It is so nice to have you helping me and looking after me."

Nevertheless, her eyes looked a little wistfully after him and Waveney when they waltzed together.

The spring days found Waveney at Cleveland Terrace again. Moritz meant to bring his wife to Eaton Square for a part of the season, and then she and Mollie would go to exhibitions and concerts and to the opera together.

Early in May Waveney was sitting in the studio one afternoon, finishing a long letter to Mollie, when Thorold suddenly entered the room. Waveney gave a little cry of delight when she saw him.

"Oh, Thorold, how delightful!" she exclaimed, as he took her in his arms. "Have you come to spend the evening?"

"Yes, if you will have me, Waveney. I have some news to tell you."

"Good news, I can see by your face." And then she asked wickedly, "Is Joanna going to be married?"

"No, my dear; no one is going to be married but you and I by-and-bye, but it is capital news for all that. Tristram has been offered a good berth at Liverpool, and, as Joanna cannot bring herself to part with Betty, she is going to keep house for them."

"Oh, Thorold, how splendid!" And Waveney's eyes sparkled with pleasure. She was overjoyed at the idea that he was free at last. No one knew better than she how uncongenial his home had been to him. Solitude would be infinitely preferable to the small carking cares and frets of his daily life. Joanna's peculiar temperament created an unrestful atmosphere round her. Tristram, who was of a blunter and more obtuse nature, was less alive to the discomfort.

Joa was always a poor puling thing, he would say, but she was very good to his Betty. And he was rather relieved than otherwise when Joanna entreated tearfully to accompany them.

"Thorold does not want me and Betty does," she pleaded.

"Joa has a little money of her own," went on Thorold, "so I think they will be fairly comfortable. The change of scene will be good for her. They are to leave Dereham at the end of July."

"That will be nearly three months hence," returned Waveney, musingly. She was fingering Thorold's coat-sleeve rather absently as she spoke. It was one of her pretty caressing ways with him. He watched the little hand for a moment as it smoothed the rough cloth so gently. Then he took possession of it.

"Dearest," he said, very quietly, "once, long ago, I was ready to ride away without telling my love like Sir Bever, but my good angel stopped me. But I find that I have not Lady Betty's patience, and long waiting would be irksome to me." And then he looked at her very wistfully. "Waveney, I want to ask you a question. When my sister leaves me, do you see any reason why we should not be married?"

It was evident that Waveney was extremely startled, and that Thorold's proposition took her quite by surprise. She grew a little pale.

"I thought you could not afford to marry for years," she returned, shyly.

"So I thought," he replied, with a smile. "You see, darling, when we were first engaged my sister was dependent on me, and at that time Tristram earned very little. Virtually, I had to keep him and Betty. But all that will be changed now. We should have to be careful and live quietly for some years to come, but I am not afraid of the future. My work is increasing, as you know. I have had to take better chambers, and our last case was so successful that I am likely to have another good brief. Tell me the truth, my little Undine. Shall you be afraid to trust yourself to my keeping?"

Afraid! Need he have asked such a question? The dark eyes looked at him with reproachful sweetness.

"Do you think I should fear anything with you?" she answered. "But, Thorold, are you sure you really wish it?"

But Thorold's reply was so conclusive and satisfying that Waveney yielded.

Everard Ward had been reading his paper in old Ranelagh Gardens that afternoon. The pleasant May sunshine had warmed and cheered him, and he whistled like a boy as he let himself into the house with his latch-key.

But his cheerfulness soon vanished when he learned the purport of Thorold's visit. He was deceived, betrayed by the very man whom he declared would be a son-in-law after his own heart. He was to be robbed of his little girl.

What a fool he had been to trust the word of a lover! His knowledge of the world might have told him that they were all wolves in sheeps' clothing. Five years' engagement! This is what he had promised, the arch-traitor! and now he was coolly proposing that they should be married in August.

Everard nearly talked himself hoarse, in his effort to point out the extreme imprudence of the whole proceeding. In his opinion, he said, it was utterly rash, foolhardy, and a gross tempting of Providence. All his life he had been an example of the sad result of an impecunious marriage; his son had been indebted to charity for education, and his daughters had been without advantages. Everard waxed quite eloquent over his theme, but Thorold refused to be intimidated. He demolished all Everard's arguments with the ease and facility of a skilful lawyer; and Waveney was on his side. Everard had no chance; from the beginning they were both against him, and at last he had to throw down his arms. Even Althea took their part, and so did Mollie; but he yielded with a very bad grace, and though he tried to hide it from Waveney, he was sore at heart for many a day.

Waveney's feelings were very mixed: her sorrow at leaving her father somewhat damped her happiness; but Mollie comforted her.

"Of course it is hard for father," she said one day, when Waveney was lunching at Eaton Square. "He hates parting with his children. Don't you remember how low he was on my wedding day? But he soon cheered up. It will be all right, Wave, so don't worry. When you are once married he will make the best of it. Moritz says he must leave Cleveland Terrace and take a nice flat somewhere near you; and when Noel is at Oxford he can divide his time between us." And this view of the case was very consoling to Waveney.

Mollie was in the seventh heaven of delight just then; she was to provide the trousseau out of her own pin-money, and this thought gave her so much pleasure that Lord Ralston declared she even laughed in her sleep.

But Lord Ralston's wedding present almost overwhelmed the young couple. He bought a house for them at Kensington and furnished it from basement to garret. When he placed the title deeds in Waveney's hands, she was speechless with surprise and joy. But Moritz refused to be thanked. "Mollie's sister was his," he said, in his airy fashion, "and it was his business to see that she was properly housed.

"Chaytor is a good fellow," he went on, "and I respect him highly, and am proud to be connected with him. I shall stand your friend and his, as long as you both deserve it. And look here"—and here Lord Ralston glanced at Mollie's delighted face—"if you and Chaytor would like to do your honeymooning at the Hut, you are welcome to it." And when Waveney repeated this to Thorold, he said that it was far too good an offer to be refused.

"Ralston is the prince of good fellows," he went on. "His generosity is as large as his purse. You will love those Scotch moors, Waveney. I have not been in the Highlands for years; it will be grand to see the heather and the grouse again."

After all, Everard Ward never had his flat, neither did he stay long at Number Ten, Cleveland Terrace; another, and far different, fate was in store for him.

About three months after Waveney's marriage he went one afternoon to the Red House. He had only just returned from Brentwood Hall, where he had made the acquaintance of his first grandson; and, as usual, he wished to talk over the visit with his old friend Althea.

For they were very dear friends now, and, next to his own daughters, he valued her womanly advice and sympathy.

In summer, the door of the Red House always stood open, and he went in as usual unannounced. No one responded to his tap at the library door, and as he entered he thought, for a moment, the room was empty.

The blinds were down, and the darkness rather bewildered him, coming out of the sunshine. But the next moment he caught sight of a grey figure in the shadow of the curtain.

Althea was leaning back in her easy-chair. There was a green shade over her eyes, and her face was pale. Everard, who had never seen her before in one of her attacks, was much shocked.

"You are ill," he said, taking her hand. In spite of the warmth of the day, it felt cold and limp. Then he looked round the room. "Where is Doreen? Surely she has not left you alone?"

"Doreen is at the Home," returned Althea, in a weak voice. "There is a committee meeting. Please sit down and talk to me. I want to forget myself. No, I am not ill. The attack has passed off, only I am stupid and dull."

Dull! Everard felt strangely oppressed. The darkness; Althea's pale face, full of traces of suffering; the disguising shade, that hid the sweet eyes; the pathos, and helplessness, and utter weariness, so evident in the whole figure;—filled him with pity. Was this what she had to bear?—she, who helped others, whose whole life was devoted to good works! who had been a guardian angel to him and his!

Everard felt a sudden impulse that seemed to impel him, in spite of himself. He got up from his seat and stood beside her. Then, as she moved restlessly, as though disturbed by his action, he dropped on one knee.

"Althea, my dear," he said, huskily, "we are neither of us young, and we have both known trouble. But, if you would have it so, I should like to devote the rest of my life to you, to wait on you, and to comfort you."

Was she dreaming? Althea pushed up her shade a little wildly. But the gravity of his face left no doubt of his meaning.

"I cannot, I dare not accept it," she returned; and she trembled all over. "It is far too great a sacrifice."

"It is no sacrifice at all," was Everard's answer. "It is I who am unworthy of your goodness." And the proud humility of his tone struck to her very heart.

"I have loved you all my life," she said to him, later on. "Everard, it shall be as you wish. It will make me very happy to be your wife. I know how good you will be to me."

Doreen was rather troubled when Althea told her the news. Their peaceful dual life was over, she thought; but when she looked at her sister's radiant face she chid herself for her selfishness.

But she soon became reconciled to the change. When Everard took up his abode at the Red House he became her chief adviser and helper. He brought his masculine intellect and energy to bear on all their philanthropic schemes, and "my brother-in-law says this" or "suggests that" was for ever on Doreen's lips.

There was no doubt of Althea's happiness. She and Everard were always together. Althea's sweet, large nature was never exacting. She knew that he would never love her as he had loved Dorothy, but this thought gave her no pain. How could she complain that anything was wanting when his thoughtful tenderness was so unceasing? when he never cared to be away from her?

"It rests me to be near you," he would say. And, indeed, there was the truest friendship between them.

Waveney and Mollie were devoted to their beloved Queen Bess, but "our boy," as Althea always called Noel, was the pride of his stepmother's heart.

And so, when her youth had passed, that faithful soul reaped its harvest of joy. "Thus the whirligig of Time brings in its revenges." But Althea's noble revenge had been much patience and much love.

Printed in Great Britain
by Amazon